P9-DHL-682

This one is for my mother, and my mother alone. Sarah Ann Remic, "Sally" to her friends, 1928-2013.May you rest in peace, my love.

PRAISE FOR ANDY REMIC

"For anyone who is missing their David Gemmell fix."
   io9.com

"Add to the mix a good dollop of battlefield humour, a good handful of Howard's style backed up with a stark descriptiveness and it's a tale that gives Remic a firm footing within the genre."
   Falcata Times

"*Soul Stealers* is fast, brutal and above all unmissable, there is quite simply nothing out there that can currently compare to Andy Remic's unrelenting, unforgiving and unflinching style. The new King of Heroic Fantasy has arrived. 5 *****"
   SFBook.com

"*Kell's Legend* is a roller coaster ride of a book that grabbed me right from the first page and tore off at a rate of knots like I hadn't seen in a long time."
   Graeme's Fantasy Book Review

"*Kell's Legend* is a novel of power and scope, able to stand as a worthy successor to the Gemmell crown. 5*****"
   Science Fiction and Fantasy Books

"*Kell's Legend* is a rip-roaring beast of a novel, a whirlwind of frantic battles and fraught relationships against a bleak background of invasion and enslavement."
   Speculative Horizons

ALSO BY ANDY REMIC

FANTASY
THE CLOCKWORK VAMPIRE CHRONICLES
Kell's Legend
Soul Stealers
Vampire Warlords
The Clockwork Vampire Chronicles [omnibus]

THRILLERS
Spiral
Quake
Warhead
Serial Killers Incorporated

SCIENCE FICTION
War Machine
Biohell
Hardcore
Cloneworld
Theme Planet
Toxicity
SIM

FOR CHILDREN
Rocket Cat

ANDY REMIC

The Iron Wolves

A BLOOD, WAR & REQUIEM NOVEL

ANGRY
ROBOT

ANGRY ROBOT

A member of the Osprey Group

Lace Market House,
54-56 High Pavement,
Nottingham,
NG1 1HW,
UK

Angry Robot/Osprey Publishing,
PO Box 3985,
New York,
NY 10185-3985,
USA

www.angryrobotbooks.com
Good to bad and back again

An Angry Robot paperback original 2014

Copyright © Andy Remic 2014

Andy Remic asserts the moral right to be
identified as the author of this work.

Cover art by Lee Gibbons

Distributed in the United States by Random House, Inc., New York.
All rights reserved.

Angry Robot is a registered trademark, and the Angry Robot icon a
trademark of Angry Robot Ltd.

This is a work of fiction. Names, characters, places and incidents are
the products of the author's imagination or are used fictitiously. Any
resemblance to actual events, locales, organizations or persons, living or
dead, is entirely coincidental.

Sales of this book without a front cover may be unauthorized. If this book
is coverless, it may have been reported to the publisher as "unsold and
destroyed" and neither the author nor the publisher may have received
payment for it.

ISBN: 978 0 85766 355 9
Ebook ISBN: 978 0 85766 356 6

Set in Meridien by Argh! Oxford

Printed in the United States of America
9 8 7 6 5 4 3 2 1

RETRIBUTION

"I'm sorry, Dek. Real sorry." The large man grimaced through his thick beard, showing a missing tooth. "I apologise. Truly. From the deepest caverns of my heart." His silhouette blocked out the roaring flames from the stacked hearth in the Fighting Cocks tavern. Voices hushed to a whisper and everybody turned eyes on Dek. Dek, the Pit Fighter. A pugilist you did not cross.

Dek rose to his feet, swaying under the influence of two large wine flagons. He turned, iron-dark eyes focusing on the newcomer and his fists clenched showing brutal scarred knuckles. He moved fast, and the right uppercut lifted the bearded newcomer clean from his feet, slamming him over the bar in a diagonal spin of smashed tankards, flying limbs and scattered stools. There came a few shouts, and some hushed curses. Somebody called for the landlord.

Weasel grabbed Dek's arm. "No! He's your brother!" hissed the little man.

"Well, I reckon I'm going to kill him," snarled Dek, spittle on his chin, and Weasel saw the light of rage ignite Dek's eyes and face and fists. He'd seen it many times, deep in the blood-slippery Red Thumb Fighting Pits. He'd witnessed it in tavern brawls and unlicensed fights down at the fish markets. He'd watched Dek's extreme violence, sometimes with despair, sometimes with horror, sometimes with approval; it depended how much coin he stood to earn.

"Not today," urged Weasel, grip tightening, even though his fingers couldn't even encircle Dek's massive bicep. "Your mother lies cold in her coffin," he said, voice filled with a great regret. "*Remember!* You're here to honour her. You're here to remember her. You're here to tell tall tales and drink plentiful wine; to salute her on her journey to the Hall of Heroes! But no fighting, Dek. You said it yourself. You promised her. You made *me* promise her. No war. Not today. For your mother, Dek. For your old mum."

Dek turned bloodshot eyes on Weasel, his oldest friend; his best friend. Weasel saw the pain there, like a splintered diamond piercing the core of the large man's skull. Pity swamped him. Pity, followed by a sudden, necessary horror. For in Dek there lurked a demon. A dark core. Of violence. Of insanity. Of *murder*.

"He's your *brother,*" insisted Weasel.

"And that's why he's got to die," growled Dek, pushing away Weasel's restraining hand as if a child's, shouldering two stocky men roughly out of his way, and leaping over the bar which groaned in protest. Dek landed, both boots beside his brother's head.

"Get up, Ragorek," said Dek. "Get up now, before I stamp your skull and brains to pulp."

"No, Dek. It can't be like this."

Dek reached down, grabbed the man's leather jerkin and hauled Ragorek to his battered boots. Ragorek was taller than Dek by nearly a full head, and Dek was big. Rag was a natural athlete, broad, lean, rangy, powerful, ruggedly handsome and sporting a thick beard. He was a man who commanded instant respect, not just because of his size and bearing, but because of some inherent natural nobility; a genetic legacy that had created a born leader.

"I fucking hate you," growled Dek through saliva, broken teeth and wine fumes.

Ragorek grabbed his brother hard, by both sides of the head. "I know, little brother. I know that. I loved her as well."

"Well, then, where the *fuck* were *you*?" His forehead slammed against Ragorek's nose, and the large man howled as cartilage splintered. In reflex, fists came up, a right overhand blow slamming into Dek's skull. Dek staggered, but shook his head as the rage of battle fell upon him like a velvet cloak, dark as eternity. He took a step back, then charged Ragorek, punching him in the throat, kicking him in the knee, then grabbing his head between both hands and thrusting his face close. "Where the fuck were you?" he screamed again, and smashed his forehead into Ragorek's face: once, twice, three times. Ragorek went down, his clutching hands grabbing Dek's torn shirt and dragging the younger man down with him.

He pulled Dek close. "You want to die, little brother? I can do that for you. I can make you suffer." And he bit down on Dek's ragged ear, ripping free the lobe in a shower of dark crimson. Dek growled, but did not scream. He was a veteran of the Pits. Dek never screamed. He rammed his fist into his brother's face, three, four, five, six, seven, eight times until the face became a glossy splatter of pig's blood. Dek's knuckles were cut by teeth. Dek's face was a contortion of rage and fear and hate and something else; something primal that transcended hate. A primitive emotion that went so far beyond civilised Man it devolved and spat itself screaming out the other side like a desolate embryo into a flickering half-life tomb-world of oblivion. Some things went beyond emotion. Some things, some murder, just had to be done. And Dek was the perfect killer. He was the widowmaker of the moment.

"Dek my lad. Stay very, very still." The voice was deep and resonant. "I love you like a son. But by all the gods, if you break up my bar again I'll put this crossbow quarrel through the back of your skull."

There came a long pause.

"That's reasonable, Skellgann. I'll take it outside," said Dek, levelly, and jacked himself backwards, standing from the coughing, groaning figure of his brother. Ragorek was helped to his feet and he scowled at Dek, spitting blood and a tooth trailing crimson saliva onto the boards.

"I'm going to break you, you little bastard," said Ragorek.

"Like you did to our weak and dying mother?" smiled Dek, eyes widening.

Ragorek surged forward, but was held back by many hands.

"Outside! Move it out to the cobbles!" roared Skellgann.

"I'm taking bets," announced Weasel, eyes glittering.

Both fighters were guided at crossbow-point from the Fighting Cocks, and a large group of men crossed ice-cracking puddles towards Heroes' Square. Here, weathered and broken statues stood, or leaned, around a cobbled central yard. They were a testament to long forgotten wars; ancient dead men; heroes forgotten.

"That mad bastard King is an amusing fellow," whined Weasel in his high, nasal voice. "This place is being flattened for a new clerks' offices. Flattened to the ground. But still. At least I'll have plenty more customers! Now, we have business to attend." He counted out five dockets and scribbled furiously with the stub of a pencil. His cracked front tooth made his smile disjointed. And despite his love for Dek, Weasel was a pragmatist when it came to coin. Dek would thank him in the morning. Perhaps.

"Break it down, drag it down," said Skellgann, his broad face flattened into a frown, his arms nestling the heavy crossbow.

"What?" snapped Weasel, frowning himself, focused as he was on odds and numbers and the clink of silver and copper.

"The statues. Our once-heroes. Soon to be smashed, torn down, broken down, destroyed."

"They're not my heroes," said Weasel, giving him a sideways glance.

"Ha! What little you young pups understand," said Skellgann, filled with a sudden great sadness.

Dek and Ragorek had moved to the centre of Heroes' Square. Here, a hundred statues of ancient warriors stared down, and Dek removed his thick wool jerkin and coarse shirt, flexing his broad chest and huge, warrior's physique. He had run a little to fat over the years, but all that did was give him extra weight. Anybody who dared called him "fat man" was soon punished with broken bones.

Ragorek had been joined by two lean ranger-types, old and scarred, battled-hardened men with whom he sometimes travelled. These were not chicks fresh from the nest, but experienced soldiers. Every movement spoke it. They helped Ragorek remove his shirt and cleaned blood from his eyes. Ragorek reined in his fury well, but his orbs were now alight with fire. With the promise of battle.

Dek, body riddled with old scars, half-finished tattoos and recently-stitched wounds, stepped into the centre of the square, fists by his sides, face calm and patient and waiting. Ragorek moved out to meet his younger brother and both men stared at one another across the ice and stone, their breath steaming like dragon-smoke through the bitter cold. Word had gone round fast. There were at least a hundred spectators present now, a few women, and even a few of the City Guard. Runners were also busy spreading the word.

"I came to apologise," said Ragorek, almost in regret.

"For what? Being a bastard?"

"She's dead, Dek. You have to let it go. It's past and gone. We had our time. Had our time with her. Now it's over. It's the end of an era, brother."

"And now you crawl out of the fucking woodwork looking for cheap copper coins and anything you can scrounge. Is that how it works in Kantarok? Is that the Kantarok way?"

"No, Dek. I came to help, I promise you. I was too late!"

"Ten fucking years too late, Rag!" Dek was staring hard at his older brother, staring with eyes the colour of iron. "You left us. To rot. And when she was dying, you never came to help. You never even came to talk. She was heartbroken, you petty little bastard, but you were so filled with jealousy. *Little brother gets all the attention, all the love.* Pathetic. How fucking old are you, man? I'll tell you how old you are – you're old enough to fucking *die.*"

Dek charged the short distance, but Ragorek was waiting. Right jab, right jab, left straight, left hook, right uppercut; a quick flurry of heavy punches exchanged, and Dek and Ragorek parted, circling, growling, scowling. Ragorek stepped in, right jab, right hook, right straight. Dek kicked him in the belly and he staggered back. Dek leapt forward, but Ragorek knocked away the boot, then the fist, and slammed a left punch to Dek's nose that made the younger brother back off. A temporary retreat.

"I'm going to burn your fucking carcass," said Dek.

"Then you'll hang, little brother."

"Then I'll hang," acknowledged Dek, eyes burning coals.

"You really hate me that much?"

"You killed our mother."

"She died, Dek. There's a difference."

"No. You pushed her. You killed her. And now you'll follow her, and father will be waiting with a helve. He'll beat some sense into you, Little Pup – down in the Furnace. You wait and see. You're going to burn for eternity, *brother*. And I'm going to send you there."

"Show me."

"As you wish."

They fought hard, exchanging blows, straights and hooks, pummelling one another's flesh and heads and bones. Stepping inside a hook, Dek delivered a headbutt that saw Ragorek blinded, spinning away, hands outstretched. Dek leapt forward, but Ragorek kicked him in the balls, had him doubled over, vomit splashing the square. There was no pride. No honour. No tribute. No discipline. No rules. No pride.

"I'll kill you."

"Show me!"

"I'll mash your fucking skull."

"I reckon you bark like a dog."

Both were bloodied bodies, staggering cadavers, a terrible bare-knuckle fist-fight to the death gone wrong. To the watchers, this was disjointed. Unreal. Even the strung-out rules and deviated regulations of the Fighting Pits were stretched, forgotten, ignored, dissolved, devolved. This was primal. Proper soul-deep hate. Brother versus brother over a matter of family...

not *honour*, but a sense of *right*. Ragorek had broken some unwritten, unspoken code. Dek felt he was there to punish him.

Both men were tired, bruised, battered, beaten. But Dek had the look of a rabid dog that refuses to let go of a meat-tattered leg. Ragorek looked like he'd had enough, but pride pushed him on, pride and stubbornness, and his bloodied stumps of broken fists were raised, his eyes focused on nothing but Dek – a symbol of hatred and family annihilation and untethered injustice, before him.

Suddenly, a sound cut through the ice night: high-pitched, and shrill, and chilling.

It severed the calm of the square, like jagged glass across meat and bone.

Heads turned, eyes swivelled, but there was a delay with Dek and Ragorek, for they were totally focused on one another; intent on delivering pain, on breaking bones, on the hurt and the agony and the death to come...

It charged, breaking into the square like an enraged bull. Its head was lowered, one bent and twisted horn from the side of its skull dropping and skewering a man and tossing him, sending him squealing, bubbling, flying through the air where he slapped the cobbles and convulsed, blood pumping out in great reverse gulps from a massive crimson hole.

It was like a horse, but not a horse. It was huge, uneven, with great lumps of bulging muscle, with twisted legs and neck and back, with a misshapen head that was too large to be right. It raised this shaggy-maned skull, then reared suddenly, great flat iron-shod hooves pawing the air as the battered figures of Dek and Ragorek, finally, dazedly, rotated and focused on the creature before them. It was big. Real big. They blinked, mouths working silently in half-drunk disbelief as the creature screamed again from inside its elongated head. It charged a gathering of men to one side of Heroes' Square, hooves trampling three, bulk crashing others from their feet. Its twisted side-horn lashed out, skewering and slashing. Blood showered the icy cobbles like rain. Blood splattered the statues of old heroes, giving them crimson tears.

"What… the hell is *that?*" squealed Weasel.

"Weapons! Get weapons!" roared Skellgann, and hoisted his crossbow. There was a heavy click and whine and a quarrel slashed across the square. It slammed into the beast, making it rear up, howling, blood red eyes spinning in its great, extended, uneven skull. But rather than drop the creature, this act of violence enraged it.

Hooves struck the ground. The beast lowered its head, issuing a deep, reverberating growl like nothing in this mortal realm. The equine head swayed from left to right, then lifted to the heavens, a long deformed horsehead that screeched suddenly like a woman on a knife-blade, and Dek and Ragorek, their feud forgotten, stared in horror at this creature of Chaos; this elemental demon from the torture pits of Hell.

It reared again, and pawing hooves hit the ground at a run, striking sparks. It charged, and Ragorek dived right with a grunt, rolling. Dek moved, but too late, and felt the impact of that great, flat, broken horsehead. The angular horn missed skewering him by a thumb's breadth. He was picked up and accelerated across the square like a child's rag doll, striking a statue which bent him in half, to hit the ground with a dull thump. He lay still, stunned, a beef carcass on a butcher's slab.

The creature pawed the ground and, with a deformed whinny, lowered its head again to charge.

"Here!" screamed Ragorek, waving his arms. The creature swayed, crazed blood eyes staring from under random tufts of black and brown fur. It turned on Ragorek, as Skellgann loosed another quarrel which thumped into the beast's back. But this time, the creature ignored the impact and bore down on Ragorek, huge jaws wide open, folded back almost, wider than any horse's mouth should ever physically be. Ragorek found himself staring into that cavernous maw, all bent and broken fangs, a black tongue curling and snapping like a spitting snake, thick strings of saliva and dead men's blood forming a glutinous web and Ragorek realised he was screaming as those huge jaws moved swiftly toward his face...

Dek slammed into the beast, shoulder first, with his speed and weight and might, and it staggered sideways, jaws instantly snapping around to tear at Dek's head. He twisted. Crooked fangs tore through muscle above his clavicle, which parted like rancid meat pared under a blunt blade, and blood pumped down his left arm in a thick surge.

"Dek, swords!" screamed Weasel, who had run back to the Fighting Cocks. Dek's head came up and his right arm reached out. The blade whistled, turning over and over, and Dek snatched the weapon from the air as huge hooves reared to crush his head.

For an instant, Dek stared at the blade as if he held some alien thing, something terrible. Every man watching in hushed horror knew Dek must be crushed by those huge, flailing legs, those crooked iron hooves. But the warrior stepped neatly to one side and hooves struck a shower of bright light against the cobbles. Dek hacked the short iron blade into the creature's neck. It snarled, head half-turning, teeth and fetid breath an inch from

Dek's blood-spattered face. Fangs snapped at him, like a lunging dog. Dek felt he was staring into the depths of some evil, cavernous pit; some charnel house, where near-dead things squirmed in pools of necrotic bowel; in pits of slithering, poisoned, headless snakes; in hollows of toxic fumes and severed cancerous growths. Dek froze to his very core as the evil magick of this beast swamped him, took his brain in its gauntleted embrace and crushed and broke his courage in half like a tortured man on a rack.

Ragorek screamed, leaping forward to hack his own sword into the creature's spine. Fangs clashed like steel in front of Dek. He blinked and, point first, rammed his own blade up through the creature's throat. Through the dark maw tunnel and strings of saliva he saw the sword slice up into the mouth, skewering the tongue; with a grunt, he jerked it up further, watching the blade slide further into the brain.

The creature reared, tearing the sword from Dek's grip – roaring, squealing – and black blood sprayed from its broken jaws in a great arc. It staggered around, hooves and claws and fangs snapping and stamping. Ragorek darted in, plunging his blade into the beast's flank. It staggered sideways under the blow. Skellgann came closer and, taking careful aim, fired a quarrel into the monster's mouth. It gave a deep groan. More men had gathered arms, and rushed in as a group, spears jabbing at the creature which accepted the blows, the wounds, the slices, the impalement, and simply refused to go down. Only when Dek took a long sword from a bearded man with fear bright and brittle in his plate-wide eyes, and with a great swing hacked off one leg, then a second, did the beast finally topple to the ground to lie, panting, wheezing, coughing blood, crazed eyes switching from one man to the next to the next as if remembering and storing their faces for some future retribution. Dek stepped in close and hacked free the other two legs which lay, oozing black blood from jagged stumps, as twisted scarred iron hooves jittered and trembled as if still connected to some crazed puppeteer. The legless body squirmed and shifted, a dark slug, moving slowly around in a circle, and Dek realised everybody was watching *him*; eyes wide, terror coiled around their limbs and sword arms, horror and disgust holding them in thrall.

"So, then, I'll do it, shall I?" snapped Dek, annoyed at the group, and spat and moved in close to those snapping jaws. And the monster's eyes were watching him, piercing into his own from that great flat head, and they made him shiver as his mouth went dry and fear flooded him. For in that instant, the orbs looked nothing less than human.

Dek's sword hacked at the neck, and it took six blows to break through thick sinews of muscle, tendon, ligament and spinal column.

Only then did the beast lie still, slowly collapsing down, deflating, onto a freezing platter of expanding crimson.

Ragorek approached, still holding his sword in swollen fingers.

"Well done, little brother."

"I reckon it's your turn next, you bastard," snarled Dek.

"Not tonight," breathed Weasel, eyes still wide. He held up both hands, palms outwards. "Not now... not after... this."

"This changes nothing," growled Dek, but suddenly his sword clattered to the ground and he dropped to one knee. He cursed, and looked at the deep glossy wound in his shoulder. He struggled to rise. "Damn it, I have a job to finish!" But blood loss left him weak, and he slumped over, onto his side.

Skellgann rushed over and rolled Dek to his back. "Who'll help me carry him back to the tavern?" Men rushed forward, and they bore the huge fighter away leaving Weasel and Ragorek standing, weak and limp, staring at the steaming carcass of the slaughtered beast.

"What is this creature?" breathed Ragorek.

"It's like nothing I've ever seen," said Weasel, rubbing his eyes wearily. He smeared stray droplets of blood across his own skin, and then stared at his hands for a moment, confused.

"I fear the world is changing," said Ragorek, gently, the tip of his sword touching the icy cobbles with an almost inaudible *cling*, "when beasts such as this can invade the home lives of good, honest men."

"Changing?" Weasel gave a bitter short laugh, like a slap. He poked the massacred beast with the toe of his boot. "This *monster* is not a product of our mortal realm. A raven-dark wind blows, Rag. I feel it, in my soul. This is just the beginning. I sense it. In my blood, like honey-leaf drugs. In my bones, like rancid marrow. There'll be nowhere to hide for the likes of us, when this thing starts proper."

"You reckon?"

"I promise you, mate," said Weasel, and turned, heading back for the tavern, the light, the warmth, the camaraderie and an illusion of sanity which promised to nurse him to a bitter, drunken oblivion.

FROM THE MUD

It was death. It was birth. It was fire. It was rape. It was exquisite murder. It was cheerful suicide. It was acid in her veins. Poison in her heart. Sulphur in her soul. A sincere abortion. A child's coffin. An army of necrotic lovers. A giggling genocide. All of those things, and yet none.

It ravaged through her, burning, burning, pure hot honey in her veins and eyes and womb, and she screamed but she had no mouth, and she cried but she had no eyes, and she fought, for that was what she knew, that was what she did, that was all she could do. She fought for life, and she fought for death, and she fought to be free of the Furnace, for they had forced her there with powerful magick charms and magick oil, sacrilegious paedophiles, religious zealots and holy bastard whores, with their blood-oil and song-magick, with their sacrifice and genocide and betrayal of the *Old Gods*, the *Bad Gods… the Equiem…* she screamed, and fought, and thrashed, and gouged, and spat, and pissed, and every fucking inch was a million fucking years, and every fucking bite another fallen star, every savage slash of claws another decadent miscarriage, every scream vomited from her solid, mercury-filled throat was another worthy charnel house of sliming fish-head corpses waiting to be filled…

But then.

Then it was done.

And the world spun cool.

She knelt, crouched naked in a ditch, in the mud, slender and white and vulnerable; like a worm; a porcelain worm. The rain slammed down with cold needles that bit her tingling flesh. Slowly, she breathed out, and then in, and then out, savouring the acidic cold air, sulphurous from the Osanda marshes. But it tasted better than any succulent honey, any vintage wine, any ripe erection; for the air was *fresh* and the air was *free*.

She was free.

She stood, uncurling fast like the strike of an albino cobra. Her head lifted, and she stared up at the cold stars through the rain. A billion miles of hydrogen and frozen, chilled light.

She lifted her head, and she screamed, a noise so high and long and loud it seemed to split the world, split the heavens, and it sliced through the night and the darkness, disturbing the peace of a nearby mudland village.

She breathed, then. Breathed deep, and low, her chest rising and falling in a rhythm she thought she had forgotten.

So, this was life.

She… remembered.

Slowly, her hands touched herself, as if in wonder. She gazed down, at her fingers, her toes, her legs, her flat naked pale white belly. She touched her own breasts, cold and white as pared fish flesh. Finally, she gazed at her finger tips.

"I am alive," she said, voice deep and musical, and she smiled, and her teeth ground together. She climbed up from the mud pit, slowly, every droplet and splash running from her skin as if her flesh was a charmed distillation and

to sully its purity a sacrilegious abomination. She stood on
the rim of the pit and watched five riders pick their way
towards her from the nearby village. They were woodsmen,
she could tell by their garb as they approached warily. The
horses snorted and stamped in sudden, raging fear as they
smelled her. Hooves clattered on rocks and ululating equine
squeals marked the start of an uncontrollable fast-rising
panic... but the woman lifted a finger and lowered her
head and the horses were instantly calm, immediately still.

"A clever trick, lady," said one man. He was large,
stocky, made even more so by his bulky oilskins to ward
off driving rain. He dropped from the saddle to the mud.
"Are you up here screaming on your own, lady, or do
you have friends nearby?" He was wary, glancing about.
There had been flashes of lightning cracking the sky. And
now... this.

The woman smiled and, quite theatrically, touched her
finger to her lips. "Shh," she said.

"You wish *me* to be quiet?" The man snorted laughter
and turned to one of his companions. "Hey, Ebram, this
wild woman of the night wants me to shut my mouth!"
He turned back and observed her. She did not move, as if
relishing his attention.

She was tall, well over six feet and, if the truth be told,
nearer to seven. She was very slender, each limb a bald
yew bough. Her skin was pale white, almost translucent,
and devoid of any mark. Her short hair, flat against her
skull, was as white as her skin. The woodsman's eyes
travelled up and down her body, and he found himself
deeply confused.

"Lady, we can leave you out here to freeze if you like.
Or you can come back down to the village. Dora's a kind
soul, runs the tavern; she'll find you clothes and blankets,

get you out of this rain and chill and give you some hot soup to warm you up."

The woman gave a single, slow shake of her head. She lifted her hand and the five men watched, eyes narrowed, until her finger came to rest pointing at Ebram's horse.

"What's the matter with you? Where did you come from? How did you end up out here like this?"

"I need a mount," said the woman, voice low, sultry, rich, musical, and her eyes flickered through a million different colours, and she felt the *power* surge within her, up, through her. Suddenly, the horse screamed and reared up, and Ebram stepped swiftly away, slipping in the mud, falling heavily to the ground with a thud where he lay, stunned, watching with mouth hung open, brain failing to decode what his eyes were witnessing...

The horse reared, hooves kicking the air, squealing like a baby, screaming like a stuck pig; then it went suddenly rigid, front hooves held high, and its skin seemed to bubble and roll with ripples like molten copper, and there came heavy *cracks* and its legs thrust out, bent into odd shapes, and a wild wind blew from the storm, and lightning cracked the sky like an egg, and the horse seemed almost to *turn inside out*, and its skull bloated, expanding unevenly, muzzle elongating and still screaming a single high-pitched note, and its body enlarged, crimson and slick with oozing blood; several of its pumping organs squirmed on the outside of its great, swollen, deformed body. The horse screamed and screamed, and its hooves hit the mud and it stood, panting heavily, nearly twice its original size, one front shoulder lower than the other, its eyes now blood red, its long equine maw twisted and scattered with uneven bent fangs. The deformed horse was a huge, malevolent, threatening creature. It grunted, shifting as if in great pain, then it lowered its jaws towards Ebram and with a quick, economical bite, snapped off his head.

Curses and shouts rang through the night, and the woman's long white finger pointed to the other mounts which screamed and reared, skin peeling, bones cracking, heads elongating, maws twisting, and the men were thrown in panic, scrabbling in the mud, then they were up and running as the twisted horses came down on new, bloated hooves with bent shoes and turned, and charged them, and ate them, bodies, clothes, skulls and all.

Blood lay heavy in hollows. Rain pounded diagonal sheets. A cold wind blew and the slender woman shivered in ecstasy as she moved amidst these five huge, threatening, newborn beasts. Her hand traced lines down their bloodied flanks, and then she leapt easily onto one creature's back and it reared, and she breathed, and it felt good to be alive; it felt good to be free. It felt good *to be back*.

"I can channel the old magick," she breathed, words drifting and lost in the storm. She smiled. "Interesting." Her flickering eyes were like fire, like blood, filled with molten magick and overflowing with an ocean of crimson tears for a distant, ancient reckoning; a violent, primeval grudge.

"Now, it is time to claim my rightful throne," whispered Orlana, the Changer.

SUGAR AND SPICE

Kiki stared at her reflection in the silver-glass mirror. Her reflection stared back with hard uncompromising eyes.

You are going to die, said that reflection, face twisting, crooked, a mocking smile of bitter ripe irony.

"No, I'm not. I cannot. I'm still young, strong, a great warrior, a beautiful woman, virile, men lust after me, want to bed me for long, rapturous hours through the night; I'm the captain and master of my own fate, and only when I cast away that belief will the stinking, rotting corpse of death arrive on his pale horse of skull-meat and squirming maggots and sever my links to this pointless, pathetic existence."

There came a long pause, and the reflection released a peal of beautiful, tinkling laughter. It was like spring petals falling. Moonlight dancing through crystal. *No*, she said, eyes the colour of iron fixing on her *her* as her lips *her own damned lips* twisted into a savage snarl of disgust. *You're dying, Kiki; you have a growth inside you, you know this is true; you heard the doctors' low panicked voices even through your pain, even through the searing agony of the hot knife blade. One said it was too close to your heart and to cut it free would be to cut your heart in two. So the surgeon left it there, and not all the gold in Vagandrak can change the fact. You are going to die, bitch. And I'm on the other side of this mirror, waiting for you to arrive.*

"What do you want from me, Suza?"

I want you. I want you here. I want you beside me. Now!

"And where exactly *are* you, *sister of mine?*"

Silence. Always silence. And that smile, crooked, disjointed, a smile of mockery and condescension. Then the image shimmered and the doppelgänger vanished to leave a *blink* and Kiki's own face and naked upper body reflected.

"Mmmm?" came a sound from behind, from the bed, murmured from betwixt silk sheets still sprinkled with fine honeyed wine and an artistic scattering of rose petals. "Come back to bed, my sweet. It's warm here. You know it is."

"In a minute."

"Come back to me, gorgeous thing. I'm waiting for you. You know I am."

"I told you. In a minute." There was iron in her voice; the same iron that dominated the colour of her eyes.

Kiki observed herself again. Long brown hair, with just a hint of silver painting a few strands bright. She was tall, elegant, but powerful with it. Creases lined her eyes, but she could ease them free with thick creams bought from the apothecary. What gave away her real age, and the wealth (horror?) of her experiences, was the pain; deep inside her eyes, like a second dark pupil of contained and casket-locked memories. Even to herself, those iron orbs looked old. Older than the world. Older than death. But then, hadn't it always been that way?

"Come back to bed, my sweet elixir of eternal pleasure." Soft hands touched her bare shoulders, and Kiki tensed. Just for a moment. Before relaxing under his gentle outward strokes. She released a slow breath, for her eye had caught the ornamental dagger on the cluttered, polished table before the mirror, no doubt for opening gilt-edged envelopes of invitation to some rich bastard's decadent wife-swapping party. Her eye had caught the dagger, and reflex alone nearly spun her, plunging the blade into the man's eye socket.

Why so highly strung? she chided herself. And then smiled, breathing deeply.

Always the killer, mocked her sister within the cage of her own skull.

"OK, Lars. You win. I'll come back to bed." She turned and stood, and he stood with her. He stepped in close, pressing his naked body to hers, and she let him kiss her again, tenderly, slowly.

Yeah. What does this slimy bastard *really* want?

Go to Hell.

They kissed, their passion igniting, and she felt him growing aroused and smiled inside the kiss. "Come on." She took his hand and led him to the tangled sheets. They were still warm and they slid into their haven, holding one other, Lars stroking her arm, kissing her, touching her, and she allowed him to warm her, allowed him to take her, and she moaned as she rolled onto her back, with him atop, entering her, and they built from a slow union of gentle rhythm to a crescendo of desperation, sweating, groaning, clawing the sheets and pillows and one another's flesh until the world no longer mattered and she screamed and growled and it was all in the blink of explosion...

Kiki lay on her back, eyes closed, listening to her own panting. His hand idly traced patterns across her skin, and worked its way to her chest and the nine inch scar she knew lay there like a raw blister. Healed, but raw inside her head. Like branded flesh. Like the cancer had marked her prior to taking her.

"Tell me again how you got this, my gorgeous."

"I never told you."

"Yes. I forgot. The beautiful lady is so *secretive*." He smiled, but not much.

"Hey, you chased me, Lars. Just because I come to your perfume-stinking bed, doesn't mean I have to divulge my life story now, does it?"

"Perfume sti… that is quite horribly offensive, my little sweetmeat; but then, your amazing beauty diverts my anger and allows you to be so abrasive and curt, wounding my heart with your silver barbs of honey-poison."

Kiki laughed, and opened her eyes, propping herself up on one elbow. "Your fine talk might work with the noble rich ladies of Rokroth, my dear Lars; but I'd wager they're simple souls. Why else would they be condemned to this backwater shit-hole?"

"Rokroth? A…" he savoured the word as he would a bitter wine, "*shit-hole*?"

Kiki laughed again, a sound she'd not heard herself produce for far too long. Lars looked wounded. Like a slapped puppy. "Sorry." She became more gentle. "I do not mean to mock. Let us be frank, good sir: Rokroth lies beside the Rokroth Marshes – hardly renowned across Vagandrak for its fine air and sophisticated culture. Wasn't it once used as an area of banishment by the Old Kings?"

Lars seemed to deflate. "I apologise. As you well know, I am heir to the Lordship of Rokroth. It… pains me to hear it belittled. But what you say is true. Sometimes, the marshes do indeed pollute the air with, shall we say, some interesting odours."

Kiki play-thumped him on the chest. "That's what I like to see! Nobility with a sense of humour."

"Hardly nobility," said Lars, blushing a little.

"Are you blushing?"

"You do abuse me so," said Lars. "Although I confess, if you hadn't saved me from that uncouth tavern brawl, I might not be here to suffer such abuse; so for that, I am eternally grateful."

"Yeah. You keep showing me."

"And will continue to do so, as long as you'll grace my table, my company and my bed."

"Mmm," murmured Kiki, closing her eyes and relaxing back. She had to admit, it was fun – for a while – to enjoy the pleasures of Lars' modest wealth. But there was much he did not know about her. So much…

"I have a question," said Lars, and she opened her eyes again, staring up into his. They were wide and pleading. She liked that. She was in control, and they both knew it.

"It's not about my name again, is it?"

"No, although I confess it concerns me I do not yet know your true identity, and it concerns me deeply you've come to my bed for two weeks now, on seven occasions, and I still cannot introduce you to my friends."

"I do not wish to meet your friends."

"But *I* want you to meet them. My father is holding a ball, no, wait, I can see your face change… hear me out, please. The ball will be an extravagant affair at Rokroth Hall, in honour of King Yoon himself! It has been rumoured the King may possibly be in attendance, and this has been the talk of many weeks throughout Rokroth Council. I would be honoured if you would accompany me to the ball." His words accelerated as he saw her face drop. "No, no, wait, it's not what you think, and if money is a problem for you then I would be more than happy to buy you a most exquisite ball gown, of fine silk. There are some incredible dressmakers in Rokroth, we could go shopping together, for shoes, and some jewellery, it would be fun–"

"No."

"But–"

"No."

"I don't understand."

"I never made you any promises, Lars. You pursued me, remember, for weeks. I was just about getting ready to stick a knife in your guts when you went and got into that stupid brawl with the eel men. Three of them. And you, there, with your perfume and your little toad-sticker. They would have hacked off your limbs and thrown you in the swamp!"

"I am expert with foil, sabre and épée." Lars looked quite wounded. "I would have bested them, I am sure."

"Yeah, in your dreams, nobleman. This is the real world we're talking about now; a world where you get stabbed in the back and left in an alley to rot after they've cleaned out your pockets and raped your wife."

Lars was silent.

"Sorry," said Kiki. She gave a narrow smile. "Sometimes I get carried away."

"I know, Kiki. I understand."

She stared at him. Humour drained from her face like the last dregs from a poison bottle, and with the intense frown she now offered Lars, colour drained from his.

"You know my name," she said, and her voice was very low, a dangerous growl, and even though the words were not threatening, not threatening in the slightest, Lars *felt* a sudden and very great presence of danger. Not some tavern brawl. This was life and death. Instant. Sudden. Predator taking victim.

"You spoke it. In your sleep. You said you were Kiki. And that means you are…" He paused, and looked at her. He swallowed, his throat bobbing. "Er."

"Go on," she said. Still, she had not moved.

"You are one of the Iron Wolves," he whispered, throat husky.

"Which one?"

"The leader," he said. He swallowed again. His eyes shone. "Look. Kiki. Honestly. This is not a problem for me. I know you're a wanted woman, but…"

"Go on."

"Stop! Stop being like this. You can *trust* me. Just because I'm some rich dandy who enjoys wine, perfumery and lustful couplings with beautiful women, doesn't mean I'm in the King's pocket!"

"*But* you said so yourself. King Yoon may be attending the ball thrown by your father at Rokroth Hall. Why would you invite me? You knew my name before you made the offer. And you're not moving, which can only mean one thing. You have a blade beneath the sheets."

She felt the cold press of steel against her ribs. Gentle, but nicking slightly. A droplet of blood rolled down her flank.

She smiled.

"IN HERE!" Lars bellowed, and she heard the clank of armoured men outside the bedroom, armoured boots muffled by thick expensive carpets. They were King's Men. King's Guards. Here to arrest her. Here to… kill her? Possibly. The problem lay with King Yoon, Tarek's direct descendant; his blood heir. Yoon wouldn't want an ex-hero of the Pass of Splintered Bones dragged through the dirt in extended shame and anti-royal publicity. One of the legendary Iron Wolves! That would be… complicated.

Twenty-five years ago, the Iron Wolves, King Tarek's elite force, held back tens of thousands of mud-orcs at the Pass of Splintered Bones; the mighty Desekra Fortress was almost overrun, thousands of Vagandrak's finest soldiers slain, and Morkagoth, an evil sorcerer with the power to shapeshift, set to wrest the throne from King Tarek. Without the Iron Wolves, the whole of Vagandrak would have been overrun, the king murdered, the people sold into slavery; or worse, slaughtered in their beds. Men, women, children. Throats cut. Hung from trees. Genocide. Now, there were no greater heroes to inspire children and adults alike than the Iron Wolves. Epic sagas had been penned by the country's finest scribes. Poems and songs were sung around tavern fires by minstrels earning their dinner. Children re-enacted the battle in endless amateur school plays. Scholars studied tactics from *The Mud-orc Siege* and *The Charge of Splintered Bones*.

When the Iron Wolves, in an epic, desperate, final battle, finally reached and killed Morkagoth, the remaining mud-orcs retreated to their pits and slime in the south; thus ended the War of Zakora, and the elevation of the Iron Wolves to heroes. King Tarek showered them with gold, jewels, land and palaces. And they had gone their separate ways...

Now, Lars, heir to the stinking backwater Lordship of Rokroth, had one of them *in his bed*. And she was wanted. *Wanted*. Not just for murder and smuggling, of which she was no doubt guilty; but also on suspicion of witchcraft, heresy and peddling the honey-leaf which was said to bring a man closer to the Three Gods and the Seven Sisters. Probably in the same kingsize bed.

"IN HERE!"

Kiki gave a short laugh. "You bastard. After all we've been through?" she muttered, without apparent irony.

"I'm sorry, Kiki. Truly. It was fun. *All of it* was fun... while it lasted."

The door rattled.

"Lord Lars," came a muffled voice. "The door! It is locked!"

"Idiots! BREAK IT DOWN!"

She moved fast, head-butting him and making him howl from a scrunched up face with broken nose. Taking the long dagger, she rammed it hard into his shoulder, through flesh and bone, pinning him to the bed. A butterfly to a board. He thrashed suddenly, screaming, legs kicking, blood frothing around the wound and the nasty black triangular steel. Kiki leapt from the tangled silk sheets and dragged on leggings and a tight black shirt as sounds of crunching wood echoed through the room. She grabbed her weapon baldric, settling it over her head from right shoulder to left hip as the door burst in and five of the King's Guard moved forward with drawn short swords.

They glanced at Lars, thrashing on the bed, moaning, and touching the handle of the long dagger with little puppy yelps. Then heads came up as they focused on Kiki, who was standing with arms by sides, completely relaxed, iron grey eyes fixed on the five men. They wore King Yoon's livery, mainly chainmail armour but with plate protecting chests, forearms and thighs. They wore tight helmets stamped with the Royal Coat of Arms. It was a good mixture, for it provided protection yet with increased mobility over full plate; Kiki gave a tight grimace showing her teeth.

"You are under arrest, madam," said the leader, who wore his black beard neatly trimmed and had dark eyes under shaggy brows. "In the name of the King."

"Do you know who I am?" Kiki said, voice soft.

"Yes, madam. No sudden moves. We've been instructed to bring you in alive, but if you force us into action we have authority to use maximum force. We are men of honour. None of us here likes to hurt a lady."

"That's good, then, captain," smiled Kiki, moving towards them, arms outstretched, hands crossed in a sign of surrender. She saw the guards' shoulders relax, just that little bit. Behind her, Lars was making gurgling noises. "Because I'm no lady."

The throwing knife went from baldric to the captain's eye socket in one swift, single slash. He staggered back as Kiki accelerated, another knife in her fist as she leapt, feinting left past a blade, kicking from the wall and punching her blade into the second guard's throat. He gurgled, ejecting blood, and she rode him to the ground as another blade whistled horizontally over her head, crashing into the shoulder of a fellow guard. He cried out as steel struck chainmail, taking a step back. Kiki hit the ground, shifting into a forward roll and leaping again with the balance of an acrobat. All was chaos. In the confines of the room the guards were crammed in too tight to use their swords effectively. One pulled his own dagger, but Kiki was too close – close enough to kiss and she rammed her blade low, into his groin between the panels of chainmail and plate. She jerked it up. It bit him like acid and he groaned, staggering forward onto her as his femoral artery was snicked open and his lifeblood pumped out to rich thick carpets. She let him fall, taking his dagger so that now she held two, and twisted away, dropping to a crouch, pausing. Her face was speckled with blood, both fists glistening crimson. Three dead. Two left. They backed away, staring at her in horror.

"Run to your mothers," she growled, rising from her crouch and stretching her back. "Before I gut you like sour fucking fish." But they could not, and she understood their hesitancy. These were King's Guards. She was one little lady, without a sword. To retreat? The King would not look favourably on such an action. In her mind's eye, Kiki pictured a large oak tree and a strong thick noose.

"Get the others," growled one guard, the senior by the grey in his beard. The younger of the two slipped through the broken door, thankfully.

They were left alone. Lars had stopped kicking on the bed and was groaning, a low sound of self-pity as consciousness slipped away. The silk sheets were crimson in a wide pool.

"Well then. It's just me and you now, woman," this final guard said.

A curious silence settled on the room as Lars passed, thankfully, into a state of unconsciousness. Outside, Kiki heard the stomping of hooves, a whinny, the patter of rain on cobbles, the shout of a distant late-night food seller.

Kiki watched him, and took a careful step back. Warily, the guard leant his sword against the wall and pulled free two long knives. His eyes were gleaming and he licked his lips. "These fools wanted to bring you in alive. But me? I'm happy to hear you sing like a skewered bird. Do you want to sing for me, pretty one?"

Kiki stepped back around the bed, and the guard advanced, both knives before him. There was a hint of cruelty around his mouth, his eyes fixed on her with a certain intensity, and Kiki got the sudden chill feeling this man was a born killer; a murderer, hiding inside the honourable livery of Vagandrak's military.

"You get off, killing women?" she said, voice husky, taking another step back. And another. She was analysing his movements; wary now. He was smooth, well-balanced, like an oiled machine. Not like the others. He had waited at the back, weighing her up. Watching her. Studying her movements. Clever.

"Men. Women. Children. There is an intimacy in death, don't you find? To drive in that knife through soft resistance. An immortal embrace. To feel the last dying breath on your cheek, like a kiss from God. To see the sparkling life-light fade from understanding eyes. It is a beautiful moment. Exquisite. Perfect. Eternal. A moment to share. A moment to be stolen."

Kiki said nothing. She was near the wall, and the window which overlooked the street. But turning to slide open the portal was not an option. Turn your back on this man and he'd put a knife through your kidney.

"What's your name?"

"Jahrell," he said.

"I am Kiki."

"I know. And we need to know these things. To share them. Before I kill you. Before you die." He smiled, gently, like a doting father to a treasured daughter.

"Before one of us dies, surely?"

"As you say."

They paused, weighing one another up.

"You don't have to do this," said Kiki.

"That's what they all say."

"You've done this before? This murder?"

"Oh yes."

"A lot?"

"Many, many times, my beautiful little songbird."

"How long have you got away with this... trickery?"

"All my life," smiled Jahrell. It was a sickly smile, when it came.

"Ahh. I see. So... you're one of those," said Kiki, darkly.

"I am not ashamed of my actions. I have done nothing wrong. I am holy in what I do. Blessed, so to speak. It is the greatest honour to take a life; and I do so enjoy earning that honour."

"I need to thank you," said Kiki.

"Thanks?"

"Yes. You've removed my guilt."

"What guilt?"

"Any guilt I might have felt at cutting your fucking throat," she said – and launched at him. His knives came up fast, for he was supremely skilled despite his psychopathic tendencies; steel clashed, singing a metal song, a series of incredibly quick blows first from Kiki, defended by Jahrell, then by Jahrell, defended by nimble fast sure strong movements from Kiki.

She stepped back.

Horse hooves stomped outside. Men shouted.

Time was… limited.

"Good," breathed Jahrell. "You're one of the best. I'll enjoy tasting you. Every, single part of you." He licked his lips, which gleamed.

"You'll have to earn it," said Kiki, sinking lower, into that place down below combat, down below war and fighting and anger and hate; she sank into a world where there was nothing more than the blades in her hands and the blades in her enemy's fists. Rain filled with ice drummed the streets. Gushed in the gutters. His eyes sparkled. She could see sweat on the stubble on his upper, unshaved lip. He was smiling.

He was sure, despite her skill.

Fuck you, she thought. I despise your arrogance. I pity your superiority. I mock your pointless dedication.

I'll show you. Show you something *new*…

He came this time, blades a dazzling blur, his movements more urgent. He knew his comrades would be dismounting, walking through the hall, climbing the stairs. And if they arrived too early he wouldn't have his fun. His playtime would be over. He had to kill her fast. Had to earn his reward. The life-light leaving her pretty, pretty eyes...

And she led him on, like an eager, spotted teenager with a priapic cock.

It wasn't difficult. She'd done it before.

That was the problem with men.

Always ruled by their petty, simple lusts.

Just... No. Fucking. Intelligence.

Blades clashed, clanged, deflected; his blade cut her upper arm and she yelped, sighed, turning to one side, injured, in pain, agony firing her eyes, deflating, and he came in fast for the kill but too fast and too eager and too ready to get the job done and finished. He was a premature ejaculation. Her knife cut into his belly and he gasped, choked, coughed heavily.

He slumped against her, his arms suddenly weak and useless. She supported him as he gasped again, and it was intimate. She looked into his eyes, blade still buried in his guts, supporting his weight. He fought to lift his own weapons, but he could not. She smiled directly in his face.

"Do you have a wife?" Her words were soft.

He gave a nod.

"And children?"

Again, a nod. He fought again to raise his long knives, but Kiki jerked her own blade and he groaned. No doubt the pain bit him like acid. No doubt it filled his mind with a bright hot fire and everything else was receding to a dull world of nothing; all that remained was the pain and the knife in his flesh like molten iron.

And the knowledge. The knowledge he was going to die.

"Sometimes," said Kiki, leaning close, her mouth by his ear, aware he could smell her scent, her perfume, her stench of recent sex, "sometimes, I hate to kill. Not like you. For me, it is a duty. Sometimes, I kill to stay alive. I kill for honour, for king, and for country. I kill so that I may live."

"Yes," he managed. Blood trickled from the corner of his mouth.

"But this time," said Kiki, shifting back a little so she could face him, to look deep into his eyes, and she kissed him then, a full bodied kiss, tasting him, tasting his decadence, "this time I love it. This time, Jahrell, you lost the game. But I will find your wife. I will find your children. I will tell them what you did. What you were. I have friends in the military; I'm an *Iron Wolf*, after all." The irony was not lost on her. "And I will have your name scraped from the Hall of Heroes in Vagan." She began to cut with the dagger, sawing upwards, opening him like a gutted fish. He moaned, dropping his knives, fingers grasping at her, clawing her, and she continued to saw like a butcher with a slab on the block, and his insides came spilling out and he stank like the dead he would soon become.

Kiki pushed away the corpse, moved away, pulled on and laced up her boots. She grabbed a sword as she heard boots on the stairs and, giving one final glance at Lars – poor dumb back-stabbing pointless Lars, whom she did consider murdering for a moment, putting him out of his misery, but then decided against it. His petty existence was his punishment, and he fucking knew it. She moved swiftly to the window. She prized open the latch with her knife, slid up the six panes and climbed out onto the narrow stone ledge.

Wind and rain and ice slapped her. She gasped, and laughed.

She was alive. *Alive*.

Alive for now, bitch, whispered her dark sister in the mirror.

For a moment, vertigo gripped her and it felt as if the whole world was moving; the whole world was crumbling, falling down in some incredible vast collapsing earthquake. Kiki breathed deeply and controlled herself, and controlled the world around her, and the vertigo drifted away like smoke from a fire.

She climbed swiftly to the roof, strong fingers finding gaps in crumbling brickwork and stone lintels, and then she was running fast across ice-slick slates. Shouts echoed hollow behind her. Shock, awe, horror. She'd emptied Jahrell like a knife-cut sack of shit.

You were right, she thought, as she sprinted through the rain and icy hail.

There is an intimacy in death. An intimacy I do not care for.

THE PASS OF SPLINTERED BONES

The Pass of Splintered Bones cut like a knife wound through the vast, savage mountain range named the Mountains of Skarandos. Acting as a natural border between the lands of Vagandrak to the north, and the deserts and grasslands of Zakora to the south, the Mountains of Skarandos numbered perhaps a thousand peaks, many reaching three or four leagues up into the heavens, the lower slopes jet black, and dark grey granite and slate, angular, steep, unforgiving, sporting little life and many dark valleys into which an unwary explorer could tumble and die and rot and turn to dust. The upper flanks and towering peaks were permanently shrouded in snow, split by vast narrow crevasses like deep throats spiralling down into Hell or the Furnace. What few routes did exist through the mountains were few and far between, high and narrow and treacherous with ice. Wolves hunted throughout the Mountains of Skarandos, and there had even been sightings of snow lions. The mountains cut across the horizon like a toothed saw blade, separating sky from land, separating north from south, and this natural barrier was the main and *only* reason there had not been more wars between the lands of Vagandrak and Zakora; for they were bordered to the west by the vast impenetrable salt plains, and to the east by the Plague Ocean in which to swim, or even sail, was to die.

And so Vagandrak and Zakora were afforded a wall erected by Nature, albeit a wall with one implicit flaw: the Pass of Splintered Bones, a valley between the towering peaks, a chasm perhaps fifty feet wide in places, as much as a hundred feet in others, weaving like a contorted snake beneath sheer walls of gleaming slate and rock. Nobody knew the true history of the pass, but it was a road of bones: a pathway of splintered femurs; broken clavicles; cracked radius; crushed vertebrae; fractured fibulas; and split skulls, many in pieces, but some part-whole, their dead black eye sockets a sober warning to those who travelled the pass, that this particular place had a very dark and nasty history.

Scholars in Vagandrak had multiple theories, many involving slave labour, ritual sacrifice and even the magick of the Equiem; in truth, nobody could even begin to know the true story of how many tens of thousands of corpses had ended up paving this twisting roadway through the Mountains of Skarandos.

However, many hundreds of years ago, after centuries of sporadic battle, after centuries of Zenta tribesmen raiding the southern villages of Vagandrak in the name of honour and earning their manhood, and with increased rumours of a united tribe army, so King Esekra the Great had conceived and built a mighty fortress, named Desekra, four mighty walls with wide battlements and high crenellations, a narrow passage and gate that could be blocked in an instant. And thus Desekra Fortress rose from the splintered bones of thousands of fallen, its stones mined from the very mountains themselves and creating a vast network of underground tunnels deep into the heart of the mountains and out like a web under the plains beyond the walls.

The Walls: Sanderlek, Tranta-Kell, Kubosa and Jandallakla – leading to Zula, a huge stocky keep, black and grim and foreboding, more like a prison than the core of a fortress. Zula meant *peace*, in the old Equiem tongue; and it had been here, on his deathbed, that old King Esekra had indeed found peace, secure in the knowledge he had built not just a protective barrier to guard his people of the north. No. It also stood as a monument to the greatest Battle King ever to walk the lands of Vagandrak.

Now, as winter caressed the horizon and rain filled with sleet slammed down from the towering Skarandos peaks looming overhead, so two soldiers from the Vagandrak Army stood on Sanderlek, having drawn a six hour night watch, from ten till four. They were not happy about the situation.

Diagonal sheets slammed down at them, rain and sleet and knives, and they huddled beneath oiled leather cloaks, hands outstretched to a half-shielded brazier on which glowing coals crackled and spat.

Sanderlek stretched off into blackness in both directions, slick and wet and vast, but the two men were more occupied by attempting to bleach warmth from the brazier than standing watch searching for possible enemies in the wild storm beyond the fortress.

Jagan was a farmer who, thanks to consistent fallow fields over three years, had lost his land holdings to the King. Whilst bitter about the whole situation, and the fact his wife and child had to move back home with her parents in distant Rokroth, he was still young and strong, and knew a career in the army would at least put food in his child's mouth until he could work out what other profession to invest his time in. Whilst not a massively intelligent man, he was intelligent enough to recognise he had few skills other than his strength and youth. His mother-in-law had suggested going to work in the tanneries or fish markets, but Jagan was a man of the land, open fields and fresh air. The thought of being enclosed made his head spin, as did the aromas from close gatherings of stench-ridden people. No. The army had seemed as good a place as any. That had been four long years ago, and Jagan had been lucky to keep his position when Yoon made vast and drastic cuts, sending tens of thousands of men back home and leaving the fortress feeling almost empty. Yes, it still had a garrison of ten thousand, but what the common man did not realise was that included staff, cooks and carpenters, builders, serving maids, ostlers and smiths. In terms of fighting force, they were perhaps seven thousand strong, and even *those* worked on rotation, with at least three thousand being out on training manoeuvres or on leave at any one time. Desekra was designed for a full complement of fifty thousand in times of war. Now, it seemed almost like a ghost town.

The second man was tall and slim, with a narrow, pointed face like a ferret. He looked dark and mean, and quite out of place in a soldier's uniform. His face was constantly twisted into a cynical sneer, and his excessive love of liquor had ended with more than one night in military prison.

His name was Reegez. In a different world, in a different time, he would have had nothing to do with the likes of Jagan, and Jagan knew it. But here and now, forced together in the endurance of a soldier's life, with hard physical training and long periods of boredom on various duties of watch, they had become good friends. Reegez had taught Jagan all he knew about cards and playing knuckle-dice; Jagan had bored Reegez with the thrills of crop-rotation and how to fix a broken plough.

On this harsh night as the storm accosted the fortress from the south, howling like demons over the plain, so their conversation was muted. They'd been on duty for three hours, and water had ingressed both leather cloaks making the men cold and uncomfortable.

"This is beyond a bad joke," moaned Reegez, wriggling under the leather, shifting his shoulders in an attempt to block out some annoying draught. "Five times this month I caught a night-time watch, and five bloody times it's rained like the Plague Ocean has been tipped over my head."

"I know. I've been with you all five times," said Jagan, shuffling a little closer to the brazier. "I think the rain will stop soon."

"You said that two hours ago."

"You're in a foul mood tonight!"

"Well, it's this horse shit weather, and this horse shit situation. Look out there! Go on, just bloody look!"

Pandering to his friend, Jagan leant sideways and made an effort to glance between the crennellations. Water slapped him in the face like an irate lover. He gasped, dribbling water, and retreated back to the brazier like an injured kitten.

"I can't see anything," he gasped.

"Exactly. What's the bloody point us standing out here in this horse shit, when we couldn't even see a warhost of ten thousand camped five bloody feet from the wall? It's pointless! They should let us inside until after the storm has passed. Get some warm tea and toasted bread down us. That would make more sense."

"You'll be asking for a warm bed on your watch, next."

"Would that be so bad? A few hours' kip. Why do they need two of us? It's bureaucracy, is what it is. The bloody generals and captains don't know what the hell they're doing; they sit there in their ivory towers…"

"There are no ivory towers at Desekra."

"…ivory towers *so to speak*, and drink coffee and smoke cigars and dream up ever more pointless ways for us to waste our time. You know yesterday? They had twenty of us scrubbing the cobbles in the east stables; *scrubbing the cobbles!* On our bloody hands and knees, we had to do it till the stone was gleaming. And what for? All so the cavalry can put their bloody horses back in there to stamp their hooves and shit on everything. It was a disgrace, it was."

"So I see," grinned Jagan, and patted his friend's arm. "But come on, it's not that bad. You have good company to while away the hours, and a good solid Vagan-built stone fortress between you and any possible enemy!"

"Pah! Enemy? What enemy? I don't see no enemy, and I'm not just talking about the darkness of the storm. We've been hearing these rumours for months, mud-orc this, mud-orc that, as if they want another bloody War of Zakora. Lots of would-be heroes in the making, frothing at the mouth for a taste of warfare when in reality, they wouldn't know what to do with a fucking mud-orc if it shoved a spear in their belly. I tell you, it's all a lot of hot air and nonsense, and the King himself says it's all good. If Yoon says it, then that's good enough for me."

"Those merchants who passed through last week seemed pretty twitched. Telling stories of being hunted by some kind of monster in the dark. It scared them bad."

"Rubbish! Little girls frightened by their own shadows."

Jagan shrugged, sending a cascade of water onto the coals, which hissed and spat. Lowering his voice, he leaned a little closer to Reegez. "Some say the King is the one who doesn't know his backside from his elbow, and that downsizing the army was the wrong thing to do. And when, *if*, an enemy were to attack then we'd surely be overrun in a matter of hours. The walls are just too long."

"Shh," warned Reegez, his eyes narrowing. "That's the sort of talk gets a man intimate with the noose."

"Ah. Oh. I wasn't thinking…"

"Who was it you heard?"

"Captain Torquata and Captain Elmagesh. I was fetching water from the Kubosa well, they were sheltering from the wind which blows down the pass. They didn't see me."

Reegez's eyes went even narrower, so they were slits in the glow from the coals. A few wisps of smoke rose from the brazier, and for a moment he really did look to Jagan as if he were some terrible bleak demon escaped from the Furnace.

"I'm not a clever man," said Reegez, slowly. He rubbed at his stubbled chin. "I never claimed to be and, if I'm brutally honest, I'm glad it's that way. Politics are for those people who have a crazy love of themselves and a need to control other people. And teacherin, well that's something I'll never understand or want a part of. But what I *do* know is what's right and what's wrong, and what I do know is when somebody's talking dangerous, talking dangerous to the extent of losing their life." He met Jagan's stare. "You keep away from people like that, Jagan. Keep away from them like your life depends on it, for surely it does. Now forget you ever heard the conversation and we'll both forget we ever had this one. I don't know whether the mud-orcs are coming or not, and I don't rightly care at this moment in time. But whatever the outcome, I'd rather not dance a jig on the end of a bloody noose. I like my neck fine, just the way it is. You get me?"

"I understand," said Jagan, quietly, hands out to the coals. "Let's talk about something pleasant. If the mud-orcs are coming, I'd hate my last days on these walls in the storm to be filled with talk about hanging and an insane king."

"Yeah," grinned Reegez, and slapped his friend on the back. "Let's talk about how I'm going to cream you at knuckle-dice at the tournament tomorrow!"

BORDERLANDS

The sun hung low in the sky, a bloated orange eye. The rolling grasslands hissed, grass dancing like a million tiny soldiers, as a cold wind skimmed the hills and howled mournfully through shallow valleys filled with large, angular boulders. These were the borderlands south of the deserts of Zakora, inhabited by the Kreell, tribes of hardened riders who lived wild in the vast, sweeping wilderness, camping in hide tents and warring often amongst themselves. The tribes were fluid, often exterminating other tribes, sometimes absorbing members into their own. None numbered more than several hundred, for often they fought, and could never forgive other tribes' long past blood feuds and death pacts.

The Horsenail tribe were one of the largest groups of Kreell who hunted the borders of Zakora. They were feared as vicious warriors who took no prisoners, raped the women of opposing tribes and beheaded children.

Benkai Tal, their chief, was a large man, his long black beard braided, a horned brass warhelm atop his shaggy head; he wore a mixture of silks and leather, and sat astride his heavy charger as if he owned the world. He certainly had little to fear in these remote borderlands.

On this cold morning, the camp was in transit. A little over two hundred mounted tribesmen, riding a mixture of heavy war chargers and geldings, with a few scattered ponies. To the rear followed twelve carts, each pulled by six oxen. The carts contained women, children, supplies, tents, extra weapons and armour, and anything else the nomadic people might require.

Benkai Tal's warriors rode in an inverted V formation, with Benkai proud at the head. He was not a leader who led from the back; but more a born warrior who beheaded his enemies and impaled their bodies on spears. He was a man of few words, and had four wives and fifteen children. His senior men joked that one of Benkai's wives had cut out his tongue to stop the other women becoming jealous of his moans during loving; but they never said it within earshot.

They approached the Sudar Valley with care. They were in no rush, and Benkai sent scouts out across the surrounding low hills to check for signs of possible ambush. He was a wary man. One had to be, even within one's own tribe.

They entered the valley, and distant horn blasts signalled safe passage. The wind howled mournfully between the hills, stirring the dusty trail which wound between huge boulders, many times bigger than the carts which carried their families and possessions.

Here, the wedge of mounted men was forced inwards, and the warriors shifted smoothly into a column formation. Horses snorted and stamped the dry earth, scattering rocks. Benkai Tal's chief general, Tuboda, cantered forward to ride beside the chief.

"I have a bad feeling," he said, through his thick beard. He was short and stocky, and wore a thick necklace of knuckle bones from the men and women he had killed.

"Hn," grunted Benkai.

"Look. Ahead." Tuboda gestured, and Benkai held his fist in the air, halting the mounted column. Distantly, the oxen snorted as cart wheels ground to a halt.

"A woman," growled Benkai Tal.

Already Tuboda was searching the hilltops, and he lifted a horn to his lips and gave three short blasts. His scouts returned his call, confirming there were no enemy riders waiting in ambush. Tuboda frowned. Unless... *unless* the enemy had ambushed the scouts and tortured them into returning the call.

"What she doing here? A long way from home, it looks."

"We find out," said Benkai.

"Hey, you not need another wife?" grinned Tuboda suddenly, and Benkai gave him a narrow scowl and kicked his horse forward. Tuboda followed, and the two tribesmen cantered down the wide track between boulders, halting abruptly before the tall, white-skinned woman with short, spiked white hair. She wore black leather trews, a white shirt, a heavy jacket of wolfskin. Her head was high, eyes watching the two warriors without fear. She was appraising them. She had some courage. Some balls. Benkai Tal liked that.

"You are in my way," said Benkai. "These are Horsenail lands. No other person come here. Not unless they wish to join my tribe. Or die."

The woman tilted her head. She smiled. But still, she showed no fear.

Benkai frowned and his temper began to slip. It did not take much. "You pale white-skins are forbidden from these valleys! You should know this! You will pay a toll. You will be whipped twenty times, then share my bed furs tonight. Then, if you are lucky, we will allow you to live."

"Share your bed furs?" said the woman, and released a
peal of laughter so confident, so full of genuine humour
that Tuboda checked the hilltops once more with growing
agitation and placed his hand on the hilt of his curved
sword. He kicked his horse forward, but the beast lowered
its head, snorted and refused to move.

The woman looked him in the eye and said, her voice
low but carrying to the front of the column, "You talk big,
for such a little man. Now, I have a deal for you. *You* will
pay *my* toll if you wish to pass, Benkai Tal of the Horsenail
tribe. These are no longer your lands. These are my lands.
I am Orlana."

"Ha! Never heard of you, bitch." He kicked himself
from the saddle, hitting the dirt, and strode forward,
unsheathing his sword smoothly with eyes glittering.
Still the smile did not falter from this woman's haughty,
arrogant, pale white face. Benkai glanced again for hidden
archers, but could see nothing. He scowled. This woman's
confidence started to worm past Benkai's guard, to chip
away at his supreme assuredness. He stopped, and lifted
his sword so the tip of the wide curved blade was only an
inch from Orlana's throat. "You not look so confident now,
pale face."

"Really?" said Orlana, and slapped away the blade.

Benkai felt his hold on the situation slipping; he was
being observed by all his men, and probably by some of the
families far behind. This woman was mocking him, toying
with him, and there was only one course of action open.

Benkai drew back the blade and stabbed out; his
intention was not to kill, but to wound her, to make her
feel pain, to suffer, to drop her to her knees – and that
would be the beginning of her torment, Benkai Tal would
see to that. As he stabbed, he had visions of hot coals in

her eyes, a back flayed of all skin, her feet with all ten toes cut free as she begged and squirmed. Yes. She would scream and moan long into the night hours...

Orlana's hand lifted, caught the blade, which was incredible because the razor-edge should have removed all her fingers, and she tugged it from Benkai's grip like a warrior taking a stick from a child. She tossed the sword carelessly away, stepped swiftly forward and struck Benkai with the edge of her hand, a vicious chop that *cracked* and went *through* his neck. The head rolled away, looking surprised, and the body collapsed in a heap, pumping blood.

Orlana looked up, and the other warriors sat on their mounts, faces grim, hands on sword hilts. This, they had not expected.

Orlana knelt, and her bloody fingers touched the dry dust, and she said, "It is here, in the land, in the bedrock, in the soil, in the dust; it exists there, has always been there. It comes from the mountains and rivers, the trees and rocks; it rides through volcanic eruptions, it surges through the great cracks in the plates of the world." She looked up then, and the tribesmen were watching her intently, unsure what to do. "Tuboda," she said.

Tuboda jerked as if stung, then slowly lifted his head to meet her gaze. His mouth was dry. This was turning into a bad day.

"Yes, witch?"

"Do you serve me, Tuboda?"

Tuboda was painfully aware of his dead chief lying just feet away, and of the two hundred swords at his back. Sweat beaded his forehead and he licked salt-rimmed lips. But some primal intuition spoke to him through the earth, through the great rocks around him, and through his connection to that woman's eyes. This was no mortal. This Orlana was... something *special*.

He dismounted and approached her, more to put distance between himself and the swords at his back. He drew his own weapon, and for a moment the gathered tribesmen were unsure what path Tuboda would take. But then he thrust the weapon point down in the dust and knelt before her.

Orlana stepped up to him and her eyes raked over the two hundred riders. The horses were stamping and skittish, and she smiled, and touched Tuboda on the shoulder, and lifted her right hand, fingers outstretched. A man screamed, and the horses began to stamp and snort and whinny, and then there came a terrible *crunch* and the beast and its rider, along with saddlebags, sword, bow, clothes and boots all folded in *together*, flesh and clothing merging and melting and folding over and through itself; blood bubbled, muscles grew and the horse hit the ground, trembling, hooves kicking violently as man and beast merged into one. Muscles filled out, swelling, becoming thicker and rippling, and the horse's head, screaming an equine cry of pain and terror suddenly mouthed silently, great strings of saliva connecting the great stretched head as the eyes turned from brown to golden, and the face stretched wider still, and the horse, and the man, became one.

Tuboda, who had turned at the screams and whines, stared in stunned disbelief as the other beasts reared and whinnied, bloating, screaming and pawing the air. They folded together with their riders with crunches and breaks, snaps and slopping sounds, as blood ran and bones broke and shifted and reformed; and then he glanced back to Orlana and her own eyes were a softly glowing gold, her fingers straight, rigid, as she channelled power from the earth and the rocks and the mountains. Down through the columns every single man and beast crunched and writhed together in some great orgy of bloated flesh, screaming men, crying horses, and the grass turned slowly crimson, and was churned into mud, and grooves filled with blood and bits of useless bone were left scattered around the carnage like useless pulled teeth. Slowly, from the mess, from the mud, from the pulsing bloated bodies rose panting, drooling creatures, thick with muscle and with jaws broken open, showing huge fangs. Many eyes glowed softly golden and had a haunted intelligent look; like human eyes after witnessing a mass killing.

"Walk with me."

Tuboda was drawn to his feet by Orlana and with open mouth followed his new mistress, down through a column which had become a charnel house; and each new creature, an amalgamated entity of horse and man, some with hooves, some fingers, some with bulging human appendages erupting from blistering horse flesh like boils, all stood large and bulky with muscle and thick strong bones. Heads were twisted and broken and wide, eyes disjointed, jaws lop-sided, and all eyes followed Orlana as she strode confidently forward, patting a beast here, stroking a flank there, her smile wide, eyes beaming in admiration for these, her creatures, her warriors, her new *family*.

She halted near the back of the column. During the savage transformation, most families had scrambled from carts and fled, children screaming and weeping, mothers holding babes close to their chests. Many of the oxen had broken free and stampeded, leaving a sudden ghost town of lost wagons. Those that remained stared on with dull, bovine stupidity, their bodies trembling, waiting to die.

Somewhere amidst the abandoned wagons, a dog barked. Orlana made a small gesture, and one of the great horse creatures turned and leapt with incredible agility, disappearing between the wagons. There came a crunch and a squeal, and it returned with a bloody limp dog carcass between those great jaws, head hung sadly to one side, great doleful brown eyes glazed.

"Your thoughts?" said Orlana, and faced Tuboda.

"I... I... I..."

"You are speechless. Perhaps understandable. I have improved your tribesmen, Tuboda. They have merged with their mounts, but in joining have become so much more powerful, and vicious, and obedient. No longer do they pursue petty rivalries and grudges; no longer do they lust after women and liquor and gold. Now, they obey me. Without question. These are the *splice*. They are my new family. They are my army. And you are part of that, now. You are part of my expanding warhost."

Tuboda swallowed, lowering his eyes. "Yes, Lady," he whispered.

Orlana shifted her gaze to the panting, drooling beasts. "Come to me," she said, and they rose, gathering round, shuffling forward, many looming over Orlana and a cowering, terrified Tuboda. All he could see were razor fangs, bloody mouths and insane eyes. He realised tears stained his own cheeks and he put his face in his hands.

"You are the beginning," spoke Orlana, looking around herself, eyes shining with pride. She lifted her hands in the air. "You are my children! And I know the Change was difficult for you, pain like you have never before experienced; and you are hungry beyond the comprehension of mortal man. Go now, find the oxen which pulled these wagons, feast on their flesh and blood and bone marrow; go now, find the

women and children of the tribe, devour them whole, feed
your hunger and be satisfied."

"No!" cried Tuboda, as the massive creatures turned and
padded off down the boulder-strewn valley. He whirled on
Orlana with wide, crazed eyes. "No, not the women and
children; you cannot do this, please! *My* wife and children
are with them!" Without thinking he found a long knife
in his hand and he stabbed it towards Orlana's heart. She
batted it aside with ease, where it thudded into the dirt and
blood at their feet. Tuboda waited to die, like the others; a
part of him welcomed it. But Orlana behaved as if Tuboda
hadn't just attempted a mortal blow.

He fell to his knees.

She leant forward and took his hand. Looked down at
him. Smiled.

"You have a new woman, now," she said, and led him
up, guiding him towards the abandoned wagons.

It was just before dawn, and Tuboda sat on the wagon
steps and cried.

All around lay Orlana's twisted creatures of nightmare,
satiated, panting, drooling, great distended bellies rumbling
and gurgling. Some slept on their flanks, huge heads to
one side, black tongues lolling free. Tuboda did not know
when they had returned, but he was sure all his tribe were
now gone, and lost, and dust.

Finally, Tuboda took several deep breaths. He glanced
behind, but Orlana was silent in sleep. Still. As if she
were dead.

Tuboda crept down the steps and retrieved his long
knife from earlier. Then he sat down cross-legged on
the ground and stared up at a bloated yellow moon. The
horizon was infused with a pastel pink. It was going to be
a beautiful, cold day.

He shuddered at the memories of his night with Orlana. Again and again she had forced him to bring her to orgasm, her nails clawing his back like knives, drawing blood. And then she had slept, and he had felt truly unclean. As if he had made love with a living corpse.

"Holy Mother, forgive me, for I am lost," he said, and pressed the knife to his wrist. One deep, hard cut, and eternal sleep would be his. He could find Darlana on the Lost Plains, and Boda, and cheeky little Eska; they would be a family again. Together again. Together in Eternity.

He shuddered and tried to cut down. But his hands would not work. He tried, again and again, until tears of frustration drenched his cheeks. But his limbs no longer obeyed his control.

He sensed her behind him and shuddered again, his body shaking with great silent sobs. She came close, naked, and sat down behind him, wrapping her legs around him, kissing him on the back of the neck.

"You don't need to do that," she whispered in his ear, breath tickling. "I have a present for you. I've been saving something special – just for you."

From the dawn gloom something moved, shifted, and Tuboda blinked. And then he *smelled* the beast, smelled its rancid vinegar piss and stinking breath filled with strips of old rotting meat. It moved closer, head low to the ground, huge tawny eyes fixed on him as if hypnotised. It gave a low, low bass rumble, and its huge paws thud-thudded on the dirt.

A lion, he thought. Holy Mother of the Plains, a lion!

"My present, to you," whispered Orlana, kissing his neck again and rising, stepping away.

"No!" Tuboda wanted to scream, as the great lion reared over him and his autonomy returned too late…

It leapt, fangs sinking into him, and they rolled together and… and everything was hot like a furnace and he was sinking into the lion and the lion into him, and his mind went blank and then flowed like thick honey; and then the pain struck him, every single atom of his body wrenching apart as dark magick burned, and he merged with the lion and all he knew was the pain – which became everything, and nothing, and seemed to last…

For. Ever.

HARSH TIMES

Rokroth was a town bordering on the size of a small city. It was busy, in that buildings crowded one another and the population outweighed the housing. The vast Rokroth Marshes to the south and west provided much employment, for they were warm and rich in fast-breeding eels; a delicacy favoured in the wealthy capital city of Drakerath, and the military capital of Vagan, and also sought out by minor nobles and dignitaries throughout Vagandrak seeking to impress by replicating the dishes on the royal table. There were other uses for the creatures; as well as food, eel-skin leather was smooth and very strong, and an eel's blood was toxic to humans and formed the basis for various apothecary drugs and poisons.

Throughout Rokroth, street gangs of homeless children ran through the mud. Dogs barked. Whores whored and dandies paraded. The rain came down hard. It always rained in Rokroth. It was an ongoing joke, although few found it truly funny. Especially those who lived there.

It was seven in the morning, and an optimistic sun was attempting to burn the mist from the streets and fields and marshes. Winter was nearly here and soon the lands of Vagandrak would be conquered by the Gods of Ice and Snow.

Kiki lay in a cellar back room. It was not an underground tavern exactly, it was just a place to go.

It was dark. The room was filled with low, comfy couches. Smoke filled the air. Thick, and choking, but ultimately, a smoke of comfort.

Figures sprawled throughout the gloom like discarded gloves.

Kiki lay on a couch against the far wall, away from doors and the narrow, ceiling-level windows. Her back rested against solid underground stone. It was the way she liked it. The way it had to be. She'd seen too many friends stabbed in the back – metaphorically, as well as physically – to squander her liver without a fight. Even under the effects of the leaf.

The honey-leaf.

A flower of beauty, honesty, power, truth, pain and misery. Kiki laughed to herself. A small trickle of brown spit dribbled from the corner of her mouth.

You survived, she told herself.

You always survive.

He was close, said her sister in the mirror. *He nearly had you. Nearly killed you. Nearly fucked you over; took your body and soul. Once, Kiki, you would have taken him in the blink of an eye.*

What are you trying to say?

Smoke drifted, thick and cloying. Voices burbled, unreal a background chatter of noise and stench and casual sex.

I'm not trying to say anything. I am *saying – you are growing old. Slow. Fat. Decadent. Pointless. Pointless, Kiki; you've changed, woman. You've changed from being a lethal awesome warrior, a killing machine, to being a slow fat slave. You rule the drug; the drug never rules you. That's what you told me. Told me a million times over. And now look at you. Look at the state of you. You're a fucking disgrace. Soon, you'll be opening your legs just for a taste of the leaf. When the money's gone. And the money always goes.*

Kiki considered this.

"Go to hell," she laughed, she giggled, and placed another leaf under her tongue. Then she put her hand over her mouth and gasped, eyes wide. "But then, how can you go to hell, Suza? You're already there, right? You had your dead child and you took your own life. Now you rot in the torture pits and you're pissed I'm not there with you; so you haunt me through the mirror. Go ahead, bitch. Do your best. Do your worst. I do not care. Life and death; who gives a fuck? What's left for me? Nothing. Nothing at all. I am as you see me: an empty shell."

People came and went. Time accelerated, then went slow. Infinitely slow.

Kiki lay, slumbering, twisting and turning in an uneasy half-life.

Lights flickered. Candles and firelight. And then, the dawn.

A shadow blocked out the light, and she covered her eyes.

If this was the King's Guard – well.

She chuckled to herself.

She was totally wasted.

"Collect your weapons."

"Who are you to tell... me... tell me, what to do?" Life, the world, infinity, all swam in and out of focus. She went as if to place another honey-leaf under her tongue, but a large hand knocked it from her grasp.

She tutted, annoyed, but did not have the energy to scrabble on the floor. It was gone and done.

Once, she would have killed the bastard for that.

A face loomed close, and if the drugs hadn't been so strong she would have flinched in disbelief. She struggled backwards on the couch, seeking to be free, and suddenly cowering in on herself, folding in on herself; suddenly brittle, and weak, and breakable, like kiln-fired porcelain.

It's the leaf, she told herself.

It's the *leaf*.

But it wasn't. And he slapped her and she screamed and struggled, but he picked her up and Kiki lay cradled in his powerful arms like a child, crying bitter, salted tears, as he carried her from the smoky den up the narrow stone steps and out into the rain.

She gazed up into his face.

"Father?" she said.

"No," he said, words more gentle now. "But I'm close enough. Come on, Kiki. Let's get you cleaned up."

WINTER SHADOWS

It was the Guild of Spice Merchants' Annual Dinner, and flurries of snow kicked down the street past the ancient Guild House. Six hundred years old, of ancient stone and black carved oak, the building was one of the oldest, and most architecturally admired, in the Vagandrak War Capital of Vagan.

The cobbled streets and lanes were dark, empty and decorated with light sprinklings of snow. Not so in the Guild House. Cheers went up and the five fat chimneys pumped smoke into a charcoal sky.

Inside, down corridors of thick, richly patterned carpets, past panels of oak and marble busts of Guild Masters dating back three centuries, drifted snippets of conversation and song, the aroma of a whole roasting pig and the clink of crystal containing Vagandrak's finest port and brandy. The main speaker, one Lord Deltari, current Guild Master, huge and bulbous, red of cheek, bald of head, and wearing a black velvet coat adorned with glittering jewels normally only found on ladies of ill repute, was just winding down his annual speech with a tale of how he'd made his fortune by identifying a niche in the market for ground and dried exotic spices from deepest southern Zakora, and from thence importing one of the most current and popular hot spices after an argument with his brother over a dog. The tale had an ironic, slapstick ending that made Lord Deltari appear witty and smart, and his brother the village idiot. And Deltari ended up with the dog. A poodle, apparently, called Charles. Another cheer went up and, amidst clinking glasses and guffaws and a discrete applause, Deltari sat down to an animated table of sycophantic chatter and over-friendly back-slapping.

In the corner sat Great Dale, William de Pepper and Lord Rokroth, from the House of Rokroth, whose main trade was eel meat from the Rokroth Marshes, but who also traded in various spiced variations of dried eel, his buying power thus earning him a place in the Guild, and therefore attendance at the Guild Annual Dinner.

"... an idiot," Great Dale was saying, and buttered himself a warm roll.

Rokroth nodded, rubbing his grey whiskers as a serving maid poured him a large measure of brandy. He swirled the amber liquid, watching the rich dance inside the many faceted crystal chamber. "The man's a buffoon. And just because he's President of the Guild, and Lord *through marriage*, I'll have you note, as opposed to direct bloodline, we have to endure his terminal self-congratulatory speech; and I use the term '*speech*' in its broadest possible sense. I don't know about you, gentlemen, but personally I'd rather stick my own head up my own backside. Or even, and this ably illustrates my despair, up *his* backside!"

They broke into laughter, but they caught the chatter at the next round table and faces soon soured.

"Pepper, what have you heard about these new tax increases? Do you think there's any meat to it?" Rokroth took a hefty gulp of brandy, dribbling just a few drops down his rich gold waistcoat.

"Not from the King himself, but the rumour mill is hard at work. If the gossip is to be believed, we are due another hefty tax hike, not just on imports, which affects us all, but on the bloody sales! And only six months after the previous inflation. It's said Yoon wishes to extend his bloody Moon Tower by another thirty levels and we, *we* have to pay for the folly!"

"A disgrace."

"Ridiculous."

"A bloody outrage is what it is."

They chatted about the changes in King Yoon's tax policies for the next ten minutes, then talk turned to the King himself.

Rokroth lowered his voice, and looked around in an almost conspiratorial manner. "Some say his outfits have become more and more garish, and more and more expensive. He has started wearing thick make-up like the players who walk the Vagandrak stage, and that he giggles at random moments like some child embarrassed about a puddle on the kitchen floor."

"There have definitely been changes to his character during this past year," said Pepper, his face growing serious. "Not only does he seem obsessed with the building of this tower, what was it called again? The Tower of the Moon? He has a thousand men working round the clock, which must be costing our Kingdom a pretty penny. But worse, you remember last winter, the army was cut back?"

"By forty thousand men," said Rokroth, grimly. "Now, we have barely enough to patrol our borders with Zakora and the Plague Lands."

"Yoon claims they can be called up in an instant, if needed; yet Desekra Fortress is manned by a skeletal force, less than ten thousand, and the navy lies hobbled far north at the Crystal Sea. Why use so many war triremes if there are no experienced crews?"

Great Dale was nodding. "It is a drastic cost-cutting tactic, I'd wager."

"But why? To build this damn tower? I tell you, the man is obsessed. But it cannot *just* be for that. Forty thousand men stood down! I swear by all the gods, if King Tarek were alive to see the mess Yoon is making of his realm." He sighed. "I miss the old bastard. He was a hard man, but fair."

Rokroth nodded. "And spinning in his ancestral tomb, no doubt, at the effeminate, gold-pissing popinjay into which his son has metamorphosed. Serving girl! More brandy! Over here, girl!"

"I swear, people are getting nervous on the streets. There is less laughter. People walk on, with hurried gait, heads down, not wishing to offend. And have you noticed the King's Guard?"

"I doubt it, he travels in a gilt-laden carriage!" laughed Great Dale, and they laughed alongside him.

"No man, but seriously," persisted Pepper. "There are more guards."

"You're imagining it, man, surely?"

"I tell you, I am not!" and he slammed down his glass so that brandy slopped over the rim.

There came a sudden disturbance at the entrance to the hall, accompanied by raised voices. There was a shine of armour and a man marched forward, King's Guard, with a short black plume denoting captain. He strode down the central carpet, and behind followed another twenty men. But what was most disturbing was they all carried swords, unsheathed, and their eyes were hard as steel.

"What is this outrage?" boomed Lord Deltari, huge frame waddling forward to meet the intrusion. "You, sir, what is your name? Identify yourself! You dare enter the Guild House with drawn weapons? I shall see you hang for this, in the name of the King!"

The captain halted and relaxed and his eyes raked the room, finally coming to rest on Lord Deltari, face puffed and red, his blood up after too much port and brandy, his velvet jacket slightly skewed.

The man was tall, powerful and had a commanding stance. Beneath his helm was neat white hair, a neatly trimmed white moustache and a hard face with tracings of pale old scars beneath a dark tan which spoke of many years in the field. "I," he said, once more scanning the room of wealthy spice barons and lords, "am Captain Dokta; Captain of the King's Guard."

A sigh escaped many present. Captain Dokta was infamous for having committed many acts of cruelty the length and breadth of Vagandrak over the last few years; acts which had, supposedly, gone unpunished, and were maybe even sanctioned by the king.

"I... I..." stuttered Deltari.

"I what, you fat buffoon? Well, I'll tell you I what," snarled Dokta suddenly, and at this point he gave a quick glance towards Great Dale, who stood up and gave a solemn meaningful nod, "this entire room is under arrest in the *name* of King Yoon. I have been sent here to serve you notice, gentlemen."

"Arrested?" managed Deltari, huffing and puffing, spittle on his chin. "But that is preposterous! On what charges? Come on, man, spit it out!"

"On the count of treason," said Dokta, voice low, words little more than a hot exhalation.

Silence fell across the Guild Hall like ash.

Lord Deltari staggered forward. "Ridiculous!" he bellowed, face frowning, his pompousness and affront returning like a surge. "An absolute mockery to the name of justice! I demand..." and his hand came up, finger poking Sergeant Dokta in the chest, but his sentence got no further.

Dokta's sword flickered up, removing Lord Deltari's hand at the wrist. The severed hand slapped on rich rugs, index finger twitching, jewelled fingers sparkling, and blood pumped out as Deltari cried out, staggered back clutching his stump, then fell over unceremoniously. There came a shocked hush, before servants rushed to their master's aid.

Great Dale moved to stand behind Dokta and his armed men.

Captain Dokta swept the room with narrowed eyes, and slowly the group began to back away. To the rear of the hall, several spice merchants and lords had tried to slip from the Guild Hall unnoticed, only to discover the rearward doors had been barricaded.

"You have all been condemned by King Yoon," said Dokta, voice clear across the finely tuned acoustics of the Hall. They carried to every guild member. They carried to every frightened man and woman, no matter what their station.

More men appeared behind the King's Guard, and they each carried wooden flasks, several with barrels, which they rolled silently across thick rugs and carpets. They moved forward and began pouring oil over furniture, carpets, and splashing it up the walls.

Lord Rokroth surged forward this time. "Captain! What, in the name of the Three Gods and the Holy Mother, *are you doing*?"

"You have all been found guilty of treason. Your sentence is to burn," said Dokta, as barrels were cast down and smashed with axes. Nostrils twitched. A flaming torch was brought forward; the gathered annual meeting of spice merchants were looking extremely panicked now. Several had drawn decorative sabres, but most were plump and old, and even if they had been swordsmen in their day, wealth and hedonistic excess had stolen any skill they might once have possessed.

The brand was tossed forward, and a *whoosh* filled the hall as a curtain of flame rose in sudden combustion. Now, every merchant and spice lord rushed for the back of the Guild Hall only to discover, as had their comrades, that they had been trapped. Shouts rang out and several men ran, leaping through the flames which ignited their clothing and perfume and powdered wigs as easily as if they'd been soaked in oil themselves. Lord Rokroth sprinted forward, leaping through the roaring fire and screaming as he did so. He landed, burning, coat on fire and sabre raised, only to be met by Dokta.

"Get back in there and burn," Dokta snarled, his boot coming up as he front-kicked Lord Rokroth in the chest. Rokroth grunted and was sent sprawling back into the flames where he screamed and screamed and quickly sank, crumpling, into a foetal position.

The tapestries and wood panelling were roaring now, the air hot and filled with smoke and ash. The ancient, six hundred year-old oak beams had caught like kindling thanks to the oil and, satisfied, the King's Guard backed from the Guild Hall as a hundred pleading screams, cries for help, and promises of wealth followed them.

Captain Dokta strode down the magnificent steps, breathing deeply on crisp, iced air. He gave a narrow smile which had nothing to do with humour, and sheathed his sword. Several small groups of people had gathered, but Dokta bellowed, "Move on! There's nothing to see here!" as behind him the screams continued. For a moment Dokta was transported back to the slaughterhouse he had worked in as a youth: the pigs, in narrow channelled rows, being dragged forward one by one on lengths of rope, and the screaming, the pigs screaming, screaming like children as he stood at the head of the tunnel, bloodied knife in one hand, rope in the other and a grim focused determination glittering in his eyes...

"Are you well, sir?"

"Yes, Glader. Secure the perimeter. Make sure nobody gets in. Or more importantly, out. Any resistance from civilians, kill them. We'll give it twenty minutes, then form a line bringing water from the river. Pass around the word."

"Yes, sir. And... can I just say something, sir?"

"Of course, Glader."

The man's eyes were shining, face almost... euphoric.

"I just wanted to say, it's fabulous to finally work with you, Captain Dokta."

THE SEER

General Dalgoran stood on the white marble steps of his sprawling, white-walled villa, back ramrod straight, short grey hair neatly combed in place, his large frame proud and his bearing still that of a military man despite this, the first day of his seventy-first year.

"Cigar, old man?" said General Jagged, stepping out into the crisp cold air beside Dalgoran, and Dalgoran gave a chuckle.

"Less of the old man, you bloody slack old goat. I'm a damn month younger than you!"

"And yet you look so much older," grinned Jagged, passing over a thick cigar and resting his hand on the hilt of his sword. General Jagged was completely bald, a short, squat, powerful man, brown face heavily creased, like tanned and wrinkled antique leather from years of outdoor soldiering. He wore a short goatee beard, white as the purest snow. Despite his age, he still carried himself well. They both did.

Dalgoran lit the cigar, and thick blue plumes engulfed him for a moment. "Ahh. But that's good. Bad for my chest, you understand, but on a special occasion like this, I'm sure one won't kill me. Not yet, anyway." He gazed off, towards the distant White Lion Mountains, silhouetted and vast and noble in the fast approaching gloom. They towered over the Skell Forest to the northeast and, if one looked carefully, one could make out the distant, high towers in the city of Kantarok.

"How's your head, Jagged?"

"Nothing wrong with my head. What the bloody hell does that mean?"

"I thought, you know, with the promise of snow in the air, the biting chill… your lack of hair…"

"Pah!"

"That's a damn cold wind blowing from the White Lions…" Dalgoran shivered theatrically, and enjoyed his cigar. "Could give a bald man like yourself a real nasty cold. I'd be covering yourself up, if I were you. Inside, Alaya can maybe find you a hat?"

"General, if it wasn't your birthday, I'd break your nose."

"Again? That would be exciting. But of course, not before I'd knocked out your teeth."

The two old men laughed, and Dalgoran leant back against a white pillar, gazing across his acres of land. Down by the distant tree line were several cottages, housing woodsmen, the cook and his estate gardeners. His eyes travelled along the tree line bordering the north of his estates, admiring the finely sculpted hedgerows, the vast flowerbeds now a riot of white and blue with winter pansies and various patterned evergreen bushes which Dalgoran had planted himself. This place was idyllic. And yet the cold wind made him shiver and the smile slowly dropped from his face as he thought again about his wife.

"I tell you something," said Jagged. "The bloody doctors in Drakerath are now saying, and I cannot believe this so-called *fact*, that smoking a cigar or pipe is bad for your lungs! What a nonsense! It clears me out a treat, I tell you."

"And of course, you know better than all the medical minds of Vagandrak put together?"

"Of course," growled General Jagged. "Without me, there'd *be* no damn medical minds, no damn universities and doctors and scholars. If I, and I concede you had a small part to play here Dalgoran, well if I hadn't been in charge of organising the King's armies when that bastard Morkagoth led his forces north... well. You and I both know, we'd be speaking and grunting in fucking mud-orc now. That, or be buried six feet under the ground."

Dalgoran, who had spluttered on his cigar, gave Jagged a sideways look. "You're a modest old skunk."

"I was a good soldier."

"I recognise the past tense."

"Just smoke your cigar and look out for the guests. I believe the cake is huge – it has to be, to fit on so many bloody candles."

They smoked in amiable silence for a while, as the winter sun sank behind the trees and painted the horizon scarlet. Pines turned to black sentinels. The shadows grew longer and eddies of snow eased from bruised heavens.

"You're a good friend," said Jagged, at last.

"Mighty fine of you to say so."

"We've been through some shit together, haven't we?"

Dalgoran grinned. "Remember Desekra Fortress? Charging that squad of mud-orcs, we thought there were a hundred men behind us, and there was just one – that simpleton Jorgrek. We were screaming, spears levelled, the mud-orcs with their wide eyes and slavering jaws, we thought they were staring in terror, but they must have been simply stunned at the stupidity of three men charging thirty."

"You hit the leader between the eyes with your spear, didn't you? And the impact popped his head from his body like a pea from a pod?"

"Aye. Made the bastards jump. Made *me* jump all that yellow jelly shit coming out of his neck."

Dalgoran stared off across his lands. "I'll never forget that look on your face when you realised you didn't have a hundred lances behind you. It was priceless! You don't get moments better than that. Not in this lifetime."

"Yes," growled Jagged, his feathers ruffled. "A bit like the time you came waltzing drunk out of that whorehouse in Lower Vagan and that half-dressed lady-friend came running out after you because you'd forgotten your hat, and she was scratching like a whole family of mice had nested in her panties! Har har!"

"I didn't realise you were there that night?"

"I wasn't. Old Sergeant Harkrock told me about it. Laugh? I think I actually pissed myself."

"I see your incontinence problems persist."

"Come on, Dalgoran. That was funny. The way she was scratching between her legs... Apparently you went so bloody pale it was said you'd pass out on the spot. You went to the battalion surgeon, still pissed, begging him to see to your groin, but he was busy building a model with his little boy and wouldn't have anything to do with you. Oh, how we all roared and slapped our thighs."

Dalgoran burst out laughing suddenly, and slapped Jagged on the back making him drop the stump of his cigar. "Yes. Funny. Good old days. Whatever happened to Harkrock? He was the one with the limp, wasn't he?"

"Yeah. Broke his ankle in a fall from a horse and it turned bad. They had to amputate below the knee."

"Ahh. Is he still alive?"

"Dalgoran, he died at the Pass. With most of the others."

"That's a shame," said Dalgoran, finishing his cigar.

"Your guests are beginning to arrive."

Dalgoran nodded, and they both watched several coaches start the long ascent up the sweeping stone drive, teams of horses straining.

Jagged gave a theatrical look around. "Why the hell did you build your villa *up here*, General? You had your pick of the King's land."

Dalgoran gave a shrug and ground the stub of his cigar under his gleaming, well-polished boot. "I like watching the horses struggle. Either that, or I have a pathological hatred of… people."

"People?"

"People in general. No offence meant."

"None taken, you cunning old bastard. You going to ask me in for a brandy?"

"Ha. Yes. No point reaching seventy if you can't drink with your friends."

General Jagged fixed him with a beady eye. "Friend? Whatever made you think that, old boy? Men like us don't have friends. Just memories, acquaintances and a wish that we'd done things differently during our youths."

Dalgoran considered this. "And you had to ask *why* I built my house up here?"

"Just curious, old boy. Just curious."

Night had fallen, and during the last hour nearly two hundred guests had arrived, old friends, new friends, family and acquaintances. Many were of military bearing; one didn't spend a lifetime in the army and not have a certain bias with regards to the trade of people one knew.

Fires roared in various wide stone hearths, and a band played discreetly in the corner: piano and strings, narrative songs about the heroes of Vagandrak. General Dalgoran circulated the several large rooms which had been set aside for his birthday celebration, smiling, chatting, kissing the odd proffered hand of a beautiful woman. Servants circulated with trays containing crystal glasses of honeyed wine, sweet meats and delicacies from as far south as Oram and as far north as Zalazar and the fabled Elf Rat Lands.

After a while, General Jagged moved to one of the large roaring fires and in his booming, parade-ground bellow, shouted, "Ladies and gentlemen, can I have your attention please?" Everybody paused, turning their eyes on Jagged, with his wide grin and a fresh cigar. "As you know, we are here to celebrate the beginning of the seventy-first year of our friend, comrade and military *hero,* General Dalgoran. You all know him as a caring man, a great father and sadly a widower in these recent months. But I tell you! I knew Farsala like no other, an incredible woman – she had to be, to put up with this stubborn oaf–" there came a sprinkling of laughter, "but I know, if she were here today, she would talk about how proud she was of this fine, strong, charismatic general who is not just a brilliant soldier, a genuine morale builder for those who follow him and an unparalleled tactician, but is above all a superb and much-loved father, grandfather, and of course Farsala would have said *husband*. I'm not going to say that, because I'll be damned if I'm going to marry the grumpy old bastard now." More laughter. "So, without further ado, I ask you to raise your glasses and wish, along with me, a very happy birthday for General Dalgoran. One of Vagandrak's finest."

"One of Vagandrak's finest!" came the cheer and, grinning from ear to ear, Dalgoran passed Jagged on the way to the slightly elevated platform in front of the roaring fire. As he passed, Dalgoran gave Jagged a hearty punch on the arm, and the slightly older man scowled.

"Thank you, Jagged, my oldest friend, comrade-in-arms and back-stabbing horse shagger." A roar of laughter. "Lock up your ponies, ladies and gentlemen, because after just four or five tankards of ale, General Jagged will be out on the prowl with a horse-whip and a dirty smile."

"Only with your help!" yelled Jagged from the back.

General Dalgoran held up a hand and a respectful silence descended. Here was a man who had genuinely saved the country and was respected by the people and kings under which he had served. Here was a man who was the epitome of strength, honour and courage to the civilians and military minds of Vagandrak. General Dalgoran was indeed a hero.

"I know many of you knew my late wife, the Lady Farsala," he said, voice soft but still carrying, even over the crackling of the large, roaring fires. "And I know that you all know of our incredible, long-enduring love. She was the light of my life, my best friend, my lover, my soul mate. I met her when I was training at the King's Barracks outside Vagan and me and a few lads disguised ourselves and snuck out to sample that fine city's finest taverns. She was a serving girl, and we gave her a hard time – right up to the point she slapped my stupid useless face. I fell in love with her the instant she hit me, for what a heart that woman had! It took me another year to woo her, but woo her I did. And now I stand here, a proud father, grandfather and soon to be *great* grandfather. Where the years went, I will truly never know. They flowed away downriver, like fine wine down General Jagged's throat! But I have so many wonderful memories; so many precious moments of time. When Lady Farsala lay dying she made me promise her one thing – that we'd had such an incredible time together, I would not cry at the end. When her last breath rattled free I cried – I could not contain myself. And it was the only time I ever broke a promise to her; my beloved. I told her I would follow her soon, for I know she awaits me beyond the Gilded Halls. It was my greatest dream that Farsala would be here to see my seventieth birthday celebrations; she made me promise to go ahead, even without her. And so, here I am and here we are.

"When she… passed away, for a long time the light went out in the world. Food lost its flavour, wine lost its taste, colour was bleached from everything I saw." He stared around the room, meeting eyes, and took a sip from his goblet of port. As he met gazes, many gave him nods and small smiles. He pursed his lips. "In one way, I feel privileged to reach the age of seventy, especially having served in some dodgy campaigns with that old goat Jagged; in fact, quite frankly, having worked with the man I'm quite astounded I reached the age of thirty, never mind seventy!"

"You look nearer eighty!" shouted Jagged, from the back. There came a ripple of laughter, especially from Vornek, who turned nearly purple with mirth.

"Maybe in age, my friend, but alas, you've put eighty pounds on your belly feasting on Mrs Melkett's fine pig pies down Baker's Alley!"

More laughter.

"However, in all seriousness, it is an honour to reach seventy; and yet with great sadness I outlived my love. I only wish she could have been here to share the celebration. So, with love, and a lifetime of fabulous memories, I stand here and ask you to please charge your glasses and take a moment to remember my fabulous wife, whom I loved more than life… Farsala." The gathered crowd raised their glasses and repeated her name, and there came a period of respectful silence.

General Jagged threaded his way to the front, and embraced his old comrade and they shared a minute of warmth. Theirs was the greatest of friendships, despite regular cantankerous banter; theirs was a friendship to kill for. A friendship to die for. Jagged pulled away and grinned at his old friend.

"You could have just shook my hand," said Dalgoran.

"You always were an unaffectionate bastard."

"Go on, go find me a drink."

"What am I, your serving wench?"

"You always were, Jagged. Always were."

"Ha!"

It was late. The barrels and bottles had been emptied, platters of food devoured, there had been much dancing to upbeat fast tempo music, then slow dances to sultry folk ballads by a master on a lyre. As the fires started to burn low, so they were stacked high again with chunks of axe-cut pine and ash; and more drink brought from the cellars. It was going to be a lengthy night.

The next hour passed in amiable companionship, even though Dalgoran's heart wasn't truly in it. As he had said, he missed Farsala with an aching heart, and it almost felt like a minor betrayal to drink and laugh and enjoy oneself when she was cold and alone in the family tomb. After several glasses of port, then moving on to port and brandy, Dalgoran felt his melancholy lift a little and he sat in a circle of old military comrades, Jagged included, and they smoked pipes and cigars, drank from rich goblets, and discussed old battles, tactics, but avoided the subject of King Yoon like the plague. Even though there were many old friends, Yoon was an uncomfortable topic. Trust was a funny thing when it came to a king sliding down the slippery slope into madness; and liable to come round and burn down your house with your family still in their beds – or so the growing rumours would have one believe.

As they sat, in a moment of comfortable silence, a servant approached and leant close towards Jagged.

"She's here, General. She's here!"

"I thought she could not come because of snow?"

"Me also. But she arrived five minutes ago in a simple black carriage drawn by two ponies."

"By all the gods!" boomed Jagged, and rocked himself to his feet, spilling wine down his finely embroidered waistcoat. "Brother in War! At last! The fun section of your birthday gift has arrived!"

"The fun section?" Dalgoran eyed his friend with deep mistrust. "Gods man, not a lady of the night? I'm seventy years old, by the Holy Mother!"

"Ha! Nothing of the sort, although I remember that Shamil dancer in Makkrappur who made your eyes stand out. In fact, that wasn't the only thing that stood out! She made you drool like a babe lusting after a sugar stick. No, no, don't panic, old goat. We clubbed together, got you a seer to tell you tall tales of your future. Apparently, she's the best in the whole of Vagandrak! Predicted Falanek's promotion, marriage and divorce – and got all three right!"

"What do you think I need a bloody seer for?" snapped Dalgoran, words tinged with anger. "I know exactly what my future holds and I'd rather not be reminded of what could be just around the corner. You idiot, Jagged. You never did think things through. That's why your battle strategy was always as sloppy as a Zagandrian's knife-opened bowels. What were you thinking?"

"Shh, she's here!"

"I don't *care*. I'm not talking to her."

"*Please*, Dalgoran. For me! Come on, it'll be the highlight of the night, I promise."

Grumbling, Dalgoran turned to the doors. Through them drifted a woman wearing a black gauze veil and a long dress that reached the floor making her appear ghostly and ephemeral. She wore black gloves and no flesh could be seen. She moved slowly, with grace, and a hush fell on the gathering.

"I am seeking General Dalgoran," came a soft voice: beautiful, and slightly sibilant on the *s*.

"I am here." He stood, holding his goblet.

She approached. "I am Allorna, a seer from Vagandrak."

"Do you bring good news, or bad? I've had my fill of bad news for a lifetime."

"I have read the runes and you intrigue me greatly, Dalgoran. I must dance for you. I must commune with the spirits. Then we shall explore the webs of your future intricacies together."

"I'm not so sure…" muttered Dalgoran, uneasily.

Jagged nudged him hard. "See! A sexy dance…"

"Be silent!" hissed Allorna, head snapping to Jagged. "Or we will talk about the inevitability or your fast approaching death. Would you like to know when you die, little man? Would you like to know when the worms begin to feed?"

Staring through that fine gauze, Jagged suddenly realised there were two dark pools where the woman's eyes should have been. She was blind, the sockets empty. He gave a long, slow shiver.

"No, no," he said through gritted teeth.

Allorna returned her attention to Dalgoran and, without further words, started to sway and gyrate. A chill wind blew through the hall and several candles extinguished.

Fires flickered and roared in the stone hearths. Not one person in that room did not have their eyes fixed on the seer.

Dalgoran felt his mouth suddenly dry, his knees trembling. He hadn't asked for this. He didn't bloody want this! Why had General Jagged done this to him? The bloody old fool. So much for fifty years of friendship! So much for really understanding another human being!

Dalgoran lifted his hand, and was just about to call a halt to the sensuous, gyrating dance when the seer said, "Hush, she walks amongst us." More candles extinguished, plumes of smoke swirling towards the high ceiling in silver spirals. The fires in their hearths burned low. A scent of lavender seemed to fill the air, and suddenly the seer went slack, slumping back, as if unconscious but held up at an odd angle by invisible wires.

Dalgoran dropped his hand as if it were a striking serpent. His eyes narrowed and his right hand came to rest on his scabbarded sword.

"What devilry is this?" he whispered.

"Not devilry," croaked Jagged, "she's for real! I thought it would be a cheap laugh about finding a fresh young woman, getting drunk and winning lots of money at cards. Not *this*."

Dalgoran stared hard at Jagged, but could not find the words to express his annoyance at the idiocy.

Still Allorna hung, suspended… And began to chant, her voice very, very old, cracked, leaden, beating out in a tribal rhythm; like a heartbeat from the depths of some ancient tombworld…

Mud born,
Blood rage,
Summoned We,

World change.
Love dies,
Hatred rise,
Fires burn,
Flesh prize.
Kings die,
Queens cry,
Five stand,
On mountain sky.
One hope,
Evil purge,
Impure love,
Wolves unite.

Dalgoran was frowning at the words, and he gave a long, deep shudder. What did it mean? These words weren't, as Jagged had at first expected, about the simplicities and tribulations of a soldier's life. No, they were... something else. Mud born? A summoning? The death of a king?

There came a sound from outside, and heads turned; it was like the galloping of a horse but with an ungainly rhythm. Loud, heavy, ponderous, uneven, crunching the stones of the drive. The heads of more guests turned towards the wide doors which opened out onto the drive and manicured lawns. Heavy curtains now obscured the gardens. They trembled gently with the irregular beat.

"What..." began General Jagged, hand on sword hilt, as *something* huge and blurred crashed through the doors, tangled in several curtains, and started viciously snarling, snapping, growling. They got a glimpse of dark grey fur, in ragged tufts, streaked with black. Jaws like those of a huge, disjointed dog were snarling and growling and snapping – and suddenly lashed out, grabbing a slender woman, stood with a look of horror on her face, crystal wine glass held limp as the fangs grabbed her round the waist and lifted her into the air, crunching through ribs and spine as adrenaline and survival instinct suddenly kicked in and she began to scream and thrash and beat at the heavily furred head.

"Jagged! To me!" bellowed Dalgoran, drawing his short sword and advancing.

The beast, struggling for a moment in the tangle of heavy drapes, staggered forward and then reared up on hind legs, the broken, limp and lifeless woman still in its jaws. It was well over six feet tall, and nearer to seven on hind legs, massively muscled, with huge cords around shoulders and spine. It was covered in thick sprouting tufts of grey fur, but its legs seemed disjointed, in slightly different places to where they should be, thus making the creature skew to one side.

"What in Hell's teeth is that?" breathed Jagged, face torn with shock.

"I don't know, but we need to put it out of its misery." Dalgoran took a step forward, but the huge creature shook the dead woman, like a dog with a bone, and tossed her across the hall. Snarling, the beast cleared the curtains and whirled on Jagged and Dalgoran, standing with swords raised.

The creature's maw opened wide, showing sickly yellow fangs, and Dalgoran couldn't help think how much like a wolf the beast was, and yet so different; twisted, with an elongated and bent muzzle and eyes of different colours: one yellow, one blue.

"Where... is... the seer?" growled the beast in a guttural dialect that made Dalgoran and Jagged take a step back.

A guard ran at the creature, which twisted suddenly, muzzle batting away the point of the sword and fangs closing over his entire head, which was wrenched free with a vicious twist trailing tendons and a short wriggling segment of spinal column.

More guards ran forward, but the wolf-like creature leapt, clearing them and scattering heavy furniture as if it were chopped kindling. Its head swayed and eyes fastened on the seer who was on her knees, head thrown forward but face raised, as if her own blind orbs could see the beast that had come for her…

"No!" bellowed Dalgoran. He sprinted forward, Jagged close behind. They positioned themselves between the creature and the veiled seer as the beast charged. They stepped apart with the precision and training of five decades, both slamming swords into the beast's flesh, but it did not break stride, even as razor steel slid under skin and muscle, broke through bone… but simply knocked both men violently from their feet, the creature stopping directly before the seer, great fetid muzzle dropping until it was inches from her face. It studied her, as one would a magnificent painting.

A guard who had fetched a spear charged, and the point slid between the creature's ribs, snapping it from its reverie. Its head whirled about and one heavy paw full of sharp black claws lashed out, slapping the man to the ground as if he were a child's doll. Claws extended, like a cat's, and punctured his screaming head like a ripe melon.

The wolf-beast turned back to the seer, who had not moved. Her lips were writhing, incanting, and slowly she raised her right hand until it was level with her breast. Now Dalgoran and Jagged had gained their feet, and their swords, and more old soldiers had run to them with blades drawn, along with yet more guards who had brought spears. They surrounded the beast in a semi-circle; a ring of jagged iron.

"What do you want?" whispered the seer.

"You know… what I… need."

The seer bowed her head, but her lips were still writhing and smoke began to pour from her mouth. The wolf-beast chuckled, lowered its maw and bit off her head, crunching through skull and teeth, brains slopping between its fangs and drooling like runny eggs from twisted mandibles. Blood arced in a fountain from the neck stump, drenching the beast and darkening its fur. A headless corpse flopped to the floor.

The soldiers charged forward with spear and sword, and the creature turned and spat a shower of brain and bone shards at them, many of whom screamed, gasped, suddenly faltered with the absolute shock. Dalgoran and Jagged ploughed on, teeth gritted, swords smashing down to hack at the creature again and again. Spears plunged into it and it howled, then, a high real wolf howl, and its claws started swiping left and right, disembowelling one man who slipped on his own entrails as he sobbed, and removing another guard's face so that he clutched helplessly, down on his knees in puddles of blood and streamers of flesh and his severed nose, clawing at a mask of shredded muscle and skin and open bone sockets where the remains of his punctured eyes lingered like pale worms.

More spears plunged into the wolf-beast and it rose, whirling about, five shafts wrenched from the hands of guards and smacking into others, knocking them from their feet. The beast staggered towards the window and the cold winter chill, riddled with open wounds, and Dalgoran grabbed a spear from a speechless guard, his face hard and iron and grim, and strode forward to where the creature, now mewling and clawing at the ground, attempted to crawl to freedom.

"Why did you kill the seer?" he snarled.

Slowly, the creature rolled onto its back, a black tongue lolling between huge jaws, and its different coloured eyes fixed on Dalgoran and it laughed, a deep-throated chuckle that was half rumble, half human.

Dalgoran placed the spear point at the creature's throat. "Why?"

"You… next… Dalgoran," it said, before snarling and trying to lurch up and forward towards the old general. Dalgoran drove the spear into the creature's throat, and Jagged was there beside him, short sword in both hands, which he lifted, then drove down through one of the eye sockets and into the brain.

The creature slumped slowly back, like a balloon deflating, and was still.

Blood pooled in a huge puddle from under black and grey fur, and Dalgoran turned, eyes sweeping the carnage and the shocked faces of his birthday party guests. He rolled his sword in his wrist, and took a cloth from a guard, wiping the blood and gore from the blade.

Jagged came up beside him, along with Vornek and Kalum, both high-ranking military officers, all with bloodied swords.

"The words, the words of the seer," said Jagged, face drained of blood.

"And now this," said Dalgoran, and gave a solemn nod. "I know what you're thinking. Morkagoth. The mud-orcs. But… we killed him, Jagged. The Wolves killed him. We drove those mud-orcs back to the slime."

"This stinks like a dog corpse," said Vornek. "We need to go to the King. We need to warn him."

"Eighty percent of the army have been stood down by Yoon over the past six months," said Kalum. "The seer said 'Mud born, blood rage'. If it is, the mud-orcs are on the march again, and Drakerath Fortress is stupidly undermanned. Yoon needs to recommission the army; we need men on those walls."

"And if the seer was talking nonsense?" said Dalgoran.

"You disbelieve her words?"

Dalgoran said nothing, brow furrowed. "Her words, on their own, would have done nothing. But that… *creature*. In fifty years of soldiering I have never seen anything like it. Where did it come from? And more importantly, are there more?"

"The times are changing," said Jagged, gently. "That creature alone needs reporting to the King. As for the seer's words? I only believe in iron and blood and soldiering. I brought her here for fun. And look what happened."

"The creature came for her," said Dalgoran. "Maybe its intention was to stop her speaking? Stop the warning? But it was too late and she delivered her message. It failed in its mission."

The men mulled this over and Dalgoran waved over a servant. "Find Granesh. I want horses saddling, with full battle gear. I want packs with food and water ready within the hour. I have a journey to make."

"I'll come with you to see King Yoon," said Jagged.

"I, also," said Vornek, and was echoed by another six or seven of the military men present.

"I am not going to Yoon. Not yet, anyway."

"Where, then?" frowned General Jagged.

"There's a war coming; I can feel it in my bones." General Dalgoran sheathed his sword, took several deep breaths, back stiff, head high. His bleak eyes surveyed each man in turn, like a hawk weighing up the kill. "And you heard the seer, gentlemen. I must go to Rokroth. It's time the Wolves came home."

OLD HONEY

You're a tart, a bitch and a cheap whore. You suck men in like a whirlpool, gain their trust, then rob them, abuse them, kill them. I despise what you have become, sister. What happened to your nobility? Your honour? What happened to the little girl who ran with flowers in her hair? What happened to the girl who sailed boats on the lake? What happened to the girl who loved her sister?

"It was never like that, Suza. You have romanticised the past. You have created fabulous scenarios that never existed; father was a tough man, a man of iron and steel. He worked us hard. Trained us hard with sword and spear and bow. We were taught to fight! How can you not remember that?"

We were children, bitch. And father simply had our best interests at heart. He was preparing us for a wicked world, an evil world, a world that does not suffer fools. And we were iron, Kiki. Tough as old leather. But what happened to you? You were his star pupil, his little girl, his little battle princess. And look at you now! There was laughter, but this was nothing to do with humour. This was mockery laced with a web of hate.

"And now it comes out, Suza, doesn't it? The real lodestone of your pathetic fucking poison. This is nothing to do with how I treat men, or how I live my life now. This is to do with how father treated me; and how he treated *you*."

Shut up.

"So, I was his little battle princess, was I? That's because *I* chose to go into the army, whereas *you* chose to marry young, tend your roses and fire out a child. Hardly *my* fault! You took the easy path. You walked with pansies, whilst I took hold of thorns and wrung their fucking necks."

Easy path! shrieked Suza. *You dare to say I took the easy path? Oh you bitch, Kiki; you absolute back-stabbing nasty evil lump of horse shit. You know my baby died! You know it turned my mind inside out with grief! How can you criticise me for that? How can you mock my pain, my trauma, my grief...*

"Shh," said Kiki, "not here, not now; I'm too tired, too strung out, the pain is back, the pain..." and she could feel it rising, a thumping drumbeat like an earthquake, that climbed up her spine from the tumour inside her, climbed like crawling vine tentacles until they blossomed with black leaves which wrapped around her brain and squeezed, gently, but with such incredible eternal pressure like sliding land plates that it made her scream.

Kiki screamed, and screamed, and screamed; and Suza laughed as she disappeared like drifting campfire smoke. Kiki's eyes opened and she groaned. Her mouth was dry. The pain thumped through her head like a horse repeatedly kicking her. The light was blinding and she closed her eyes again, breathed deeply through rat-breath, tried to calm the trembling in her hands and arms and entire body.

Honey-leaf, screamed her body.

Give me the honey-leaf.

Kiki forced her eyes open again, knowing that if she could just find one single leaf, or even a portion of a leaf, and ease it under her tongue like a magic pill then the world would fade away, and it would be a gentle release, dissolved, not this mortal agony which raged through her like a shamathe's elemental storm. She clawed herself into a sitting position and realised the light was not actually bright; just cracks from around the curtains. She blinked and licked her lips. She needed her pouch. Her little black pouch. She scrambled across the tangled bed sheets and stopped, suddenly, mid-crawl.

There was somebody else in the room. He was seated in the single comfort chair in the gloom.

Images of Lars and violent guards came flooding back through the treacle of her memories and Kiki launched herself off the bed to where she kept her sabre – but it was gone.

There came a small, rhythmical tapping sound from the chair.

"Looking for this?"

A deep voice. Male. Strong. It filtered through clouds of pain. It wormed through Kiki's withdrawal with just a tiny hint of recognition.

"Who are you?" Her words were slurred. She staggered, fell to the bed, and she felt more than heard or saw the man stand and lean her sabre against the wall. He moved towards her, and she lashed out with a fist, but he stepped back and she fell to the bare floorboards and groaned.

"Kiki. It's me. Dalgoran."

"Dalgoran?" She looked, face scrunched, flesh pale, hair lank and filthy. "It is really you?"

"It's really me," he said, and knelt, and took her in his arms and she began to cry, great sobs which came from deep inside her, welling up and bursting free with a decade of fear and frustration and terror.

Kiki snuggled into his arms, sobbing, and could smell smoke, and horses, and the oil he used to sharpen his iron blade; and a world of memories came rushing in, an eternity of memories came rushing back, hard days on the parade ground, marching, mock combat, training to be Wolves. Training to be Iron Wolves…

"I missed you," she said, eyes full of tears, and drifted away into sleep.

When Kiki woke again, it was to the smell of frying bacon. She yawned, and at least the banging in her head had gone, although she was still trembling. More importantly, Suza had left her in peace; which meant pleasant – silent – dreams.

She sat up slowly, and realised she was dressed in a long, soft, cotton nightdress. She dug around the untidy room, pulling out socks, trousers, boots and a thick woollen shirt. She glanced out the window to see a thin scattering of snow on the street down below. There came a series of clangs from the smithy across the street, and the rattle of horse hooves over cobbles as some noblemen rode past.

In the small kitchen, Dalgoran had lit the cast iron stove and was frying bread in lard. Kiki stepped in and leant against the door frame, watching the old general. He was just as she remembered; like the last time they had spoken. Well. *Argued.* Only now his hair was grey instead of black with streaks, his face a little more lined, but still strong, proud, almost ageless in its cast. He wore a smart black uniform but without insignia, and it was bulked, betraying a chainmail vest beneath. His boots were polished to a shine and this, strangely, made Kiki feel scruffier than ever.

"Bacon? Fried bread?" he said, without looking up.

"Yes. Thank you." Kiki moved almost humbly to the table, and sat, and pressed her hands down hard against the wood to stop them shaking. Her mouth was dry to the point of ashes and she poured herself a wooden cup of water from a clay jug.

"I am… surprised," he said, slowly.

"By?"

"By this," said Dalgoran, and gave her a sideways glance. Then he went back to turning the bacon in the pan. It hissed and sizzled and the smell made Kiki feel suddenly nauseous. It was always the same after the leaf. All you wanted was another, to take away the pain. She fought it.

"This room? This house? This life?"

"Yes, this room. Have you really pissed away everything King Tarek gave you?"

"No. No." Kiki shook her head, sipping water and watching Dalgoran over the rim of the cup. "I could buy this town ten times over. Every building in it. I like it here. Above a bakers. Across from Big Jon the Smith, who always shouts hello when I step out onto the cobbles. Back in Ganda, in my wonderful marble palace, I just rattled around like a pebble in a bucket." She stumbled into silence.

"How did you find me?"

"I followed the honey-leaf fumes," he said.

There was an awkward silence. "Oh," said Kiki, finally.

Dalgoran scraped the bacon and fried bread onto a wooden platter and carried it to the table, placing it in front of Kiki. It was all she could do to not heave up the acid contents of her belly and she turned away for a few moments, taking deep breaths, trying to calm herself.

Dalgoran grabbed a rough-sawn pitch pine chair, reversed it and sat, arms folded at chest height across the back. He stared hard at Kiki, then, stared hard with those old eyes and she squirmed under the stare.

"Stop it with the guilty horse shit, will you?" she said, finally, and pushed a piece of bread around her plate.

"Eat it. It'll make you strong again."

"I am strong!"

"In your dreams, maybe," said Dalgoran, more harshly than he meant.

"I could take you, old man," she said, eyes flashing with anger. "I wasn't your captain for no fucking reason and you know it." She pushed her plate away, wood scraping wood.

"Is that what you want? To hurt me? To stick that pretty little sabre through my guts and watch me bleed like a pig all over your floorboards?"

"No." Kiki retreated. Her eyes had huge dark rings. She looked... hunted. "What I meant, was..."

"Or do you want this," said Dalgoran slowly, and pulled a small black pouch from his pocket. It was still fat with honey-leaves. Kiki's breath caught in her throat, and the trembling in her hands returned.

"Give me that," she said.

"No."

"I need it," she said, and raised her eyes to Dalgoran's. The pity in his gaze nearly floored her. She considered that pity. From the greatest man she had ever known. From somebody she considered not just her general, but also her friend. Not just her friend, but her *father*. She shouldn't have responded how she did. Instead, she felt her anger building. What was the old fool doing, coming to her after all these years, making judgements about where she lived, what she did with her time, the people she met, and the... the leaves she chose to ingest? Who the hell did he think he was? He had no right! They hadn't spoken for ten years, and even then the words had been heated; again, his criticisms about how she lived her life. He was her general, not her damn bastard mother, and she was sick of it!

"No." He stared at her with his hard eyes.

"No?" she shrieked, rising to her feet, face contorting into something near pain. "The leaves are mine! I bought them. They belong to me. I can do with them as I like, and I need one *right now, old man."*

"It's got you that bad, has it?"

"Ha! What would you know? I haven't seen you for ten years. What do you care about my life and the way I'm living it? And now you break into my world, and I'm sure you think in your head you're doing the right thing, come here to save me from myself and all that stinking rancid horse shit." Dalgoran's face had not changed. He was still rigid, poised, focused. "Unless… of course." Realisation dawned. "You need me for something, don't you, General?" She saw the flicker in his eyes, and she gave a laugh. "Last time I saw you, you began to preach like an old Church Priest on a mission to purify me. I said I'd break your jaw and you stalked off, huffing and puffing like one of those oil engines down in the factories. But now, *now* something has changed. What is it, General? Your wife left you and you need me to hunt her down? Somewhere warm where she's frolicking with her new and *much younger* lover?"

"My wife died," said Dalgoran, face stone, voice level. "I am on my own now, but not for the reason you say."

Kiki paused, then shrugged, and inside a little part of her died and she hated herself for it. *This is a man you love,* she imagined Suza saying. *And you're on a mission to make him slit your throat.* But that wasn't it. She simply wanted…

"The honey-leaves. Give them to me." She held out a hand, locking her eyes to his.

He met her gaze for long moments, then turned swiftly and threw the pouch through the open door of the stove.

There came a sparkle and the pouch flared in the heat of the fire amongst the glowing coals, flaring into a bright splash of silver and gold.

Kiki's cheeks flushed red and she leapt across the table, stretching for the pouch. Dalgoran caught her and she snarled and he pushed her back, hand outstretched, fingers open, but eyes hard and locked.

"You need it so much you'd lose your hand?" he said.

"You bastard. You know, know how much I need it..."

"Then it's damn well time you stopped. Yes, you are right, there is something I want you to do. You are Kiki; Captain of Wolves. I came looking for her. Looking for my captain. But... maybe I was mistaken?"

"Maybe you were."

"It was my birthday. As a present, some old friends brought a seer. Her prophecy spoke of mud-orcs marching, blood being shed, soldiers slaughtered; it's happening again, Kiki. The bastards are gathering; I can feel it in these ancient bones. At the end, the chant spoke of one hope – to reunite the Wolves. That's you. And me. And the others."

Kiki relaxed back, sat on her chair and stared long and hard at Dalgoran.

"I don't believe you," she said, finally.

"Shortly afterwards, our party was crashed by... a creature." He went on to explain the fight and the creature biting off the seer's head and spitting the mangled bone and brain at the charging men. "I have never seen anything like it, Kiki. In all my long years. I don't know where it came from, what dark magick conjured it from Hell or the Furnace; but it was real and it took some hard killing." He lapsed into a brooding silence and stood, hands on hips, staring at his former captain.

"What was the full prophecy spoken by the seer?"

Dalgoran repeated the chant as best he remembered it, his eyes down, voice a low rumble. And then he glanced up to see Kiki smiling.

"That could mean anything, you old fool," she laughed, voice full of mockery, reclining on her chair, rocking it back on two wooden feet and stretching out her legs.

"You think so?" snarled Dalgoran, losing his cool. "I've come halfway across fucking Vagandrak to find you; I was looking for my captain, looking for the hard woman of iron I knew so well, a woman I loved like a daughter, so we could gather the Wolves and take them home; back to Desekra; back to the Splintered Bones. But instead, I find a whore sleeping with petty noblemen, murdering King's Guards and filling her cheeks full of the idiotic narcotic favoured by mindless simpletons – the useless, the weak – and using the cancer in her heart to fuel her constant whining and constant fucking self-pity."

"You know about that?" growled Kiki.

"Yes, soldier," snapped Dalgoran, then stepped suddenly forward and smashed a hard slap across her face. The blow knocked her from the chair and her head snapped up fast, eyes glowing. She leapt at him, small blade in her fist – Dalgoran didn't see it drawn – and within the blink of an eye had it pressed against his throat. Kiki was dangerously close.

"You've been watching me?" she whispered.

"A purse of silver coin buys a lot of information, in these parts."

"Some things earn an immediate death sentence," said Kiki, voice low, menacing, hands trembling in rage.

Dalgoran looked deep into her eyes, her face and her soul. "I have nothing but love, admiration, honour, time, patience and respect for Kiki, my Captain of the Iron Wolves. But I see you are not her. I see she left this place a long time ago. Lady, I bid you good day."

Dalgoran knocked the blade aside as he would an annoying insect, gathered his heavy overcoat and scabbarded sword, and made for the stairs. As his boots thumped, so Kiki slumped to the floor, tears streaming down her face, knife clattering on the boards, and she lowered her head and cried into her hands and thought about his biting words: *But instead, I find a whore sleeping with petty noblemen, murdering King's Guards and filling her cheeks full of the idiotic narcotic favoured by mindless simpletons – the useless, the weak – and using the cancer in her heart to fuel her constant whining and constant fucking self-pity.*

"No," she whispered, into tear-stained hands.

But yes, sister, mocked Suza. *He's right. And you know he's right. And the truth hurts, doesn't it, bitch? Bites you like a toxic snake. Stings you like a scorpion strike. You've just pissed away your last and greatest friendship. Watched him walk out the door for the love of the leaf. I don't need to despise you any more, sister. You have enough hate in your cancerous breast for the two of us.*

"Leave me alone!" she screamed, sobbing, and she could smell the aroma of honey-leaf in the air from the oven, just a hint, just enough to tease and her mouth began to water and she could taste it on her lips, under her tongue, in her brain; she had coin under the bed. All she had to do was grab a handful and head for any six or seven places she knew so well, better than the back of her hand. Better than her own face. Better than her own friends.

She forced herself to her feet, wiping her eyes, and shoved the knife in her boot. She swayed a little, feeling suddenly, violently nauseous. Dizziness swamped her and she staggered, but grabbed the jug of water and forced herself to drink the entire contents. Then she stood there, panting, breathing deep, and ran for the stairs, taking them three at a time and nearly stumbling where she would surely fall and break her neck.

She slowed, then burst through the rough wooden door and out into the bright street. Her boots slid on snow-kissed cobbles and she looked frantically up, then down past the bustling people. She couldn't see Dalgoran. Damn it, she couldn't see the old general! Where was he?

The voice, when it spoke, made the hairs on her neck stand on end. She shivered, a deep feeling of vulnerability between her shoulder blades, and suddenly her eyes caught sight of two archers lurking in the shadows of the upper windows across the street.

"Hello, Kiki," said Lars, and Kiki turned, slowly. The nobleman had his arm in a sling and his face was pale and grey; but not his eyes. His eyes were red-rimmed and burned with hate, and fury, and bitterness.

"I see you got the knife out," she said.

"You should have stayed to watch the fun," he growled, and grinned, and only then did she notice the drawn sword, and hear the clatter of boots on cobbles. Two men were behind Lars, but swiftly another ten approached. These weren't King's Guards. These were mercenaries. Tough bastards. Outside the Law.

And then there were the archers…

"Can we talk about this?" she said, stalling for time. Why hadn't she grabbed her sabre on the way out? Why? *Why?*

Lars grin turned sickly. "Do you realise how much I suffered, *whore*? The surgeon says I will never use my arm again. Think about that. I am now a cripple. I am now to be mocked by the ladies, instead of bedded by them. So. I… don't think words are enough, my sweet." His body

tensed for the killing strike, eyes narrowed, tongue wet
against blood red lips...

"Hold your blade, son," came the deep, authoritative
voice of Dalgoran. He stepped from the deep shadows of
an arched doorway and eyed the twelve men.

Lars' gaze flickered to him. "Keep out of this, old man."
He made as if to move forward. When Dalgoran's words
came to him, they chilled him to the core.

"Take another step, lad, and your bowels will decorate
the street. Know this. I am General Dalgoran, of Desekra
Fortress, former chief of the King's Armies. I was killing
men and mud-orcs before your suckled your mother's
tits and not one man has ever stood against me and lived.
So, back down, take your mercenary scum, and fuck off,
before I take exception to the lot of you and cut out your
livers for fun."

"Brave words for one old man defending an addicted
honey-leaf bitch."

Lars eased back towards the gathered mercenaries, then
yelled, "Kill them!" The mercenaries surged forward, and
in one smooth movement Dalgoran unsheathed his blade
and cut upwards across the face of the lead man, who fell
back, blood flushing his eyes. On the downward stroke
he caught the second man between shoulder and neck,
cleaving him from clavicle to sternum. A huge flap of flesh
and attached arm folded out and the man hit the cobbles
dead. Kiki grabbed the knife from her boot and ducked
under a wild sword swing, coming in close, ramming her
knife into the man's groin to twist and *nick* the femoral
artery. She carried his weight for a moment, taking his
sword, then allowed him to flop to one side grappling
at the flush of warm blood down his cotton trews. She
blocked a downward sweep, kicked the mercenary in the

groin, and stuck her adopted sword point straight into his throat where he gurgled on the wide arrow of iron for several seconds before Kiki front-kicked him from the point of her blade.

There came hisses, and black-feathered arrows appeared in the backs of two mercenaries, who grunted and fell forward. A second later, they were joined by two more. In a few heartbeats eight mercenaries were dead; townsfolk were lining one side of the street, hands to mouths, eyes wide in horror at this sudden surge of violence.

Lars stood, stunned, four men still behind him but his fury transcending normal logical thought. "You bitch!" he screamed, and launched himself at Kiki. She stood her ground, tall, graceful, head held high, eyes burning. She was back on the battlefield, armoured men bearing down on her, their swords slamming towards her head. She blocked Lars' horizontal sweep and sparks showered the cobbles, blades sliding together until their hilts locked.

"Say goodbye, Lars. You were fun... whilst you were breathing."

Kiki stepped back, disengaging blades, and what followed was a stunning display of swordsmanship. Lars, despite his fancy clothes and noble birth, had been taught by some of the finest swordsmen and fencing tutors in Vagandrak. But he was not a soldier. His contests had been for prizes, be they monetary, or the warm bed of some grinning, slack-jawed beauty. This was different. This was real. This was to the death...

The blades rang in song, hissing left and right, diagonal cuts, thrusts to the face or groin; Kiki and Lars moved back and forth on the cobbles, faces locked in concentration but with an increasing look of panic creeping into Lars' features. He licked his dry lips and found himself madly defending against a dazzling attack, blades clashing and grating together, until Kiki's sword cut a line across the side of his neck. Blood flushed warm down his collar. An inch deeper and she would have cut open his windpipe…

He took a step back. "I withdraw," he said, voice shaking.

"Not this time," said Kiki, and launched a final attack, a dazzling smash of blades that left Lars' weapon clattering across the cobbles, then a *thud* as his decapitated head landed face down, followed by his collapsing, deflating body.

Kiki's head snapped up. The remaining mercenaries held up their hands and glanced at Dalgoran who gave a nod. Slowly, they backed away from the scene, sheathed their swords and disappeared down the nearest alley.

"The archers were yours?" said Kiki, smiling bleakly.

"Of course. Basic military strategy dictates at least one form of backup when entering any known confrontation. It's textbook."

"Yes. General Dalgoran. *Father*. Thank you. And… I'm sorry." She took a deep breath. "I have been a fool."

He stared hard at her. "It was good to see you fight again, Kiki. Good to see my captain in action once more. You still have it; a bit rusty on the lower left defence, but not something that can't be ironed out."

"You asked me a question. You want to reunite the Wolves? You want to take on this new menace?"

"Yes. You'll come with me, Kiki?"

"I'll come with you, Father. But I have to warn you, the others… they have fallen on bad times. Harsh times."

Dalgoran nodded. "It's been too many years, Kiki. But whatever state we find them in, you're still my Iron Wolves, still the best elite unit in Vagandrak. And I'll skewer any man who says otherwise."

"Some might say you're living in the past," whispered Kiki.

Dalgoran sheathed his sword and held up his hand as the City Guards approached. Seeing his rank, the squad of six stopped suddenly, snapping to attention, salutes held in place. Nobody demanded more respect than Dalgoran.

Nobody, except the King.

"We shall see," growled the old general, and gestured for the guards to clean away the bodies.

RED THUMBS

Dek sat on the wooden bench, staring at the ale tankard before him. The tankard, in turn, sat on a wooden plank. The wooden plank was attached to other wooden planks, and the wooden planks, rough sawn, still carrying speckles of sawdust and the heads of large iron nails, were hammered together to form a crude box. It was a coffin. And inside the coffin lay Dek's mother.

Dek's face was grim, battered, bruised, scowling. His knuckles were grazed and swollen, and one of his ears was missing a lobe and had been roughly stitched. Directly opposite him, also with a growling visage, sat Ragorek, although Ragorek held his tankard in his bandaged fists. The two men stared at one another. The grand living room was filled with menace and a promise of impending violence. A single brand on the wall flickered, filling the space with eerie light and long dancing shadows.

"I came as fast as I could," said Ragorek, finally.

Dek took a drink. Foam lined his upper lip. "Eighteen fucking days. It's a day's ride, Ragorek. You unfeeling bastard."

Ragorek stared at him. "I was busy."

"Too busy to see your dying mum?"

"I... didn't realise how serious she was."

"I told you."

"I didn't understand."

"Horse shit! You're a bastard, Rag. A boneless, spineless, worthless son. I can't wait for the day you die. Dad's going to be there, wielding a helve and waiting for you to pop up your stupid grinning head. He'll cave in your teeth, then your skull, and break your spine; and you'll deserve every single damn blow."

"You said that. Wait. Wait!" Dek settled back again, violence a cloak. "You're being too harsh," said Ragorek, and sighed, and placed his tankard by his side on the bench. "I came here to help. To help, Dek. To bloody help! Don't you understand?"

"Horse shit," growled Dek. "You thought you'd wait it out like a piece of shit coward, like a fucking rat at the bottom of a barrel of liquid shit. You thought you'd wait until she was dead, then poke up your stupid flat head and come on down for the money and the house. Well, here we are. And the house is here. But you know what, Ragorek? You can stick mum's house up your rectum. You're not having it."

"That's not your decision."

"Now, there's a wager."

"She lodged it with legal men in Drakerath. It's a legal procedure. Seconded by the King and the Law of the Land."

"Fuck the Law of the Land." Dek's eyes were glowing. "And fuck the King."

"I have the law on my side," said Ragorek, not unkindly. "You are blinded by grief. I understand that." He slowly stood. "I can see it was a mistake me coming here." He rubbed his aching jaw, and his tongue probed an extra missing tooth. "I'll be gone. You'll get the paperwork through soon enough."

Dek surged up. "YOU'LL FUCKING SIT DOWN AND DRINK YOUR BEER AND FUCKING SEND OUR MUM OFF RIGHT, OR I SWEAR BY ALL THAT'S UNHOLY, I'LL SNAP YOUR FUCKING SPINE OVER MY FUCKING KNEE!"

The two men glared at one another.

Brothers.

Brothers in hate.

Gradually, resentful, grumbling, Ragorek sat back down.

Dek subsided, his eyes wild, his face a contortion. He glared at Ragorek, then drank his drink, then slammed his tankard on his mother's coffin.

"You show her disrespect," said Ragorek, voice low.

"No. I was here. *HERE*. I did it all. I sorted it all. I held her hand. I told her I loved her. I listened to her rants. I kissed her tears. I listened to her laments. She wailed, and begged, and cried, and asked why you, YOU, you fucker, asked why you weren't here."

"You were always her favourite," said Ragorek, softly.

"Fuck you. Man, how old are you? What horse shit. That's because when Dad died, I was there for her. I was always there for her. You fucked off. You went playing your pathetic little games of life in another town, another city, another world; but I knew, I knew she was dying and I stayed and I helped. You did not. Would not. You would not help. And I swear, man, by all the unholy gods, I swear I'll make you pay for *your* disrespect."

"Not that again. Not the fight, again. I'm tired, Dek. Too old and tired for this."

"Well, wake up, old man, because I'm going to kill you."

They glared at one another over the rough sawn planks of their mother's coffin. Around them, the house gave a soft creak, as if awaking. Outside, the wind howled and a storm hammered. Rain and sleet battered the windows. A lantern swung wildly, its yellow glow casting crazy patterns on the stone gravel drive.

The house was large and detached, stood in three acres of its own land. Dek's father had been not just a career soldier, but a trader in ancient texts; he'd made his money and saw his family well provided for before his untimely, early death. The house had been their family home. Dek and Ragorek had played there as children, exploring the nooks and crannies, learning its many secrets. Now, it was worth a pretty penny on the Vagandrak property market, and Dek knew Ragorek had a gleam in his eye for the incoming coin.

Dek gave a sinister smile. Well. He had news for his brother.

Dek drank. And slammed down his tankard.

"Don't do that."

"Why? You think I might wake the dead? I wish I could, brother. Wish I could."

They sat in uncomfortable silence for a while. The type of sour silence that invades a gloomy church ceremony. The atmosphere of a cuckolded husband listening to his wife's weak excuses. The silence at a child's funeral.

"I sat," said Dek, slowly, "and held her hand."

Ragorek stared at him. He didn't know what to say. But he knew something was coming. Something bad.

"I sat and held her hand. And I watched her struggling; not to live, I think. I think I was watching her trying to die. She looked like a corpse. Her face was drawn, gaunt, stripped back to the bone. She hadn't eaten for forty or fifty days. I don't know. I lost count. I was too busy fucking crying. Crying and wondering where the fuck you were."

He cast a sideways glance at Ragorek, but his elder brother said nothing. "She'd lie for a while and look like she was at peace. But then she'd grasp my hand, crushing my fingers – which was incredible, because all the weight had fallen off her. She was skin and bone. She squeezed the hell out of me, but that was good, *good*, because it showed fight and it showed strength. The will was there. I'd cheer her on. '*Fight it!*', I'd scream. '*Fight the fucking thing*'. But of course, it gets us in the end, don't it? We can only hold out for so long, no matter how bloody hard we think we are. And so I held her hand, and she squeezed me, and I watched her contort, writhe, arching her back, her mouth open in a silent scream. I wept, cried silently, as she screamed silently, and we were mother and son in misery as well as in flesh and history. I waited for her to die. But more. Much more. I *willed* her to die, you know? I begged for it in the end. Down on my knees by her bedside, as she screamed and moaned and shit herself. She was suffering and there was nothing I could do to make it right. I begged for the gods to take her, but of course the gods are all fucking sick, and I mock them, piss on their rancid false effigies. And so, in my madness I started to think about killing her. About taking that fat duck-feather pillow and smothering her; because I could; because I couldn't bear it, but more importantly – and this is where you fucking need to listen you selfish bastard of a brother – because *she* couldn't bear it."

Ragorek stared at him questioningly.

"Did you kill her, little brother?" he asked, eventually.

Dek held up his hand. "No, no, come on, please. I did not, although I contemplated it for long days and longer nights. But who am I to play a god? It is not for me to judge, to kill her, no matter how much she suffered."

"I am surprised."

"Why?" A plunge into immediate anger. Hate. Violence.

"You've sent enough to their deathbeds. In the army. In the Wolves. As a fighter in the Pits. I know your reputation. I've seen you take men apart limb by fucking limb. You're a madman, Dek. A madman."

"Only when the rage is on me. But I can control that now, I reckon. I'm better now."

"Yes. We'll see."

Dek drank his ale. His small eyes were the colour of cobalt. He slammed down his tankard, which slopped over the sides, splashing his dead mother's coffin.

"That's disrespectful," said Ragorek again, words slow and direct as pointed barbs.

"Fuck you. Fuck the man who fucks off for weeks when he knows his mother is dying. Fuck the man who doesn't visit, doesn't help, doesn't care. Fuck the man who fucks off on his own little mission and only re-emerges when she's dead and cold and gone, and he thinks he's going to get his money, thinks he's going to get his slice of the Estate. Fuck him."

"It wasn't like that, Dek."

"It looked like that."

"It didn't play out like that."

"Fucking looked like it, you big bastard."

They stared at each other. Time passed. Worlds died. Stars were born. They did not speak. Eventually Dek smiled. A broad, friendly, humorous smile that was totally out of place. He drank his ale leaving a foam moustache.

"What's that smile mean?"

"Ha! Get fucked."

"No. Seriously, Dek. What's going on inside your head? Except the blindingly obvious?"

"We have a problem."

They stared at one another.

"What kind of problem?"

"A serious kind of problem," said Dek, slowly, and threw his tankard to one side. He rose, ponderously, for he was a big man. He stared hard at his brother. "You have, of course, heard of the Red Thumb Gang?"

"Yeah. Nasty scum. When they kill somebody, they leave a bloody thumbprint on the victim's forehead."

"Yes. That's them. They rule pretty much all the gangs and shite in Vagan, Drakerath, Kantarok, Zaret... all the major cities. Well. Let's see. How can I put this... I owe them some money."

"How much money?"

"A lot of money." He grinned. "A *lot* of money."

"What did you do?"

"Gambling, mostly. After the fights in the Pits."

"And you lost?"

"Yeah. More than that. I lost. And I lost *this*."

"This? What's *this*?"

"This house. *This* fucking house."

"It wasn't yours to gamble!" screamed Ragorek, surging to his feet. "It belonged to our mother! It was her home! How could you gamble her fucking home? You little bastard shit."

"At last! A show of emotion! Is the fear of losing your inheritance stinging you, little boy? Yeah, I bet the house on the pit fights, and I know what you're going to say; you're going to whine and moan and bleat like a fist-fucked goat. You're going to say now, *now* our mother is dead, then half the house is yours. By the Law of the Land. The Law of our fine King Yoon. By all the courts and the Law of Vagandrak, yeah yeah. But unfortunately for you, you old bastard, the Red Thumb Gang don't listen to the Law of the Land. They're going to come here. They're going to come here tonight and take what they want."

"I don't believe it!" raged Ragorek.

"You'd better believe it. I made a few mistakes. This house is forfeit. But then, that's academic because our mother, *our fucking mother*, is dead. And the only loser I can see here, and now, is you." He laughed out loud, and grinned at Ragorek. "I believe the gods show their pleasure in numerous different ways."

Ragorek stood. He drew his short sword. "I'm going to kill you."

"Be my guest. There's a fucking line of bastards waiting to do it!"

There came a shout from outside. Firelight flickered from brands; many brands.

"They're here!" hissed Ragorek.

"Yeah. I know." Dek poured himself another tankard of ale. "Funny, ain't it?"

"Oh, you bastard! You knew they were coming, you knew the Red Thumbs were coming and you let me sit here and drink and talk! Oh Dek, you're the lowest form of horse shit."

"And that's where we disagree." Dek rose and drew his own short sword. "You see Ragorek, you owe me. You owe me in blood, and in honour, and in your pathetic show of compassion; you owe me in family shame. You owe our old mum. Now, I'm happy to let you die here. By the sulphur of the Furnace, I'm willing to die here myself. By all the gods, I don't rightly give a shit."

"Hoy! You in there! Come out and throw down your weapons! We have a warrant from the Red Thumb Governor."

Dek grinned. "But tonight, by all the gods, I'm going to burn this place down and cremate our mum. It's where she wanted to lay. She wanted go by fire, here, in the grounds where our father is buried. Now, you can help me, Rag, or I can cut off your fucking head and do it all by myself. What's it going to be?"

They stared at one another, across their mother's coffin.

Ragorek's face contorted. He gritted his teeth, and growled, and then spat.

"You cunt, Dek."

"Never said I wasn't," rumbled the big pit fighter.

"I'll do this. For our mum. And to show you I never was interested in the money."

"Your face betrays the words that puke from your mouth like disgorged maggots, but whatever. Let's get to it, if that's the way it's going to be."

"What's the plan?"

"We need to entice the Red Thumb boys inside. Deep inside. Lead them into the Heart."

"Then what?"

"Then I've taken care of it," said Dek, grinning, and showing his missing teeth.

Dek stood. His face narrowed.

Firelight glittered in the courtyard from many brands. Ragorek stood, and the two men looked out the window. There was a large group, dressed in dark clothing and bearing many weapons.

"There must be twenty men," said Ragorek, and gave Dek a sideways look. "Shit, brother. They must want you pretty bad!"

"I did say I owed them money."

"But... *twenty* men?"

"Let us say my reputation precedes me."

"What's the plan?"

"Get out your sword, follow my lead."

Outside the group had gathered. Firelight shone on damp cobbles and various ancient, moss-darkened statues from the family's distant past. One man foregrounded himself; he was a tall, athletic man, a warrior by his stance. He held his brand high and the firelight shone from his brown forked beard.

"Dek, this is Crowe," he bellowed. "Come on out. We know you're in there. Show yourself. You have some questions to answer, old friend. You have three minutes."

"This way," growled Dek, and ran through the dark and shadow-filled house. Both men had spent their childhood there. They knew every corridor, every step, every stairwell, every room and cut-through and nook and cranny, every cupboard and wardrobe, every window and which way they opened, every statue and pillar and panel and table and hideaway. Even in the dark, intuition kicked in, from a childhood playing at being soldiers and heroes, of fighting mock battles with sticks and small wooden figures, of lying in the dark, long into the night, talking excitedly about strategy and how they would both join the King's army and help rid Vagandrak of evil wherever it may be found! Now, some of that evil, members of the Red Thumb Gang, Vagandrak's biggest underground scourge, were here to do them harm. It was an ironic turn of events.

Dek slowed, and Rag mimicked his younger brother. They were approaching the rear of the house and the servants' kitchen, quarters and entrance. As they entered the long kitchen which had, in former glorious years, been able to cater for more than a hundred guests, Ragorek's nostrils twitched. What was that smell? Lantern oil?

Dek and Rag approached the rear door, solid oak, and,

even as they arrived, so a narrow, flat, paper-thin blade was inserted through the crack and jiggled the lock. Dek gave a two strike gesture with his index finger, and in the darkness Rag nodded. They separated, swords out, moving to stand with backs to the cupboards that flanked the door. Dek crouched, and Rag did the same. The door creaked open on purposefully un-oiled hinges.

Three men crept in, bearing swords which had been blackened with gun-oil and soot, and as they came into range Dek let them move past, then reared up, his own blade hacking at the rearmost man. The blade tore into his neck, grating on bone, and the man gave a ragged cry, trying to turn. Dek front-kicked him away, and smashed his blade in a backhand sweep, cutting the second gang-member's throat. He went down on both knees and Dek slid the sword into his eye socket. During this, Ragorek cut down the third man, ramming his sword into the man's back. He followed the gang member to the floor, kneeling on his back and plunging the blade a second time through his kidneys. The man lay still, blood leaking out onto ancient stone flags.

"He's here! He's here!" came a scream from outside. They saw dark shapes running towards the rear door.

"An excellent plan," murmured Ragorek. "Discovered immediately."

"No. It's perfect. Come on."

Dek pounded through the house, and Ragorek glanced back. Men were flooding through that thick oak door, past the large grooved preparation table on which ten thousand carcasses had been skinned and gutted and carved over the decades; and past a stack of barrels. Barrels?

There came the sounds of smashing glass, from several parts of the building. And the splintering of wood from the front door.

"This way."

They headed for the cellar steps, but five men blocked their way.

"Dek!" bellowed Crowe. "Stop! Don't make me come after you!"

Dek said nothing, but veered right with Ragorek close behind. They pounded down the wide main corridor, back to the central living room where their mother's rough-sawn coffin rested. Dek moved to stand behind the coffin, as did Ragorek. Both their swords were bloody, and only then did Ragorek realise the room stank of oil. Lantern oil. He blinked in the gloom. In the short time they had been away, the coffin had been soaked in oil. And now, several barrels flanked the coffin, and a cool breeze drifted into the room from the window behind.

Crowe and ten of his men entered, bristling swords and knives and grim faces.

"Welcome, old friend," said Dek.

"What horse shit is this?" scowled Crowe, rubbing his forked beard. "You know what you have to do, Dek; you need to give me good hard coin, and lots of it! Killing my men will not find you favour with the Red Thumb Gang. And you fucking know we control every damn town and city from here to the Skarandos Mountains in the south, and all the way up to Kantarok and the Skell Forest. You are fucked if you don't cooperate, Dek. You and your pretty brother." He gave a nasty grin which showed his tombstone teeth. "Unless, Ragorek, you wish to come and work for us? We always have use for pretty boys like you. I'm sure we can come to some kind of understanding."

"Listen," said Dek, holding his hands apart, an interesting vision of placation because his sword still dripped blood. "The way I see it, Crowe, it's like this. Yes, I gambled away a life's fortune when I was pissed. And you bastards allowed it. Even *you* allowed it. Old friend. But I recognise a debt is a debt, and as you see, here's my old mum in her coffin, dead, and now this house here belongs to me and my brother here. I reckon this house is good enough to settle my debt. What do you reckon? You can have it."

"Dek!" snarled Ragorek.

Crowe raised his dark, shaggy eyebrows, and withdrew some of his aggression. He looked around, eyes widening, nodding in appreciation.

"That's good, Dek. I see where you're going with this. And I see you have at last come to your senses. This sure is a fine house. I'm positive the men in charge, the people I have to answer to, I am *sure* they will value this as being a good way to paying off some of your debt. Then you won't have to die. Not yet, anyways. So yes, a wise move, and the sensible option, my old comrade."

Dek smiled a narrow smile. "Yes."

Crowe's eyes were fixed to his. "I knew you had history, but didn't realise you had such good family… *connections*. You kept them from me. All those years ago." He smiled. "Lucky for you. It's saved your life."

"Crowe. I think we misunderstand one another," said Dek, face relaxing into a sombre expression. He licked his lips and his eyes gleamed in the flickering light from the single brand.

"We do? How so?" Crowe frowned.

Dek suddenly lunged, grabbing the flaming brand from its bracket. "When I said you could have the house; I didn't mean by selling it and allowing you to reap the financial rewards. I meant that it would be your final resting place. Your grave. Yours, forever." Dek dropped the brand to the coffin and a wall of flame shot up. Searing heat lashed out and Crowe and his men suddenly realised they were standing on carpets soaked with lantern oil. Fire roared, billowing out, igniting the carpets, the oil, and the suddenly screaming men. Clothes caught. Beards and hair flared in ignition. Fire, a dancing demon, leapt from man to man to man, scorching flesh, burning, burning bright, and each man screamed and grabbed at himself and tried to escape in a blind panic of desperation and sudden, incredible terror.

Dek and Ragorek stumbled backwards, towards the open window. Bright fire blinded them. They turned and leapt out, boots thudding into soft earth. Weasel and a group of men were waiting. Weasel's face was deadly serious.

"Are they all in?" snapped Dek.

"Yes. We've still scouts out, but these boys didn't think to leave anybody outside to keep watch. Not too bright, these Red Thumb idiots."

"Nail it up."

Men ran forward and started hammering planks over the window from which Dek and Ragorek had escaped. Bangs and thuds echoed across the gardens and cobbled driveway, reverberating from the boles of nearby ancient trees.

"You sure you got all the doors?" asked Dek.

Weasel nodded. "As soon as you lured them all in through the kitchens and started leading them away, we began then. And when you lit the coffin, I gave the signal to the others."

Now, they could hear the roar of raging fire and the crackling of timbers. Dek walked away from his family home, from his mother's house, from *his own* house, and when halfway down the drive he stopped, and turned, and stared up at the magnificent stone edifice which had been in his family for five generations. Now, in his grief, and in his desperation, he'd torched the place.

Ragorek approached. His face was grim and soot-streaked.

"I can't believe you did this," he said.

Dek stared. The whole lower floor was on fire, and even as they watched flames could be seen caressing the upper storey. A man leapt, burning, screaming, from one of the upper windows. He hit the ground with a dull thud and Weasel and three men ran over and plunged long knives into the burning body, which lay still, flames flickering.

"No escape," whispered Dek. "None of them can escape."

"They'll still know you did it. The Red Thumbs, I mean."

Dek shrugged. "I no longer give a fuck."

They watched the house burn. They watched their home burn.

The roof had caught now, and the whole place was a roaring inferno. Nobody was getting out of the place alive. But then, that had been the whole idea.

Weasel approached. "We're done, Dek. The whole lower floor is nailed up tighter than a whore's... yes. Well."

Dek grasped the small man's hand. "Thanks, Weasel. To you and your boys. You done me proud."

"Anything for you, Dek," grinned Weasel. "You sure you'll be okay?"

"Yes. Any stragglers come staggering out, and I'll give them a bit of Dek loving. Ragorek here will go with you. I have some business to attend to."

"Ragorek is staying where the hell he wants," growled Ragorek, staring hard at Dek. "It's my damn house too. My damn mother who's burning."

Dek gave a single nod. "As you wish, brother."

Weasel and his men melted into the night, and Dek and Ragorek stood for an hour, watching the house burn. Flames roared high illuminating the estate almost as if it were day. But here, ten miles north of the city, there weren't any neighbours. Dek and Ragorek were left alone to watch their mother, and their fortune, burn.

Eventually, Dek sat down cross-legged on the cobbles. Ragorek sat next to him.

There was a mammoth roar as the roof collapsed inwards, shooting a million sparks up into the freezing winter sky. The fire seemed to calm a little then, and the core of the house was glowing white like the centre of a blacksmith's forge.

"It was a good send off," said Dek, finally.

"For mother?"

"Yes."

"I didn't realise that was the plan."

"That was always the plan," said Dek, giving Ragorek a skeletal grin. "The Red Thumb Gang – well, they just got in the way, and this was a convenient way to settle an old score."

"That Crowe man?"

"Yeah. The bastard."

"You know him?"

"Oh, I know him, all right," said Dek, eyes filled with sorrow. "Used to be my best friend."

They sat, their backs freezing, the heat from the burning house throwing out enough energy to make them sweat like armoured soldiers in the sun.

"I miss her," said Ragorek.

"You do?"

"Yes, of course I fucking do!"

"And there was me, thinking you were a heartless, jealous, childish bastard."

"Maybe I'm that as well. So, what do we do now?" Ragorek asked.

Dek shrugged and lay down on the cobbles, placing his head on his arm. "Don't know about you, mate, but I'm going to sleep. It's been a long day. A long week. A long fucking life. And I'm staying here till mum's gone and done and ashes."

Ragorek nodded, and stayed up for a while, watching the stones begin to glow.

It was a cold chill bastard morning. The sky was grey and bleak, like iron. The puddles lay frozen in tiny platters; like dead fish eyes.

The house smouldered. The four main walls were still standing, along with the skeletal infrastructure of supporting walls. But that was all that remained. Windows and doors were toothy gaps. The entire innards of the house were gone and several walls had collapsed to form mounds of rubble. The core of the house glowed, and heat emanated to warm the surrounding cobbles. Ash lay in concentric circles spreading away from the centre, and the great mounds were stirred by gentle gusts of winter breeze, glowing bright occasionally as oxygen breathed life into old fire.

The figure trod carefully up the cobbles, looking left and right, nostrils twitching at the scent of charred timbers and wood smoke. The figure stopped, staring at Dek and Ragorek, lying on the ground in uncomfortable slumber, still warmed by the dying embers of their family.

The figure gestured back to another figure, an old military hand signal, and then approached very, very carefully. Eyes took in the two big men, and the empty bottle of whiskey which lay between them.

Dek was snoring, but the snoring stopped abruptly as the long sliver of steel rested against his throat.

He showed no sign he was awake, but she knew he was.

"Are you here to kill me?" he rumbled, finally. His eyes flickered open. "Because if you are, get it fucking done."

"I'm not here to kill you," said the woman, gently. "I'm here to rescue you. From yourself."

HORSE LADY

Orlana rode a huge, jet-black war charger, sitting, back straight, every inch the queen. To her left padded Tuboda, a massive, magnificent example of man and lion crushed together, warped together, with patchy white skin and tufts of golden fur. Every so often his tawny eyes shifted to gaze up at Orlana, with total love, total obedience, and she would smile and nod in his direction, acknowledging his love. Behind, came the two hundred or so horse beasts, the splice, padding along with heavy feet and paws and mangled iron hooves, some running with odd angular movements due to legs of differing lengths, or a twisted shoulder or pelvis where the fusing of man and beast had not gone completely smoothly. But whatever their deformities, whatever their *perfection*, whatever their *evolution*, all cut a terrifying spectacle. All oozed threat and menace and a promise of oblivion. A merged cavalry unit from ancient tales of horror. From the Before Times. From the millennia rule of the Equiem.

Approaching a walled town at dusk, Orlana said nothing but simply *focused*, and the beasts around her surged forward, snarling and growling, and inside the stockaded walls an urgent bell began to chime in panic from a tall, angular wooden church. The high town gates were dragged shut and Orlana could hear shouts and yells and the clanking of arms. As the splice neared, a small group of men lined the walls with bows drawn – but it was too late. The splice smashed through thick wooden boards barely breaking stride, and those without such heavy, powerful bulks leapt, iron hooves scrabbling to scale the twelve foot planks, and over, and into the town. Once inside, screams echoed and the slaughter began. They charged through the streets, hooves crushing skulls, bulks charging men and women, crushing them against walls where they toppled into the mud and their heads were cracked open. Huge jaws bit off arms, showering the ground and village cottages with blood. The massacre was over in a few minutes, and the splice padded around, hunting out any survivors.

The gates were opened as Orlana approached, Tuboda by her side. Two of her creatures had found the town chief cowering inside the church, and they dragged him out, careful not to rip his arms from his round plump body.

Orlana looked him up and down, and smiled. "You know who I am?"

"No, no, I apologise, we have done nothing, we are a simple people..."

"Tell me, who is your king? Your queen?"

"Zorkai, King of Zakora. You are in his lands now."

"His capital city is Zak-Tan, yes? In the desert, yes, close to the Mud-Pits?"

"The Mud-Pits are forbidden," said the chief, shaking, eyes fixed to the ground as if his subservience might save him. Occasionally he glanced up at one of the quivering, snarling splice, as if maybe he thought he dreamed a nightmare and would wake up soon. But he didn't wake up. It was real. And he stared at the ground again, wishing it would open and swallow him.

"Why forbidden?"

"It is said the Mud-Pits spawned the mud-orcs of old, when the evil sorcerer Morkagoth strode the world. It is one of our Dark Legends."

"Ah, yes, old Morkagoth. A fool. How many men does this King Zorkai command?"

"I… I am not sure. Thousands. I am not a military man, I swear, I do not know such things…"

Orlana nodded, as behind the town chief the splice had rounded up every horse in the area. There were perhaps a hundred, their eyes glassy, ears laid back in fear beside their bulkier, larger, more fearsome counterparts. Orlana held out her hand, and closed her eyes, and the horses began to rear, whinnying, screaming, hooves pawing the air as they suddenly… began to change. Legs cracked, spines rippled, skin and muscle folded in on itself and the town chief stood with mouth hung open, eyes wide in horror and brain shutting down because he knew; knew he would never be able to sleep again.

After the change was done, Orlana let out a breath and turned to Tuboda.

"We must rest now. This place will be fine. Tomorrow we march on Zak-Tan."

"Our army… we not… have enough," said Tuboda, carefully, forming his words past huge, misshapen lion fangs.

"We shall see," smiled Orlana. "Now pass the word to rest."

"What… I do… with him?"

"Are you hungry?"

"Always," rumbled Tuboda, eyes narrowing.

The rotund town chief looked up suddenly, a snap of his head as understanding kicked him. He squeaked in fear. He began to back away, hands held out. "No," he said, "No, please no, have mercy!"

"He's yours."

Tuboda leapt, huge jaws fastening over the town chief's head. There was a pause as they seemed locked, motionless, a snapshot in a stark flash of lightning. Then Tuboda ripped the head free, crunched easily through the skull and brain, and swallowed. The body hit the mud, and Tuboda placed a heavy paw on the dead man's chest and looked up, lifting his great shaggy head to roar at the sky; in majesty, in exultation, in acceptance.

Then, lowering his muzzle, he burrowed through the man's sternum and drank, and fed.

He ran through the long grass, excitement and joy thundering in his breast. She had said yes. Yes! And she was *so beautiful!* He could not believe it.

"She will meet you by the Scorched Willow, in one hour," said Juranda, his best friend, grinning and patting him on the back. "You be good to her, or her father will knock out all your teeth!"

Now he ran, stretching out his muscles as he pounded the dirt track, cutting left onto a grassy hillside which he climbed with easy, loping strides eating the distance. He reached the top of the grassy slope and was momentarily blinded by the sun. He paused, shading his eyes, staring down the long grassy slope to the fast-flowing river they called the Zerantarillo, or "Loop of Life". He could see a figure standing under the angular black branches of the Scorched Willow, which was a traditional meeting place for young lovers of his tribe when they camped in this area.

Calming his thundering heart, the racing, skipping beat having little to do with his exertions, he forced himself to walk even though he wanted to sprint as fast as he could and sweep sweet beautiful stunning funny Darlana up in his arms and deliver the biggest kiss he could. Yet he knew that would never happen. He was far too shy. Far, *far* too shy!

The sun was nearing its zenith and beat down with glorious warmth. The grass hissed under a cool breeze from the south. And with his heart filled with joy, he knew today was a good day to be alive.

He walked down towards the Scorched Willow, and she had her back to him.

As he got closer, he said, words so soft they could hardly be heard above the hiss of the grass, "Darlana?"

She did not turn, did not register him, and for a moment his heart fell like a rock down a well. Was Juranda playing some cruel joke? Was this some evil jest dreamed up by the other young men of the tribe? He felt his temper rising, and his fists clenched, and he would show Juranda what was funny, and what was not; *that* was a promise!

Then Darlana turned, and she saw him, and she smiled. Her whole face lit up!

"Juranda, well," he said, "well, I was passing… and I saw you, and I thought." He cursed himself and closed his yapping mouth. The more he spoke, he knew, the more he would bury himself in the dirt.

"Tuboda," she said, softly, her voice music; the sound was the most beautiful thing he'd ever heard. "I have been looking forward to meeting you."

"And I you."

"You can step closer. I won't bite." And she giggled, and his heart melted, and he knew then he desired this woman more than life itself. For all eternity. He stepped closer. She reached out, shy then, lowering her eyes to the ground, her hand snaking out to stroke the back of his.

"You are the most beautiful woman in the tribe," he said, at last.

She looked up, dark eyes flashing. "Really? But Zarind is dazzling! And the most athletic girl I've ever met. She can hurl a javelin two hundred paces!"

"Beside you, Zarind is a haggard old woman with a moustache," said Tuboda.

Darlana giggled and stepped a little closer. She looked up at him, her eyes shining with humour, her eyes glittering with love. "Tuboda? I have a question."

"Anything, my sweet."

"Why... *why* have your eyes changed colour?"

He frowned. "What?"

"And, your face... it is changing, growing, expanding..." she gasped, stepping back from him in horror, and black storm clouds rushed across the sky and he could see the fear and disgust in her face as thunder rumbled and pain slashed through him like a silver sabre, and he bent, bones cracking, falling to all fours as the *lion* absorbed him from the inside out, and he jerked and fitted spasmodically, limbs growing, filling out with massive cords of muscle, huge curved claws ejecting from his fingers and slicing through soft loam.

Darlana screamed. "Get away! Get away from me!" and she stumbled away, crying.

Tuboda tried to speak, but realised his bent and twisted fangs were in the way. He forced the words out, but they were deformed and broken. "Cme... ba... ck..." he managed, and her scent filled his nostrils and his eyes narrowed and he realised he no longer wanted to hold her and kiss her; no. Now, he wanted to feed, to taste her blood and hear her bones crunch and feel her warm muscles slither down his throat.

A darkness flooded his mind, like it was in water, billowing in great expanding clouds.

What have I become? he thought.

What monster? What terrible, awful beast?

Tuboda awoke, great head on his paws, his patchy golden fur wet with tears. He stood, slowly, stretching out his legs and spine, and then forcing himself back and up onto two feet. He wasn't sure which was more comfortable, but some lingering memory of being a man stuck with him and, for now, at least, he wished to walk upright despite the pain in his hips and lower spine.

It was near dawn. He walked through the town, down muddy streets now filled with nothing but overturned carts, the odd stray weapon and a chicken or two which clucked and ran when they noticed his approach.

A great thirst was upon him, and he moved to a well, picking his way between ten sleeping horse beasts, all lying on their sides, snoring, spluttering, drooling. Reaching the well, his claws clasped the bucket – like a tiny cup in his great paws – and he dropped it. The wheel spun, rope whining, and there was a splash.

He wound the handle awkwardly, and when the bucket arrived he stared for a long time into the shimmering reflection of his great tawny eyes.

He'd had… a dream.

He'd remembered… a woman. But even now, even as he remembered it, it floated away, like smoke on a strong breeze.

He drank.

"Are you ready for today?" said Orlana, from close behind.

Without turning, Tuboda nodded. "Yes, Horse Lady. I am ready."

"Wake the splice. It's time to ride."

YOON

Chief Engineer Isvander sat on the flat stone summit of the unfinished Tower of the Moon, cross-legged and tapping carefully at an intricate carving with his hammer and stone chisel. He ignored the sounds of his mason team which surrounded him in a bustle of activity, the grinding of stone blocks being fitted together, the chimes of chisels on marble and the scrape of careful, studied refinement. Of skill, and precision, and stonemason *engineering*.

Three hundred masons, five hundred and thirty labourers, and *still* it would take two years to finish the tower to match existing plans, despite nearly six years of Isvander's life already spent cutting blocks, carving the greatest figures of Vagandrak heroes (including, it had to be acknowledged, three hundred individual carvings of the great King Yoon himself), engineering intricate arches and fluted columns, and formulating a magnificent tower greater than anything previously created. *Ever.*

Isvander, as Chief Engineer on the project, was promised immortality in this vast stone creation by King Yoon. However, whereas King Yoon promised his modestly ageing Chief Engineer would be remembered as Isvander the Inventive, he was sure with a wry and painful smile, and a nod to popular downtown opinion, that in all reality he would also be known as Isvander the

Idiot. Yoon's Folly, they would name the tower. Or even worse. Isvander's Pointlessness.

The Tower of the Moon, commissioned by King Yoon after a spate of drunken orgies, was to be the tallest single structure ever built. So tall, that on clear nights to stand on its summit one could see clear across the distant Pass of Splintered Bones, through the valleys of the Mountains of Skarandos and from there into the southern lands of Zakora.

Zakora. The Three Deserts. Uncultured, uncouth, a land of *death*...

The Tower of the Moon was so prohibitively expensive, King Yoon could have built another ten extravagant marble palaces and still have change for another of his hedonistic parties (with painted horses, mounds of honey-leaf narcotics in bowls of Ice desert crystal and a flood of naked girls and boys smeared with oil and tongue paint of different flavours). The stone had been mined in the White Lion Mountains in northern Vagandrak. Yet more stone had been mined from the heart of the Mountains of Skarandos, to the south; those mighty great peaks which acted as a natural border and defence against their subdued and controlled enemies, the desert people of Zakora. The stone for the tower staircases, inlaid with minerals and swirling blue and white patterns, had been dug by slaves from the Junglan Mountains in the northwest. It was even said, in hushed whispers by the more reckless members of King Yoon's court, that sacred Crimson Stone from the Blood Teeth Mountains on Blood Isle was being imported for a special summit bedroom chamber. A thousand ships would transport the almost transparent red stone from far to the south, following the dangerous jagged coastline of Oram, up round the Cape of Zangir to dock at Old

Skell in Port Crystal, where King Yoon would specifically build good roads to transport the stone to the Vagandrak capital, Drakerath. "An extravagance, yes," King Yoon was reported to have said, "but one cannot skimp and save copper coin when one is putting one's life work, one's genius, into molten flesh."

Isvander finished the small stone piece he'd been working on, lifted it to the sun and blew a skin of rough dust from the surface, then ran his finger down the arched flank of the carved angel. Perfect, he thought. As perfect as I can make it. And he had to admit, no matter how insane he, or any other member of his team of sculptors and masons found the King, he was certainly giving them a world canvas and a chance to be remembered in the Tomes of History in the Red Circle Library of Drakerath.

Isvander stood and stretched his weary back. Pain was troubling his lower spine, had been for a couple of years now, growing progressively worse, especially in the last few months. Still, he would finish the Tower of the Moon; he was damned if he was going to bow out before the job was done. Then, only then, would he consider retiring with his sweet wife, Anador. They would grow old together in the Quiet Sector in Drakerath; also known as the Flowered Quarter. It was peaceful there, and beautiful, and the perfect place in which to relax and grow old. King Yoon's gold would secure them a perfect little cottage. It would be... idyllic.

A cool wind blew, and dust drifted across the flat stone platform. Isvander glanced back, at the fifty or so masons working on this wide summit level beside him. He caught Granda's attention. The one-armed mason grinned at Isvander, and waved his stump. Amputation in battle in his younger, wilder, military days had done little to dampen Granda's twisted sense of humour; he was probably making a rude gesture.

Isvander walked across the stone platform, carefully circling the hole leading to steps which spiralled down beneath them for a good distance. Around Isvander, from his stunning pinnacle, the capital of Drakerath drifted away like some distant, wonderful painting, a rich scene of bustling city life. Drakerath. The greatest of the Marble Cities!

Even at this height, the Tower of the Moon was taller than any structure ever built, but that was still not good enough for King Yoon. He wanted it taller. Taller. Taller taller taller…

"It's a hot one," mumbled Granda, as Isvander came close, and took a cup from the water bucket. Isvander nodded, drinking noisily and spilling a little down his tunic.

"That's it, my friend. And the more we build, the closer we get to the sun. I fear one day we'll all burst into flame!"

Granda snorted a laugh and continued to chisel away at the block on which he worked. With only one arm, Granda's ability to chisel stone was an art in itself; he had fashioned himself a series of special tools, which he sharpened every night without fail. Isvander had once asked what he'd do if he lost his other arm, and Granda had said he'd chisel with his mouth and teeth. He claimed there were only two things that could possibly stop him working – decapitation, or marrying a rich whore. Maybe both, he conceded, when pushed. But preferably the rich whore first.

"Is Anador well?"

"Aye, aye," said Isvander. "She's got it in her head she's going to embroider a map of the whole of Drakerath! I think, sometimes, the woman is obsessed."

"Not like her husband, then?"

Isvander laughed, and replaced the cup in the bucket. "Most certainly not. What are you trying to imply?"

"And the boys? How do they fare?"

"Dagron is at the university in Kantarok. He's doing extremely well, or so his letters confidently proclaim. But then, he always did know how to pull the wool over his old dad's eyes. Did I tell you about the time he re-directed the neighbour's toilet drain into the kitchen of a local Syndicate man who was extorting money from several old women? Got into a lot of trouble over that one, but I always knew he'd become an engineer or an architect – from the very moment a shoal of turds flooded Dak Veygon's evening dinner."

The two men laughed and then were quiet, reminiscing on their younger days.

A call came drifting up the spiralling stone steps from far below. "A number eight chisel," came the shout, and it was repeated several times by different masons and labourers. Isvander cursed. This was their coded language. There was no "number eight chisel". It meant King Yoon, the noble and extravagant King of Vagandrak, had arrived below with his entourage for one of his random "inspections". He would certainly spend several hours in the Tower of the Moon. And, more worryingly, he would no doubt question Isvander long into the evening, thus eating away any free time the Chief Engineer had hoped to spend with his lovely wife.

"That mad fool," snapped Granda, frowning.

"Shush, man! He'll have you flayed! Or worse. You know how… *touchy* he has become of late."

"He makes my skin creep."

"Keep your thoughts to yourself, Granda. After all, he is our… king."

Granda nodded and went back to work, thankful King Yoon's attentions would be focused on his friend and superior. Isvander was a patient man. And from what Granda had seen of King Yoon recently, Isvander would need *all* his skill and patience to survive.

First came the drifting sounds as King Yoon and his entourage swept up and up the spiral steps towards the summit of the construction. There were giggles from Yoon's sycophantic hangers-on, there was raucous braying and chatter, loud obnoxious voices that made Isvander and Granda exchange worried glances. This wasn't just Yoon; this sounded like his entire bloody court!

Next came the smell. Expensive perfumes imported from Zalazar and the southern Ice deserts of Zakora. Isvander wrinkled his nostrils. They might as well be distilled from the rotting fish-guts of the Rokroth Marshes, for all the pleasure they offered the Chief Engineer.

And finally came the King himself. King Yoon strutted from the staircase, head high, a light sheen of sweat on his pale waxen brow from the climb, but still proving he had hidden stamina, for the climb was a long, hard one, and during its course he'd left half his retinue behind.

"Isvander!" boomed the King, voice an uneven shrill as he strode forward trailing red silk and lace, and embraced the Chief Engineer awkwardly. "I see your work progresses apace." He laughed, and the trailing members of his court (some of them still wheezing from the climb), laughed and giggled alongside him as if they'd caught some strange, foreign plague of comedy.

Isvander eyed his King and Monarch with a wary eye. King Yoon was tall, well over six feet in height, and as broad and athletic as his warrior heritage would suggest. After all, was King Yoon not a direct bloodline descendant of the incredible Battle King, Tarek, the very king who fought and was victorious over thousands of invading mud-orcs during the War of Zakora? Had King Yoon not been trained in sword, spear and bow from his earliest childhood moments? He could fight as soon as walk, and had proved himself a warrior on many occasions, leading skirmishes south into Zakora when regular uprisings of the nomadic people threatened either the watching Garrison Towers, or indeed, even the Desekra Fortress which guarded the pass through the Mountains of Skarandos.

Had King Yoon not shown great courage in battle? Great leadership and tactical skills? Great physical strength and, indeed, honour and loyalty from his soldiers earned by his love and concern for them? It was even said he'd fought a lion, and slain it by standing his spear against a rock and letting the beast charge him. Not the actions of a coward.

Yes, decided Isvander, as he watched King Yoon strut about the tower summit, wandering dangerously close to the edge, which had no barriers and gave a dazzling, vertigo-inducing view – straight down to the waiting city below. Yes. King Yoon was all those things. *Had been* all those things. But he was changing. It was subtle, but he was changing.

Now, King Yoon had his long, thick, shaggy hair dyed an unrealistic deep black in order to disguise the grey. He wore a thick, white makeup, accentuating his already pale skin and filling the wrinkles of his ageing face with excess. It caught in the creases of his skin and made him, along with the false gleam of his panther pelt, look more like an out-of-work stage actor than any noble King of note. He wore a robe of thick red velvet which ran from neck to ankles, but had strategic vents at both front and back that, when Yoon moved, and if one were to catch an unfortunate glimpse, displayed flashes of his genitalia and backside, depending which way he turned. From his throat and sleeves flowed long scarves of silk and lace, and again all Isvander could imagine was some actor in a contemporary stage piece relaying a part from foreign shores. The Drakerath Empire was traditional. Men wore leather, cotton, chainmail; its foresters wore greens and browns; and in the Marble Cities even dandies wore more subdued colours of green and red. King Yoon's current fashion statement was... odd.

With sinking heart, Isvander watched the rest of the entourage assemble. There must have been twenty men and women. The men wore ornamental armour and silks, with many a decorative carved leather codpiece on show, whereas the women dressed in gauzy thin cottons and laces which flowed and described succulent curves and revealed a worrying lack of undergarments.

Isvander licked his lips, as many of the entourage giggled for no apparent reason.

"Highness! Please, stay away from the edge!" cried one young man, moving forward and resting his hand casually on his own protruding, quivering codpiece. Isvander winced. The movement was too oddly familiar to be natural.

"Listen to me, Pepp. I am *divine!*" intoned Yoon, solemnly. "I will walk where I will, for none shall *dare* take my life, not god, thief nor beggar!" Yoon edged closer and stalked along the very edge of the platform. Tiny stones, scuffed by his silk sandals, clattered away into the vast, awning abyss.

Isvander coughed. "Still, Highness, I think... *Pepp?* I think he may have a point. It would be a sad day if you were to fall."

"Nonsense!" Yoon stopped, turned suddenly, and a breeze whipped his silks away behind him, far over the edge of the precipice. "I *will not fall!* Indeed, I *cannot fall!*"

A low wind moaned, kicking up stone-dust on the platform, which swirled past King Yoon and disappeared into the distance. Isvander licked his lips again. Nervous now? He didn't want to be even vaguely responsible for Yoon's death, no matter how tenuous the link. And he was instinctively aware that if Yoon fell, somehow, no doubt some *way*, he would end up shouldering the blame.

"Highness, look at this!" cried one woman. She was kneeling by a half-finished stone-carving of a gargoyle. "Isn't he cute? Isn't he divine?" In her crouch, her short silk skirts had ridden up revealing, in Isvander's opinion, far too much pale white thigh-flesh and the quivering pink of revealed puckered lips.

Yoon strutted forward, a walk so far removed from the battlefield as to be alien. "Yes, indeed, it is determinably cute and bulbous. As are you, Jamanda, my sweet ripe fruit." He took the woman's hand, and she rose, and he kissed her deeply, tongue in her mouth, apparently unaware that he had an audience; an audience that did not presently include his wife and queen.

Jamanda broke away and swooned, and her hands eased out and stroked King Yoon's flanks in an over-familiar way. "Would you like to, Highness?"

"Later," coughed Yoon, and seemed to remember where he stood. He turned to Isvander. "You there. Chief Engineer. I see progress is being made at a considerable pace. I am happy with the work. Although," his hand swept an empty area, "I would like more gargoyles. More gargoyles on this level."

"Sire?" enquired Isvander, softly. "I think you'll find you have already specified an inordinate amount of gargoyles for this level. Indeed, I think the plans show the current number of gargoyles to be… Granda? Do you know how many gargoyles we are carving for this level?"

Granda flashed Isvander a filthy look, as if to say: *don't drag me into your dirty sycophantic warbling.* "Three hundred," he growled, and lowered his head again, as if the rancid, thick perfume in the air was making him sick. Which it probably was.

"Three hundred, Majesty," said Isvander, with an easy, open smile.

"Not enough," snapped Yoon, and clicked his fingers in rapid quick succession until a young man in bright green silks ran up to him and produced a long tube from a long leather satchel. Isvander felt his heart begin to sink.

"Surely, not more plans, you simple, giggling, face-painted bastard? Just stick to dyeing your hair and humping your many and varied mistresses, both men, women and young boys if all accounts are true, and we'll get this bloody tower built on time, you fucking imbecile, right?" That's what Isvander *wanted* to say. Instead, he held a tight smile to his tight face, and muttered, "Surely, the plans are *locked*, Sire. To make more changes could further jeopardise a stable foundation which, I assure you…"

"Nonsense." With a swipe of one hand, Isvander's concern, and indeed, engineering skill, was dismissed. Pepp and the green-silk architect unrolled the plans on the floor, and King Yoon crouched, his cock dangling obnoxiously from the venting slit in his red robes.

Isvander glanced to the other masons on the wide stone platform. Wisely, everybody kept their eyes down, hands busy on their work. Isvander moved to King Yoon.

"More gargoyles?"

"Yes! More gargoyles! I want *two hundred* extra gargoyles! And we have also revised the height of the tower. I require the Tower of the Moon to elevate for another thirty levels."

"*Thirty*…" Isvander stood, mouth open, unconsciously staring at his monarch's child-maker. He snapped out of his shock. "But Highness, the sheer *weight* of another thirty levels would guarantee a necessitated modification to the foundations… we'd need extra footings, capable of supporting *vast*…"

"Nonsense! Krolla! Explain it to him."

Krolla, the man in green silks, explained it to a solemn, narrow-eyed Isvander. What he explained was insanity. This was a man who did not understand the simple relationship between the size of a building's foundations, and its subsequent allowable height and weight. The math he proposed was illogical. Wisely, Isvander kept his mouth shut and his eyes from the bare naked breast which King Yoon was stroking idly, then licking, in open view of his braying entourage.

Krolla finished his architectural and mathematical lecture with a wagging finger. Chief Engineer Isvander gave a single nod of tight-lipped acquiescence. What was the point of arguing? Who could argue with the insane? And indeed, what was the point being Chief Engineer if nobody listened to your engineering *experience?*

"So, as you can see," Yoon was strutting around again, sunlight gleaming from his black hair, his heavy robes swaying regally around his silk sandals, "not only will the Tower of the Moon be *named* the Tower of the Moon, one day, it may even *reach as high as the moon*!"

Somebody giggled.

Isvander kept his face painfully neutral. And realisation struck him. Surely… surely Yoon didn't think he could really build a tower that high? Was that his aim? Truly? *Gods, he's getting worse! He's plunging fast into a deep pit of madness, and he has the money to do it and sustain it. What can I say to bring him back to reality? How can I help the King?*

Pepp stepped forward. He had an inordinately high forehead, greased back curls, and a laugh that could crack glass at fifty paces swifter than any crossbow quarrel. "Surely, Highness, a tower could never touch the moon?"

There was an awkward silence.

King Yoon took a threatening step forward, and glowered down at Pepp, who shifted uneasily in his long, pointed, black leather boots. When Yoon spoke, his voice had dropped to a low, animal growl. "If I say the Tower of the Moon touches the moon, then touch the moon it shall!"

"But, that's impossible," said Pepp, like a stubborn dog with a rotten bone.

Yoon's hand slammed out, grabbed Pepp by the throat, and in a few shocked seconds he dragged the choking nobleman to the edge of the platform where he held him out over the vast drop. Pepp's boots scrabbled on stone, scarring their highly polished leather. Pepp choked and kicked. Yoon's arm was rigid, muscles standing out like iron.

"See that? Down there, you pathetic little maggot? You see my city? My country? Do you see my whole *world? My fucking world*?"

Pepp tried to agree and choke at the same time. One boot slipped and his body swayed out over the drop.

"It's MY WORLD!" screamed Yoon, and gave a short giggle. "Do you want to see it more closely? Well, Pepp, that can easily be arranged! Oh yes!" His fingers opened their grip.

Isvander watched in grim horror as Pepp seemed to suspend for a moment, a look of dismay on his stupid painted face. Then he fell, screaming like a little girl having her hair pulled, arms and legs swimming as if he might paddle his way back to the tower's summit.

Most of the entourage rushed to the edge of the platform and gazed down, watching Pepp fall. And land. He landed hard. There came a distant *slap*, muffled, almost unheard. But disconcertingly *real*. His body seemed to separate into many different pieces.

Isvander heard it. So did Granda. Both men exchanged a solemn glance. *This is getting out of control,* said Isvander's gaze.

This is already out of control, came Granda's grim response.

"So then," King Yoon slapped Isvander on the shoulder, his voice merry, as if they had just shared some jolly triviality, a glass of port, a humorous anecdote about a turnip, and now they were parting as old friends and comrades. "You can do five hundred gargoyles, lad? Surely?"

"Of course, Majesty," said Isvander.

King Yoon strutted to the steps. His entourage, talking happily, trailed after him. From somewhere, one had produced a crystal decanter of wine. Several were drinking, their lips slick, glasses waving gaily. King Yoon stopped. The entourage stopped. They walked when he walked. They stopped when he stopped. They were a gaily coloured, perfume stinking *shadow.*

"Well, we understand one another perfectly, then, Chief Engineer Isvander." Yoon's dark eyes seemed to gleam as he stared hard at Isvander for just *a little bit too long*. They drove into him. Seemed to worm inside his brain... and turn it inside out.

"Perfectly," said Isvander, mouth full of ash.

King Yoon stepped onto the spiral of stone steps and descended three. Then he stopped again. He glanced back at Isvander. "Oh yes. Be a good boy, and send somebody out there to clean up the mess, won't you?"

"I will see what I can do, Great King," croaked Isvander.

Yoon smiled, and along with his gaudy group of giggling followers, disappeared from view.

ZORKAI

King Zorkai was a tall, powerful man, early thirties, with a forked black beard, thick bushy black hair and piercing blue eyes. He was an incredible swordsman, archer, bareknuckle fighter, and had hunted and killed lions, tigers, bears and wolves for sport with nothing but his bare hands and a short spear. He lived to fight. He lived for war. He lived to die. With three wives and seven children, he had secured his bloodline, his longevity and now, in the prime of his health, and strength, and ferocity, with an able experienced army to back him, nothing was a threat to the King of Zakora. *Nothing*.

And the fact he had killed all three of his brothers and seven cousins who could potentially fight for the crown also added comfort to his present Kingship. King Zorkai was a man who knew where he stood. He was a man who did not like surprises.

Which is why, when the scout reports came in, he listened, frowning. The reports spoke of a woman with a hundred or so "rabid, twisted creatures", advancing rapidly through his domain. They were challenged by a cavalry unit of three hundred, who engaged them in battle, according to one report, although – insanely – the scrawled message spoke of "horses turning on their riders and eating them". Zorkai's men were killed. All of them.

Zorkai sat, rubbing his whiskers in thought, and refusing to immediately dismiss the report, although he knew he would have the scout flogged in the city square, then nailed to the Betrayal Cross. Horses turning on their riders and eating them? He'd been heavy on the grain spirit, no doubt.

Zorkai stood and walked to the rough sandstone windowsill of the Desert Palace, looking out over the city. *His* city. Zak-Tan. Fifty thousand sandstone dwellings, mostly two storeys high, many painted white to reflect the heat of the sun. Here and there Prayer Towers rose from the throng of buildings, and great swathes of people moved amidst the narrow streets and alleyways. He could hear music from a nearby bazaar and the shouts of traders selling silks, spices, honeyed milk, salted fish and many sweetmeat delicacies. The city was a thriving ants' nest and he enjoyed watching the scene, listening to the people, soaking up the atmosphere of the place he had helped build, helped create! His father, the late King Zentak, had brought together ten wandering desert tribes, sowing the seeds of the Zak-Tan dream. They had conquered other tribes and built a city of tents. As they expanded, and built up their army, they had invaded neighbouring desert areas, conquering and becoming wealthy beyond their dreams. Architects were drafted from "more civilised" lands to build, initially, a fortified palace – which is where Zorkai now stood. Despite being surrounded by the soft flowing desert, there were also the Salt Plains to the south and southwest: hard-packed, lifeless and unforgiving. But able to bear cavalry. King Zentak was the first of the desert kings to buy horses from the northern lands of Vagandrak, to learn the secrets of breeding and cross-breeding, and to expand his army with cavalry. Within ten short years, his army was unstoppable. Eight thousand foot warriors and nearly three thousand cavalry soldiers with long spears and expert training; there was no other force for a thousand miles that could challenge his supremacy. Except Vagandrak. But they hid behind their mountain walls, the Skarandos Range; hid behind their massive fortress, cowering like children.

"Is everything well, my love?"

Zorkai turned, and frowned again. It was his wife, Shanaz, dressed in flowing red silk and leaning seductively against the wide arched doorway.

"No, it is not. I have garbled reports of some mad woman with a collection of monsters and horses that eat themselves."

Shanaz considered this. "That is… strange. Still, come to my bed and I will take your mind from such petty distractions."

Zorkai stared at her. Shanaz was his most recent wife and, he suspected, a trouble-causer. His first two wives had certainly not taken well to her, and he'd caught the three squabbling on occasion.

"There you are, Shanaz! We've been looking everywhere for you."

Hunta and Marella came through the door, both wearing long black silks and shawls, and Shanaz did not turn, instead looking towards the king as she said, "I was here asking my husband to bed, as you two had announced you were going to the market to buy vegetables."

"Ridiculous!" snapped Hunta. "We said no such thing! We told you not to disturb *our* husband, the King, for important reports had come in from his scouts. And you blatantly ignored our instruction!"

"You are giving me instructions now, are you?" Shanaz whirled, eyes blazing vicious fire. "Just because you have been married for longer, and yes, are suitably *older*, does not give you superiority over me!" She padded towards Zorkai, bare feet slapping the terracotta tiles, and grasped his arm, looking up with those wide, pleading eyes which had so captured his heart at the annual Feast of Warriors. "Tell them, Zorky; your other wives are being mean to me! They always are, when you're not here."

"Ha!" snapped Hunta. "Zorkai, you simply would not believe what we have to put up with in your absence. You have married a little bitch, that's for sure! She wanders around in her bare feet, crowing like a cockerel that she has a better time between the bedsheets with you. She says we are sexually inferior to her and she knows how to play you like a *zanda trell*."

"Ladies!" snapped Zorkai. But Hunta was on a roll.

"She's also bragged about how, if you were to choose one queen, you would choose her over us, because she controls you like a puppeteer with a little king puppet. She says she pulls your strings."

"Horse shit!" yelled Shanaz, whirling on Hunta. "How *dare* you try and sabotage the special love I have with my king! Just because you feel you have grown old and wrinkled before your time, your tits sagging to your waist and your flower becoming dry and barren…"

"Why, you little sparkly bitch," said Hunta, eyes narrowed. "I'll…"

"Stop them, Zorkai, stop them both!" pleaded Marella, and the King threw his hands in the air. "They both love you for your money; I am, truly, the only one who loves you for *yourself*."

Hunta and Shanaz were staring at Marella.

"Oh, you back-stabbing whore," snarled Hunta.

"LADIES!" thundered Zorkai, both fists clenched, face suddenly purple. "You will ALL stop your bickering, or I will have you ALL flogged! I am sick to the back teeth of this constant yapping! Now get out of my sight, I have an important issue to deal with; you are not helping the situation!"

The three women, heads held high, haughtily withdrew from the King's Chamber. The doors swung shut, snugly clicking into the arched doorframe. The minute he heard that click, there followed urgent hushed voices beyond and Zorkai glanced, just for a moment, towards his short sword.

His mother had warned him. "Only an idiot marries three," she had said, unblinking eyes fixed on him. "You'll be taken in by their young, supple limbs, their luscious hair, their pouting lips, their shining eyes, their writhing hips. But ultimately, my son, they'll bring you more pain than pleasure. I promise you. I know these things."

He had ignored her. He was *the king* after all. But oh, how she had been right!

"Sire! I have urgent news!"

It was Jendakka, one of Zorkai's most feared generals. Vicious, merciless, a hard man without compassion for anything or anyone. Zorkai shook his head, clearing his thoughts. Gods, he hadn't even heard the man enter!

"What is it, Jen?"

"Further sightings of this tall, white woman. It is said she rides a lion beast and is followed by monsters. And she is heading straight towards Zak-Tan. Either this is really happening, or the whole country has been drinking ether spirit."

"She's heading across the South Salt Plains, then?"

"According to scouts."

"Send message to the barracks. Saddle three thousand mounts. Let's see what this woman wants."

They rode hard in a wedge formation with King Zorkai and General Jendakka the point of the wedge. Behind, in perfect symmetry, rode three thousand highly trained warriors on horses bred for war. Hooves drummed the salt plains sending up clouds of salt. Each mount had damp cloths over muzzles to protect them from the dust, and warriors had heads and faces wrapped with finely woven keffiyeh. Zorkai pushed them hard for an hour, then they dismounted and walked their mounts for twenty minutes, resting them. Mounting once more, they continued south following directions given by Jendakka's scouts.

When they saw the enemy force, it was much larger than they'd anticipated and Zorkai drew rein, his huge stallion rearing and dropping to stamp the salt plain. His eyes met Jendakka's. "How many?"

"At least five hundred. At *least*."

"That's what I was thinking. Suggestions?"

"They are intruders in our lands, Sire. I suggest total annihilation."

Zorkai nodded. "Battle formation!" he bellowed. "Long lances, we'll hit them from the front, split and wheel in the Ram's Horn; come in from both sides to mop up any survivors." Men pulled on battle helms and unhitched lances. "Any questions?" shouted the king. "Then ride hard and true, my boys! For Zakora!"

"FOR ZAKORA!" they thundered, and kicked their horses into a matched canter, building swiftly up to a gallop. They stampeded across the salt plains, hooves drumming, great clouds rising behind them, and as they came close so visors were lowered on helms and lances levelled in readiness for impact...

Screams echoed across the salt plains, high pitched and piercing and King Zorkai *felt* more than saw or heard the chaos behind him, and cast a glance back. What met his gaze was, truly, an impossibility, for his entire battalion were sat astride rearing, thrashing mounts, stampeding around on rear hooves, pawing the air, huge maws open showing lolling thrashing tongues and gleaming long teeth as lips quivered and the men clung on grimly. It felt, to Zorkai, that the entire world had gone suddenly mad. And then the horses started to break apart, bones crunching, flesh running, blood splattering, and he cantered to a stop, lance and sword forgotten, mouth hung open as three thousand men and mounts merged together, folding in on each other, and then they hit the salt plains in a thrashing screaming mass and great salt clouds rose up to engulf the savage horrific spectacle and Zorkai cantered a few steps forward, then halted again, lance suddenly slippery in his grip. He turned to Jendakka, to see if he was crazy, to see if Jendakka's eyes mirrored his own. Jendakka threw off his helm, was panting heavily, and that look told Zorkai everything he needed to know. He was not a victim of dark seed, liquor or some horrible imagined nightmare. This was real. This was *happening*...

"We have to help them," shouted Zorkai over the sounds of thrashing, squealing, thumping and squelching. "What, in the name of the Sacred Fire Orchids, is happening?" But Jendakka's mount suddenly reared, and Zorkai watched him merge with his horse, the beast's back opening like a huge wound and sucking the man inside, plates of armour melding with the horse's back and flanks; it hit the ground on its side, Jendakka's boots kicking and then becoming slowly absorbed and sucked into the expanding, bulging mass as horse and man became one: one creature, one monster.

Zorkai leapt from his own mount, eyeing it suspiciously, and with a sudden horror remembered the large enemy force they'd been about to engage. He swallowed, mouth desert dry, and to a symphony of merging flesh and metal and thumping slaughter, turned and looked upon the enemy.

She walked towards him in utmost serenity.

She was beautiful beyond belief.

And deadly. Zorkai sensed her intrinsic killer streak, and panic welled in his breast like a fast blossoming cancer, opening dark petals to swallow his heart and soul. Beside her padded a massive beast, a twisted, deformed lion with... Zorkai swallowed. Its features were almost human. Almost. But it was neither one thing nor the other, and great yellow fangs poked unevenly from a broken lion's maw. Huge tawny eyes settled on him and he held that gaze for a moment, recognising human emotion, intelligence, mixed in a golden pot of unabridged violence and a need to kill and feed.

Zorkai met the woman's gaze.

"I am Orlana," she said, voice simple, quiet, unchallenging.

"I am King Zorkai. What have you done to my... men?"

"It is a thing of the old magick. I cannot explain in your language, for it is more of an essence, of land and rock and sky. Let us say I can channel such power; and I can *shift* men and beasts together, splice them into one beast which will serve me unfalteringly until death. Do you understand?"

"I understand," said King Zorkai. "And yet, you have not done this to me?"

"No. I need you."

"You *need* me?" Zorkai was frowning. He glanced over his shoulder, at where the splicing of Jendakka and his mount was complete. A short, squat, powerful horse beast stared back with evil, dark eyes. Black fangs nestled like razors in a too-big equine maw. From one set of claws Zorkai could see a bulging lance point, and he shuddered. Man, and horse, and metal. All made one. He turned back to Orlana. With voice little more than a croak, he asked, "What do you need of me?"

She stepped forward and placed a hand on his chest. He was breathing fast. He still held his sword, but some intuition told him she could kill him faster than he could raise the blade. After all, she'd just disabled three thousand hardened warriors. And swelled her own ranks in the process.

She leant close. "None can stand against me," she whispered in his ear, words tickling, and suddenly, curiously, he felt aroused. This woman, this witch, this dark shaman; she excited him in ways he had never dreamed.

"Yes," he said. "I can see that."

"You can either join me, and I will become your Queen. Or you can… serve me, as your warriors here now serve me."

Zorkai turned once more. The salt dust was settling. He wished it wasn't.

Turning back, he suddenly dropped to one knee and took Orlana's long, slender fingers. He kissed the marble white skin of her hand.

"Welcome home, Queen Orlana."

"You may stand, my King."

Zorkai stood and eyed the beasts arraigned behind this tall, beautiful woman. He swallowed, then looked deep into her eyes. "What happens next?"

"Take me to our palace at Zak-Tan. We have plans to formulate."

Orlana strode through the Main Hall of the Palace at Zak-Tan, head held high, eyes surveying the finery of the surroundings: carved marble, vibrant paintings, busts of stone, rich tapestries imported from the far east, wooden statues from the deep south. She swept up the steps towards Zorkai's chambers, the king trailing ten footsteps behind, his mind still in a whirl from the madness he had witnessed. On the streets of the city, the returning forces had not been met with the same enthusiasm as when they had left. Men and women and children, running in blind panic, amidst screams and shouts and general chaos. Now, the streets were deserted, and patrolled by the horse beasts of Orlana. And whilst they were not exactly under orders to attack, Zorkai had quickly got the general impression his people weren't willing to put it to the test.

"I like," Orlana said, pointing to a huge tapestry at the top of the sweeping stairway. It depicted a huge battle between mud-orcs crawling like worms from the Mud-Pits, and defenders on the walls of Desekra Fortress at the Pass of Splintered Bones. Zorkai had always found the work depressing, but it had been a favourite of his late father and so he'd kept it to remind him of the stern old man.

"I always found it... brooding, dark, violent."

"Those were dark, violent times."

"You were there?"

Orlana met his gaze and gave a small nod. "Let us say I knew Morkagoth. He was a man possessed." She smiled.

"He was killed by the Iron Wolves, right?"

"Not exactly *killed*," said Orlana. "More *banished*. He carried the blood of the Equiem. Now, there is a race that's hard to destroy."

Zorkai glanced down the stairs, to where Tuboda had set up guard by the massive entrance doors to the Main Hall. The great lion-creature had settled down on its twisted haunches, leaning slightly to one side, and the tawny eyes met the king's. He shivered. That look was far too intelligent for his liking.

"Zorkai! You're back! Why didn't they ring the bells?" Shanaz ran down the steps, hair bouncing, silks flowing, bare feet slapping, a wide smile on her pretty face: her gleaming red gloss lips, and evocative, dark ochre eyes. Then she saw Orlana and stopped dead. "Who is that?"

"This is Orlana."

"Your new queen," said Orlana, voice soft, eyes glittering.

"*What?*" screeched Shanaz. "Hunta! Marella! Come quickly! Come NOW!"

She needn't have shouted, for both women were already on their way, unwilling for Shanaz to spend too much time alone with their *shared* husband. The two other wives paused at the top of the steps, eyes widening at this new complication, then slowly descended to the mid-point landing and the huge tapestry depicting the War of Zakora.

"This woman! She says she is the new queen!" babbled Shanaz, near hysterical, head turning from left to right, hair flying, eyes suddenly wild. "Have you ever heard such rubbish? Zorkai! How could you? How could you bring another woman here? We three are not enough for you? After all those wild nights I spent in your bed making you moan, my nails clawing your back, my performance better than these other two *bitches!*"

Orlana looked at Zorkai, then back to Shanaz. "Is this woman ever quiet?"

"Don't you dare do that!" screamed Shanaz, and Zorkai took a step back, paling. "Don't talk about me like I'm not in the room. Oh no! So tell me, *bitch*, go on, how long have you been seeing *our* husband? How long have you been *fucking* my king?" She strutted towards Orlana, and only then did the small, jewelled blade become visible in her hand. It glittered with gold and precious jewels, but the blade was razor sharp, the edge thinner than paper and honed religiously by a fanatic.

Hunta and Marella were silent, but they leaned forward eagerly, eyes shining, thrilled at this new turn of events. It seemed like a situation which could only benefit them; Shanaz was building herself up into a frenzy, and whether she killed this new woman or not, she was not painting herself in a modest light. Zorkai did not like such displays amongst his wives. Whatever the outcome, Hunta and Marella were going to benefit. Especially if Shanaz *killed* his new woman...

"It's a disgrace!" shouted Hunta.

"Go on, Shanaz, show her we won't be dishonoured like this!"

Zorkai threw them an evil glare, and placed his hand on his sword hilt. "Shanaz, wife, calm yourself!" But there was no soothing Shanaz. Her temper was up. Her face was flushed red with fury. Her eyes glittered brighter than her dagger blade.

Orlana still made no move as this spitting, snarling ball of dark energy approached. She wore a narrow smile on her face, but her hands were by her sides, her soft flesh apparently unprotected.

"Bitch queen!" spat Shanaz in Orlana's face, having to stand on tip-toe to reach her. She was close now. Close enough to plunge in the blade. But she paused... her flapping tongue had not yet finished.

"You think you can come here and open your legs and take my man, well I'm here to tell you something; he belongs to *us*, we worked hard to get him, *I* worked hard to get him. And I'm not letting some skin and bone arrogant whore suck and slime her way into his bed and take the wealth we – *I* – have worked so hard to acquire! Have you any last words before I gut you like a rotten fish?"

Orlana considered this. Her small pale tongue moistened her pale, almost translucent, lips. The smile had still not left her face. Quietly, she said, "Do you always mewl like a fist-fucked kitten?" before back-handing her down the stairs, a movement so swift none saw Orlana even lift her hand.

Shanaz spun, over and over, limbs and torso slapping hard against the marble edges of the steps, her jewelled razor dagger clattering away ahead of her. She hit the bottom hard and lay still, and broken, a skin bag of crushed bones.

Slowly, she groaned, and pushed herself up a little, but slumped back down to the white marble floor. The small pool of blood which leaked from her mouth was dark crimson, a stunning contrast against skin and white marble.

Zorkai said nothing, but took another step back, as if to distance himself from this act of violence. Whilst he did not actively dislike Shanaz – she was a wild Hellcat beneath the sheets, for example – he had no real desire to see her come to harm. And despite her pulling a blade on Orlana, her words had been hot air. In a real world of real violence, one acted, not flapped lips. Shanaz was full of hot words and insults. He did not believe she would have used the blade.

Now, Orlana lifted her gaze to Hunta and Marella. The two women had turned pale.

"Come to me, little chickens," said Orlana, and stretched out her hand, and half closed her eyes.

"Zorkai, no, don't let her hurt us! We're your wives! Please!"

Zorkai clamped shut his mouth and lowered his eyes, as against their will, both Hunta and Marella began the long, long walk down the marble steps towards the woman with pale skin and soft, glowing eyes...

NARNOK

The corridor was plush and expensive, in a cheap and nasty way. The wallpaper was maroon with golden swirls, but in poor condition, damaged on doorway corners and scuffed near skirting boards. The red carpet, whilst once thick and rich and obviously expensive, now had various tattered patches and various unrecognisable stains. There were quality fake busts made from cheap plaster, and an over-abundance of gilt on archways and decorative vases which, rather than add to the allure of the décor, gave the opposite effect. It was the sort of corridor decorated and dressed by somebody who had never seen wealth before; which was ironic, because Narnok was one of the wealthiest men in the city.

None of this mattered as the panicked screams bounced down the long passage, from which ten doors led to ten independent "suites" housing a variety of young ladies with differing hair colours, styles, breast sizes and tastes in the extreme. The Pleasure Parlour catered for most.

Narnok sprinted down the red carpet, boots thudding to stop by Room 9. Without ceremony, the large man kicked open the door to see Luleyla cowering beneath the gathered black sheets, backed up against the headboard of the overlarge bed, her face framed in horror and bobbed red curls. The thin, hairy man, naked but for his socks, held a short serrated knife and he spun around, eyes locking to Narnok's brutal scarred face. Narnok took a threatening step forward.

"Lose the weapon, friend," he rumbled.

The man, weasel-faced with a short, forked beard, grinned, eyes glittering. He might have only been of slim build, but there was a wealth of nasty experience in those dark gleaming eyes. Narnok immediately disliked him. But then, Narnok immediately disliked most men.

"I'm not your friend, *fucker*. I paid my coin, and now I'm going to get what I paid for. A few little cuts won't hurt. Will it, sweet cheeks?" He turned to Luleyla, grinning.

"He wants to hurt me, Narn. Please don't let him!"

"Nobody's going to hurt you, Lules. Go over there and get dressed."

"Don't – fucking – move." The man turned back to Narnok, and the fact he'd had the balls to turn his back on the large man with his broad, powerful chest, hulking shoulders and fists like shovels was a testament to his courage; or his stupidity. He stared into Narnok's brutally scarred face, with its criss-cross of thin white razor scars and the one milky white eye, and his face relaxed into a languid smile. "Why, you're a pretty one. You're Narnok. I've heard of you."

"Only bad things, I hope," growled the huge warrior.

"On the contrary. I know you know my people. Therefore, you should know me. I am Galtos Gan."

"Never heard of you. Now drop the knife before I really lose my temper."

"I am cousin to Faltor Gan. I'm *Red Thumb*, see? And I always get what I pay for."

"Not this time."

"I was told this girl likes to play rough. I'm ready to play rough. If you don't like it – well, you can kiss my rosy backside. You know my boys will be round in the hour to torch this place if I just say the word." He reached forward and patted Narnok on the shoulder. "So, be a good lad, and clear off. There's a woman here needs a little bit of slicing."

As his hand retreated from the pat, Narnok's own hand struck swiftly, grabbing Galtos Gan's hand and twisting it savagely against the joint, whilst lifting it high. Galtos was immediately forced down on one knee, a squeal of shock and pain erupting from his lips, his other hand dropping the knife and slapping the floor hard. Narnok held him like that for a moment, then let go, stepping back, scarred face narrowed.

"That's your warning. Get your clothes and leave. Maria on the desk will give you back your coin."

In silence, Galtos Gan pulled on his trousers and fine silk shirt, and a heavy overcoat of rich dark wool. He pulled on his boots, and stooped to retrieve his dagger, but Narnok trod on the blade.

"You must have missed our 'no weapons' sign on the door when you came in, friend. You can leave that there. Give us your address and I'll have it sent on. After all, I wouldn't like to *upset* the Red Thumb boys now, would I?" Narnok gave a crooked smile, as if he really didn't have a care in the world.

"That's fine," said Galtos, straightening his heavy overcoat. He threw a look towards Luleyla, along with a narrow smile. He winked. "Be seeing you sooner than you think, sweet cheeks. After all. A perfect body like that needs a little scarring."

As he turned back, Narnok delivered a powerful low right hook to the man's ribs. Three broke with audible cracks, and the man doubled over, grunting, as Narnok's knee rose into his face, snapping his head back with a splash of blood up the walls and breaking his nose in the process. Galtos fell back, gasping, whining, both hands clutching his face as he stared up through a mask of blood.

"You bastard! You broke my nose!" He clutched at his side and tried to rise. His fine silk shirt was sodden with blood.

Narnok reached down, grabbing the man's hair and hauling him to his feet. "You threaten my girls again," he growled, pulling him close enough to kiss, "and I'll snap your fucking neck. You understand, you maggot?"

"He's got a knife!" screamed Luleyla, as the blade slashed for Narnok's side. He batted it away and head-butted Galtos on the broken nose, making him slam back into the wall, slipping down to the carpet, weeping and holding his broken face.

"Get dressed, Luleyla. And gather the girls together. Tonight is a good night to close early, I think."

Luleyla ran from the room and Narnok took the knife and examined the blade. Fine silver steel, honed to a razor. This man was wealthy; there was no doubt. But was he really part of a Red Thumb Gang?

The Red Thumbs were notorious throughout Vagandrak, and every city or large town had a syndicate run by a collection of the most wealthy crime families in the land. They specialised in extorting simple, honest people from their hard-earned coin; either as "protection" money or by open threats and injury; even murder. They ran gambling houses, dog- and wolf-fighting pits, whorehouses, honey-leaf dens, and even resorted to open robbery if the reward was high enough. They were a jagged splinter in the side of every City Watchman, and an embarrassment to King

Yoon who seemed, with every passing month, to ignore their presence with renewed vigour. It was a well-known fact you didn't cross the Red Thumbs, for their name had come about from the people they had murdered. Each corpse was left with a bloody thumb-print in the centre of the forehead. Hence the name, and synonym with violence.

Narnok had had his fair amount of trouble on the streets of Kantarok, but always studiously avoided the Red Thumb Gangs if at all possible. A man didn't need that kind of concerted trouble. Narnok ran his whorehouse with efficiency, kindness to the women, and an honesty which brought him little attention from the City Watch. But now, it would seem, the Red Thumbs had come calling on him, whether he wanted their attention or not.

Narnok pocketed the knife, and hauled Galtos to his feet. "Come on, friend. Let's escort you out to the street."

"You'll die for this," said Galtos, through his bloody face.

"You never know when to shut up, do you, son? Well, if I'm going to die for this…" Narnok delivered a heavy punch to Galtos' belly, making the man groan, and another solid overhand blow to the man's face, pulping the cheekbone within. Galtos sagged under Narnok's grip, as he hoisted the half-conscious man behind him and strode down the corridor towards the reception where Maria sat, face pale.

"Is it true? Is he Red Thumb?"

"Possibly, although he may well be full of horse shit. A lot of these people are. Get the girls together and go down to Tanor's Tavern. I have good credit there; he'll let you share a few rooms until I get this thing done."

Maria stood and grabbed Narnok's massive bicep. "What are you going to do, Narn?"

He grinned, then, a quite terrifying sight from behind an insane criss-cross of thin white scars below a milky eye. "Don't you worry you none," he growled. "This bastard had it coming. Nobody treats my girls like that and walks away."

"Yes, but... the Red Thumbs..." She gazed at him, terrified.

"We shall see," said Narnok. "Lock the door behind you."

"Are you sure you'll be all right? I can call my brother, Gellund..."

"Just do as you are told, woman!" Narnok dragged Galtos to the door, and peered out. The cobbled street was silent, for the hour was late. Distantly, he heard drunken shouting, but boots thudded away and silence returned.

Narnok hoisted Galtos Gan up, draping one of the man's arms around his broad shoulders as if helping a drunken friend home; then he stepped out into the winter chill.

It was dark, and a biting wind cut through the streets. Narnok walked Galtos, who was groaning and mumbling, for a good ten minutes until they reached the wide street which ran alongside the Kantarok River. Narnok could feel the chill from the deep, fast running waters and he shivered.

He looked up and down the street, eyes picking out the occasional yellow glow of a fish-oil lantern. Then he walked the mumbling man across, propping him against the low stone wall which had been built to protect the city from flooding. In past decades, the Kantarok had been swelled by snowmelt from the White Lion Mountains to the northeast, bursting its banks and flooding the cellars of half the city. The late, great King Tarek had funded the floodwall from his own royal coffers; but then, he had been a king of the people, loved by the people. Not like the latest dandy idiot, thought Narnok soberly.

He listened carefully. A wind howled from the mountains and for a moment Narnok was lost in their snowy embrace; he'd fought several campaigns over the mountains and the crossings, especially in winter, had been no mean feat. And yet... yet he loved the mountains with all his heart. No compromise there. Just iron. And rock. And ice. But equally, no ego, vanity or back-stabbing friends. Maybe that's what he should do. Sell the whorehouse. Or even better, give it to the girls. Head off into the hills and build himself a lonely wooden cabin... Then he wouldn't have to deal with situations like this.

You attract trouble like a fresh-laid turd attracts flies, Dek had once said. Narnok had bridled, but Dek grabbed him in a bear-hug. *Look at you! Too bloody handsome by far! If you weren't so good looking I'd break your bloody face!* They'd wrestled over that. A mighty contest. Narnok won eight silver pennies.

The memories drifted away like smoke on the biting, bitter wind, and Galtos Gan mumbled again. Narnok listened, but could hear no signs of the Watch. Just what he needed right now, some nosey guard sticking his big bloody nose in.

"What... what yer doing?" mumbled Galtos Gan, through a mouthful of blood and teeth shards. He drooled it down his already soiled silk shirt.

"Listen," said Narnok, holding the man by the front of his heavy coat, good eye narrowing. "Tell me for sure, now. Are you really a part of the Red Thumb Gangs? Be honest with me, because a lot depends upon it."

"Aye man, yes, so let me go or you will suffer greatly!" mumbled Galtos, easing the words out from his damaged face.

Narnok sighed, his heart heavy. "That's what I was worried about." He pulled free the expensive dagger, checked around once more, and pushed it slowly into Galtos Gan's belly. The man felt the cold bite of razor steel and his eyes went suddenly wide, his body and mind suddenly fully awake as adrenaline and awareness flushed his lethargy away. He started to struggle, legs kicking, fists smacking weakly at Narnok, but the big man held him tight, and cut upwards with the knife, opening Galtos Gan like a fish on a block. The man wriggled, but the knife opened his heart and he spasmed in Narnok's hands, then went suddenly slack. His mouth was open in an "O" of horror.

Narnok looked left and right again, and leaving the blade in the body, crouched, and hoisted it to the top of the thick stone wall. With one final look, he pushed the body into the Kantarok River. There was a splash, and he was gone in the blink of an eye, swallowed and carried away on powerful currents.

Narnok stared down at himself. Blood wet hands, and his own shirt stained.

Time to light the wood-burner in the cellar, he thought. And he'd not had to do that for a long time.

Not since Katuna. Not since her betrayal.

Narnok thought about his wife as he trudged home, hands deep in pockets to hide his murder. He thought about his *ex*-wife. He remembered her as she had been. Prettier than any woman he'd ever met, long black hair in natural curls, flashing dark eyes, skin the colour of olives! He'd been hailed as a hero back then, wealth and land showered on him by King Tarek after the killing of Morkagoth. Endless parades through the city streets, with people cheering and throwing flowers. Saved them all, he had, from a mud-orc massacre! The people loved him! And Katuna had loved him more. But then, he mused, his thoughts darkening, anger clouding his mind, fists clenching in his pockets, *no wonder* she'd loved him – when he had all that money!

They'd wed quickly and spent blissful weeks locked away in Narnok's huge country retreat just outside the city of Drakerath. A ten-bedroom house, some two hundred years old and in its own mature grounds of thirty acres, with stables and a lake stocked with trout. Those had been days of bliss! Days to melt a man's heart!

And Katuna! Loving! Doting! And a Hellcat between the sheets like nothing he'd ever experienced! His skin rippled with goose-bumps just thinking about her. But then… where had it gone wrong? His brow creased into a frown beneath the scars. He knew exactly where it had gone wrong. Other men. And greed. And a true Hellraiser attitude to life in general. She'd started spending mornings away from the house, but he'd hardly noticed, as Narnok was busy recruiting a new battalion for Tarek which kept him more than busy away from their love nest. When Tarek asked him to tour various towns giving his "Narnok the Axeman! Hero of the Desekra Fortress!" speech, he could hardly say no. He was gone for a little over a week, returning one Sunday morning just as the sun was rising. He'd picked wild flowers from the garden by the lake, where'd they'd made love frequently during the summer months, and crept up the stairs to their bed chamber to surprise her…

And found Katuna in their bed with another man.

In the darkness of the curtained room, Narnok had bellowed in rage, and there had been a savage fight, smashing up the furniture, curtains torn from rails, and for once in his life Narnok found another man who was a match for his strength, speed and aggression. They'd burst from the bedroom, tumbling onto the landing where lanterns still burned, and through bloodied teeth, Narnok saw–

Dek.

His sword brother. His blood brother. His *friend*.

He'd been stunned into inaction; felled, as if by a pick-axe handle. And Dek, with tears streaming down his face, whispered, "I'm sorry, Narn," before fleeing down the stairs and out into the early dawn light.

For a long time Narnok simply stood, then he'd strode down the hall to his armoury, kicking open the door and hoisting his double-headed axe from its pride of place above the panels of armour and chainmail. The large weapon was dull and black, the blades nicked from years of combat and real-world battle. But the blades were razor sharp, the balance perfect, the axe a *part* of Narnok.

Katuna ran into the armoury. "No, Narnok! No!" She grabbed his arm, and he back-handed her across the room.

He strode down the hallway, but she came after him with a long knife, leaping onto his back trying to cut his throat. That's when he lost it. That's when his rage swamped his mind and the next thing he remembered, he was sat astride her, her face bloody and broken, her eyes filled with… not terror, exactly, but a cold understanding. He'd never seen a look like that on another soul, and knew he never would.

Leaving his axe, for fear of what he might do, he saddled a horse and went on a three day drinking spree around the seedier districts of Drakerath. When he arrived home, filled with remorse, and apology, and regret, still half-drunk from the many flagons of wine he'd consumed in the city, they were waiting for him. A hammer blow to the head saw him unconscious and when he came round they were in the old stone cellar, his hands and feet bound by wire to a sturdy oak chair.

Six men, large, swarthy, with the eyes of killers. They carried helves and knives. One carried a bottle.

At first, Narnok had no idea what was going on. Until from their midst stepped Katuna, his lovely, beautiful, sexy Hellcat Katuna! Her face was still bruised, and when she spoke the words were like ice spears through Narnok's heart.

"This is Narnok, my husband. He betrayed me with a long line of bitch lovers, then beat me again and again and again." Narnok could hear the growls of anger from the mercenaries. "You can still see my bruises," whimpered Katuna, lowering her head as if in great shame; as if she regretted this whole sorry business. "Now," she said, words a low whisper, "he wants to cheat me out of what is rightfully mine. He won't allow me to leave. He won't give me money, but I know he has plenty hidden in the house."

The right hook knocked Narnok, and the chair, over. He hit the ground hard, smacking his head. Two men rushed behind and hoisted him up and his eyes flashed with anger.

"Don't listen to her. It was not I who cheated, but her! She lies, I tell you!"

A small man pushed to the front of the group. He was narrow and quite old, his head bald, features pointed. He smiled at Narnok. In his hands he carried a cork-stoppered bottle. "You need to listen very carefully, Narnok. Very carefully indeed. I am Xander. I used to work King Tarek's dungeon; my chief responsibility was torture, pain, confessions. Now, I am freelance – it would seem Tarek no longer wishes to rule his people by fear and punishment; a foolish choice, but his by right of monarchy, I believe. Still, that is history. What should concern *you* right now, is that we are in this young lady's employ. You have been most dishonourable towards her…"

"Yes, he has," whimpered Katuna, patting her bruised face.

"But in all truth, this is a paid job. If you do not tell us where the money is, then we do not get paid. So, we will begin with blades. And if that does not work," he held up the bottle. "This is acid. I will burn out your eyes."

Narnok started to struggle violently, but a helve blow to the back of the head stopped that, knocking him once more to the ground, half unconscious. He came around real fast when the razor cut a strip of flesh from his face…

His screams lasted long into the night.

And in the end, he told them where the money was.

Narnok stopped by the door to the Pleasure Parlour and checked around with his one good eye. He spat a heavy ball of phlegm, as if by removing the bad taste from his mouth he could remove the bad memories of Katuna, his ex-wife, from his skull.

I wonder where you are now, he mused, and opened the door. Hopefully, some scumbag has cut your throat and left you dead in an alleyway.

And Dek. Oh, you bastard of a bastard. I wonder if you still breathe our fine Vagandrak air? Or did some pit fighter break your spine? Maybe gouge out one of your eyes? See how you like it?

Narnok's final words to his sword brother, blood brother, friend, had been screamed in hate across the army mess as men sought to restrain them both, and a runner was dispatched for Dalgoran; "I'm going to fucking kill you!" bellowed Narnok, "and when you do fucking die,

I'm going to ride into Hell and the Furnace looking for your bones and your fucking soul, and I'm going to tear you apart again!" before he was dragged out by warriors and threatened with military prison by General Dalgoran.

Old days.

The *bad* old days.

Long gone, down, lost and forgotten; but not too readily forgotten. Not now. Not in times like this.

He unlocked the door and stepped carefully inside, closing it with a click and waiting in the darkness, allowing himself to acclimatise and his vision to adjust. *Were the Red Thumbs waiting for him? Did they know?* But of course, they did not know, and Narnok descended into the basement, screwing up paper balls and building kindling into a small pyramid before adding larger chunks of wood to the burner. Soon, flames were crackling, slightly damp wood popping, and Narnok set an iron bowl of water to heat on the hob whilst he stripped his clothes free, tossing them into the fire.

There, naked, covered in blood, he thought again of Katuna.

And he thought again of Dek.

A week had passed, and Narnok thought he'd got away with it. He opened the Pleasure Parlour as usual, and Maria arrived. She seemed edgy, tired, with huge bags under her red-rimmed eyes, but Narnok thought little of it. The girls arrived on time, and Saridia was complaining of a sore back; but then, she always did that.

Narnok sat in his "office". He let Maria perform the front of house work, as his heavily scarred face and milky eye had the effect of putting many with a weaker constitution off the act of copulation. Once, a drunk had grinned, saying, "If that's what happens to your face when

I sleep with one of your girls, I'd better recommend this place to my enemies!" He left with a broken nose.

So, Narnok sat in his office; it was a quiet night. At about 10 o'clock Maria brought him a cup of warm milk and sugar, his usual evening tipple, and he sipped it as he read the book before him detailing a history of Zalazar, penned by the esteemed scholar Kazellius, Professor of History at Drakerath University. Narnok didn't drink alcohol when he was working, because if there was any trouble, it would impede his performance when he most needed it. Not that they had much trouble at the Pleasure Parlour. News, like Narnok as a leg-breaker, got round most taverns pretty quick.

Which was why, after a half hour or so, Narnok found it strange to feel dizzy and extremely sleepy. He rubbed his temples with big, strong fingers, yawned, and frowned at the page where letters seemed to drift and shift and swirl. "That's not right," he mumbled, and got slowly to his feet. His left leg buckled at the knee but he caught himself, hands flat on the old scarred desk. He yawned again. "Not right at all."

He didn't hear the door open; movement caught his eye. They came into the room. There were eight of them, big men, each carrying a pick-axe handle or iron bar. They flooded the office and Narnok grunted, turning towards his axe on the bench behind, but the whole world was spinning, and he felt like he'd drunk a barrel of wine. Narnok hit the ground like a sack of shit, but the impact didn't bother him, because darkness had already fallen. The first thing he noticed was the sour taste in his mouth, and a gritty feeling on his tongue, like the dregs of some bitter pill. *She drugged me,* he realised. *Maria! Faithful old Maria!* Had she turned against him? No, he thought. She was as reliable as clockwork. So, they had a hold over her. Something small and hard filled Narnok's soul. The Red Thumb Gang. Red Thumbs. He scowled, anger rising. So, they wanted a war, did they? They wanted a fucking *war?*

He listened, and could hear the heavy, slow flow of deep water. He was cold, shivering in fact, and some intuition told him he was underground. A cellar? But a cellar *where*, though? He listened, but could hear no voices. Were they standing there, waiting for him to wake up so the pain could begin?

Narnok's head was thumping, and he resisted the urge to frown or wince. It beat inside his skull, like a trapped lion roaring to get free.

He was seated on a hard wooden chair. His feet were tied together, and his hands bound behind his back; to one another, as well as to the chair. Not good. A torturer's position, and that was a place Narnok had been in once before. It was a place he never wanted to visit again.

Gently, he tested his bonds, but they'd been entwined and knotted by a professional.

Reluctantly, Narnok eased his eyes open. He was in an underground warehouse of some kind. A huge stack of crates lined one wall, stamped in a language he'd never before seen. To his right, and emanating cold, flowed a deep, fast river. However, these were just subliminal background images. What interested him – or horrified him – even more was the man seated directly before him. He was a small, wiry man, with a bald head and pointed features. His aged face was lined, indeed lined considerably more than the last time Narnok saw him. Yet he was still instantly recognisable. After all, you never forgot your first torturer.

"Good day, Narnok. I am sure you remember me."

"Xander!"

"You're looking well. I see my handiwork scarred nicely."

"Fuck you."

Xander smiled. "So crude. So brutish. So very much what I expected. I see your scars and acid-kissed eye did little to improve your manners. And yet, the romantic part of my soul truly believed my… *gift* to you would calm you down a little; teach you a grade of…" he savoured the word, "*humility.*"

Narnok heaved against his bonds, and his chair scraped across the stone-flagged floor. Behind him, the river hissed. He was growling, spitting hate, wanting so bad to get to the man who had not just caused him intense physical pain, but effectively, in Narnok's mind, ruined his life.

Finally, he calmed down enough to speak. He was a deep crimson, fists clenched and straining against the arms of the sturdy oak chair. His single working eye was narrowed and focused with unalloyed intensity at Xander. If looks could kill, Xander would be chopped pieces in a bucket.

"I'm going to kill you," said Narnok, gently.

"Ah, yes. The threats." He stood, revealing a small wooden table containing an opened leather case. It was small, the sort many doctors carried. Narnok caught the gleam of polished steel. Sharp steel. Needles. Knives. Curved dental equipment. The tools of Xander's trade. "They always come first. In fact, you should remember! This is how we began last time. And yet it ended so differently, did it not?" He moved closer and Narnok jerked against his bonds, trying to reach the man who had taken his face and his eye. "And now I work for the Red Thumbs," said Xander, voice low and intimate, "and in a massive twist of comedy, and fate, I believe, I find you seated before me once more. Oh, how I do believe the gods like a joke as much as the next man!"

"Bastard! I'll rip out your throat! I'll tear out your fucking spine!"

"Tut-tut." Xander smiled, as if berating a squawking tantrum child. "I fear I must remove some of this foulest of language. One way, I have discovered, with other guests, is to begin with the teeth... and then we'll talk about Galtos Gan – whom you murdered – and the fact that he *was* cousin to Faltor Gan, one of the three rulers of the Red Thumbs." He reached out and picked up a pair of heavy-duty silver medical pliers, normally used by battlefield surgeons. "Although, of course, you *won't* be able to speak. But you can grunt. And spew blood. And spit teeth. And sign a declaration of confession." Narnok's eyes came to rest on that tool, on that weapon, all the time straining at his bonds. His muscles writhed along his arms, neck and chest, and his thighs and calves burned with the effort of straining against the chair legs.

A cool breeze drifted through the underground warehouse.

The river hissed by, on its journey to the ocean.

Narnok could smell distant fire and hot oil. All his senses seemed to come suddenly alive. As if he knew he was about to suffer incredible pain and then die, horribly. This was his last chance. He could smell Xander's sweat and a lotion the man used to soften his skin. He could smell his own sweat and fear and piss. The river carried some sewage, which prickled Narnok's nostrils. The subdued light came from fish-oil lanterns, and the light suddenly burned Narnok's brain. But this was as nothing, he knew, compared with the pain to come...

He grunted, heaving with all his might as Xander drifted closer, those silver pliers in his wrinkled, liver-spotted hand.

Xander smiled, and it was a smile with no humour; it was the smile of Death.

"Welcome back, Narnok," whispered Xander, with the intimacy of a lover. "I missed you."

AFTERSEED

It was dawn.

Pale light filtered around the edges of the great iron shutters surrounding the Main Hall of the Zak-Tan Palace. A huge bonfire glowed in the centre of the hall, blackening the marble. An hour earlier it had been roaring, filling the great chamber with dancing light and frightened shadows; but now the coals pulsed with orange and white, and most of the log chunks had burnt away.

Three carcases, with spears from anus to mouth, still roasted by the edge of the fire. The skin was golden, blackened in places, and meat had been cut free in generous quantities; but even now, the three roasted creatures were still vaguely recognisable as Shanaz, Hunta and Marella, King Zorkai's former wives.

Zorkai himself sat on a blanket by the edge of the fire furthest away from the roasted women. He felt confused, and just a little sick. Not just from partaking in a flesh feast of his former lovers and the bearers of his children; although that did trouble him deeply. No. He felt both pure and impure, hallowed and yet tainted, free and yet enslaved by his coupling, and his conversation, and his future plans with Orlana, the Changer; whom some called the Horse Lady.

Before the murders, she had taken him to his bed. A bed he knew so well, and scene of thousands of pleasant evenings of sexual couplings with his women. But this had been different. His lust has been all consuming, so great it blinded him, so great it blanketed his fears and sent his mind to another place, where he was no longer in control of his actions, no longer in control of his feelings or self-preservation. Orlana had removed her clothes, and that fabulous body welcomed him into its soft, warm, supple, powerful embrace. He entered her, and it had been fabulous, the most amazing sex he'd ever experienced; but then it stepped up to a new level, and he'd gasped, and felt a physical sensation so pure and beautiful he could not believe this was simply sexual congress with a woman. It felt as if they merged, there, rutting, twisting on the black silk sheets. He vaguely remembered looking down, and it was as if their legs were one, the flesh melted together, their flesh sucked together and inside one another; not just a fuck, but a complete organic joining, a total melting together, a unique experience of the flesh. With clever muscle control she held him in thrall, denying him ejaculation until it became painful and he wanted to scream and beat at her with his fists. The pain grew and grew until this was no longer sex but a massacre, no longer enjoyment but pure white hot fire filling every atom of his body. And just when he thought he could contain himself no more, when he thought he would have to reach for a blade and slit her throat just to end the agony, so she relaxed and allowed him to fill her with his seed. His ejaculation went on, and on, and on, until he felt like he must have emptied himself totally into her, not just his sperm but his blood and water and organs and bones. And then he lay, panting, and realised suddenly that he was still alive. He hadn't emptied his flesh inside Orlana; but he had surely emptied his soul.

After what could have been minutes, could have been hours, Orlana stepped from the bed and pulled on a robe of white cotton. Its simplicity heightened her beauty and Zorkai watched him from his slumber. She glided from the room and his heavy-lidded eyes folded and were closed.

The scream brought him awake with a vicious start. It was so high and pure, even though muffled by walls and doors, that King Zorkai believed he would never sleep again. Sword in hand and naked, he pounded down tiled corridors with high-arched ceilings and an excess of gold and crimson. He skidded around several corridors, making for the stairs to the Main Hall, and he leapt down the top set of steps and then froze at the sight which greeted his disbelieving eyes...

Orlana stood, Marella held out with one hand, half bent over, as Orlana forced a long spear into her anus, twisting with each thrust and subtle crunch; Marella had gone limp, but was held erect by this forced internal brace. Her mouth and eyes were still open, but she no longer screamed, and even as Zorkai watched, Orlana made a final thrust and the slender spear blade emerged in a shower of blood from her mouth, tilting her jaw wide open.

Orlana tossed Marella aside, where she slapped the marble beside the already skewered figure of Shanaz who was, incredibly, still shivering and shaking, clinging to life with some final, desperate threads.

Orlana reached out, grabbing a cowering Hunta, whose eyes suddenly fixed on her husband and King.

"Zorkai! Please! Help me! By the Seven Sisters, please stop this!"

"No!" screamed Zorkai, kicked into action. He sped down the steps, bare fleet slapping, and charged Orlana with his sword held high. She glanced at him, made a casual gesture and it appeared as if he were struck by the side-swipe of a giant, invisible hammer. Folded, in half he crashed across the Main Hall, connecting with the wall and slamming to the floor, groaning. Orlana hefted the final spear, grinned at Hunta, and said, "No more carping from you, bitch," before shoving the spear blade into the woman with a rectum-tearing *crunch*.

When Zorkai had awoken, he'd felt groggy, and for a moment wondered exactly how much spirit he'd consumed, before recent horrific events came rushing back in a blink of disbelief. Surely, it had all been a terrible nightmare? Surely, this Orlana, this *Changer*, was a rabid element of his over-stressed imagination and bad dreams? But the raging, roaring fire at the centre of his marble hall had told him something different, that and the sight of his three dead wives roasting over the flames as Orlana idly turned an improvised spit and hummed a gentle tune more in keeping with flowers opening their petals, or moonlight skimming over glimmering ocean waves, than the cooking of her lover's dead wives.

Orlana had lifted Shanaz's ornate, razor-sharp dagger and cut a piece of flesh from the dead woman's thigh. She'd tasted it, thoughtfully, as if she were a chef deciding how much seasoning to add to the broth.

Zorkai had staggered to his feet and grabbed his sword – before realising the blade was bent nearly in two. He'd cast it down with a clatter and moved warily towards Orlana, his steps dragging. He'd touched the back of his head and his hand had come away with blood.

He'd halted before the open flames. "You cooked them," he'd said, for it was all the imagination he could muster.

"Yes. It stopped their mewling. Care to taste some?" She'd held a slice of pink meat towards him, and he shuddered. The meat had been tender, and steaming gently.

"No."

"Yes."

"I cannot! They were my women!"

"No, they are dead flesh, dead meat, there to be savoured and enjoyed. We, the victors, have that right. They wished me dead; I killed them. Now, I eat their flesh, their souls, and they will be my slaves for eternity."

"Truly? Eternity?"

"Or until I die."

Zorkai's eyes glittered.

"Before you get any ideas," said Orlana, voice a gentle hum, "please remember the old magick flows through my veins. I bested three thousand of your warriors. With a click of my fingers, I could have them leaping through the walls, and by through I actually mean *through* just to get at your flesh and bones. So, ask yourself this, King Zorkai. Are you willing to rule by my side, as my king; or do I do it alone?"

"A king has his orders obeyed," said Zorkai, eyes dark.

"And of course, I will allow such power. But for now, with this, I need total command. You can rule with me, here in this realm, Zorkai; I want it so. We will expand your Empire; we will smash north through the Pass of Splintered Bones and take Vagandrak, we will travel east and conquer the Plague Lands, for with me by your side there is nothing to fear! From thence, we will take Zalazar – I know the White Lion Mountains well – and finally head for the Mountains of the Moon!"

Zorkai had considered this. He pushed back his head and rolled his neck and thought of his mother, and his father, and his brothers and sisters and cousins, who had all perished for him to become king. And now, yes, he was King of Zak-Tan; King of Zakora! But where to go? The southern tribes were a thousand motley groups of wandering warriors; hardly worth the effort. And Vagandrak was guarded by the Desekra Fortress: four massive walls and a keep at the narrowest section of the pass. Vagandrak's army was an incredible fighting force, indeed had beaten back the first mud-orc invasion when Morkagoth had walked the realm. Zorkai had been a mere child then, but he remembered Morkagoth: tall and oozing dominance, with a flowing white beard and piercing black eyes, he had terrified toddler Zorkai, but also excited the young child, with his sheer electric presence. He even now remembered his father being in thrall to the sorcerer. Now, he was being offered a chance of expansion, of Empire! To take Vagandrak, the bastards who had been a thorn in his side, with their sneering and superiority, their powerful navy and their alien ways.

King Zorkai could conquer Vagandrak.

Smash the Desekra Fortress that had shamed his father, his people.

"We will need a bigger army," he'd said, moving closer and warming his hands by the blaze.

Orlana had nodded, cutting free another strip of meat.

"I can help with that. You have witnessed what I can do. What I did to the horses. The riders."

"Even with such beasts, the walls of Desekra are high and brutal; even Morkagoth failed, with his legions of mud-orcs."

"We can do better than that," said Orlana, voice hushed.

Zorkai had taken the meat and eaten. It tasted good. His mind had been working hard, and he'd turned suddenly to Orlana. "You would bring back the mud-orcs, then?" he'd said.

"Yes."

"You have such power?"

"Yes."

"What do we need to do?" he'd said, chewing thoughtfully, his head full of raging thoughts, of betrayal, and violence, and Empire. If King Zorkai did this, his name would crash through history for the next ten thousand years. He'd smiled and he'd chewed, Shanaz's thigh meat caught between his teeth, her bubbling fat running into his beard.

In a low, husky voice, eyes glowing by the light of the fire, Orlana had said, "You must round up from Zak-Tan the ill, the lame, the crippled, the diseased, the slow of wit and slow of body; and you must bring together every second child. We must take these to the Mud-Pits. There, I will perform the Rites. There, we will summon the mud-orcs."

"My people must suffer?"

"We must feed the Mud-Pits."

"I cannot travel to the Mud-Pits. It is forbidden. The flesh will peel from my bones. Blood will pour from every orifice. I have seen this with my own eyes. The Mud-Pits are a place of evil. A place that is forbidden to mortal man."

"I am not mortal," whispered Orlana, "and you will have me by your side. You: the king. And I, your queen. Are you ready for this? Do you seek empire and immortality?"

"I do."

"Then gather your people. It is time for them to die."

THE NORTH

It was dawn, and the Rokroth Marshes stank like a five day corpse in the sun. Kiki, riding at the head of the group, glanced right. The ground was rocky and undulating, with several large boulders of black granite; but beyond this short stretch, this rocky natural *barrier,* the marshes stretched away eastwards, a putrid plain of coarse grasslands and stagnant water. There were narrow paths through the marshes, as used by the Dagran eel catchers, but they were a guild secret and jealously guarded. For most mortals, to attempt any kind of serious crossing of the Rokroth Marshes was a guaranteed death.

"Wait up!" Dek nudged his horse into a canter and drew alongside Kiki. His horse snorted, pawing the rocks as if annoyed at this short burst of speed. Dek leaned forward and patted its muzzle, muttering calming words and wincing as his shoulder stitches pulled tight.

They'd headed east from Vagan, the War Capital, which was now two hours behind them, and Kiki was glad to be away from the oppression of the city. With a nomadic soul, it rarely took long for Kiki to grow tired of a place, and even before the incident with Lars and the City Watch, she had grown deeply tired of Rokroth, and similarly tired of Vagan. After leaving Vagan behind, they had angled northeast until they hit the marshes, which did nothing, if not remind Kiki of her recent encounter with Lars.

"You okay, Dek? You look like you've been in a fight."

"Yes. Very funny."

"No. Seriously." Kiki wiggled her finger in front of her own face. "Your nose is bent, you've a cut above each eye, bruising to your cheeks. And you're favouring your arm; a soldier notices these things."

"Thanks for the appraisal," he grunted, rubbing his nose and wincing. "I'll make sure I ask for your advice next time I need a new wardrobe."

"Fancy. Been hanging around courtiers, have you?"

"Well, I've fought a few in the Pits. You get some pompous, rich, arrogant fuckers; a few drinks, a few fight lessons, think they can take on the world. Usually they have a few whiskies for courage, then come and meet me." He grinned.

"I expect you beat them all?"

"Yes." He frowned. "Of course."

Kiki leaned towards him and smiled. "I was talking to Ragorek. Earlier."

"I thought you might."

"And you can take that look of thunder from your face, Big Man. He's your brother, by the Seven Sisters."

"Go on. Spit it out."

"Well, he's your *brother*. He loved your old mum as well."

She watched the storm accelerate across Dek's face, and the pit fighter seemed to swell. His eyes narrowed and he gritted his teeth. Then he forced himself to be calm, and slowly, very slowly, regained control of himself. "I'd rather not talk about it," he growled, at last, glancing at her with a sudden embarrassment. His cheeks flushed red.

"That's fine," said Kiki, softly. "I meant no offence."

"I know. I know! It's me, Kiki. It's just, Rag knew our mum was dying. And he chose to do nothing. Nothing! I sat with her, holding her hand day after day, week after week, and she asked me again and again when Ragorek would arrive. She wanted to see him one last time. Before it got too bad. Before she went away." He stumbled into silence, and Kiki realised he did not have the words to articulate his feelings.

"Maybe he had his reasons," she said, eventually.

"Yeah. Well. He stabbed her in the back. He stabbed me in the back. There's no forgiving some fucking crimes. Change the subject, Keek, or I swear by the Chaos Halls I'll turn this beast around and ride over the horizon and away from here."

Kiki bit her lip, and sighed, and stared at Dek. She knew him, knew him better than a brother; knew him better than he knew himself. And yet she *did not* know him. How long had it been? Fifteen years? *Sixteen?* A lot of things changed in that amount of time. Gods, how she knew the truth about that! Where was the honey-leaf when she needed its sugar and spice? Where was Suza now, a dark god mocking her every decision? Abandoned by her Love, and her Hate. Shit.

"*Shit.*" She took a deep breath and changed tactics. "Rag told me about the… creature. The horse thing that attacked you both and near chewed off your arm."

Dek spat out a laugh, and rubbed his bristles. "Yeah, that bastard. That was one hard beast to kill."

"Did you tell Dalgoran? He has a similar story."

"Really?"

"Some kind of wolf beast, with an enlarged, twisted muzzle. Killed the Seer who made the prophecy; the reason he's here to collect us like bad and rotting apples from the bottom of a broken barrel."

"You have such a way with words, Keek. You always did."

They rode in silence for a while, the stink of the marshes in their nostrils, a cold winter wind blowing from the north. Far to the northeast, they could just make out the distant tips of the White Lion Mountains, the huge, unbroken wall that effectively bordered Vagandrak and cut them off from Zalazar, the lands of the fabled Elf Rats. Kiki shivered. Tall tales to frighten small children. Her uncle used to frighten her with those. Until the day she put her knife in his eye. But that was for a very different reason.

"Are you well?"

"Yes. I'm fine. Just thinking of the Elf Rats."

Dek laughed again, but this time it was genuine humour. "Me and Narnok used to joke about them; wondered what the women would be like." He fell into silence. Then, speaking so quietly his words could hardly be heard over the wind, said, "This is your bastard fault. I haven't said his name in ten years!"

"Well, you're going to have to talk to him."

"It's never going to happen, Kiki. I'll come on your damn mission with you, and I'll do Dalgoran's dirty work. But I do it for *you*, Kiki. Only for you. And you know why?" Kiki nodded. "Damn."

"What happened with you and Narnok?"

"Let that one lie, little lady."

Again, Kiki nodded. Then she laughed. "When did it all get so complicated?"

"We were children, back at Splintered Bones. We did the training, obeyed the orders, did the fuck what we were told. And we... endured the curse." He glanced at her, but she looked away. "Then we took Tarek's gold and we... we were forced to grow up. Afterwards. It's a bad world out there when you have a purse full of coin."

"Yes, Dek." Her words were soft. "But I want you to talk to Dalgoran. I want you to trust him. He's a good man. He believes in this country. To him, Vagandrak is a vulnerable woman in need of protection. And we are the iron to forge the blade."

"He's lost in the past," said Dek, not unkindly.

"Maybe so. But his heart is in the right place."

"All men's hearts are there," said Dek, bad temper returning. "That's what makes them so easy to kill."

Night had fallen, and they'd built a fire within the lee of a huge, L-shaped group of rocks. Distantly, wolves howled. Ragorek, on Kiki's advice, was out collecting more wood and she stirred a pan over the flames which contained a thick broth, which bubbled gently. Dek had found some wild onions and Dalgoran added beef and salt. It smelt fabulous, especially out in the open air; out in the wilds.

I missed this, she thought idly to herself. The bite of the cold breeze. A night under the stars wrapped in blankets. A harder life, for sure, but a more fulfilling one. No comfy beds, weak handshakes and false back-stabbing smiles. The life of a soldier for me.

But not for long, said Suza, sliding into Kiki's mind like a snake slides into a sleeping woman's chamber. *After all, you have the cancer; you have the growth beside your heart, and I can see it, Kiki, watch it growing, expanding. Can you not feel it? The pressure in your chest? It's going to grow and grow and finally consume you. You will die, Kiki, coughing your bloody mispumping heart up through your mouth, to vomit it on the floor at your blood-spattered feet.*

"Leave me alone." The words were soft, calm, gentle.

Why? Why should I? You tortured me! You would not listen, after all I went through, after all the horror I suffered. I was in trauma! But did you help? No, you were too busy running off playing at soldiers… were the men there a good fuck, little Kiki? Because that's the only way I can imagine you surviving in such an environment.

"I saved the country," hissed Kiki through gritted teeth. "I saved you! Saved you all from the mud-orcs."

Is that what they tell you? Is that what you really believe? Her mocking laughter echoed as it faded away, and Dek approached, arms full of firewood, eyes fixing on her and making her shiver.

He reminded her of… a better time. A better place. When they had been…

No.

"When will the broth be ready? It smells fabulous," said Dek.

"It's ready when it's ready," replied Kiki, a smile taking the sting from her tone.

"Yes – but when?"

"Soon. Stop nagging. You never did know when to give it a rest. Go and sharpen your sword or something."

She got up and moved over to the horses. Her grey mare snorted softly, dipping her head. Kiki patted the creature, whispering into her ear as she loosed the cinch on the saddle and laid a blanket across her back.

Dalgoran came and sat by the fire, holding his hands to the flames. Dek studied the old general. His hair and beard were white, eyes hard and grey. His face was deeply lined, and by the light of the fire he suddenly looked like a marble statue: noble, erect, unbreakable.

"How goes it, old timer?"

Dalgoran glanced up. "I can still kick your skull from here to Kantarok, no matter how big you are, Dek lad; so I advise you to wire that mouth shut before I knock your few remaining teeth right out of your skull."

Dek burst out laughing. "Still the cantankerous old goat, I see. By all the gods, that parade ground bellow of yours still haunts me in my dreams! Sometimes, I wake up in a mad panic, thinking I'm late for drill. Can you still do it?"

Dalgoran grinned, then. "Yes, Dek; I can still do it. There're some things that bastard, Old Age, will never rob. By all the gods, that broth smells good. Where's Kiki gone? Kiki? KIKI? Can I dish out this broth? Look, you're going to burn it. Dek, get the ladle, lad, dish it out. She's going to burn it."

"You're joking? Haven't you learned? Never, ever touch that woman's food before she gives permission. Do you not *remember* Jester Scolls? She threw him *off* the battlements."

"What, at Desekra?"

"Yes. Admittedly, he only broke an arm, but she'd warned him before."

"I don't remember that," said Dalgoran, softly.

"Ahh, you were too busy running the damn fortress. Although I do remember you had time to sample Kiki's bread."

"Good days," said Dalgoran.

"No. Those days were full of horse shit. Polished boots and shining armour. But I reckon we sure saw off them damn mud-orcs, didn't we?"

"We did, lad. We did. Listen. Kiki mentioned the beast that attacked you. Sounds like a familiar story. Was its head too long, twisted, full of fangs? A big, heavily muscled bastard, like something escaped from the Chaos Halls, or the Tales of the Black Blade?"

"It took a lot of killing," said Dek.

"Yes. Ours also." They pondered this for a while.

"You think they're coming back, don't you?" said Dek, finally.

"The mud-orcs? Yes."

"And Morkagoth?"

"Possibly. There has to be a leader, a focal point. That's the way the Equiem work."

Dek made the sign of the Protective Cross. "I thought we sent Morkagoth screaming into the Furnace?"

"We did, lad. But some things are too bad to burn."

Kiki returned, and her face was sombre. She ladled out broth to Dalgoran and Dek, and then seated herself cross-legged, a bowl in her lap, a thick chunk of black bread in one fist. She started to eat.

"Are we waiting for Ragorek?" said Dek.

"I thought you hated him?"

"I do. And I'll kill him one day, for sure. But the man still has to eat!"

"He's collecting more wood."

"How much wood do we really need? Are we cooking a pig?" Dek stared hard at Kiki, then grimaced. "I see what you did. You're playing at being matchmaker again, aren't you? Think you'll keep us apart and avoid any trouble. Hah!"

"Isn't that a good thing?" said General Dalgoran, words gentle. "She cares about you, Dek. I care about you."

"Horse shit," said the large pit fighter, his temper starting to rise. He threw his bowl to one side and stood. "You're patronising me, and I'll not be standing for it. If me and Rag start brawling, well that's between us brothers. But you people come back into my life after all these years, at this fucking time, of all times, and expect me to roll over and let you tickle my belly? No. Not happening. Fuck you."

Dalgoran stood, and stared hard at Dek. "You need to stand down, soldier, before you say something you can't take back. I haven't ridden half way across Vagandrak for this sort of raw recruit behaviour. I've come for my Iron Wolves. The men and women I remember were hard, they kept their mouths shut, they did the job that needed doing. All I've seen of you so far, boy, is an argument with a brother over a dead mother, a few corpses and a burned down house. You tell the big tale of killing the creature, but I'll believe the actions when I fucking see them."

"Yeah?" growled Dek, looming close.

And then Kiki was there, her hand on his massive arm. "We're on the same side," she said.

"No, we're not," growled Dek, eyes still fixed on Dalgoran. "He's come here spouting his tale of woe, of seers and prophecies and horse shit. What do we really know? What evidence? Just this old man's intuition. It makes me fucking sick, the lot of it."

"Is that how you're going to be?" said Ragorek from the edge of the camp. His arms were laden with thick sticks, and he let them fall with a crackle. He walked forward until he stood before the flames; stood before Dek. Then he slapped Dek, hard, across the face. Dek's head came up, eyes narrowed. "Stop being a bitch, and behave like a soldier!" snapped Ragorek, his face a snarl. "You got the chance to change the world, and you did it. But you left me at home looking after mother, didn't you? You ran off to train with the best army in the world, under the best fucking general. And you fought the mud-orcs, and killed Morkagoth, and you're the hero they teach to the little children in schools. You became a legend, Dek. A *legend*. They built statues of your ugly mug. But not me; I was left out, despite my sword-arm being just as strong as yours. You know how that felt, little brother? Watching you fly into the sky, soaring like a bird, whilst I was down in the shit with the worms. You were fighting at Desekra

Fortress; I was cleaning out the shit from Shankell's Pig Farm with a shovel. And now, your old friends are here and they need your help... so get your head from up your backside and *help them*."

Ragorek slumped down, and accepted a bowl from Kiki. Head down, he began to eat, trembling either from rage or tears; it was hard to tell by the firelight.

With a snort, Dek stormed off into the huddle of darkened trees. Kiki rose to follow him, but Rag touched her arm. "Best let him go. Let him cool down." Then he grinned. "He always was the hot-headed one."

Kiki nodded, but looked after him into the darkness. A cold wind blew. Kiki shivered. "General?"

"Yes, Captain?"

"Do you really think the mud-orcs are coming?"

"I'd bet my life on it."

"Just on the words spoken by the seer?"

"I can't explain it. It's in my bones. In my soul. We've been at peace too long; the timing just feels right. As for that creature that attacked us... it wasn't anything from this mortal realm, Kiki, my dear."

"Well, I hope you are wrong."

"I, also. Truly I do. I want to die knowing my children and grandchildren have the safest of futures. I am too old to be fighting another war. But those mud-orcs are coming; or something far worse. And Desekra is our only bastion against our enemies in the south. We need to petition Yoon; rebuild the army. We need to oppose them."

"You think he will listen?"

"General Jagged is heading there now. If anybody can persuade Yoon, Jagged can. We will talk tomorrow."

Dek stood in the trees, listening to the darkness. It began to snow, and a sideways breeze made the snow hiss against dry, brown, winter leaves. He crunched forward until he came to a clearing, a former campsite. Logs had been dragged around a central fire pit and Dek sat on one of the logs, stretching out his long legs. A break in the clouds above allowed shafts of moonlight to fall through the snow, illuminating him. He smiled and imagined his mother was looking down from heaven.

"Can I join you?"

"I knew he'd send the woman."

"I'm not just any woman."

"I *know* that." But he patted the log beside him and Kiki moved forward, hand on her sword hilt, boots crunching through a thin layer of snow and frozen dead pine needles.

"It's getting too cold to camp out," she observed, making conversation. Dek was a huge, threatening bulk beside her.

"Dalgoran says we'll camp at Skell Fortress tomorrow night, if the snow continues."

Kiki shivered. "I think I'd rather freeze to death."

"Don't be foolish, woman."

"Woman, is it?" grinned Kiki, drawing a long knife with a hiss of steel. "Once, I would have thrown *you* from the battlements for a comment like that. Broken your leg. Cut off a finger. I didn't earn Captain of *this squad* without cracking a few big dumb skulls."

Dek turned towards her, his face painted white, ghostly, in the moonlight, in the snow. She tried to read his features, but could not. A long silence developed between them, until Dek leant a little closer and she felt the warmth of his body.

"You used to love me," he said, gently.

"I still love you," said Kiki. "Despite being just *a woman.*"

"Ha. Always a quick joke to avoid what needs to be said. You were always this way."

"Really? Well, I remember giving my heart and soul to you, and I remember you betraying me. And not just me: Narnok. Your sword brother. Your blood brother."

Dek remained silent, and then lowered his head, rubbing his face with both hands.

"How did it get so messed up?" he said.

"You messed it up," said Kiki, regretting the words the minute they passed beyond her lips. She cursed herself, and felt Dek stiffen. She placed a hand on his arm. "I'm sorry. It was a long time ago. Best to forget."

She thought about the honey-leaf, then. Her addiction. Contemplated her own betrayal; more subtle, but still a betrayal of her unit, her lover, herself.

"Can I kiss you?"

Dek moved close in the darkness, and reached towards her, and she placed a hand flat on his chest but did not push him away. He came close, and kissed her, and his lips were unexpectedly soft, his kiss surprisingly tender.

He pulled away.

"Don't get any ideas," said Kiki.

"I needed that. Our parting words were... harsh. *Your* words were harsh."

"I'm sorry. Actually, no, I'm not. You slept with Narnok's *wife*, Dek. You abused his trust and mine. You broke us all up. You killed the Iron Wolves more effectively than Morkagoth ever could."

"It was a seduction," he said softly, large eyes filled with sadness. "She drugged me. I was out of my mind. And I never meant any of what followed."

"Have you seen Narnok? Since it happened?"

"No."

"Have you seen what she *did* to him? What those bastard mercenaries did to his face?"

"No. But I heard."

"Hearing isn't enough," said Kiki. "But you'll see. You can apologise firsthand to his fucked-up face. That's if he doesn't kill you first, of course."

"I'm a hard man to kill," said Dek.

"We're all hard to kill; that's why we're Wolves."

Dek stood, a sudden movement. "I still love you, Kiki. We've been apart... too long. We can leave. Leave this place: now. Saddle our horses and simply ride away. We don't need no trouble. We don't need another battle, another war." He came close, kneeling before her, bathed in moonlight, shoulders dusted with snow. "I'll take you away, Kiki, to the mountains. Build you a cabin. We can live out our years together. It'll be like we were never apart, like none of those bad things ever happened."

"We can't. Dalgoran needs us. He has a dream, a vision."

"Big swinging horse bollocks to his vision! We have a right to happiness, Kiki. We did our fighting for Vagandrak, for Tarek. We spilt blood and cracked skulls and gave everything to rid the land of Morkagoth. But you know what I learned? Nobody truly gives a damn. The people, I mean. Those bastards I supposedly fought for. Ungrateful fucking City Watch; moaning teachers, shit-spouting academics, back-stabbing politicians; even the fucking farmers! Happy for us to do the dying. Not so happy if we needed their bloody help. I learned it real fast, Kiki. As long as they all have their warm beds, their ale and wine, soft open legs and one another to rut with, snotty nosed children to care for, they just get on with it, and leave the killing and the dying to the likes of us. We're fools, Kiki. We need to get out of this life. Out of this world. We're too old for this horse shit. What I'm trying to say, is, that I always loved you, even through the long lean years, and I always will love you. You're my soul mate. I should never have let you slip through my fingers. And now it's time; now it's time to retire, and let others do the fighting. And the dying. Especially the dying."

Kiki stared up at him, bathed white and pure. In this light, on this evening, she could see past the scars and broken features. She could see the young man again, giggling with her on the first wall of Desekra, Sanderlek, whilst they waited for the enemy horde. Young, foolish, full of their own legend-to-come.

He wants you, whispered Suza, a black snake in the night grass. *You should take him. Use him. Get rid of him. You've done it a hundred times before. Piss him away, in the same way he discarded you.*

No! That's not how it happened!

It's exactly how it fucking happened. I was there. I saw everything.

How could you possibly be there?

I've always been a part of you, Kiki. We came from the same broken egg. Sisters. Twins. Only you got all the luck, all the breaks, all the favours from father; I was left to rot and burn and crumble. And then, when I lost my...

Don't start with the sympathy shit again. Why can't you leave me in peace? I want to be at peace!

I will make a pact with you, said Suza, words a gentle caress. Like a blade kissing a sleeping throat.

Go on.

When you are no longer an Iron Wolf, then I will leave you alone.

That's a hard ask.

I'm a hard bitch.

I noticed. A traumatised one, too. Well, how about this? I'll put up with your constant whining, your reluctance to let go of the past, your exaggeration of anything petty and bad that ever happened to you, and when I finally die, and I see you in the Halls of Chaos, or the Furnace, or wherever the fuck Den of Hell I end up... well, I'll stamp out your teeth and break your skull and send you to oblivion. How does that sound, sister bitch?

"I'm going back to the fire," said Kiki, shivering.

"Stay with me. Come away with me."

"No. Dalgoran needs me. He is like a father to me."

"And I can be a husband to you. And a father to your children."

He turned and she looked up into his face. He doesn't know, she realised. But then, only Dalgoran knew, and if he blabbed it to cheap whores and word got around, she'd cut his throat like all the other scum who'd abused her. No. Dek didn't know. How could he know? She stared at the hard brutal features. Once, he'd been ruggedly handsome. Now, he was just rugged. She could live with just rugged.

"I'm dying," she said, softly.

"What?"

"I have a cancer. Inside me."

"Have you seen a doctor? A surgeon?"

"Of course I have, Dek," she said, and stepped in close, putting her head to his chest, holding the big man. "They can do nothing."

"Who did you see? Did you see Corialis of Vagan? He used to tend the King. I have money." He thought about this. "I can *find* money. As much as you need. I can help you, Kiki. We'll get you the best!"

"Remember all that gold showered over our heroic heads by King Tarek? I already paid for the best, Dek." She took his hand, pressed it to her breast. "They cut me open. Here. To remove the growth. But it was too close to my heart. They said to remove the cancer would be to kill me on the operating table. And so they sewed me back up and it's there, growing, poisoning, consuming: eating me from the inside out."

Dek pulled away and stared down at her face. Snow settled on her upturned gaze. "That cannot be, Kiki," he said, with great gentility.

"It's a hard fact. So, I would ask you, Dek, in all and total unfairness, having laid this great news at your feet, that you do me several favours."

"Anything, Kiki. I'd do anything for you."

"Make an effort with your brother, Ragorek."

Dek remained silent, though his teeth ground together.

"Make an effort with Narnok, when we see him; no matter what your reasons, in his eyes you stabbed him in the back. You betrayed his friendship, his brotherhood and his love."

"And the third?"

"Come with me. Follow Dalgoran. Let's see where this adventure leads. But together. I want you by my side again, Dek. I've been alone for too long."

He leant forward and he kissed her. And she sank into his embrace.

The snow was coming down thick and fast. Dalgoran was pushing a fast pace, and Ragorek cantered up beside Dek, horses kicking through snow. "He's a hard bastard for such an old bastard."

"Tougher than you could ever know," grunted Dek, eyes straining to see through the thick flurries. "By all the gods, this snow will be the death of us."

"We are fools to still be on the road."

"Dalgoran reckons it's another hour and we should hit Skell Fortress; haunted, empty shit-shell that it is. But still.

A broken roof and crumbling walls are better than another night in the open. I could barely sleep last night!"

"Because of the cold, or because of the extra warmth?"

Dek eyed his older brother. "Don't get smart, fucker, or I'll knock out some more teeth."

"Ahh, your friendly banter is ever a tonic for this winter chill."

They rode in silence for a while. Finally, Ragorek said, "Listen, Dek, I wanted to explain something. I want to…"

"No." Dek held up his hand. "Let's stop there. The fire burned hot and took her away. Let's leave it there; draw a line in the sand and walk forward from this point on. How does that sound, Rag?"

"It sounds good, brother."

Dek nodded, and they both returned gazes to the trail.

"You have been to Skell Fortress before?"

Dek nodded.

"Isn't it… haunted?"

"Worse than haunted, brother; Skell carries the souls of demons. It's a real bad place, through and through," and with those words he huddled under his cloak, and tried to ignore the cold, the wind, the ice and the snow.

SKELL FORTRESS

Wind screamed across the land. Night had fallen. Thick snow swirled in a harsh blizzard. Skell Fortress, a thousand years old, at least; crumbling, abandoned, it loomed from the snow and dark with a shocking suddenness and a distressing, massive oppressiveness. As if it were some great and terrible beast that would suddenly reach out, plucking them from their mounts and crushing them totally.

Cowering against the weather, they plodded under the massive entrance archway where once a huge gate had stood. Now, its tattered, shredded remains hung from rusted iron hinges thicker than Dek's waist, and did little to block the gathering snow drifts.

Kiki stopped just within the arch. She'd heard the stories of Skell Fortress. Or Skell's *Folly* as it had become known; but had never visited this supposedly haunted relic. Until now.

It was big.

No.

It was *huge*. Bigger than any fortress had a right to be.

Kiki's head lifted back, chin tilting to the dark heavens as she surveyed the massive, vast array of towers and bulkheads, walls and blocks and warehouses. Desekra Fortress guarding the Pass of Splintered Bones through the Mountains of Skarandos was BIG; four walls and a keep

BIG. Skell had only one surrounding wall and a central keep, but its vast vertical size was something to blow a soldier's mind.

"What was it guarding against?" she said, words whipped away by the dog-snapping wind.

"Who knows?" said Dek.

"But... here. Beside the marshes. There is nothing worth guarding."

Dek nodded. "Maybe the landscape changed?"

"Or the mountains grew legs and shuffled away? Who would build such a thing? Here, on a flat plain, on the edge of the Rokroth Marshes. What's the damn point?"

"They had a reason," said Dalgoran, looming from the darkness. He kicked from the saddle and boots thumped old, weathered cobbles. "Or they wouldn't have put in so much effort. Come on. We can stable the horses up here."

"And build a fire," said Dek, shivering. Not because of the cold. Dek could stand the cold. This was more to do with the... ambience. An umbrella of protection. From... bad things.

Kiki dismounted, and calming her horse, walked the mare towards the low-lying stable block ahead. Again, age-old stone, a thatched roof that had almost caved in and was bowed under a weight of thick, glistening snow.

They stabled the horses, each in silence and thinking strange thoughts. For Kiki, she contemplated the walls of the stable as a starting point. The whole structure of Skell Fortress felt... *wrong*. Wrong in her skin, her flesh, her bones, her brain. It was subtle, she had to admit; like a gentle infusion. But it was there, tugging at the corners of a person's mind; at their vision, and twisted imagination. There was something deeply *wrong* about Skell Fortress.

Rubbing his horse with a handful of straw, then settling a blanket in place, Dek listened to the howling wind, and the over-bearing silence of fallen snow, then cocked his head at Kiki. "What is it?"

"What do you mean?"

"It's subtle, I'll grant you, but something is out of place here; out of joint with the world."

Kiki wanted to disagree, but found she couldn't. She felt light-headed, like the time she came around from the operating table and found a cluster of doctors, surgeons, nurses, tending her. Bright lights. Feeble excuses. A surreal experience; not of this world.

Without speaking, she stepped from the stable block and simply stared.

The wall was high and thick, gloss black, some sections crumbled away forming huge Vs of erosion. The original stone masonry was exquisite; or would have been in its day. Even now, many hundreds of years later, it gave a feeling of solidity, robustness, so if this place had to be held against the enemy, it would still have the...

Mass, she decided. The word was *mass*.

"What are you thinking?" asked Dek, stepping out beside her, his arm snaking around her waist.

"I'm thinking the walls are not straight."

Dek stared. "By all the Gods, I think you're right!"

"You *think?* Look at them! A blind man could make out the irregularities. But do you know what's really strange?"

"Go on."

"I think it was by design. I think Skell Fortress was built this way."

Dek stared long and hard at the subtle, disjointed walls. Angles were not quite right. Nothing obvious,

but it seemed like the whole place had *shifted* slightly.
Was maybe built on soft foundations. But there were no
cracks, no breaks, no missing mortar.

"But… why?"

Kiki frowned, and brushed snow from her long leather
coat. "How the hell should I know? I'm just an unwilling
observer. But it's weird. Everything is out of place. Every
joint and angle is just that little bit wrong. Like Skell was
built in a different time; in a different world."

Dek held on to Kiki's words as they moved across a vast
courtyard that was insanely proportioned; far too large to be
practical. It was more of a…

"Killing ground," said Kiki, filling in Dek's blanks.

He grinned, and slapped her on the back. "I like a girlfriend
who takes in the details and understands military strategy."

"Girlfriend?" The words held more ice than the entire
battlements of Skell Fortress.

"Well, you know, you are my… friend, and you're…"

"A girl? Really? Dek? Are you truly that goat dumb?"

He slapped her on the back again, dislodging some snow,
and gave a laugh like a short bark. "I could call you my
wife, but then I'd have to marry you." He grinned, showing
several missing teeth.

"Is that supposed to be a joke?"

"Er… yes?"

Tossing her head and carrying her saddle, Kiki stalked
away, disappearing down a wide avenue of massive stone
blocks, all of which had been cut at irregular angles and yet
which still fitted together perfectly, despite the centuries.
Dek stood, looking confused for a moment before General
Dalgoran came up behind him.

"Son, you'll give up your whole life trying to understand
them."

"Am I being a simple sheep herder, here? I studied military tactics under Szen Thu!"

"Ahhh," said Dalgoran, knowingly. "This is the Art of Women, not the Art of War. And I'll give you five big gold pieces if you can decide which one is the more complex."

"War?" suggested Dek, and grinned again, wiping snow from his nose. "Come on, Dalgoran. I'll buy you a drink in the mess."

"I've a feeling your money's no good here."

Dek scowled. "With my reputation, my money's no good *anywhere.*"

"This is a bar full of ghosts."

"I don't care! As long as there's some hard liquor!"

Kiki, yawning, padded down long stone corridors after Dalgoran. He still wore his armour and his sword was sheathed at his hip. He carried a fire brand, the light of which cast deep shadows on damp stonework. He turned, smiling at Kiki, face lit like a demon, and she returned with a tilt of the head, and a questioning smile of her own.

"We must go to the chapel," he said.

"But it's the middle of the night, General."

"I need to show you something."

The walls contained large patches of damp and were covered with black mould and green moss. Underfoot, the large stone flags were uneven, buckled, bent, and Kiki traced her fingers down a rough hewn block wall. Again, the angular cuts fitting perfectly together. She frowned. It would take an absolute genius to cut such stonework. That, or an absolute madman.

They reached an archway, and a terrible cold draft cut through. Water dripped. A wooden mantle had warped and swollen, bulging with a bright white fungus.

Kiki ducked warily under the bloated wood, and they entered a narrow corridor with a sandy floor which led steeply downwards.

"This way."

Firelight danced from the walls as they passed a hundred recessed alcoves bearing small, magnificently carved statues, angels on one side, demons on the other. The corridor ended after a hundred paces and Kiki got a real, tangible impression she was underground and the sheer vast *mass* of the old fortress squatted above her, threatening to collapse and bury her alive. She shuddered and something deep in her soul, some primeval fear, went *click*.

They reached a door. This time, there was no damp, no infiltration of water or fungus. It was bone dry and Dalgoran pulled a large iron key from beneath his leather coat. He slid it into the lock and it turned with the tiniest of neat snicks. The door, a good foot thick, swung silently open.

Kiki ducked a little, peering inside as Dalgoran moved forward and went around the circular chamber, lighting brands set in stone brackets. Kiki stared in wonder. The floor was bare stone, the walls hung with fabulous intricate tapestries, twelve feet in height and showing battles and conquests from Elder Days. There was a small, discreet stone altar, very basic in design, and low stone pews in double rows leading back from the altar to where she stood. The whole chamber felt... Old. Pagan. From Before Times.

And then she looked up, and her awe was complete. The entire arched roof was lined with precious stones of all types: emeralds, rubies, diamonds, sapphires, and the criss-crossing arched beams were inlaid with beaten gold.

As Dalgoran lit the brands, and fires blazed, so the ceiling sparkled and glowed and light swept in patterns across the… words.

"What does it say?" asked Kiki, words no more than a whisper.

"*An haerarch Equiem*," said Dalgoran, lighting the final brand and moving to the altar, where he placed the burning torch in the open mouth of a demon.

"Which means?"

"*In praise of the Equiem*. They were the Old Gods, Kiki. The *Bad Gods*. Or so it went."

Kiki moved forward, and gave a little shiver. "Why are we here, Dalgoran?"

"I need to speak to Jagged. And to show you something."

"Why *here*?"

"How can I explain this? There is magick, in the land, in the rocks and earth, in the seas and the mountains. Forget the tales of childhood, with sparks and streams of fire and glowing eyes and all that other horse shit; this is an *energy*, a dark energy, based on the four elements of the universe which complement one another, run in harmony. It oozes through the world, deep in the lines. It is a circuit, Kiki, and we can tap into it. One can use it; if one knows how."

Kiki nodded. "I have dreamt about such things. A long time ago. When I was a child." Dalgoran removed his coat and helm, placing them to one side. She watched him. "Is this dark energy safe?" she finally managed.

"Of course it isn't safe," he snapped, then checked himself. "We are dabbling with a great power, Kiki. Have you ever watched a fire consume a forest? Have you ever ridden the sea in a violent storm? Nature is awesome, violent, unpredictable. And this is a direct chainway to the Equiem; if they still exist, of course."

"I thought they were just an ancient myth," said Kiki, voice low.

Dalgoran, eyes hooded and masked by shadow, shook his head. "They lived, Kiki. Tens of thousands of years ago. They lived and they ruled. Not something you learn about in Vagandrak history, for the arcane Lore is illegal. Too much power and too much knowledge are a very dangerous combination, eh girl?"

Kiki nodded again, eyes shining. She had always worshipped Dalgoran; followed him as a general, despite the curse of the Iron Wolves, and listened to him like a father. But now she was learning there was more to the old man than she could ever know. He wasn't just some old soldier in love with nostalgia and middle-aged has-been heroes; he was something unique. A part of the ancient *magick*...

Dalgoran drew his sword and approached the altar. He knelt on the single step and said three low words Kiki did not catch; then he stood and moved to the stone plinth and suddenly, in this light, in this place, to Kiki's already sparked imagination she realised it was not a table; not a *table*, oh no. It was a sacrificial altar. A place of death and energy and channelling and magick.

Dalgoran lifted the sword, gripping the pommel, blade a vertical shimmering totem carved with ancient runes from the general's considerable ancestry. Only then did Kiki see the brass circle in the floor before the altar's platform.

Dalgoran inserted the point of the blade into the slot, and with great care, lowered the sword until only the hilt was visible. But still he gripped the weapon, with both hands, his muscles trembling. Kiki waited patiently, but nothing happened. After a few minutes she began to grow impatient, and realised a slow cold was creeping into the chapel. She began to shiver, and realised her toes inside her boots were frozen.

"Dalgoran?" she asked, quietly.

There was no response. She blinked, then realised ice was shining in his grey hair and beard.

She took a step towards him, wondering if this was normal; whatever normal was supposed to be.

Her boot slid on ice.

"Dalgoran?"

And then he spoke, voice loud enough to make her jump and seeming to boom around the hollow stone chapel.

"Jagged? Is that you?"

"It is I," came the reply, but it was metallic; hardly the voice of a man.

"Have you reached King Yoon?"

"We are a day away. He is camped thirty miles east of Drakerath with thirty thousand infantry and a thousand archers. If we are right about the mud-orcs, then he could support Desekra. With forty thousand men in total on the walls, we would stand a much better chance. All depending on how many of the filthy bastards are coming our way, of course."

"Make a strong case, Jagged."

"Be sure, Dalgoran, I will. Have you found the Wolves?"

"Kiki and Dek. We go now for Narnok."

"I hope you're right about them."

"I am right."

Dalgoran went silent, hands trembling on the sword's pommel. Then he spoke, more quietly now. "Kiki? Go in my coat pocket. There's a pouch. Bring it to me."

She did as she was bid, shivering now, her own hair filled with ice. The pouch was leather and contained...

something soft. Organic. Like meat. She carried it to
Dalgoran, and he held out one hand.

She tipped the contents into his palm, and almost
recoiled. It was a dark meat, containing skin, tufted fur, and
a small fragment of bone. Dalgoran closed his fist around
it, then suddenly turned, looking at Kiki. "Come here,
hold the sword's pommel with me. We will look into the
future together. We will see where this beast originated."

Every atom in Kiki's body wanted to scream a refusal,
but ever the soldier, she obeyed Dalgoran's command.
Climbing onto the altar, she knelt in the ice and grabbed
the sword with both hands, covering Dalgoran's large
fingers with her own.

"Now close your eyes," he said, and drifted into words
from ancient language that were soft, musical, but turned
slowly harsh and guttural. Kiki felt goosebumps scatter
across her flesh, and the hairs on the back of her neck
stood up good and hard.

"We will see, we will see…" he said, *and Kiki found herself
drifting, and looking out from alien eyes onto a world that seemed
different, curved around a small globe, corners shining, and she
was running with a pack, and glancing left and right she saw
other huge horse creatures, twisted, broken, bent, deviated: huge
equine heads stretched wide open showing row upon row of razor
fangs… and they were screaming, the horses were screaming, and
she realised she was screaming with them as they thundered on
broken hooves out from the borderland and onto the plains before
Desekra. Dawn was breaking, winter sun streaming over high
mountain ridges gleaming with black rock, snow and ice, and she
ran, huge muscles pumping beneath her so she was in a flood, a
huge dark flood of screeching, drooling mud-orcs…*

She let go of the sword with a start, and gasped,
coughing, leaning forward on her knees as Dalgoran

withdrew the sword, which was now rimed with ice, and slid it into its sheath at his waist.

He stood, and reached down. Kiki took his hand, looking up at him in horror.

"Will that happen? Truly?"

"I do not know. With the flesh I held, we were linked: to the past, the present and the future. But at least it confirmed one thing. The mud-orcs *are* back."

"How many?"

Dalgoran shrugged and turned, heading for the door. Then he stopped. Glanced back. "More than last time," he said. "Come on. We need to reunite the Wolves. We are running out of time."

A thousand miles away, in a black silk tent, Orlana's eyes opened in the darkness with a *click*. Outside, the splice were howling. Zorkai snored beside her, his handsome face troubled in sleep.

"I see you," she whispered, and stretched out her hand which coiled with serpents of mist.

"I know you," she breathed, licking her blood dark lips.

"Come to me, Iron Wolves. Come to Orlana."

MUD-ORCS RISING

The Oram Mud-Pits. More than a thousand individual hollows, each one a small lake of ooze. They stank of sulphur, bubbling softly in huge craters amongst the violent upthrust of savage rocks; Nature's natural daggers.

King Zorkai stood on a rocky plateau, looking off towards the setting sun, a huge orange orb slowly dying over the vast horizon. It was bloated, like a seven day corpse. Suddenly, Zorkai felt as if he was going to vomit. He closed his eyes for a moment, calming himself internally; and then took a deep breath. He wished he hadn't, as sulphurous fumes filled his lungs and he spent the next three minutes choking.

Finally, wiping tears from his eyes, he glanced off across the Pits. They stretched away from his vantage point for as far as the eye could see; huge clusters of vertical jagged red rocks, each a sentinel mound guarding a vast elliptical chamber filled with mud and oily water, some black, some red, some a murky, metallic rust colour, some green like pus from a gangrenous wound. Many bubbled. Some were stagnant. But one thing was for sure: nothing lived here. Nothing could survive in this godforsaken place.

Orlana was standing out in the midst of the Mud-Pits, a tiny stick figure in flowing white robes. She should be dead, Zorkai knew; he was on the verge of puking his internal organs out and he knew from experience to move any further in would be to perish. And yet there she stood. The witch. The demon. The bitch. Zorkai smiled. But she was his key to becoming an Immortal Legend.

Hearing a whimper, followed by a deep-throated growl, he half-turned, but then paused and turned back to observe Orlana. He forced himself. She was walking toward him, bare feet treading lightly on the scorched, razor rock.

A pang of guilt rose in Zorkai like bile, but he quelled it savagely. Had he not killed his brothers and sisters? Had he not slit the throats of cousins lying in their beds? There was a time for feeling, emotion, pity, understanding and love; and there was a time for brutality, and savagery, and greatness. Now, he knew, was a time for greatness.

Behind, on the paths leading to the Oram Mud-Pits was a huge stream of people. His soldiers had emptied the hospitals, toured the streets of Zak-Tan proclaiming a new incredible Healer had come to the palace, and how she would cure diseases, deformity, blindness, deafness and any other ailment a person suffered. Thousands had poured from their homes and had been led west away from the city with carts of food and wine, with promises of healing. How many had Tsanga said? Fifteen thousand, so far. And that didn't include those being brought on carts from the hospitals and the asylum.

Only now, the *splice* had arrived, savagely tearing apart several runners as an example to the others, and the huge group had been split into sections and escorted west; brought *here*.

Be strong, Zorkai told himself.

Soon, this abomination will be over.

And things can only get better.

He watched Orlana approach, and she gave him a cursory smile and passed him by, leaping up the rocks to stand at the summit, looking down on the winding paths and the plains beyond, and the huge gathering of the ill, the deformed, and the crying. She lifted her right arm and the splice began snarling, their huge heads lowered and weaving, nudging the people forward. Crying and begging, they began the trek up the remaining pathways until they reached the summit. A woman tried to run, turning and fighting her way free, but a splice bit her in half at the waist, showering women and children with crimson arterial gore.

"Feed the Mud-Pits," whispered Orlana, eyes bright.

Men, women and children were pushed, jostled and urged over the summit where they began to choke from the fumes, disorientation fast overcoming many. These were dragged by the splice and dumped unceremoniously into the many huge ovals of bubbling mud.

At first, Zorkai could not watch. Each scream pierced his heart. But then curiosity got the better of him and he opened his eyes, cutting off the cries and the begging, to stare down at these: the weak, being given a second chance.

As the sun sank, and darkness descended, so tens and hundreds were fed into the mud pools, where they sank, silently, without trace. Orlana stood beside Zorkai, watching impassively.

A woman screamed, arms outstretched towards her king. She was lame, he could see, with a twisted foot, hobbling urgently to get away from the snapping fangs of a splice which took her to the edge of a mud-pool and butted her, sending her into the slime. She thrashed for a moment, screaming, the thick red substance flowing into her mouth and throat – and then she sank, and was gone.

"The Mud-Pits need to be fed," repeated Orlana.

"I know," said Zorkai, both fists clenching, his left coming to rest on a sword hilt.

"This will build you an unstoppable army. You will see."

"Yes."

The work went on long into the night. Several fights broke out, mainly men, old soldiers, who formed small squares and refused to move. They were broken in seconds, dragged screaming and bellowing by their ankles up over the ridge and down, where they were tossed into the pools.

Men. Women. Crying children, their faces streaked with soot and dark sand. Even babes, wailing, squawking, and Zorkai gritted his teeth, muscles in his jaw tight, as they were tossed away, spinning: hurled into oblivion.

Finally, the numbers had thinned and the splice were taking the few remaining hundred further away, down rocky aisles between the hundreds of Mud-Pits which dominated the plain.

Orlana glanced at Zorkai. "It is not enough."

"You said…"

"I know what I said. But it would appear you are a healthy people." She smiled sardonically. "Tuboda!"

The great lion beast was there in an instant, his huge bulk bounding up the rocks, where he settled, gazing adoringly at Orlana. "Yes, Horse Lady?" he managed between his fangs.

"We need more."

"Your will, Horse Lady."

"Round up every second woman and child. We need the men for the merging…"

"Yes, Horse Lady."

"No!" snapped Zorkai, his eyes flashing.

"Rule with me, or…" Orlana lifted her head, gesturing to the massacre, "join them."

Zorkai's eyes narrowed. "You are destroying my people!"

"You will grow again. *This* will make you stronger. You will not just rule Zakora; you will rule Vagandrak, Zalazar, Lartendo, even the Plague Lands. They will speak your name for ten thousand years!"

"And what do you get out of this?" said Zorkai, suddenly.

"My plan goes much deeper than simple domination," said Orlana, and watched a hundred splice charge past, over the rocks, on their way back towards Zal-Tan, and the unsuspecting, sleeping population.

Zorkai awoke. For three days he had sat on the plateau, at first watching Orlana's splice feed thousands more into the mud, across the whole plain, across hundreds of massive pits which bubbled and accepted the gift without sign. He kept telling himself it was something he had to do; this mass murder was for the greater good. But some small sliver of his heart did not quite believe it.

"Your people will rise again!" Orlana soothed him, kissing his neck.

And slowly, she had eased away his doubts, and he found the sliver of disbelief, and sorrow, and extracted it, tossing it away like a lost pin. He hardened his heart, focused his mind, and knew he fucking *knew* this was what had to be done. To become strong, there had to be sacrifice. To rule, there were always casualties.

Night had fallen.

Fires burned out on the plain, and down amongst the Mud-Pits.

Now, all the screaming was gone and done.

Now, Orlana said, all they had to do was *wait*.

"The mud-orcs are a creature of flesh and bone and magick; they are as old as the world, a primitive seed held in the Mud-Pits of Oram where they can be summoned, and grown, starting with the flesh of others as an agent to stimulate rebirth. They are not strictly born, but are a resurrection of past mud-orcs; so even when they are young, they retain incredible fighting skill combined with a savagery rarely seen amongst Men."

"Why will they serve you?" asked Zorkai, eyes wide.

"Because I channelled the magick of their rebirth. I am their Mistress. I am their Lady. I am their Queen."

And now, he watched as the pits started to bubble with an intensity he found alarming. The ground shook. His lungs were scorched from the hot air and the sulphur. And now it grew worse, and huge clouds of vapours, of gas and fire, erupted from the pits. There came a movement, a surging of thick mud and something, *something* emerged, climbing up the jagged rocks to stand, naked and proud, bigger than a man by more than a full head, with wiry limbs and a wide chest and narrow hips; its skin was a pale green with streaks of red like open wounds; its head round and hairless, eyes jet black, tongue blood red, fingers tapered into long crooked claws, feet the same; and its first words were growls of blasphemy and it lifted its head to the moon and howled like a wolf...

More came, climbing from the Mud-Pits and Zorkai's hackles were standing on end, his heart thumping hard in his chest, mouth dry, bladder full, as these creatures, these visions from nightmare, from the darkest dreams of terrified children, climbed from the Mud-Pits in their tens, then their hundreds. Gradually, the whole plain of rock and pits was alive like a writhing, shifting ant nest as the mud-orcs were reborn, climbing gleaming from the lakes of mud, and they moved in a great stream of green and blood-red flesh towards Orlana, where she stood, arms apart, palms outwards in greeting, smiling at the abominations emerging before her...

"Is there a captain amongst you?"

"He will come, Lady," hissed, and growled, and spat one mud-orc with long yellow fangs and a dark, intelligent gaze.

"Go, assemble on the plains below alongside my war tents, and when your leader arrives, send him to me."

They moved like huge cats, agile and supple despite their size, loping off down the trails towards the fluttering white tents Orlana had erected. A huge stream of mud-orcs flowed down onto the plains and, without instruction, they began building their own camp. Tuboda was down there, giving out weapons and tools. Before long, several units headed off to distant stands of woodland; maybe a hundred mud-orcs in all.

"What are they doing?"

"Building a camp for when their captains arrive. The captains will come later; and you'll know about it, when they do."

"Big, are they?"

"Big, and mean, and more than a match for one of my splice."

"You sound like you're a fan," said Zorkai, weakly.

"I am. We've worked together before." She took his hand and tugged him towards her. "We have time. Come down to the tents. I have need of you."

Zorkai could feel the need emanating from his new queen, and in deep shame, and his own deep lust, he could not bring himself to refuse her.

It was the middle of the night when Zorkai rolled from the blankets and furs, in desperate need of a piss. He could see the flickering of many fires beyond the canvas walls, but what he witnessed as he opened the flap and stepped outside made him gasp...

The mud-orcs spread away across the plain like a dark ocean, their fires burning, their low, grunting songs chanting with a primeval rhythm. Drums beat, and the screeches of stressed steel reached Zorkai's ears.

"What the hell are they doing?" he muttered, and then turned – to find himself an inch away from the silent mud-orc captain, with its arms folded, eyes watching him. The creature was massive, and stank like a corpse. Zorkai looked slowly upwards, from the heavily muscled chest, with its thick, rippled green and red skin, full of warts and lesions, up to the wide brutal face and head, where tusks protruded from the lower jaw and gleaming black eyes surveyed him with an intelligence he did not enjoy.

Slowly, the mud-orc captain lifted a great, swarthy hand and pushed Zorkai in the chest. His hand went to his sword-hilt and the mud-orc gave a wide, evil smile. "Where is Horse Lady?" he rumbled.

But before Zorkai could speak, Orlana was there, her hand on his arm, nuzzling his ear. "Don't upset him," she said. "He's very, very hungry."

"Hun...!" but Zorkai snapped his mouth shut.

"Reporting, Horse Lady," said the creature, fangs chomping, a huge string of saliva drooling from his face. "Can I eat the human?"

"Not this one. I need this one."

"Oh." The mud-orc looked crestfallen.

"What is your name?"

"Vekkos."

"This is your order, Captain Vekkos. Take your battalion, scour the country for a hundred miles in every direction: every hut, every village, every town; find weapons, and armour, and food; but more importantly, bring me *people*. We must still feed the Mud-Pits. We must still build your ranks!"

"What we eat? We hungry! We mud-orcs need feed!"

"Pigs, cows, camels, snakes, whatever you find; but not the horses, Vekkos. Never kill the horses." Orlana smiled, cold eyes glittering. "Bring them to me," she said. "I have a very special treat in store."

The days passed. The mud-orcs brought hundreds of people; thousands of people. All were forced struggling into the Oram Mud-Pits. The mud-orcs made their own weapons, and their ranks expanded; and this larger force headed out, further afield, bringing back hundreds and thousands more. Only Zak-Tan remained totally unmolested, and the remaining population stayed in their homes out of sheer animal terror. The more mud-orcs were born, the more fresh battalions headed out scouting for flesh, now with carts for the living, piled high and soon to be fed into the mud.

And the wind howled mournfully. A song for the dead. For the dead.

After a month, Orlana called Zorkai to him. She was dressed in full battle armour, all black; a stark contrast to her beautiful white face.

"Yes, my Queen?"

"Now for the real test. We have forty thousand mud-orcs, and near five thousand of my beautiful splice. We will head west, across the borders into Kenderzand; they have been your blood-oath enemies for millennia. We will slaughter them. We will enslave them."

Zorkai lifted his head, eyes reading the madness in Orlana's face. But he smiled, and licked his lips, and said carefully, "We are not at war with Kenderzand; we currently have good trade relations. They are a much more prosperous people than we. We have contracts. We have treaties."

"Fuck your contracts and treaties. When we slaughter them, and take everything they own, and feed their flesh into the Mud-Pits, then you will see; then you will *know* that we cannot be stopped. This is our first real test, Zorkai; this is where we trial the mud-orcs, to see if they're as brutal as they look. To harden them in battle. To ready them, for the real war."

"There are three passes through the Kender Straits, all protected by high walls, and with sea to either side."

"Well," said Orlana, pulling on a plain black helm. "This is where it begins."

THE WAREHOUSE

"Welcome back, Narnok," whispered Xander, with the intimacy of a lover.

Narnok had been rocking the chair to which he was tied. He had felt the weakness in the front leg, and kept levering his weight on the flawed joint, until... There came a *crack*, and the chair leg snapped. Narnok was jerked forward into Xander, who jumped suddenly as Narnok lurched and his head struck Xander's nose. Xander went down hard, blood gushing, and Narnok kicked free one leg from the broken chair, the rope unravelling from his other ankle, and he stamped down on Xander's balls, then on his sternum, then on his face with three hard sudden blows.

Xander squealed, a long high pitched noise, his hands not knowing where to grab, and a door opened somewhere amidst the crates. The eight heavies who'd abducted Narnok back at the Pleasure Parlour piled in, armed with iron bars and helves; one also carried a sword. Narnok eyed the weapon coolly and stamped free of the broken chair legs and rope.

"Ahh, my lovely boys," he said, grinning, and delivered another heavy stamp that broke three of Xander's ribs. Xander groaned, wheezing.

The men spread out as Narnok backed to the tray of Xander's torture implements, grappling with a scalpel. It parted the rope and the remains of the chair fell away, rope trailing from both of Narnok's wrists. "Come on then, let's see what you've got," he rumbled.

The men were all a touch taller than Narnok and more heavily muscled. They sported a range of beards and pock-marked faces, and wore rough woollen clothing and cheap boots. But their eyes glittered with the promise of a coming fight and they were secure in numbers. The man with the sword gestured, and two men with iron bars approached warily. Narnok still held the tiny scalpel in one hand, the broken chair in the other. The two men rushed towards him and he hurled the chair, took an iron bar on the forearm and slashed the scalpel across his attacker's eyes in a horizontal stroke. The man went down screaming and Narnok kicked the other in the knee and took his iron bar as he writhed on the ground, leg folded back the wrong way. He cast the scalpel aside with a bright tinkle of steel and weighed the bar thoughtfully.

Narnok rolled his shoulders and tilted his head left, then right, with terrifying cracks of released tension. The two men at his feet were groaning at different pitches, and Narnok stepped over them, testing the weight of the bar and muttering, "Not as good as the axe, but it'll do." He looked up. And grinned. "What's it to be, then? Two at a time or all six at once?"

"Get him!" screamed the swordsman, and the heavies charged. The rest was a whirl of chaos with Narnok at the centre. He ducked a helve swing, jabbed the edge of the bar into a man's throat, kicked another in the balls, leant back to avoid a sword swing, smashed a left straight to another's nose, smashed a man straight over the head with his bar, took a blow on his shoulder, smashed his bar across a man's knees, jabbed his outstretched fingers into

another's throat, deflected a sword swing, charging
forward so the bar ran up the blade with a shower of
sparks and his knee came up in the man's balls, his
fist hammered him to the ground – and he took the
blade. He threw down the bar, swung the sword in a
whistling figure of eight, then glanced at the four men
still standing. "Let's finish this," he growled, and in five
strokes left four corpses bleeding on the stone flags.

Silence descended, except for occasional groans
from the wounded, and Narnok bent over, ripping a
man's shirt free. He cleaned the blade, admired the
weapon, then looked up as a figure stepped through
the doorway.

It was Kiki. Kiki!

Narnok did a double-take, then grinned from behind
his scars and milk-eye. "Well, well, well; don't tell me
you're behind this little skirmish, Captain?"

"You did well, Narnok." She moved closer, and he
read the pity in her eyes as she gazed upon his ruined
features. "Those were pretty severe odds." He nodded.
"For a normal man, at any rate."

"But then I'm not a normal man; I'm a Wolf," he
said, softly.

He reached out, and they grasped hands, and Kiki
stepped in yet closer, hugging the big man. Into his
shoulder, she said, words a little muffled, "I missed
you, Narn. Like you wouldn't believe."

"You too, little Kiki." He pulled back and gazed
down adoringly. Then he seemed to remember his
scars, and he pulled away from her grip, turning his
back on her. "I'm sorry you've got to see me like this."

"Like what?"

"Don't patronise me, Kiki."

She grabbed his arm, pulling him back to face her. Moving close, she repeated through gritted teeth, *"Like what?* Yeah, so you have your scars. We all have scars. Yours are on your face. So what? The point is, you're still an Iron Wolf, and you can still fight like a bastard. That's all I need to know."

"How did you find me?"

"Maria. She was a Red Thumb sympathiser, shall we say. I persuaded her to explain where you might be."

"Ahh. I confess. That… *surprises* me. I trusted that one." He grunted, and turned back to stare at Kiki. "So, you have a mission?"

"I like that. Straight to the point. No, 'Where have you been the last ten years, Kiki?' or 'You're looking younger and slimmer than ever, Captain'. Yes, I have a mission. One of considerable… challenge. I need you, Narnok. I need my axeman."

Narnok stared at her for a long time, and she met that gaze, unflinching at the milky eye, the horror-show of razor lines and criss-crosses, some white, some red, some puffed and infected, some narrow and healed and permanent; a crazy patchwork duvet of the flesh.

"Is it paid work?" he said, at last, watching her.

"Yes. Of course. As much loot as you can carry in an ox-pulled wagon."

He shrugged. "I don't need the money, you understand; but it's nice to be appreciated. Dalgoran set this up?"

"He's waiting with the others."

"Others?"

Kiki paused, biting her lip. Then she blurted, "Dek's here."

Narnok stared at her. "I've had better news." One of the wounded attackers suddenly reared up behind

Narnok, a knife in his fist. Without a word he turned, and back-handed the sword across the man's throat. Blood spattered like rain, and the body flopped to the ground. "Dek." Narnok contemplated this. "I remember what he did. That bastard."

"You'll have to put that behind you."

Narnok blinked, slowly, like a cat. "I'll think about it," he rumbled, then seemed to come out of a daze. "I need my axe," he said. Then glanced around. His eyes fell on Xander. His smile was not a pretty one. Even without the scars, it would have been horrific. Now, it was obscene. "And I need five minutes with that bastard."

Kiki gave a nod. "Make it three. We've got fifty Red Thumb bastards on their way. Bad news like you travels fast."

"Well, I reckon three minutes will be long enough," rumbled Narnok, stooping to pick up a glinting, silver scalpel, a toy in his huge bear paws. Then he moved towards the quaking figure of Xander, who tried to scramble backwards, away from the looming axeman.

Kiki was waiting outside. It had started snowing. The world smelt fresh and new to Narnok and he took great lungful's of bitter cold air. "Still alive," he muttered, then turned on Kiki. "Where we going?"

"Timanta."

"What, by Zunder? That's a dangerous city, Kiki. What's so important we need to go to that shit-hole?"

"Trista."

"Trista!"

"And Zastarte."

"Oh. Him."

"Yeah. But don't be getting any ideas about Trista; she's harder than she used to be. Apparently."

"Well, that's one diamond-hard bitch, then, because she was unbreakable and unreadable before I ever met her."

"Yes. What did you do to him, Narn?"

"Who?"

"The old torturer. Back there."

"I, er… I returned an old favour."

"What favour's that?"

Narnok grinned. "I cut out his fucking eyes. When I get my payback, I like it with a little bit of interest."

After detouring to the Pleasure Parlour, which was silent and dark, front door open, lanterns extinguished, a smell of blood in the air, Narnok got his axe – his huge, black, double-headed monster of a weapon. He followed Kiki back into the snowy street and, pulling on heavy leather cloaks, they headed across the city, Kiki a few steps ahead of Narnok, the big man constantly checking over his shoulder.

Dalgoran had rented a suite of rooms in one of Kantarok's larger taverns, but at this early hour of the morning the revelry was done, the drunks ejected, the floors scattered with sawdust, and candles now burned low and few. Only a complicated series of knocks and taps got Ralph the Landlord to open the door. Ralph had a big round head and a wide friendly face. He was portly and boisterous, even at this unholy hour, his body big and round, his cheeks puffed red behind a bushy black beard. He was a naturally happy soul, content with his role in life; that of drinking heavily, and getting others to drink heavily, whilst experimenting with the Joy of Food – "*All Food!*" he would studiously point out – as he watched his two girls grow into adulthood, like trees growing and spreading their branches, before they progressed out into the world.

Ralph eyed Narnok's axe with utter distaste. "No weapons in here, son," he said, finally, voice quavering a little as that milky eye seemed to fasten on him and suck out his very soul.

"I think you'll find I'm the exception," said Narnok, coldly.

"He's with me, Ralph. He's OK. I'll vouch for him."

"He doesn't bloody look OK to me," muttered Ralph, fumbling to lock the tavern door before leading them through the large main drinking area, gloomy and filled with shadows, and to the foot of the wide bare-board stairs. "I'll leave you here, Kiki. And you, er, whatever your name is." He glanced at the axe again.

"Don't worry. We just need sleep, then we're heading out in the morning. Well. Maybe around noon." She reached over and pecked him on the cheek. "Thanks for all you've done. It's much appreciated."

Ralph blushed a deeper red.

"My pleasure, Kiki, honestly, it's a great honour and..."

"Who is it?" screeched Ralph's wife, Beth, from the ground floor bedroom.

"I'm coming, love of my life," hollered back Ralph, and grinned apologetically. "Wedded bliss! Only for the mad!" he said, before disappearing behind a thick oak door, where heated words were exchanged.

Kiki heard phrases like, "...let them walk all over you," and "at this unholy hour of the morn!" She grinned again, almost forgetting that Dek and Narnok were about to meet for the first time in ten years. And the first time since... the incident.

She climbed the stairs, Narnok close behind, and onto a broad landing. They stepped through a door to the left, which she locked behind her, and a short corridor led to a square communal area with carpeted floor and low comfortable couches, and four separate doors leading to four separate rooms. On a table at the centre of the couches was bread, cheese, pickled onions and a glazed roast ham, along with several flagons of Vagandrak Red. Narnok dropped his axe with a *thunk*. "Food! Fabulous!" He ambled forward, grabbing a carving knife and sawing a thick slab of ham, which he skewered on the end of the knife to gnaw like a dog.

"Help yourself," said Kiki.

"Thank you, I will," mumbled the huge warrior from behind a mouthful of bread and meat.

"I'm turning in. Now remember! Be nice to Dek."

Narnok stared at her, and carried on chewing, and did not reply. Tutting, Kiki disappeared into her own room. She shut, and bolted, the door.

Narnok grinned. "So much for sisterly trust," he muttered, cutting a thick slab of cheese. It was creamy and soft. "By all the Gods, this is fine cheese!"

"Beth bought it especially for us, down at the farmer's market." Dek's voice was soft and low. "They love Kiki like a daughter. They dote on her. Lucky for us, or it'd be rancid pilchards and maggoty bread."

Narnok said nothing, but continued to chew, his back to Dek, his mind in a whirl. He'd imagined this moment a thousand times, *ten thousand times!* What he would say, what he would do, the violence he would inflict, the curses he would spit like venom. But a gauntlet of confusion grabbed his brain and squeezed hard and his mouth was dry and cheese dribbled down his scarred chin and he remembered, by God, he *remembered*...

Finding him rutting in bed with her, her black curls scattered across the pillow and down her pale naked body...

The fight; massive, massive fight…

And Dek's face, cheeks wet with tears, eyes wide in absolute horror…

"Do you remember the last thing you said to me?" rumbled Narnok, slowly, rolling back his shoulders and then turning. By the bright flickering candlelight he saw Dek standing in the doorway to his room, feet bare, wearing cotton trews and a loose, white cotton shirt. He was as big as Narnok remembered. But then, Narnok was no little girl.

"I said I was sorry," whispered Dek, iron eyes hidden by shadows.

"I went and got my axe. I was going to kill you."

"I know."

"Instead… well. Katuna was not pleased with her beating. She thought it unjust, despite fucking my best friend behind my back. And she wanted my money, the whore. She did this to me, Dek; she fucking did THIS to me!" He strode forward, kicking a couch out of the way. Dek did not move. Narnok thrust his scarred face, his milky eye, into Dek's impassive gaze and screamed, "SHE FUCKING DID THIS TO ME! CAN YOU SEE? CAN YOU UNDERSTAND HOW MUCH I HATE YOU?"

Ragorek and Dalgoran, in the other room playing cards with a bottle of brandy, stared at one another over their tumblers of amber fire.

"Maybe we should intervene?" said Ragorek, gently.

"No," said Dalgoran.

"They might kill one another."

"Yes, they might do that," said Dalgoran.

"Then surely we should stop them?"

"My old mother used to have a tomcat. A vicious, nasty piece of shit it was, scratch your skin from your bones given half a chance. A real heavyweight bruiser: stocky, with tattered ears and liquid hate for a stare. Her friend moved to another city, and she had another tom herself; left it for my mother. Mother put them both in a room together and locked the door until they'd sorted it out. It was messy."

"These are not tomcats," said Ragorek.

"The principle is the same. We have to let them get it out of their systems. Let them sort it out their own way. So it is, sometimes, with men."

"Do you know what they did?"

"No. But they'll sort it out. Trust me."

Back in the communal area, the two men stood toe to toe, nose to nose. Narnok was shaking with rage, but Dek was calm, breathing deeply, his eyes locked to those of his old best friend.

"I won't fight you, Narnok."

"But I'll fucking kill you!"

"So be it."

Narnok stared at him. "Damn you, you bastard!"

"I'm sorry, Narnok. Truly. If I could take it back, I would. What happened was bad; it was wrong. I have my excuses, but I'm pretty sure you don't want to hear them. And... your wounds. I did not know about that. Not till years later. If I had known, we could have hunted them down together; tortured them together."

"But we did not," said Narnok, softly. "Instead, you fucked my wife."

"Yes."

"Was she good?"

"Yes."

"Were *you* good?"

"No. I was out of my skull on honey-leaf and whiskey."

"I don't believe you."

"Those are the facts, brother."

"Don't call me your fucking *brother!* I've heard how you treat your brothers. Well, this one ain't going to lie down and die. This one is going to kick your fucking teeth out in this very room."

Dek stared into Narnok's eyes and realised this wasn't going to end without bloodshed. Narnok's pain, both psychological and physical, was too great. He wanted his payback, and Dek had to say, had to admit it from the darkest reaches of his soul, he could not blame the man; couldn't blame him at all. Well, if that's the way it was going to be, then that's the way it was fucking going to be.

Dek rammed his head forward, breaking Narnok's nose, and the big axeman spun away, arms outstretched, blinded. He stumbled back over a low couch and knocked a flagon of wine from the table, where it glugged onto the carpet.

Dek stepped forward and cracked his knuckles.

"Well, *brother,* fuck it, if that's what you feel you have to do, then that's what we must do. Come on, you big bastard. Get up and fight. Or are you down and out already?"

Narnok climbed to his feet, snarling, and charged Dek with arms outstretched. Dek threw a right hook, but Narnok jerked his head, avoiding the blow, and cannoned into the pit fighter; they both slammed back against the wall, and Narnok punched Dek in the belly as his arm circled his throat. Dek grabbed Narnok round the waist, lifting him into the air and throwing him back. Narnok twisted like a big cat, landing on his feet, and as Dek charged him a front-kick checked his advance.

They circled, down into the communal area. Narnok growled and, using the table as a spring board, scattering

bread and cheese across the carpet, launched himself
headlong at Dek, grappling the man to a low couch. They
were punching one another: heavy body blows. Dek tried
another headbutt but Narnok twisted, and slammed his
own head into Dek's face, breaking *his* nose. Now both
had faces covered in blood, and their pummelling slowed
a little as blows thudded home. Narnok cracked one of
Dek's ribs. Dek bit into Narnok's shoulder and the axeman
howled, clubbing his fist into Dek's broken nose… and as
Dek pulled away he tore a strip of flesh in his teeth.

"You dirty stinking fucking cheating bastard," said
Narnok, grabbing the torn flesh.

"It's a free for all in the Red Thumb Fighting Pits."

"This ain't the fighting pits!" bellowed Narnok.

"Well, you turned it into one. So, here we are."

They circled, and Dek hooked his foot under the table,
flipping it up at Narnok and charging after the barricade.
Narnok went down under the roast ham and a wine flagon,
which spun across the carpet disgorging fine red, which
glugged as it escaped. Atop the table, Dek jumped up and
down as Narnok wrestled to be free, suddenly tipping the
platform and sending Dek twisting sideways.

With a growl, Narnok ripped a leg from the table and
hurled it at Dek, whose arm shot up, deflecting the blow.
Narnok ripped another leg free and the two men, now armed
with short wooden clubs, advanced on one another…

"I think it's time you put up your weapons," said
General Dalgoran, from the doorway. "You've done
enough damage."

"Fuck off, old man," hissed Narnok through curtains
of rage.

"Or I can run my sword through your back, if you like."
He said it so casually, nobody disbelieved him.

"Do what you will," growled Narnok, and launched at Dek, and the clubs met with a heavy thud. They locked, sliding together, and both men's faces were inches apart.

"I should have hunted you down ten years ago," said Narnok through spit and blood.

"What, so you could die ten years younger?"

"I'm going to mash your face, you wife-shagging bastard."

"Looks like somebody already did that to you!"

Howling, Narnok took a step back and the table leg caught Dek between neck and shoulder, dropping him to his knees. His arms came up but the next blow smashed through them, hitting him in the face and knocking him onto his back where he lay, panting fast, blinded by blood.

Narnok towered over him, the table leg in both bloodied fists. He, also, was panting fast, and had a murderous gleam in his eye, his face a wrinkled, scarred mask of hate and rage. He lifted the table leg high into the air... and Kiki's voice floated to him through a sea of crimson.

"If you do that, you will regret it. Forever."

Narnok paused, club raised, hate burning in his heart.

"Don't do it, Narnok. You're better than that. He was your best friend, once. Let him prove himself to you."

Her voice was like music; and magick, as well. It soothed the savage beast in his soul and Narnok tossed away the club, where it bounced from the wall. Dek was scraping blood from his eyes and, blinking, looked up at the huge axeman.

Narnok stretched out his hand.

"You satisfied, now?" said Dek, and spat out a piece of tooth.

"No. I'll never be satisfied. But Kiki here wants it so; and at the end of the day, we're both Iron Wolves. That must count for something."

Dek took Narnok's hand and the axeman hauled him up.

They stared at one another for a while and Dek laughed, shaking his head. "You should do some stretching exercises. You're a little slow on the lower left. I'd put that down to old age, though."

"Yeah? Well I kicked your hairy cunt, *Pit Fighter*," said Narnok. Then he turned suddenly, to see Kiki, Dalgoran and Ragorek all watching. "What?" he snapped. "Get some more wine! This clumsy fucker has spilt it all!"

Narnok had drained a flagon in one, and went to clean himself up. Kiki sat, a bowl on her lap, cleaning the blood off Dek's face as the pit fighter tested each tooth in turn. "I hate breaking a tooth. Do you know how hard it is to find a good dentist? Last bitch almost burned off my tongue with her bloody hot steel tools. I broke her jaw for that one."

"It occurs to me, that you are not a subtle man," said Kiki, dabbing a cut above his eye.

"Aye. Well. Some of us are made that way."

"You weren't like that on the walls of Desekra Fortress when the mud-orcs screamed and charged towards us. 'Tall he was, noble and proud, a cloak he wore as if a shroud; his shining armour blazed like fire, the enemy burned on a funeral pyre!'"

"Fuck *off*, Kiki; that was a bad poem back in its day, and unlike wine, it has not matured with age. Whoever wrote it should be killed."

They stayed in silence for a while, and Kiki dabbed the cloth into a water and blood filled bowl, and slowly cleaned the blood around Dek's mouth.

"You let him beat you, didn't you?"

Dek met her questioning gaze. "I don't know what you mean," he said, eventually.

"Narnok is a fearsome warrior with an axe. And a formidable man in a fist fight. But I've seen you in the Pits, Dek; you're a machine. You're unstoppable. You scare *me*."

"I don't know what you're talking about," said Dek, gently, and smiled. "The point is, Narnok got some kind of a revenge. A small one, I'll grant you, but up here," he tapped his head, "it'll do him the world of good. And now we can travel, can we not? Now, we can head for Timanta."

"Good. I think it's time we got some sleep."

"Together?"

"Nice try, mister. But not tonight. Not in this life."

"But we…"

"No."

A commotion came from downstairs. A crashing sound, followed by a repeated banging, as of wood on wood.

"Narnok fall down the stairs?" grinned Dek.

"No…" said Kiki, frowning. "That was far too loud…" She gathered her sword and moved to the door leading to the stairs. Dalgoran came from his room, his own blade in his hand, closely followed by Ragorek.

"What is it?"

Kiki gave a shake of her head and opened the door. Another crash echoed up the stairway and Kiki ran to the top of the wooden flight; Ralph was at the bottom, backing away, hands outstretched. "No," he was saying, hands trembling, "No, please, no!" and then he turned, and saw Kiki and his face contorted and he screamed, "Please, help me!" as something *big* hit him hard and fast, a blur of movement that shocked Kiki so much she took a step back. A ruptured shrill scream pierced the tavern and the creature, a twisted, grotesque deviation of horse and *something else* lowered its head and bit straight through Ralph's red puffed cheeks, allowing his brain slop to spill out like jelly from a bowl.

It screamed again and shook its head from side to side like a dog with a bone. Then it looked up, its elongated equine head, with a huge lump to one side and random tufts of black spider hair sprouting, fixed on Kiki.

"By the Seven Sisters," she said, voice hushed, taking a two-handed hold on her sword.

"Ralph! Ralph, Ralph!" wailed Beth, rushing forward bearing a carving knife.

"Keep back!" yelled Kiki, but with one swift movement the horse beast turned its head, and a huge arm/leg came up containing long black claws that sprouted through a buckled iron horse shoe; it lashed out, claws decapitating Beth. Her head rolled down the corridor and her body hit the wall to leave a crimson smear against the patterned flower wallpaper.

Kiki growled and took a step down towards the beast.

"I'm going to cut your fucking horsehead off," she said.

"Wait!" hissed Dalgoran, and touched Kiki's shoulder. From behind the twisted horse creature appeared two more, pacing forward like hunting lions. These, also, were part horse and part *something*, and each one was broken and twisted in a different way, each one wore different coloured skin and had crooked fangs of various diseased colours. One had a tusk in the side of its head.

"What in hell's balls are those?" boomed Narnok, and hefted his axe, pushing to the front of the group.

"They move fast," advised Dek, remembering Heroes' Square. "Go for the eyes and the brain."

Narnok nodded, for once lost for words.

And with a clattering thunder of broken hooves and claws, the splice lowered their heads, screamed a high-pitched alien wail and bounded up the stairs towards the grim warriors above…

JAGGED EDGE

The vast, rolling plain lay dull green, frosted with white. Heavy bruised clouds dominated the sky, with various towering cumulonimbus killing the winter sun and threatening snow with clenched fists and thunder. Banners bearing the crest of Vagandrak fluttered and snapped in the wind, and as General Jagged breached a rise he felt his adrenalin pump as the army spread out before him; thirty thousand camped infantry ranged in twenty-two individual battalion camps, each with their own cooks and armourers, servants and whores. At the centre was a large white tent, surrounded by the smaller tents for the generals and captains, and Jagged's eyes narrowed at the black and white pennant of King Yoon.

"So, here you are, you bastard," he muttered. Jagged leant back in the saddle with a creak of leather, and both Tuokhane and Kerran gave him a nod. Big serious men, born warriors, they were not to be taken lightly and rode their mounts like born cavalry, backs ramrod straight, dark eyes masked in storm-shadowed helms. "Now, there's an army of Vagandrak iron, eh lads?" he grinned, but the two men said nothing. Jagged shrugged. They were here as bodyguards, not to swap pleasantries, and they took their roles with the utmost seriousness of the professional soldier.

"Yah!" Jagged kicked his horse into a canter and within thirty seconds ten riders broke away from the camp, galloping with lowered lances to meet the three men. As they came close, their lances lifted and Captain Gerander of House Trantor smiled at General Jagged.

"You're a long way from home, General!" He saluted. "I thought you'd retired? What brings you all the way out here?"

"I seek an audience with King Yoon," said General Jagged, watching the cavalry captain's face for signs of... what? Well, if the rumours were true...

Captain Gerander stiffened a little, and his eyes lost their humour. "The King does not enjoy the company of unwanted guests without appointment," he said, carefully. "I would urge the general to reconsider the need of such a meeting, and only approach our beloved King if the meeting is of the utmost urgency."

Jagged urged his mount forward and he patted Gerander on the shoulder. "It is, lad. It is. Don't you worry. Take me to him."

"You will have to surrender your weapons," said Gerander, voice carefully neutral.

General Jagged stared at the captain for a long minute, then gave a nod, his smile gone, his mouth a line, his eyes hard. "If that's the way it has to be," he said, and gestured to his two bodyguards who reluctantly drew swords and knives, handing them over to the Vagandrak riders.

Jagged rode beside Gerander through the sprawling camp. Soldiers glanced up from their tents, swords or bowls of soup as the group passed by, and many gestured, waved or nodded to General Jagged. Jagged was an old soldier, a veteran of many a campaign. He smiled at a great many men, often making comments like, "I see you there,

Belfour, you young pup," or "you missed some rust on that blade, Falazar; sloppy work, man, sloppy work!" and there were a few grins. But Jagged's overall impression was of an army not at the pinnacle of its morale.

Thunder rumbled distantly as heavily armoured guards took reins from Jagged. Gerander saluted, and said, "I must leave you here, General. It was good to see you again."

"And you, Captain. If you're ever north of Vagan, feel free to call in on my estates."

"A very kind offer, sir. Maybe one day I will."

Jagged's guards were bid to wait outside, and Jagged ducked under a tent flap and stopped, his mouth open.

King Yoon's war tent was... exquisite.

The ground was covered in thick patterned rugs and several mounds of fur had been built up, giving what Jagged could only presume were areas in which to be pampered. Several braziers burned, set on marble plinths, and gold and obsidian busts had been set around the tent's interior on low stands. Silks and tapestries hung from horizontal tent-poles, some fluttering from unseen breezes or updrafts. Incense burned, lavender, orange and... Jagged frowned. Was that *honey-leaf*? The fact it soon filled his head with muddy thoughts, slowing his reactions, gave him the answer. There were long tables containing rich cakes, salted meats, flagons of wine and crystal decanters of amber liquor, and deep within the haze of the tent Jagged suddenly realised there were women reclining on a low bed; three of them, completely naked, oiled, moving with the ease and languor of sun-lazy snakes as they slowly crawled over one another, kissing, touching, caressing...

"Your Majesty?" inquired Jagged, uncertainly. The honey-leaf stank in his nostrils worse than any burning city. It made him want to gag.

And then he realised with a start that the King was seated, watching the three oiled women. He was totally focused on their oiled bodies. His long shaggy hair was just as black and unkempt as Jagged remembered, and the joke around court was "that bloody king should get a good haircut!" only not to his face. He seemed to be wearing some kind of baggy outfit like jesters wore, fashioned from diamond panels of brightly coloured silk.

Jagged moved forward. "Your Majesty?"

"Ahh, Jagged."

The King stood and moved around the oiled beauties; for they *were* beauties and Jagged's breath caught in his throat. He coughed, feeling it inappropriate to speak about what they thought was an impending invasion in front of such… debauchery. He coughed again, but King Yoon loomed close, bending over at the waist but peering upwards toward Jagged's face. It was a most unnatural position, and Jagged took a step back.

"Your Highness. I come with missives of great urgency."

"You do, eh, General?" Yoon grinned at him, and fluttered a hand as if waving away a buzzing insect. "But more of that later. What would you like? I have some spiced wine or whiskey with ice. What'll it be, hmm?"

"Highness, I come with news of grave importance; information regarding the security of the realm!"

"Ahh, and what is it, then? We need more City Watch, do we, lad? We need more money in the royal coffers?" He gave a small giggle, which he stilled with the back of his hand, then gave a cough. He moved to the table where flagons were lined, and poured out two generous measures of something amber with tiny black things floating in it.

"No, Highness." Jagged took the glass but made no effort to drink. He could still see the oiled bodies in his peripheral vision. "Maybe you should dismiss the… ahh, performers, and we can sit down and speak of matters of war, of life and death; and of Desekra Fortress."

Yoon sighed and leant against a thick tent pole, sipping his drink. He rolled his great dark eyes and shook his shaggy mane of hair. His face was painted white, Jagged could see now in the light of a fish-oil lantern, and it made the creases of Yoon's face ever-deeper. To Jagged, this man looked little like a king, any king. But he was, and Jagged would have to work with what he had.

"It is a fact, Highness, that the army has been somewhat thinned at Desekra."

"Yes, yes, what of it? There is no threat from the south. I have papers from Zorkai to that effect. In fact, I believe I may be marrying one of his illegitimate daughters. When she grows by another ten years, ha ha."

"Highness, I bring word from General Dalgoran, your most trusted servant and former General of the King's Army."

"Dalgoran. Yes. I liked him. Nice man. Too tall. Never trust a too tall man, that's what I say."

"But, Sire," said Jagged, flustered.

"Oh yes. Message from Dalgoran. Do go on. You don't mind if I drink, do you? It's this damn weather. Plays havoc with my joints. Not that I'm getting old, you understand. It wouldn't do for my adoring and loving public to think I'm getting old. *You* don't think I'm getting old, do you, Jagged?"

"No, no, of course not, King Yoon."

"Do go on. You don't mind if I drink?"

Drink yourself to death for all I care, thought Jagged but, kept his face straight. "No, Highness. Please. Don't let me stop you."

"And your message?"

"A seer visited Dalgoran on his seventieth birthday. We thought it a fun game, a bit of frivolity for the old man, but her words were deadly serious, and she foretold the return of the mud-orcs from the south."

"I wouldn't worry about such ramblings," said Yoon, swaying his glass from left to right, his eyes watching the ice cubes chink.

Jagged frowned. "Not ramblings, Majesty. A *prediction*. And we would have been highly sceptical if we hadn't been visited within a few moments by the most horrific of beasts from darkest nightmare. A creature, part-wolf, broke through the party and killed the seer; we eventually put the monster down, but it took a lot of killing."

"A lot of killing," murmured Yoon.

"Yes, Highness. It was like nothing I have ever seen, in all my years of soldiering. It was twisted, broken, but almost like man and wolf had been merged together…"

"I think you were mistaken," said Yoon, flapping his hand, a movement accentuated by the silk and lace. "Now, if you don't mind, I have more pressing matters to attend to," and he'd already turned, eyes fixed on the oiled, gyrating women, his feet in brightly coloured soft slippers stepping away from General Jagged. His point was obvious. *The meeting is over. Please leave.*

Jagged gave a cough, any meekness he may have suffered now deserting him. His parade ground brusqueness returned, and returned with a vengeance. His eyes narrowed, and five decades of shouting at big men stomped to the front of his brain.

"King Yoon," said General Jagged, and something in the tone of the old man's voice halted Yoon and made the dandy king turn. "If the seer was correct, and there really is an army of mud-orcs heading for the Pass of Splintered Bones, their intention the raiding of Vagandrak, the slaughter of its civilians, the emptying of the royal coffers, the despoiling and slaughter of Vagandrak women; then, the king who would allow such a thing to happen would become a laughing stock; more, indeed it could be argued a rebellion might form and seek to overthrow some weak, selfish, narcissistic monarch who chose personal gratification over the safety and security of the country's people. You camp here, only a week's march from Desekra, with thirty thousand well-trained soldiers, and yet Desekra stands at quarter-compliment with only ten thousand. You can man the walls with this force, Majesty, and be seen as the king who did the right thing, thus preserving his honour and popularity with the people! Now, General Dalgoran entrusted me with this message, and you and I both know he deserves at least an answer from yourself, Highness. You must understand, we seek to offer no disrespect, but I beseech you, this is a time of urgent national security, if nothing else, send scouts south, seek out Zorkai and his princelings; for something sinister is afoot in our lands, King Yoon, and we cannot stand by and watch evil grow and invade."

Yoon considered this, walking forward, swirling his drink, his dark eyes hooded.

"Jagged?" he said, almost amiably.

"Yes, Majesty?"

"I have a gift." His arm came back, lace ruff puffing out, and for a moment Jagged thought the king was going to slap him. But it was worse than that. Much worse. The ruff concealed a slender black dagger, which slashed for Jagged's face and the old general leapt back, mostly from instinct and decades of training, for he had not seen the concealed weapon, nor even anticipated such a blow.

"Yoon!" yelled Jagged, mouth open in shock.

Yoon lunged forward again, and Jagged's arm came up. The blade slashed across his forearm and the straps which held his greaves; steel bit flesh, drawing blood, nothing serious, but pain forced Jagged to gasp and take two more steps back.

"GUARDS, GUARDS!" screamed Yoon suddenly, "ASSASSINATION!" and in a heartbeat five huge armoured men were there, swords rammed up against Jagged's throat, their sweat palpable, their breath stinking of onions as they bore Jagged to the ground and he went down under a sudden weight of men and armour.

A wall of iron filled Jagged's vision, and an incredible pain crushed his chest. His heart pounded in his ears and his mouth was suddenly dry. Why would Yoon do this? *Why?* And the answer came and the answer was a simple one.

Madness.

For long moments Jagged could not move, and his brain swirled in confusion. The King had quite obviously gone insane. But what to do? How to get out of this predicament with... he smiled grimly. His life.

He had to get word back to Dalgoran.

He had to warn his friend.

The weight shifted a little, and he heard barked orders. The steel armour shifted again, and some of the pressure released. A sword blade was held against his throat, and the soldiers slowly removed themselves. With a blink, General Jagged realised it was Yoon that held the blade.

"You think to come here and mock me?" sneered Yoon through his white mask of paint. "You use words like 'rebellion' and 'overthrow' and think this is acceptable language to use in front of your king?"

"Majesty, I..."

King Yoon raised the sword, half turning, and General Jagged started to lift himself up on elbows. But Yoon whirled back, the blade slamming down, hacking into Jagged's throat and opening a huge wound. Jagged gagged, eyes rolling, blood flushing from the huge crimson slash. Yoon lifted the sword again, dark eyes gleaming, and hacked down again, severing Jagged's head. The body flopped to the rich rugs, pumping out blood from a ragged neck stump, and the head rocked a little, tongue poking out, the features suddenly very, very old.

Yoon's soldiers stood by, uneasily. They knew who this great general was. But if King Yoon chose to execute him for talk of rebellion, or for attempted assassination, who were they to stand in his way?

Yoon was panting, lank hair in his eyes, sweat on his brow making trickles of white paint run down his face. He glared suddenly at the soldiers, and it took massive courage to not take a step back under that gaze, for there was murder in Yoon's eyes. Instead, he said, "Take his head outside, place it on a lance point, and stand the lance at the edge of the camp. *No man* tells me how to run my country. No man talks of rebellion. No fucker tells me *what to do!*" He screamed the last words.

The soldiers came forward, lifting Jagged's head and body and bearing them from the tent.

Yoon returned to the wide bed, sword dripping a trail of blood across fine rugs, to where the three

oiled ladies had halted their drug-infused ecstasy.
Yoon waved the blade. "Continue. And you." He
pointed with the bloody weapon at a shocked, oiled,
painted lady. "Open your legs. Open them wide. I need
some entertainment."

WOLVES BITE

Kiki and Narnok stood shoulder to shoulder as the splice bounded up the wide stairs; but it was too narrow for them to fight. "Behind me!" bellowed Narnok, and Kiki stepped back, twirling her short sword to loosen her wrist as Narnok tensed and hoisted his axe, hammering it down. It glanced from the shoulder of the beast, bouncing from thick hide as jaws snapped an inch from Narnok's face. The second splice, accelerating close behind, leapt left, claws digging into the plaster of the wall and launching past Narnok. Kiki ducked a swipe from a knife-sharp split hoof and rammed her sword up into the beast's belly. It screeched, landing next to Kiki on the landing. The first splice took Narnok's axe in its flank, roared, and hit him with a back-hand blow that sent Narnok flying through the banister spindles, cracking the wood, to topple to the hall below.

Kiki withdrew her blade, ducked another sweep of claws and thrust it higher this time. And Dek was there, his own longsword smashing overhead and cutting the creature down the middle of its skull. Still it came on, fangs gnashing, and with a twitch wrenched Dek's sword from his grip. Jaws clashed a thumb's breadth from Kiki's face and she wriggled right, sword trapped in the splice's chest.

"There's no room!" bellowed Dek. The third splice, halfway up the stairs, turned and leapt at Narnok, who was sitting, shaking his head, stunned. As it bore down on the dazed axeman, Dek leapt through the gap in the banister, both boots slamming into the creature's head and knocking it to the floor, Dek atop. But it reared suddenly, and he clung on as its head twisted round, snapping at him in an attempt to remove his face.

"Dek!" screamed Ragorek, and threw his sword. Dek caught the weapon in both hands, rearing up as if riding a horse, and plunging the blade down through the top of the beast's head. Narnok came from below, a knife in each fist, stabbing them forward into its belly and cutting upwards, opening it like a gutted fish. Bowels slithered out like an overturned barrel of eels, and the beast wailed, making a high-pitched keening sound, then slammed a hoof into Narnok's face sending him bouncing hard from the wall and down a long black well into unconsciousness.

Kiki was fighting a rearward retreat from the splice with her sword in its chest. She held two long knives; its claws slashed left, right, then diagonally, trying to open her from shoulder to hip. Dalgoran stepped alongside her, cool like no man had a right to be, and as the beast slashed for Kiki's face Dalgoran's sword slammed down, cutting the twisted appendage free with a crack of cut bone. Blood spewed out, drenching Kiki. Dalgoran drew back his blade, and rammed it hard through the creature's eye, leaning his full weight against his sword and driving it deep into the brain beyond. The splice hit the ground twitching, leaving just one creature standing on the landing.

It eyed Kiki and Dalgoran, who had his boot on the slain beast's head as he pulled free his blade. Ragorek was weaponless behind them, grim faced through his bushy beard, his fists clenched and ready. Below, Dek hacked his sword through the wounded splice's throat until its thick twisted head came free. Narnok was groaning in a heap.

The final beast screeched and leapt up the stairs towards Kiki and Dalgoran, taking his sword across one bent horseshoe with a shower of sparks, long equine teeth snapping for his face as claws raked across Kiki's armour and both were pushed back by the creature's sheer size and weight.

"Dek!" screamed Kiki, slamming her sword into rancid horse flesh. That great head swung towards her, teeth gnashing to chew through the skin of her shoulder like the gears of some ancient machine. She screamed as pain hit her like a hammer, twisting away, and shoved a knife into its eye. Dalgoran hacked at its neck two-handed, but its head dropped and slammed upwards with a snort of blood, ramming Dalgoran against the wall where the back of his head slammed stone, and he toppled to the side, stunned.

Ragorek ran forward, stooping to grab Dalgoran's blade, and together with Kiki he hacked and slashed as claws tried to cut their faces from their skulls and open their bowels and arteries. Kiki leapt over a slashing claw, slammed a left hook to the beast's face snapping a fang, and as Ragorek skewered its throat, holding its thrashing head in place, Kiki took her blade double-handed and hacked again and again and again, as blood and bits of brain and chunks of skull fell to the wooden floorboards. Eventually, the great moaning gnashing creature sank to the boards and was still, and Kiki stood, legs apart, still holding the sword with both hands. It was embedded in the dead splice's head.

"A bad business," muttered Ragorek.

Kiki nodded, and tugged free the blade with a crunch. She moved to Dalgoran, who was sat up, a trickle of blood at his temple. "How do you feel?"

"I'll live," he grumbled, and let Kiki help him to his feet.

Dek and Narnok moved up the stairs. Their faces were grim.

"I think we should leave now," said Dek, voice gruff. "There could be more of them."

"Yes. Get your shit together and meet me out front in five minutes," said Dalgoran, wiping his blade clean. He stared down at the headless body of Ralph, and the torn cadaver of Beth, his wife. "It shames me to leave them like this, but Dek is right. We are trapped here like rats."

"Do you think they're hunting us?" said Kiki, softly.

"I didn't. Now I do," said Dalgoran.

The wind was a harsh, cold, biting mistress. She snapped and whined, whistled and howled, slapping faces and bare exposed skin, chilling armour to torturous levels, and making the members of the group squirm uncomfortably in saddles, tugging at bits of clothing and cloaks and wrapping thick scarves around faces.

A thin layer of snow covered the undulating, rocky ground. Now, to their left as they travelled south from Kantarok, then angling southeast, stood the massive, vicious, daunting White Lion Mountains. They passed through the lower foothills, with thousands of hidden gulleys and valleys, towering stacks of rounded rock and huge angular boulders, which must have once been a part of these mountains. It was a dangerous journey, for there were many hidden opportunities for a horse to break an ankle, or stumble and throw a rider; the wind made it hard to see and so their progress was slow. Added to this, the recent battle at the tavern left none in the mood for idle banter.

That evening, huddled around a camp fire in the lee of a group of boulders, Dalgoran and Dek fought to secure some tarpaulins from boulders to ground to give shelter from the still falling snow. The snowfall was thin and sporadic, whipped about by the wind, but the promise of a heavy fall was imminent.

Narnok sat warming his hands, then returned to the flat rock on his knee where he sliced onions for the stew. Kiki was shredding dried beef into the bubbling pan, and glanced up as Ragorek returned, arms stacked with blackened wood from a nearby lightning-struck oak.

"Smells good," he grunted.

Kiki nodded, as Ragorek settled by the fire.

"Why don't we head west out of this broken ground? I'm constantly worried my horse will break a knee and throw me head first onto a tooth of the White Lions."

Kiki shook her head. "The Rokroth Marshes spread like a bad disease, right up to the rocky ground we now find ourselves trapped in. I've tried sneaking through many times before with various units, during my soldiering days. Always bit me on the backside. You either end up lost in the stinking mist when it inevitably descends, or find yourselves trapped in some bottle-necked gulley and have to back-track for half a day. This way is best, trust me. I've ridden it before."

"But man, this is good ground for an ambush," observed Narnok, and stood up, scraping the chopped onions into the stew. He placed his flat rock chopping board down, and grabbed his axe, as if the great weapon afforded him some comfort. It certainly gave him the same great protection afforded by any razor-sharp double-headed axe. He grinned at Ragorek.

"Who would want to ambush us?" asked Ragorek, softly.

Narnok shrugged. "I'm just saying, that thing back at Ralph's tavern. That killing. Was it just a random chance meeting? Seems funny to me, is all."

"How funny?" said Ragorek.

"Well, Dalgoran's off on some personal crusade to reunite us old bastards, no matter what our scars. He says the mud-orcs are coming back. Now, I'm a cynic. Only have to take one look at my face to see why. But things don't feel right. I know Dek described these beasts from his fight in Heroes' Square, but seeing them in the flesh..." Narnok shuddered. "They was not what I expected."

"No, I suppose not," said Ragorek, and rubbed the bristles on his chin. The bruises on his face from his fight with Dek had pretty much healed, but his nose was still buckled. He touched it tenderly and Kiki saw the movement.

"How's things with you and Dek?"

"Calm," said Ragorek, eyes fixed on Kiki. "Can I ask you something?"

"Depends what it is." She smiled to take the sting from her words.

"You and Dek. You were together, once, weren't you? At Desekra? During the War of Zakora?"

Kiki gave a short nod, averting her eyes. "We thought we faced certain death. At times like that, people can find... *unlikely* company. Not that I'm saying Dek is unlikely; he was certainly ruggedly handsome back in his day."

"Just as you were wildly pretty?" butted in Narnok, grinning a broad grin.

"I like to think majestically beautiful," smiled Kiki. "But it fades. It all fades. Things change. We were young and doomed to die. It drove us together seeking warmth and comfort in the lonely night hours of downtime, when there was no killing to be done."

"Wasn't that a court martial offence?"

"Ha, yes, but when there's tens of thousands of mud-orcs snarling and drooling and screaming curses, waving their swords and axes and spears and trying to remove your head; well, then you tend not to bother about such things. Neither do your officers, especially those newly baptised in war." She gave a little shudder. "It's something no person should have to go through."

"And what about now?" asked Ragorek, eyes still fixed on Kiki.

"Well, if you were asking me about *now*, I'd tell you to mind your own fucking business, or I might just pour this stew over your damned head. Understand?"

"Oh I understand all right," smiled Ragorek, and suddenly Kiki realised how much like his brother he really was. It wasn't in their build or colouring, or even facial structure; they looked modestly different. But it was in the *set* of their features, the way they occasionally smiled, the subtle gap between their middle lower teeth. It was a hint, nothing more.

"What I want to know," said Narnok, resting back, his axe on his lap like some long lost son, "is Dalgoran reckons these thousands of mud-orcs are on their way back, to invade Vagandrak or whatever, which seems mighty improbable to me; especially just based on the word of some mad old woman probably high on the honey-leaf." He rubbed idly at one facial scar with his thumb. "Ach, but this bastard itches. Listen, I just don't understand it. So some twisted horse creatures have been attacking people, and maybe we aren't targeted, maybe we are; but that doesn't mean there's a link. These beasts could be from the Plague Lands; have you ever visited the Plague Lands? A barren, evil place, everything twisted and dead, and all the trees are black. Poisoned. Broken."

"You went there?" said Kiki, aghast.

"When I was younger, and wilder," nodded Narnok. "Nobody tells Narnok that he can't do something. You know what a stubborn mule I was. Am. You know what I mean." He grinned again, a quite horrific vision.

"You're insane," said Kiki.

"Just insanely curious."

Kiki shrugged. "Well I don't give a bucket of horse shit what you think; I trust Dalgoran with more than my life. And his intuition, in all the years I've known him, has always, *always*, been right. His skill, and knowledge, damn, his *sixth sense* got us out of more trouble than you could believe possible. You know this, Narnok. You were there, man! With the Kultakka Raids, with the Zorkai Princes, and that time we nearly all died on the West Salt Plains. He saved us. Every time. And you all know what happened with Morkagoth…"

"I agree, Dalgoran seemed like a damn mystic when it came to Morkagoth. And he helped invoke the cur…" Narnok suddenly shut his mouth, glancing at Ragorek.

"What is it?"

"Balls. I speak too much for a man without a face."

Kiki stood, and moved to Narnok, reaching out to gently place her hand against his cheek. "Stop it," she said.

Narnok pulled away, eyes narrowed, then stood and stretched. "I'm going for a walk before that smell drives me insane with hunger. I'm a big lad, I am. I needs my food."

Narnok ambled off, axe still in one large fist. After the beasts back at the tavern, Kiki could hardly blame him.

Kiki went back to the pot and stirred the contents with a wooden spoon.

"What did he mean?" asked Ragorek. "About *invoking* something?"

Kiki glanced up, iron eyes dark and gleaming. Ragorek recoiled from the anger there.

Forcing herself to remain calm, Kiki said, "Some things are best forgotten, Rag. Some things are better left dead," and she moved off to her horse to unpack her saddle-bags. Snow was falling heavy. Kiki dreamed of a life where there was no war, no horror, no thrusting a sword into a mud-orc's guts and watching its bowels spill out over your blade as it writhed and screamed and clawed its way up the sharp iron, pulling your blade more and more into itself as its claws grappled for your throat... she dreamed of being young, and healthy, and pretty, training at the new recruit training ground west of the capital city, Vagan; so proud to have been picked for her fitness, strength, agility, swordplay... and there was Dek, a wrestler, a pugilist, broad-chested and athletic; expert with sword and spear, powerful, handsome, with booming laugh and infectious smile. But to fall in love was forbidden, and the soldiers were worked damned hard to drive away any such carnal desires. Later, much later, they stood on the battlements. The mud-orcs were coming, so the scouts said. "We might die here," said Dek, and he touched her shoulder, a light movement for one so big, so heavy, so brutal. "Yes, I know," she said, and gazed up into his eyes and fell into them. Their sex back in the barracks had been gentle at first, then hot and hard and filled with need not want. But then the mud-orcs arrived, and the killing began, and there was little thought of romance...

She turned over in her sleep, hugging her cloak tight about her.

Snow had gathered on the stretched-out tarpaulins and had started to bow them. Outside, a fox padded into the camp and paused, muzzle to the ground near the fire. It found a morsel of beef and ate hurriedly before padding onwards. A few miles out into the forest it halted, nose twitching, scenting something... *strange*. Whatever the scent, the fox changed direction and sped away, head low, paws running silently across fresh fallen snow.

You should tell him you still love him, said Suza, voice like a snake in Kiki's bed. *Tell him you are dying and only have days left; then he will take pity on you and come to your bed. A pity-fuck. That's what you're used to, isn't it, you hateful wide-legged whore?*

"Why can't you just leave me alone?" She turned in her sleep, arm falling free. Her brow was creased, eyelids twitching.

Tell him Dalgoran is right, and the mud-orcs are coming. Tell him they are here, and you want him for those last final moments before their claws tear out your eyes, their spears pierce your body, their brutal black swords hack off your head. Then he'll come to you, naked and lean and hard. Imagine him pressing against your naked body, Kiki. Imagine his powerful hands opening your legs as you roll onto your back like a yelping puppy; imagine him kissing you, his hands moving down over your breasts and belly and touching you there, teasing you, his fingers gliding into you...

"No! Stop it! Suza, you are a wicked, evil poison; get out of my head, get out of my dreams! Leave me in peace..."

You'll be left in peace all right, bitch, when the mud-orcs arrive...

"And when is that?"

Yeah, Kiki, when, when, when. They're expanding even as you lie here like a cheap strumpet; expanding their ranks, forging swords and spear points and axes; they feed the living to create the twisted, they feed the mud to give birth from the mud. Orlana has sent out scouting parties. And she has sent out killing parties. Vicious mud-orcs looking for certain people; looking for those who might oppose her in these first days.

"Is this true?"

Would I lie to you, sister of mine?

"How could you know such things?"

*The barriers between their world and my world are not
so hard to cross. I watched Orlana; watched her take Zorkai
to bed like a pimply eighteen year-old virgin. She ate him in
many ways; just after she'd eaten his wives.*

"So, Dalgoran is right?"

*He might be. Or maybe I just like playing games with
your pretty little stupid head.*

"Damn you, tell me the truth!" raged Kiki, and
Suza's mocking laughter peeled out and Kiki blinked,
realising she was awake, and cursed. She kicked herself
quietly from her blankets, pulled on her cloak and
crawled from the tarpaulin protection. A cool breeze
chilled her and she moved to the remnants of the
camp fire, noting the fox prints and smiling. "I hope
we left you something," she muttered, and stoked the
glowing coals.

Then something, a tiny bad feeling, crept into the
back of her mind.

*Tell him Dalgoran is right, and the mud-orcs are coming…
scouting parties… killing parties…*

A noise echoed from the boulders to the right. Kiki
moved back to her tarpaulin, grabbing her short sword
free. She moved to Dek, nudging the large man with
the toe of her boot and he grunted, rolling smoothly
from his blankets and drawing his own blade.

"Trouble?"

"I don't know. Something's not quite right."

Dek roused the others as Kiki moved to the fire and
its sanctuary of warmth and flickering flame; then she
moved beyond, into the trees, where she settled into
a crouch allowing her eyes to adjust to the darkness.

A cool breeze eased through the boughs bringing the scent of pine needles. Wind hissed through brittle brown leaves far off to her left. And then... she *heard* them coming. They moved swiftly through the gloom, angling towards her and the fire behind. Kiki kicked up from the snow and ran back to where Narnok was weighing his axe, face a horror-show by the light of the glowing embers.

"What is it?"

"Mud-orcs!" hissed Kiki.

"You're joking?" snapped Dek.

"Do I look like I'm the village fucking idiot?"

The Iron Wolves formed a line, rocks to their backs, weapons before them. The remnants of the fire flickered and crackled gently.

The trees sighed and creaked.

Their smell came first; it was rotten eggs, it was bad milk, it was sour cheese, it was open gangrene, it was the maggot-filled corpse of a strangled cat. Putrefaction washed over the group and they gagged, and then the mud-orcs sprinted from the darkness and they were big, and moved with agility and aggression and no fear and Kiki gasped as memories slammed into her mind and she was back on the walls of Desekra Fortress in the Pass of Splintered Bones while the war-horde chanted and screamed on the plains below...

Mud-orcs...

They came through the darkness, a large group, perhaps forty strong, moving with inhuman speed in a ragged line. Within twenty feet they began an unholy howl, mouths like muzzles lifted to the sky, breathing ragged and panting like dogs; they were bigger than men, with spindly limbs and carrying rough-edged swords and axes.

"Stand strong," came Dalgoran's voice – steady, authoritative – as the mud-orcs, growling now, became visible. Their skin was a sickly green and streaked vertically with red and crimson, as if their flesh had been hacked wide open. Their eyes were glassy black, and they had painted war markings on their flesh with white clay and mud ochre. All four limbs ended in long, curling claws as they powered through the forest...

And then they were there, and Kiki screamed and leapt over the fire, an axe rushing past her head as she swayed and her sword clubbed between glistening eyes. The mud-orc went down in a tangle and she leapt its body, slashing her blade left into another's eyes, then right across a throat, opening it like a wide smile gushing blood. To her left, Narnok waded in with his axe, cleaving skulls left and right, splitting them down the middle like melons so brains splashed out over his axe blades, over his jerkin, over his scarred face. He fought in silence, features a terrible grim mask.

All was madness in the dark forest. General Dalgoran, despite his advancing years, fought with a mechanical accuracy gained from half a century with a blade in his hand. He was cool, calculating: each movement, each block and strike and cut performed with minimum effort, maximum efficiency. The mud-orcs, larger in numbers, and each one bigger and heavier than their human foes, were used to using their bulk and weight and power to devastating effect. But Dalgoran used clever little twists of body and blade, small accurate side-steps, neat movements of head and shifts of weight to manoeuvre himself out of danger, and skewer his opponents on his short sword. Whereas Narnok bludgeoned his way to victory, each massive blow cutting limbs and heads from bodies, in contrast, Dalgoran's blade seemed hardly to touch the mud-orcs: a throat cut appeared nothing more than a thin red line delivered on the tip of his blade, but then unzipped like a jacket spilling out oesophagus and vocal cords in a shower of blood. Dalgoran stabbed one raging massive mud-orc in the chest, a simple flicker of in-out, his blade intruding barely more than a couple of inches into the mud-orc's flesh; and yet with unerring accuracy it pierced the mud-orc's heart and dropped it like a sack of shit.

Dek was mid-point between Narnok and Dalgoran; he fought with accuracy, but also with a primitive joy in battle, hacking and slicing, twisting and moving with great agility. He also used his fists, elbows, knees and boots, effective in dirty bouts in the Red Thumb Fighting Pits, and just as effective in a melee in the darkened woods.

And finally, Ragorek fought on the right, not as skilled as the others with his blade, but just as ferocious as being Dek's older brother would suggest. His great mane of hair seemed aflame by the dying light of the fire, and he bellowed through his beard, half in rage, half in fear, as the mud-orcs seemed to come on in a great flood of green flesh like some necrotic army, and he found himself in a sudden island of fighting, completely surrounded by mud-orc flesh and armour and dirty great battle-axes. Rag felt himself starting to panic. He blocked a downward axe sweep, kicked the mud-orc between the legs, making it grunt, but its weight carried it forward and it crashed into Rag. He tried to side-step, as he had seen Dalgoran do, but the mud-orc's arms wrapped around him and both went down in a flurry of limbs. Rag lost grip of his sword and screamed as a knife slid across his ribs. He head-butted the creature, breaking its already buckled nose, and twisting, crawled atop it, grabbing its windpipe, thumbs pressing in deep, throttling it. Now the mud-orc slammed a knee up into Rag's balls, and a throw sent him flying. The mud-orc leapt across him, grinning down, eyes gleaming, long strings of saliva drooling down onto Ragorek's face and open mouth. He thrashed, but the mud-orc was incredibly strong, and heavier than Rag. He threw punches, left and right, left and right, huge heavy blows, but the mud-orc pushed its head back out of reach whilst still delivering that windpipe crushing grip...

Stars swam. Red ran through black, like blood disseminating through a night lake. Ragorek was choking, his vision gone now, his tongue protruding like a stalk, his legs thrashing. The beast was incredibly strong; stronger than Rag.

This is what it's like to die, he thought through rivers of pain.

This is where it ends.

THE STREETS

Vagandrak's more southerly capital, Drakerath, was less militarised than Vagan, and concerned itself more with being a hub for the arts and culture. In societal terms, the Vagan people considered themselves tough, no-nonsense, strong of body and mind, whereas those who chose Drakerath in the south were soft and weak and more concerned with man loving man. Of course, those in Drakerath considered themselves sophisticated, educated, more prone to think than to fight, whereas their neighbours in "the second capital" were boorish, uncouth, aggressive and proved their stupidity by a lack of appreciation of the arts and response to criticism with violence.

On this night, however, as a few flurries of snow kissed the winter gardens, the tree lined avenues, the beautiful tall houses of the rich quarter, and King Yoon's Drakerath Palace's sculpted battlements, white marble walkways and narrow, picturesque purple towers, so Drakerath's citizens had something rather more serious than neighbourly insults to contend with…

A scream echoed from the darkness. Followed by rushing footfalls.

A woman appeared at the edges of the golden glow of a fish-oil street lantern, face twisted in terror, one shoe lost. Then something in the darkness, growling in a low burble, reached out and plucked her from the light, dragging her back into black. She screamed again, and there came various tearing noises, two cracks and a heavy thump. Then, more slow tearing and a sound like a long-drawn out deflating sigh.

Captain Horsell, of Drakerath's City Watch, stared at the mound of paperwork forlornly as the door to the watch-house burst open and screams echoed through to his office and the cells beyond. Horsell groaned, rubbing his already weary eyes. It was going to be *one of those nights*.

He heaved himself up and walked swiftly through to the counter, where Jarred was nobly trying to calm the woman. She was dressed like one of the many prostitutes who worked the Lower Quarter of the city, down by the river where the tanners, fish markets, cheese factories and fighting pits tended to operate their slightly noisome trade. She wore brightly coloured silks and a yellow scarf, but on this night it, and her face, were sprinkled by a delicate tracing of blood.

Jarred had moved round the counter and had the woman held by both upper arms in a gentle but firm grip, and was trying to talk her down from her fast, impenetrable babble.

"Madam," said Horsell, "you need to calm down." For some reason, his deep, resonant tones brought a sudden hush to the watch-house front desk. He moved closer to her, and Jarred released her, taking a step back in deference.

"Did she tell you anything?" asked Horsell.

"All I got was *'wild animal'*. He gave Horsell a sideways glance, for they'd already had two reports of some kind of huge dog, or maybe wolf, loose in the city. Eaten one lady's poodle, apparently. Scared some children. Savaged a drunk down by the rice warehouses. It was midweek. It should have been a *quiet night*…

"OK, calm down, lady. First, can you tell me your name?"

She gave him a suddenly shifty look, for the Watch were not renowned for their leniency when whores strayed from their designated areas. He waved away her look. "Just so I know who I'm speaking to."

"Galina, sir."

"And is that blood on your scarf, Galina?"

"It is, Captain Horsell. Well the thing is, I was out walking the streets with Jade, we were standing under a streetlamp, stamping our feet for 't'as grown terribly cold now winter is coming fast, and this carriage pulls up. He was a right portly gentleman, and balding, with a face like a pig's anus, but his carriage was sleek and black, the two horses in good health…" she took a deep breath, and her eyes grew haunted, "and we hears this growling sound, like a big dog, and it leapt and brought down the two horses in one bound, crushing them, snapping with long fangs, like, and it was rightly terrible. It turned on the carriage, biting at the wood, and we ran, and we heard the portly gentleman's screams and the thing *came after us*…" She paused, gulping, as Jarred placed a wooden tankard of water before her. She took it thankfully, draining it in one.

"What happened next?"

"It came down Groper's Alley, and I am ashamed to say I ran from Jade, cutting right and heading here, like. I shouted for her to follow. But she didn't. I heard some screams. They must have been her. Oh please, Captain Horsell, please go and look for her. Take your sword!"

"You say this wolf brought down *two horses* in one leap? No wolf can do that."

"It was not a wolf, sir." Her words were soft, her chest rising and falling fast in her panic above a tight corset the colour of blood.

"What was it?"

"It… it was like a dog, but big as a lion. But, twisted. Its head was twisted to one side. It bit a horse's head clean off!"

Horsell took Jarred to one side. "Have you smelt her breath?"

"Gin?"

"Aye, I reckon. And too much of it by the sound of her. But that is blood on her scarf, so we'd better check it out. Have Darka and Lantriack checked in?"

"No, sir. They're due."

"This is what we'll do. You stay here, I'll head down Groper's Alley and try and retrace this woman's footsteps…"

Boots pounded the cobbles outside and Lantriack spun into the watch-house. He looked dishevelled, panicked, and that was not like Lantriack. Lantriack was the calm professional who could both talk any enraged drunk down, and had the natural presence to command respect when he decided to crack heads with his Peacemaker. Lantriack did not panic easily, and yet here he was – red in the face, eyes wild, lips wet, breath coming fast.

"Captain Horsell! You'd better come quick. There's been some murders!"

"*Some* murders?"

"Women." Lantriack gulped. "Seven women!"

Horsell rounded on Jarred. "Stay here. With her. Don't let her leave." He grabbed his Peacemaker, stared at it for a moment, tossed it aside and grabbed his short sword. This was not a night to be half-prepared.

Reena's Palace was just down Fisherman Black's Lane, across from the Fish Hex Market. It wasn't, as the name suggested, a palace at all, but rather a narrow two storey house wedged between a spice shop and an open-fronted food pit which sold slabs of roasted pig for two copper pieces.

Captain Horsell was panting as he arrived, and a light falling of a snow was frosting the cobbles in white. Darka was standing in the doorway, eyes wide, stamping his feet to ward off the cold, and behind him was a young pretty girl of no more than sixteen years; obviously a "lady in training".

"Upstairs," said Darka, grimly, and his face told the tale. Horsell stooped to speak to the girl. "You called this in?" She nodded, mute with terror.

Horsell took the stairs three at a time, long legs eating the ascent, left hand holding his scabbard tight against his trews to stop it slapping. He stopped on the landing, a sudden movement as if he'd hit a portcullis.

The first woman lay a few feet from the stairs. Her hands were stretched out towards Horsell, as if in pleading; as if she'd been crawling to escape when… *whatever it was* had bitten off both her legs. Thick puddles of blood, gore, stray ligaments and tendons and wispy straggles of torn skin led like a trail in a V from the woman's body trunk. Horsell met her glassy eyes, and looked away.

Carefully, he stepped over her remains, but could not avoid the blood. It was everywhere. Horsell had been in several battles, and witnessed various murder scenes; but this was something else. Like somebody had tipped buckets of blood over the floor. It was obscene. And unavoidable… he left bloody footprints on his way to the main room of the brothel, and stood in the doorway for a moment, shaking, eyes wide, before stepping to one side and throwing up his supper.

Lantriack came in, stepping over the first body.

"Are you all right, sir?"

"Yes. Yes." Their eyes met. "By the Holy Mother, what in hell's teeth did this?"

"I truly do not know," said Lantriack. He stood alongside Horsell, and together they once more surveyed the scene. There were six bodies – or so they would discover the following day, after the pieces were laid out on sheets in the street and crudely put back together again. Here, though, and now, they were strewn around the room. No single body was intact. Legs, arms, hands, feet, heads, teeth, hair, all were mingled with buckets of blood, with torn clothing, with shoes and jewellery that glittered under the oozing crimson. As Horsell's gaze moved slowly around the room, looking for clues, looking for *any* clue, he saw a finger here still wearing a ruby ring, a section of face there (which appeared to be smiling but in reality was probably screaming), there, an unrecognisable lump of meat, there a...

"What *is* that?" said Horsell.

"It's a breast, sir."

"We need to find who did this, Lantriack." Their eyes met. "And kill him."

"Or it, sir."

"You think a wild animal did this?"

"I used to live on a farm when I was a lad, sir. We kept horses, cattle and also chickens. One winter's night, a fox broke into the chicken pen; thirty it slaughtered, in a frenzy of killing madness. It couldn't possibly eat that much, but it murdered every chicken in that hut. This... this scene kind of reminds me of that. A wild animal gone crazy with bloodlust."

"Whatever it is, it's powerful. To pull a woman apart like that..."

"What shall we do, sir?"

"Emergency call out to all guards. And send messages to General Caltor at the garrison barracks. We might need their help. And, I expect, we should inform King Yoon."

Lantriack met Horsell's eye for a moment. "That won't do any good, sir," he said, his words quiet and neutral. "In fact, in might do a lot of bad."

"And yet we must," said Horsell. "Go on. Get on to Caltor first; he can summon more men than I."

Lantriack saluted and back-tracked down the stairs, boots thudding. Horsell looked around the room at the dismembered corpses, then up and out of the small panes of glass at the window. Outside, snow had started to fall heavy.

"Winter's coming," he muttered, and he meant it in more ways than one.

THE PRINCE

Prince Zastarte lifted the glass of ruby wine and smiled from that handsome, round face framed by long black curls and topped by an expensive felt hat containing a bright red feather. "A toast to you all, my dears! To such fabulous hosts!"

There came a gentle round of applause from the family members of the Wellton Estate and their friends, and servants circulated with silver trays bearing crystal glasses of finest port, brandy and the ruby wine which still glistened on Zastarte's lips.

In the corner, under the glittering lights of a chandelier, Ember, youngest daughter of the Wellton family, struck up a lively piece on the glossy black grand piano, and Zastarte was just about to approach the young lady, face made up to look more than her enticingly sweet sixteen years, when Ember's mother stepped before him, her hand lifted and clutching a lace kerchief.

"You may ask me to dance, Prince, if you wish," she said, smiling to show slightly over-large yellow teeth.

"But why, of course!" exclaimed Zastarte, beaming a gallant smile, and began whirling Lady Wellton giggling around the large dance floor, her ample bosom bouncing, his feet jigging to the tinkling upbeat piano number, her laughter cackling out like a strangled hyena. Zastarte's curls bounced in rhythm as his hand found her waist and squeezed just that little bit inappropriately through the lace and fanciful crochet-work of the tight white bodice she wore.

They danced around the room to four piano pieces, as Lord Wellton gradually drank himself into a state and retired to the library with seven other men of good-breeding and tweed for a smoke and a brandy.

Sweating now, Zastarte excused himself from the dance, leaving Lady Wellton red in the face, hand on her bosom, and headed off down a cool corridor towards the gentleman's room, hand on the hilt of his rapier to stop it flapping against his legs.

Zastarte passed a full length mirror amidst the acres of dark oak panelling and he stopped for a moment to admire himself, as he always did. Tall, broad-shouldered, narrow-hipped, long of leg and upright and stiff, he was every inch the soldier, every inch the prince, every inch the *hero*. Oh how he had regaled all present with his tales of zig-zagging the point of his weapon to remove the surprised eyebrows from a mud-orc at Desekra Fortress; how he had reprimanded a drunken brigand in the street, his sword licking out to cut the buffoon's waistband leaving his trousers around his ankles making everybody in the fish market laugh and point; and how his many previous infamous parties had led to (at his last count!), twenty-five pregnancies, seventeen divorces, three murders and one dancing dog. The dog wore red ribbons, danced on its hind legs, and made everybody roar with laughter.

Zastarte looked himself up and down. Tailoring of the finest quality, imported fine-weave cotton from Zakora, a silk blouse from Zalazar, Junglan lace ruffs at wrist and throat, with a thick Vagan top-coat of jet black wool, and of course, bright red Drakerath three-quarter length pantaloons tucked into bright white socks and glossy black Drakerath court shoes with golden buckles. He chuckled. *Some* fashion statements would never change. He really did look the part.

Zastarte looked into the reflection of his eyes, iron grey and piercing, set in a strong, lightly tanned face, square jaw, rugged hero looks, no scars (oh how he had protected his face in the days of battle!). He was every inch the dashing, well-matured fellow, noble and honourable, with impeccable history and a grand noble heritage. Had he mentioned he was noble? He was *damned* noble, with extra lashings of honour.

He tugged his coat a little, then moved to the gentleman's room where he took his generously proportioned cock in one hand and pissed through the wooden hole in the floor as he hummed the piano tune played by Emba Wellton. He pictured her, with her tiny white features and hair in pretty blonde sausages. What a delightful child! At sixteen, soon she would have the suitors queuing to bring the gifts and desire of courtship. Grumpy old Lord Wellton would have a riot on his hands, that was for sure!

Zastarte chuckled, stowing his manhood away, then washed his hands and, taking a powder brush from its bowl, applied a light brushing of white across his cheeks. Then he stepped from the chamber and closed the heavy oak door behind him, with a click.

A hand grabbed his wrist, dragging him round the corner, and Lady Wellton pushed him hard against the wall. His head thudded the panelling.

"Lady Wellton!" he proclaimed, feigning shock.

"Oooh, you animal," she said, hands rubbing up and down his arms and chest. She clutched at him eagerly, like a virgin on her wedding night.

"But… but what about Lord Wellton? This is an exceedingly compromising position you place us in!"

"Fuck me," she hissed, grabbing his coat hard and pulling him down into a kiss. His lips found hers and she kissed him with the passion of a middle-aged divorcee after a decade of celibacy; she grabbed his hand, forcing it between her legs, panting; and he found she was exceedingly wet.

"Fuck me! No! Here! Now! Just FUCK ME!" she breathed, eyes wild, and now it was Zastarte's turn to push Lady Wellton against the opposite wall, unzipping his bright red pantaloons and producing his engorged cock for her eyes to feast upon.

"Ooh," she said, again, licking her lips. "Can I touch it?"

"Touch it, taste it, ride it, it's time we got to business," panted Zastarte, dragging up Lady Wellton's skirts. He thrust inside her without foreplay, after all, time was of the essence, and she groaned and bit his shoulder, and her breasts wobbled against his chest, and over her shoulder Zastarte's eyes gleamed and he grinned as he gave her what she wanted, hard and fast.

"Delightful evening, old chap!" said Lord Wellton, puffing on a cigar as Prince Zastarte stepped onto the stone steps at the front of Wellton Hall in a stretched circle of glowing orange lamplight. "Shame we don't have more civilised company like you, hey?" He swayed a little, seriously the worse for wear after at least ten port and brandies.

A servant had brought Zastarte's carriage around, and the four horses snorted in the cold night air, one pawing the loose stones of the driveway. Most of the guests had already left, and Zastarte gave a salute to his driver.

He shook Wellton's hand vigorously, coughing a little on cigar smoke. "It's been a mighty fine evening, old chap," he beamed. "Very robust. Very energetic. I've found myself *invigorated* by the delightful company of your *delightful family*!"

"Good lad, good lad," beamed Wellton as Zastarte stepped briskly to one side to take Lady Wellton gently by the arms, and deliver a petite kiss to her cheek.

"And Lady Wellton, it's been a pleasure."

"No, no, the pleasure was all mine," she beamed, showing those slightly over-large yellow teeth.

"No, I insist, rarely have I enjoyed myself so thoroughly at an engagement! I find myself swollen with delight! Wet at the lips! I feel like an over-excited schoolboy who's had all the sweets from the jar. Thank you so much for your wonderful hospitality. I've come into your life as a stranger, and leave the richer person."

"You shall have to come again," said Lady Wellton, giving a little curtsy.

"Indeed, I should love to come inside your home many, many times!" Glancing over Lady Wellton's shoulder, he caught sight of Ember Wellton being fussed by servants and then heading for the stairs and, no doubt, bed beyond.

"Well, Zastarte," said Wellton, punching him on the shoulder. "Don't be a stranger."

"I shan't. And if you can convey my goodnight wishes to your fabulous daughters, and that very sweet little morsel, Ember. What a delightful pianist! Talented and skilled."

"She gets her strong, agile fingers from her mother," grinned Lady Wellton.

"I am sure she does. I am sure she does. Good night! Farewell!"

The room was a cool, dark place. Bare candles flickered in little alcoves in the grey stonework, and it had the feeling of a cellar, or dungeon, although it was dry and did not suffer damp. The floor was made of uneven stone flags, worn in places from centuries of boots and work. Along one wall there were several old, rusted iron chains. Occasionally, a gentle draught made iron links clink against the stonework, a subtle accompaniment to the heavy silence of this deep underground place.

At first, there was darkness.

Then light came to her, and it was the tender yellow light of hazy flickering candles. She blinked lazily, and yawned, and wondered where she was, what was happening, and why her surroundings had changed so drastically. Her mind tried to leap-frog facts and she could not focus, could not concentrate, could not *comprehend*. Where was her thick white duvet and plumped up pillows? Where was the frame of the dark oak four-poster bed? Where was the drifting gauze of the curtains that surrounded her little palace of sleep?

She realised she was on her back, and this was strange for she never slept on her back. Indeed, she was more the sort of person who snuggled deep under the covers and cocooned herself against the ice and the cold, against the dark and the savage real world. But here she was, arms and legs stretched apart...

She tried to turn over, but was restricted. Her mouth tasted fuzzy and metallic; like copper or blood. She worked her lips and tongue, and tried to move again. Something rattled. Something metal.

Awareness started to come to her, as if her mind had been full of smoke and gradually it was clearing. She realised with a start that she was naked, and that the place, the underground chamber, was warm. She heard the crackle of coals, with tiny hisses and pops. She frowned.

"Hel... Hello?" she managed through dry lips.

"Why, hello, my little darling," came a rich, resonant voice, and she frowned again, deeper now, for she recognised that voice; it was a fabulous voice full of life and love and laughter. Where had she heard it before? And *where was she?*

"Er, why… where am I? What happened?" She tried to lift an arm to rub at her head, but again felt the restriction, heard the jingle of chains. Her eyes were swimming in and out of focus, and she turned her head to the left… and her world dropped out through the bottom of her soul like a body in a tarpaulin dropped down a well.

Two people hung against the wall, their wrists in thick iron shackles, both naked, both unconscious, both slumped against the chains, which had been fastened to thick iron hooks hammered into gaps between the stones.

One was a woman, her body filthy, bruised, and… bloody. Strips of skin were missing on her belly and breasts. Her toenails, also, were missing, her feet brown where the blood had dried. The second figure was a young man with short blond hair. His wrists and arms were streaked with blood, presumably from struggling. He had no marks on his naked body, but ducking down a little, she could see his face was heavily bruised.

Now there came a sigh from behind her, and a figure stepped into view. He was tall and handsome and gallant and noble, and her heart leapt, for surely the wonderful Prince Zastarte was here to rescue her?

He grinned at her, then, a look of genuine good humour. He tilted his head, eyes locked on hers, as if trying to decipher what was going on in her head. Then he licked his lips, and she saw he carried a pair of tongs, their end punctuated by a hot coal glowing orange, sizzling softly, and offering threat implicit.

"Prince!" she said, startled. Then pulled against her chains.

"Ahh, sweet Ember Wellton." He moved closer, puckering his lips at her as if she were some little cry-baby and he was about to mock. "You are such a pretty little thing, yes you are. I bet that little mind is all tumbled over and so confused, isn't it?" He screwed up his face.

"You have brought me here?"

"I would clap, but I fear this coal would burn off my flesh." His voice sounded more authoritative now. It was like a knife of iron had suddenly eased through him, and the glint of humour had gone.

"Why? Why would you do this?"

"Questions. Always the questions." He moved yet closer and rested his hand lightly on her soft, naked, pale ankle.

She licked her lips, and then looked up at him. "Seriously, Prince Zastarte," she managed, although her voice was a little cracked, "why have you brought me here?"

"I would like to say it was for the money, little Ember. I would like to say it was because I was in great debt at the hands of the Red Thumb Gangs, and thus driven by despair to desperate ends, taken to kidnapping young wealthy individuals in order to extort large amounts of finance from their bloated, over-stuffed parents." He smiled, and trailed his hand from her ankle, to her knee, then halfway up her thigh. She shivered. He smiled at the response. "But then, that would be a lie."

His hand continued its journey, moving up her thigh, sliding slightly inside so that his trailing fingers gently teased against the edge of her pubic mound, slowing a little, as if they might explore further to an intake of her breath, but then circling, and moving up her flat white belly to rest gently on her ribs.

"I would like to say I am overcome with lust for your amazing and fabulous tight little white body. Your bottom is so firm and strong, your breasts pert, nipples erect with fear even as we speak… and yes, your eyes and lips are all perfect, your hair oiled with the finest of lotions, your legs long and straight, your quim an absolute exquisite joy to behold…" he came close, fast, face looming into her, "and yes, of course I would like to fuck you just as I fucked your mother, twice, hard and fast against the wall, her hands on my rump pulling me in harder faster deeper as she bit my chest and neck and just couldn't get enough; then later, up in your father's bed whilst he drank himself stupid down below on port and brandy, pulling out at the last minute to eject my seed all over her tits and face, rubbing my juice into her lips, into her mouth, watching her taste me and her together, our sexual honey converged and mated forming the sweetest elixir; oh yes, sweet Ember, I could do that to you, I could give you the forbidden fruit and watch you drink it so deep. Alas, sex is something that bores me. To fuck you, yes, it would bore me very much."

Ember stared hard at him, mouth open, pink lips dry, unable to comprehend what was actually going on. Then slowly she closed her mouth and the terror came, and it was a terrible dark worm coming up from the pit of her belly, through her heart, into her mouth like a dead scaly thing, sucking out her life.

Understanding had arrived.

"Please don't hurt me," she said, voice barely more than a whimper.

"Hurt you?" he shouted, whirling suddenly away like a dancer, the glowing coal leaving traces of bright swirls before Ember's eyes. "Of course I won't hurt you!" He returned, and rested a hand near her throat. "Not yet, anyway, my sweet darling."

He turned and moved to the two people hanging against the wall, ducking a little to look up into the young man's face.

"Aha! So you are awake, you cheeky little scamp. You thought to fool old Uncle Zastarte with your playground play acting?" He grabbed the man's hair and jerked his head up roughly. Then he glanced over to Ember. "See, Pestrat? You have an appreciative audience now, my friend!"

Ember gasped, for one of Pestrat's eyes was gone revealing nothing but a black, empty socket. The young man started to whimper, then to wail, and Zastarte slapped him hard across the face, knocking his head to one side and silencing the noise.

"Enough of that, fucker." He lifted the tongs, with the glowing coal, until it was near Pestrat's face. The man started to squirm, trying to get away from the terrible heat. "What's the matter, cat got your tongue?" Then he gave a low laugh. "Of course not. I've got it. In a jar, over yonder." He pointed with the coal to somewhere behind Ember, who was slowly pissing herself, her urine dripping from the bench upon which she was chained.

Pestrat's face began to glow with a gentle soft light as the coal came closer once more. His remaining eye was wide in absolute terror.

"Don't do it," croaked Ember.

Zastarte half-turned, but he was focused on his task.

"Please, don't hurt him anymore!"

"Why?" snapped Zastarte, whirling about and stalking towards her. He thrust the glowing coal towards her face and she squealed, trying to back-pedal, to get away. "You want to take his pain for him?"

"No, no, I just don't understand…"

"And you think I expect you to? You think I *care* whether you understand why I bring you people here? You are the dregs at the bottom of the barrel, and yet you float at the top. You wade through your lives stepping on all those around you, using them like cattle in your factories, your tanneries and fish gutting plants, your slaughter-houses and sewers; and you take the money, the profit, and let them live in filth and squalor and poverty. You abuse your fellow human beings and you think there will be no retribution? Well, I am here to show you not everybody is afraid! I am here to show you the poor and the weak and the abused, they can fight back, they can turn on their masters and make them suffer just like the poor and the weak of this world suffer."

"I have done none of those things!" wailed Ember.

"No," snarled Zastarte, "but your family have, they have built their wealth on the backs of the poor, and for that, my sweet little girl, they must be punished. And they will be punished. Through you. Through your pain and through your exquisite suffering."

He advanced on Pestrat, and thrust the coal into the man's remaining eye. Pestrat screamed a deformed scream, a strangled, cauterised wail, his bloody tongue stump waggling, his head lifting high as if praying to a god who didn't love him for a miracle that couldn't happen.

It took a minute, but to Ember the minute lasted a lifetime.

Then Zastarte turned, grinned at her, his face a sheen of sweat with a few smudges from the coal brazier. His iron grey eyes were gleaming. He said, "Then again, that whole 'for the good of the people' horse shit could just be all be… horse shit. After all. Some of us just like to watch people suffer."

Captain Zelt of the Timanta City Guard looked up from his desk as Feest, one of his men, entered. Feest's eyes were gleaming. A single candle burned, and outside snow fell. The wind howled outside the single pane of glass.

"We've found him," said Feest.

"You're sure?"

"A whore heard a cry and looked out of her window. She saw a man matching Zastarte's description lift what looked like a body from his carriage and carry it down into a cellar under a shop on Fish Market Lane."

"To hide the smell."

"That's what I thought."

"Get the men together."

"All of them?"

"All of them. We're going to hang this bastard. All we need is evidence, no matter how weak. You and I both know he's guilty."

Feest stared into Zelt's eyes and did not see justice there. No, this was way too personal; it had been going on for far too long. Young men and women, sons and daughters of the wealthy in Timanta, had been disappearing for nearly a year now. There were sixteen cases of missing persons and not one body had been found. However, in the last month the numbers of abductions had increased; as if the kidnapper, or indeed killer, was getting greedy. Or overconfident. Whatever, there was massive pressure on Captain Zelt and his men to catch the bastard. And not just catch him. The clamour of the wealthy demanded serious payback.

"Let's go. And warn the men. This Zastarte, he's one dangerous fucker."

"What shall we do we when get him?"

There was a moment of pure, unspoken understanding.

"Let's just say he can't be allowed to leave the building with his heart still beating in his chest."

RIPPLES

The raven circled high on the air currents, gliding under a cold, vast, blue dome of sky. Its glossy black feathers glowed beneath a winter sun, and its black eyes were like glass, observing the world below it, a huge gameboard spread out for its sole entertainment.

It gave an echoing croak and changed direction, dropping a little and giving slow, flowing wing beats. To the north the mountains reared, distant and massive, the rock black, peaks white and cloaked in a single massive layer of mist that stretched away across the world. The raven croaked again, and circled, dropping in height. Its eyes fixed on the plains to the south and the far northern city of Pajanta Kin. Thick black columns of smoke still rose, and the raven could make out fires burning. It could not miss the destruction; the whole city burned.

And from the south came a slow flood of darkness oozing across the land. Like ants, they progressed across the gameboard, watched by the raven with nothing more than idle curiosity. There were thousands of them, marching at a steady pace. There were tens of thousands: mud-orcs in mismatched armour and bearing rough-forged weapons. They did not march with any structure; there were no ranks or units, just an untidy straggle seemingly as wide as the horizon and many ranks deep.

The raven flapped towards the seething mass in the distance, like giant insects that had overrun the huge city of Pajanta Kin and absorbed its citizens into their own numbers, growing them massively; and onwards they came. Marching, marching, boots stomping the hard barren earth as they headed ever north.

The raven blinked, black eyes moving past the mud-orcs. If it could have counted numbers, it would have realised they had swelled their ranks, and were now close to one hundred and sixty thousand green-skinned beasts. And behind them came the splice, galloping disjointed, most either swollen, distorted horses, some a mix of horse and man; or a few other clusters where Orlana had used her shapeshifting magick on wolves, or bears: huge broad-shouldered lumbering monstrosities with tufts of orange and black fur and muzzles twice the length of a normal bear with hooked crooked black teeth. In total, Orlana's army neared two hundred thousand creatures, and they moved across the land like a plague of insects, taking everything, destroying everything, creating nothing.

The raven beat its wings, heading high above the marching army. It stank, and the raven gave a final croak, eyes gleaming. The raven was intelligent enough to know that when an army travelled, it was often followed by battle. And after every battle, it was time for the raven to gorge.

Zorkai slumbered, and awoke with a start to see Orlana, her head resting on one hand, propped up on her elbow, as she watched him. He licked his lips. Fear was an ever-present shadow, like a stain across his soul, but he tried to pacify it with thoughts of conquest and victory and immortality and strength and power. Somehow, there was always an imbalance. Somehow, he never felt pure.

Orlana was naked beneath the thick silk sheets, and Zorkai's eyes travelled down. One breast was exposed, small and firm and pale white, like delicate porcelain. She saw him look, and he quickly transferred his gaze. Orlana's sexual appetite was insatiable, and Zorkai's lust and strength and stamina were prodigious; and yet... and *yet* after every single act, he could not help but feel a little bit – dirty. Not dirty in a sexually frisky sense; but in a purely physical one, as if a fine oil residue was left covering his entire body after the act. An oily film of perversion he could never, ever wash free.

"What are you thinking?" she asked, suddenly, voice low and melodious.

"I am thinking our army is massive beyond belief."

"And still it grows."

"For how long?"

"Until I have enough."

"For what?"

Orlana smiled, then, and reached forward, kissing his head as she would a simple child. "You do not need to worry yourself about such matters; soon we will be at the Pass of Splintered Bones and we will smash the Desekra Fortress. Even now I have splice and mud-orcs crossing the mountains by treacherous, hidden paths; many hundreds will not succeed, but enough *will;* and these will hunt down those I know oppose me. These will work to open the Desekra gates from the inside."

"This I know," said Zorkai.

"Come here, my lover." She leant forward and kissed him, and he returned the kiss. But he was getting tired. Not just physically, or sexually; but in his soul.

"I have a question."

"Nothing more dangerous than a man who thinks."

"Ha! You think I built my own fucking empire by not using my mind? You think I murdered my brothers and sisters, my cousins and their cousins, without having a single element of strategy in my body? You frighten me. Yes, I know that you know. And yet you thrill me, also, and your promises are an incredible drug; not promises that I trust, but a heady drug aroma which entices me on for more and more and more. I am not a stupid man, Orlana. I see your power. I watch your army. I recognise I was a puppet that helped get things started; and I will be faithful and true to you for as long as I live, for yes, I am a vain man, yes I am in love with power and an eternal line for my children. I know you can achieve your dreams, Orlana; but I cannot help you do this, and secure my place by your side, if I do not know what those dreams really are!"

Orlana considered his words. She looked at him in a new light.

She reached out, fingers curling around a fine stem of crystal and drinking deeply of the strong red wine within.

"Very well," she said, finally. "Ask your questions. And I will not patronise you. I will treat you like a man. I will treat you like a general. I will treat you like a king."

"You have built a massive army. There are paths over the mountains; you do not need to take the fortress. And yet I think it is faster to take the fortress than risk the high passes. Correct?"

"Yes. Go on."

"Why Vagandrak? You do not need this land. What do you seek?"

"I seek to pass through."

"On a road to where? To what treasure?"

"I seek to travel the Plague Lands."

"Why?"

"There are three long deserted cities. Ratad, KaCarca and Eyusdan-Fall."

"What lies in these cities?"

"A terrible weapon," said Orlana, her voice low, eyes hooded. She drank again from the crystal; wine stained her lips, which glistened crimson, as if tainted by blood.

"But this is a race? Against time?"

"There is a time element, yes," said Orlana softly. "And I also need to continue to build the army. To expand. The people of Vagandrak will act as fodder for my mud-orcs. A genetic base. Food for creation. We will expand until there is no room left for us... and then..."

"Yes...?"

"I cannot speak now. My enemies are great. My enemies are terrible. To even think the thought is to risk annihilation." She stood and glided naked to the tent's flap, which she snapped back. The mud-orc camps spread away as far as the eye could see, hundreds and thousands of camp fires, burning, roasting meat, roasting human meat, boiling bones and eyes in huge cauldrons, talking in guttural growls.

Zorkai stepped up behind her, pressing in close, his hand tracing a curve down her spine. She shivered and he smiled. It made her seem more human, although he knew deep in his heart that she was not.

"So, the people of Vagandrak, they are just an obstacle?"

"Yes. We will smash Desekra Fortress and finish the business Morkagoth could not."

"There will be many deaths," said Zorkai, his heart filling with sadness for the days of blood and horror to come.

"You all die eventually," said Orlana, without emotion, and turned, returning to the silk sheets.

Torquatar held up his fist and the riders thundered to a halt behind him. Night was falling, and they were far from home, tired to the bone, their mounts exhausted, but General Vorokrim Kaightves had been most explicit in his instructions after receiving the message from King Yoon. The general's face had paled just a little beneath his thick blond beard, and his ice eyes had turned on Torquatar and the five other cavalry captains gathered in the high draughty chamber at the Keep of Desekra Fortress.

"The King assures us there is nothing to worry about," rumbled Vorokrim, his face like carved stone, his eyes hard, his vocal inflections offering nothing beyond the facts of his actual words. "He is adamant there is no army of mud-orcs advancing on our fortress, despite many messages from panicked merchants fleeing the south and seeking shelter beyond our walls and beyond our fortress. King Yoon... *reassures* us that all communications with King Zorkai of Zakora are friendly and in place, and that nothing untoward is about to occur. He says we are not at war. He claims all stories to the contrary are simply wild rumours spread by unsympathetic agitators intent on destabilising his monarchy."

Vorokrim's eyes swept the men before him. All good men. Strong men. Men who had proved themselves time and again in skirmishes against Zorkai's warriors in what was a never-ending border war, perpetuated not because of necessity, but down to the pride of the warrior-hearts of Zorkai's tribesmen.

Ineilden coughed into his gauntleted fist. "With all due respect, General Vorokrim, the King's assurances seem... *poorly researched*, and thus perhaps flawed, in the current climate of panic spread by merchants seeking shelter in Vagandrak."

Vorokrim considered this.

"In this missive," he gestured with the crumpled parchment in his fist, "King Yoon expressly forbids us sending out scouts to the south. He states he is in delicate talks with Zorkai over the future of our borders, and that he does not wish our foolhardy headstrong riders to incite an incident that could jeopardise his talks."

He allowed that to sink in.

"So, the King forbids any men travelling south?" said Ineilden, voice and eyes guarded.

"Exactly so," said Vorokrim.

"Then, what do we do?" rumbled Elmagesh, running a hand through his long, sweat-streaked hair. His dark armour gleamed by the light coming through the keep's archer slits. Outside, the grey light was fading fast.

"Obviously, I hereby forbid any of you to head south on a scouting mission. I forbid you to take your pick of the finest mounts from the stables, and to take your pick from the men available. We only have ten thousand left after King Yoon disbanded three quarters of the standing force."

He gave a narrow smile.

"What is our expressly forbidden mission, then?" rumbled Elmagesh.

"You have three days," said Vorokrim, "to *not* search out any possible enemy mud-orc movements. On this mission that does not exist, I would advise you do not engage any possible hostiles unless absolutely necessary. And of course, any information on possible advancing numbers, if indeed there are any, would be treated in a strictly confidential manner."

"When would you like us not to leave?" grinned Ineilden.

"I would like you not to leave immediately," said Vorokrim, eyes hard. Then he softened. "I love you all, like brothers; may the gods smile on your mounts, your sword arms and your children."

"Mounts, sword arms, children," intoned the men, and left the high room of the keep one by one.

Finally, General Vorokrim Kaightves was left alone. He moved to a slit in the thick stone and peered down at the long sections of killing ground between each wall, and then out, past the seemingly impenetrable fortress to the vast expanse of plains beyond, dotted with jagged rocks.

Silently, his servant Moshkin approached. "A drink, General?"

"Thank you."

"You think they will not succeed?"

The general barked a laugh. "I know they *will* succeed. And that, my friend, is the problem."

Now, they had found the mud-orcs. They were camped across the horizon as, in the far distance, the city of Pajanta Kin burned. And it was a big city. A *vast* city.

Hell, thought Torquatar with bitterness, sadness and a low-level, impending horror. Camped across the horizon? They *are* the horizon. His blood was chilled. Never had he seen so many campfires, never mind campfires belonging to a mud-orc enemy horde. Their dark shadows moving around the flames were the stuff of nightmares.

Covertly, the Vagandrak men returned to their mounts and rode hard and fast north. But they'd been spotted, and mud-orc units sent in pursuit.

"Captain, they're circling us."

"Wedge formation. We will ride fast."

"*They're* moving fast."

"I *know* that," hissed Captain Torquatar.

They rode hard for another twenty minutes, until their horses were about to keel over and die there on the hard-baked plains of northern Zakora. The men dismounted and walked their mounts for a while under a bloated yellow moon which filled the plains with a ghostly, ethereal light.

"It feels like we are dead and walk the shadow world of ghosts," said Xubadar, shivering.

"Thank you for sharing that," grumbled Torquatar.

"They're coming!" screamed one man, drawing free his sword. And they saw the enemy up close for the first time. The mud-orcs, numbering perhaps a hundred, had crept along a low ridgeline of rocks which formed the lower foothills leading to the Mountains of Skarandos. Now they had managed to get ahead, and were streaming out from the rocky cover, forming a wide line, three ranks deep, axes and notched swords at the ready.

"Mount up!" bellowed Torquatar and, alongside Ebodel, formed the point of the wedge. They unhitched lances, and kicked their mounts into a wild charge under the yellow moon, hooves galloping across the dusty, near-frozen plain, moonlight making it difficult to spot uneven ground and holes that would break a mount's leg.

Bravely, the Vagandrak cavalry charged an enemy four times their size.

As they came close, Torquatar heard the growling, the muttering, the slobbering. He saw the dark gleaming eyes, the spools of saliva, the twisted inhuman faces, the slashes of red through green skin like opened crimson wounds. They seemed not like a hundred mud-orcs, but like a thousand with razor-edged swords waiting under the yellow moon, the terrible moon, to rip and tear and slash and kill.

"KILL THEM!" bellowed Torquatar as they thundered towards the enemy, and the mud-orcs broke into a ragged charge and the two forces raced towards one another under the moon, smashing together with an unmistakable crash and cacophony of metal on metal, metal slicing flesh, hoof beats, cries, noises of shocked surprise and an element of chaos, always an element of chaos when foes collide; Torquatar slammed his lance point into a mud-orc's face and blood splattered him and he caught sight of the twisting snarling features up close but then he was amongst them, and his sword slashed up and clear, then down and bloody into a snarling face. He blocked a low cut and back-handed his sword across a black/green throat, horse still ploughing onwards with the speed and weight of the charge. He cut a head from a body and then he was free, free of the mud-orcs and the weight of the cavalry forced through and swords slammed and smashed up and down, staining the dry desert plains with orc blood. Axes and swords crashed into men and horses in retaliation sending squeals echoing out across the plain, but then the Vagandrak cavalry unit were through and galloped hard across the baked earth, only slowing another mile away where Torquatar turned in his saddle and peered across the eerie, moonlit plain.

The mud-orcs were not in pursuit.

"Dismount!" bellowed the captain, and the men thankfully slid wearily from saddles. Many were splattered with blood. Many had haunted eyes.

"Captain!" saluted Sauo, approaching.

"How many did we lose?"

"Six, captain. Along with their mounts. Eight wounded, but they can still fight."

Torquatar gestured for his men to gather round. "You did well today, my friends. We had the first taste of the enemy."

"Tell that to the dead! Yoon has a fucking lot to answer for!"

"No, what is important here is we *know* the enemy are approaching: fact. And more. We know they are closer than we could have imagined. Yes, the dead do not appreciate this information; but their families will when we petition Yoon for more soldiers and stand strong on the walls of Desekra Fortress. Now, no more talk that makes me think of deserters and sacrilege; we will walk our mounts for a half hour, then head back to the fortress. We have the information General Vorokrim Kaightves did not request."

"Are we at war, then?" shouted one soldier.

Torquatar waved his hand. He was tired. Tired to his bones. He smiled a grim smile. "Let's just say, if we are not, within a matter of days the blood will start to flow."

BEAUTY & THE BEAST

Ragorek thrashed and kicked and choked with the powerful mud-orc claws around his throat, and slowly, slowly died...

And then the mud-orc's head vanished, and the grip relaxed, and Dek pulled the creature clear of his brother, grinned darkly through a mask of blood splashes, and offered Ragorek his blood-slippery hand.

"Better stick with me, old man. Don't want you getting killed!"

Rag rolled to his feet and grabbed his sword, rubbing at his heavily bruised windpipe. When he spoke, it was a husky croak. "Thanks, Dek. I mean it."

Dek looked at him hard. "Yeah. Well I reckon nobody gets to kill you except me," he grunted, and launched a blistering attack at two mud-orcs which returned it with deafening bellows, charging the pugilist. They clashed in a flurry of blades and blows, leaving one dead, the second staggering forward without its axe-arm. It carried on past Dek, and Ragorek stabbed it through the eye.

"Right," he muttered. "I'll remember that."

Kiki felt wooden and clumsy. She had two left feet and two broken thumbs. Her short-sword seemed too heavy, her boots full of lead, her head full of residue from the honey-leaf, which came back to haunt her, a gentle pounding, a persistent tugging. Smoke me. Taste me. Eat me.

It had been years since she had been involved in a proper, full-on battle. A real fight. To the death.

Was it always like this, she thought.

Of course, mocked Suza. *You were always shit.* But after her fifth kill, suddenly a weight lifted from her shoulders and in a moment of red-mist epiphany the skies cleared, her mind found clarity, her body found equilibrium.

And then she danced...

She spun, and twirled, and her sword was a natural extension of her arm. She ducked and weaved with incredible grace and speed, her body flowing like liquid, her mind dropping into a zone where she no longer *thought* about combat, it just *was*. It was everywhere. Everything. Every moment that had ever existed. Every moment to come. Kiki *became* death and she moved like a ghost, a shadow, a ballerina of slaughter. Her sword flickered and the mud-orcs fell and one by one, Dalgoran, then Ragorek, then Narnok, then Dek, killed their final foes and watched Kiki dance amongst the final three beasts, killing them with such consummate ease it was a crime to pitch so few against her.

The last axe-blade was deflected, eyes cut out with a neat sideways sword slash, ending with the blade thrusting straight into the mud-orc's throat. It quivered erect, gibbering and drooling on the end of her blade as she looked fast, left and right, seeking more foes, before she front-kicked the beast from her blade and spun it lightning fast before guiding it back to its sheath.

Beneath her feet, the earth seemed to tremble. The trees spoke to her, whispering promises as their roots coiled through earthsoil, through worldrock, and Kiki's fingertips tingled and she could taste copper.

Her eyes came up. She met the admiring gazes of the other Iron Wolves. Then a great heavy sudden darkness slammed her, and she hit the blood-soaked, limb-scattered battleground of the snow-peppered frozen forest floor.

She could hear them speaking before consciousness fully returned.

"What happened to her?"

"It was too much. The excitement. She has a joy of battle, that one." She could almost sense Narnok grinning.

"No." Dek sounded worried. She could hear the rustle as he rubbed his stubbled chin. "This was something different. She's ill. Really ill."

"Yes," said Dalgoran, softly. Now she could hear the crackle of flames like music, and her left side was gloriously warm from the fire. She could still smell blood and stench from the slaughtered mud-orcs. Her fingers twitched, as if seeking a blade. "I cannot betray her trust, I cannot tell you exactly what ails her. But she is very, very ill."

"Is there nothing we can do?"

"No. Except look after her when times like this occur."

"What happens if it's in the midst of battle?" rumbled Narnok.

"Well, my friends, my Wolves, we must keep a close eye on her!"

The Iron Wolves rode fast for Timanta, pushing their mounts as hard as they dared. It had stopped snowing and the morning was bleak, grey, and what blue sky could be seen through the haze was the icy blue of a frozen lake, hostile and threatening and waiting to swallow an unwitting person whole into deep dark murderous depths. They stopped at noon for a cold lunch, stretching backs and chewing through tough dried beef strips and chunks of black bread. Narnok brewed a pan of water over a small fire and made sweet tea to ward off the cold, and for this the Wolves were thankful.

Kiki felt strange, and burrowed deep down into herself, alone with her thoughts rattling around her skull. She knew she was a possible weak link in their group; what would have happened if she'd collapsed during the battle with the mud-orcs? It was things like that which could get a person, or one of their companions, killed. She'd seen it before, several times, comrades-in-war dying whilst they tried to protect a sword-brother. Kiki didn't want the deaths of any more friends on her conscience.

And now they were racing to Timanta, before cutting southwest through The Drakka and then west to Desekra Fortress. The appearance of mud-orcs had given their mission to reform and get to Desekra a new urgency. If a roving band of mud-orcs had managed to get as far north as this, then they were closer than Dalgoran could have believed possible.

The journey for the rest of the day was a brutal thing, a test of endurance as great as any had endured before. The ground was still rocky, forcing each member of the group into hard-focused concentration, and each also had to be alert for mud-orcs or splice. The world suddenly seemed a very different, and hostile, place. Their comfort blanket of expected safety had been stolen away, and now each warrior was feeling particularly exposed, looking over their shoulders constantly.

They passed a burned and gutted village. People had been slaughtered like cattle, stabbed in the back, eyes put out. Every building had been put to the flame, and Narnok dismounted, his one good eye surveying the tracks.

"Mud-orcs," he spat, following the tracks off to the north. "Obviously the same group we slaughtered. So, they were on a mission to murder innocents, were they? I'm glad I split a head or ten open with my trusty axe."

They left the village behind, each with a heavy heart. There was nothing worse than seeing murdered villagers, men, women and children, to really make a soldier question the nature of the world, and existence, and life. One thing was for sure. The mud-orcs were real; the threat Dalgoran promised was coming to fruition.

As they approached the city of Timanta, a sprawl of grey and black buildings nestling under the protection of the White Lion Mountains where they curved away to the east like some great sweep across the face of the world, each drew rein and sat for a while, marvelling at the beauty of the city. Then Dek turned and pointed silently, and to the west they saw the massive, black oppressive bulk of Zunder, the long extinct volcano and centrepiece of many a historical tragedy on the stage and in literature. It had long been a fascination of playwrights and poets, and historically Timanta was built on the ruins of a previous city which had been destroyed by a pyroclastic flow. Geological surveys from the University of Vagan had shown that Timanta was indeed built *above* the previous city, and that beneath them lay a massive network of caverns and ancient streets, buried houses and temples from a different age that had been claimed in one mighty, long-forgotten volcanic eruption.

Dek lowered his arm and they turned their horses towards the black-walled city.

The sun was disappearing over the mountains, a glowing orange fireball which lit their faces with golden light.

"Let's ride," said Dalgoran, head high, face stern, and they broke into a canter, eager to reach a tavern, warmth and civilisation before nightfall.

The twisted screaming was gone and done. Zastarte sat on the floor, his own shirt torn and tattered, his head drooping wearily, dark curls touching the stone. Ember thought he was asleep, and in her long-drawn panic dreamed of escape, or rescue. Anything to get her away from this madman whom she had just watched kill Pestrat – murder him with nothing but a burning coal, pushing it not just through the man's eye, but onwards, deep into the brain as he screamed and screamed and thrashed and twitched, finally slumping forward, dead, and gone, and at some kind of peace; if nothing else, at least an oblivion away from pain.

Pestrat's body hung limp in chains. Zastarte was silent, brooding.

Ember noticed several candles flicker as a draught eased from somewhere deep in the cellar system. Her heart leapt. Had a door opened? Was somebody here to rescue her? Was she going to be saved? Please, by the Holy Mother and the Seven Sisters, *please* let it be one of the handsome guards from the City Watch! Heroes! Men of Iron! But then, and her brow twisted into a frown, wasn't *Prince Zastarte* supposed to be one of the Iron Wolves? Wasn't *he* supposed to be a Hero of Iron?

Footsteps came through the cellar, and Ember's heart leapt in joy. It was a woman! Sweet Mother of God, it was a woman! Come to save her! Come to take her away from the cruelty and torture and death.

She was tall and athletic, a natural warrior by her catlike movements. Her hair was bobbed and brown, her eyes dark in this gloomy subterranean vault. She glanced at Ember, but no emotion passed across her face.

Ember felt her soul fall away into darkness.

The woman approached Zastarte, then stopped. When she spoke, her words were low and gentle. "Prince? You have fallen a long way, my friend."

Zastarte chuckled and his head snapped up fast. So much for him being weary, or asleep. His eyes met those of the woman and for a long, long time they both remained silent. Then the woman's head turned and she surveyed the handiwork of the ruined cadaver chained to the wall.

"What *are* you doing?"

"Righting wrongs."

"I'd like to believe that. But what about her?" She gestured backwards with her thumb. Emba's heart fluttered in panic.

"Don't judge me, Kiki. That was always the problem with you; you were a fucking judgemental bitch who had far too much to say." He stood, and pushed past her to drop the glowing coal into the sizzling brazier. Then he turned to a bowl of water and washed his hands, then splashed water into his face. Taking a towel, he dried his skin before glancing at Ember, then looking sideways at Kiki.

"What do you want? I'm busy."

"Dalgoran is reforming the Iron Wolves. Vagandrak is about to be invaded by mud-orcs and terrible creatures. But obviously, you are far too busy here with your..." she glanced around, face wrinkled in distaste, "*playthings*, to be worried about the good of the fucking people. What happened to you, Zastarte? You were a noble man, once."

"Noble men grow tired, and bitter, and cynical," he said, throwing the towel to one side.

"You can walk away from this. From this kind of life."

He gave a bitter laugh. "You think so? You think I don't have a commitment here?"

"A commitment? What, to torture?"

"To putting things right," he said, dark eyes hooded. "I wouldn't expect you to understand. I wouldn't expect *any* of you bastards to understand. Heroes. Ha! They called us heroes because we were good, we were fast, we were hard; putting a blade into the eyes or throat of a living creature doesn't make you a hero; slicing somebody's throat, cutting open their bowels, hacking off arms and fucking legs. What's heroic about that? War is justification for inhuman slaughter."

"The mud-orcs *were* inhuman."

He flapped a hand. "Just a formality. It wouldn't have mattered to the politicians and the King if it had been men instead of scary beasts. Whoooo! Stories to frighten small children with. Murder to achieve votes. If I didn't know better, I'd say Tarek engineered the whole fucking incident, had Morkagoth on his fucking payroll, set the whole thing up to secure his throne against insurgency. After all, it was good old Tarek who saved the people, saved Vagandrak; without him, the people would be enslaved, or dead in their beds. They had a lot to thank him for. No wonder they showered us with jewels! But then, there never could have been a doubt. It was all a sham."

"Is that what you really believe? Then you're more twisted than the cancer eating my soul."

"Oh, cancer is it, now? Don't be trying to pluck at my heart strings. All my strings snapped a long time ago. Left them entwined on a distant battlefield with a dead sorcerer and my honour pissed out through my boots."

"You took the money, the jewels, the lands, Prince."

"Oh yes," he said, and moved closer.

Kiki tensed. Zastarte had always been an unpredictable son of a bitch.

She could smell his sweat, smell his perfume, smell his pleasure. Her eyes narrowed. If he tried anything, she'd kill him.

Well. She'd try…

He circled her, like a predator. Then took a step back.

"What's Dalgoran offering?"

"A chance to redeem your soul," said Kiki, softly.

"Done!" Zastarte clapped his hands suddenly, and laughed. "I was getting bored, anyway. There's only so many ways to torture a person. Only so many platitudes they can wail and scream and bubble." He moved behind the trembling Ember, and grabbed a fresh silk shirt, pulling it over his head. The lace ruffs at neck and collar were pristine white. He dabbed a touch of perfume on his skin, then moved in front of Ember. He looked down at her. "What am I going to do with you, my pretty?"

"P… p… p…" she managed.

Zastarte glanced back at Kiki. "You think I should release her?"

"You do what you think is right," said Kiki, eyes hard.

"I'll release her," said Zastarte, and undid the shackles with an iron key.

Ember climbed up from the bench, rubbing her wrists, eyes darting from Zastarte to Kiki and back again, as if this was all some cruel joke. She licked her lips and took an experimental step sideways.

"Go on, my chicken. Off you cluck." He pointed. "That way. Down the tunnel. Can't have you using the front door."

"Wh… where does it lead?"

"Don't worry, it leads out to another cellar and there are steps up to a different street. But… and this is a promise… don't tell anybody what happened here." He grinned, and stroked his chin. "Or I'll come and find you. So, hush. Yes? Now go. Before I change my mind."

Ember ran into the gloom, and quickly vanished.

Kiki looked at him. "That was the truth, wasn't it? You've not sent her off into some terrible trap?"

Zastarte spread his hands, eyes sparkling, mouth a wide smile, face the humorous mask of an astonished nobleman; in an instant he was transformed from evil to joy, from torturer to regent. Kiki frowned, annoyed at how easily he could switch on his charisma. It made him a dangerous individual.

"Would I lie to you?" he purred.

Kiki led the way, stepping out onto the cobbled road slick with ice. A wind whipped down the street, bringing little flurries of snow. Kiki looked up and down the street, eyes narrowing, hand on sword hilt, as Zastarte came out behind her. He lifted his hand to his carriage, parked a little way down the street, and the driver flicked reins. Wheels rattled on cobbles and the carriage approached, pulling alongside.

Kiki and Zastarte found themselves looking at the tensioned points of three crossbows, in front of three grinning faces wearing helms of the City Watch. Boots thudded on cobbles and more men poured around the corner, and from a doorway across the street. Moonlight gleamed on steel.

"See what you've done?" muttered Kiki.

"Damn! They must have been onto me! Either that, or you led them here with your big flapping boots and loud vulgar peasant voice."

"Don't tar me with your twisted perversion," snapped Kiki.

"OK, my pretties, put down your weapons, real slow like," came a careful, authoritative voice from behind the dark gleam of a full face helm.

Kiki glanced at Zastarte, who gave the faintest of smiles as they… *connected*.

They kicked apart as three clicks and *whines* hummed and three crossbow bolts ricocheted from the building behind in a shower of sudden sparks. Swords erupted in smooth arcs, Kiki's trusty iron short sword, Zastarte's too-delicate rapier that looked as if a decent strike would see it shattered into a thousand brittle pieces.

The rapier jabbed through the window, taking out a guard's eye, who squealed as Kiki charged the gathering of surprised guards; they had expected submissive captives under the threat of three crossbow bolts, now Kiki was amongst them, sword slashing left and right. The guards were grouped too tight, a huddle, and Kiki waded right into the middle moving like a whirlwind, blade slamming out, cutting necks and faces, arms and thighs and jabbing between the joints of armour at groin and armpit. Zastarte spun around the back of the carriage, leapt up the iron-rung ladder and thrust his rapier up into the spine of the driver, withdrawing it fast. The man cried out and toppled from the seat, and Zastarte leapt to take his position, sheathing his weapon and grabbing the reins.

"Yah!" he screamed, and the horses whinnied and charged the melee, slamming guards out of the way with their sheer weight and bulk.

"Get him!" yelled the captain, and there came a whine and a smash of wood as a bolt appeared between Zastarte's legs and hissed up into the flurries of snow falling vertically.

The prince paled, and kneeling, stabbed down with his rapier once, twice, and on the third strike hit flesh. He grabbed the reins and drew them hard. The two lead horses reared up, hooves clattering on armour as a guard went down.

"Kiki!"

She was fighting in a frenzy, but his words came through to her and he flicked the reins once more. The horses powered forward, knocking two more guards from their feet and as the carriage accelerated Kiki whirled and leapt, catching the ladder. Her eyes were glowing. She laughed a maniac laugh as they slammed down the street, iron-rimmed wheels thundering on cobbles, the guards milling behind her – with eight men down, dead or injured, their blood in the gutters.

Kiki clambered to the top. Zastarte met her gaze.

"I'm wondering if Dalgoran can even pay me enough," he said, tossing back his curls.

"I just *saved you* from the City Watch!"

"No no, sweet Kiki; I believe *I* just saved you from your madman rage. Yes? Surely not?"

There came another click and whine, and a bolt smashed thoguh wood, passing between them in close proximity and cutting the cloth and lace ruff of Zastarte's sleeve, before whining off into the night.

"There's still a guard in the carriage?"

"Sorry, I did mean to mention it."

"Zas!"

"Have you seen my shirt? Do you *know* how hard it is to get a good tailor around here?"

Kiki sheathed her sword, grabbed the rim of the carriage and leapt, body spinning over, twisting, boots slamming through the door and into the carriage. There came several thumps, then the door opened and the unconscious guard was tossed to the icy cobbles where he rolled over fast, breaking bones.

"I could have pulled over, you know," said Zastarte, talking down through the crosbow quarrel's hole in the roof.

Kiki's curses were unintelligible through her snarls.

Trista was tall, elegant, and incredibly beautiful. She wore the richest of pink silk ballgowns, a magnificent dress which billowed out from her waist in a huge globe of shiny loveliness, glittering with stitched sequins. Her shoes were a glossy pink, expensive exclusive items made to measure by Hitchkins of Drakerath. She wore a gold watch on one wrist, which glittered with inset precious stones, and a diamond bracelet on the other, which sparkled as it caught the light. Her face had high cheekbones and a natural nobility, her cheeks flushed with just the right level of pinkness, her lips painted with just the right pastel shade of red, her earrings glittered with yet more diamonds set in molten tears of gold, shown off ably by a hairstyle that piled atop her head, luscious blonde curls stacked and skilfully interwoven to add at least a foot in height to her already tall frame. She was smiling, her teeth perfect and white and even, and her eyes sparkled as brightly as the diamonds at wrist and ear and throat.

In the distance, music played, a slow-beat rhythm of strings and piano. Behind her, the banquet was nearly over, the large banquet hall with trestle tables covered in white and gold linen, decimated after the two hundred or so guests had taken their greedy fill. Red wine traced patterns on the linen like droplets of blood.

Trista sipped pink wine from a tall crystal flute, which glittered and sparkled, reflecting the light from a hundred glowing candles. She was stood at the top of a wide set of stairs in the largest, most fabulous, most expensive tavern in Timanta, music like a rolling, grumbling ocean filling the space behind her.

It had been a fine wedding. The bride in white, the groom in black. They were both beautiful people, sparkling people, his laugh a soldierly rumble without much humour, her laugh like that of a castrated donkey (or a donkey being castrated). They made a perfect couple. A beautiful couple. The service had been immaculate, a triumph of decoration, good dress-sense, perfect timing, "ooh"s and "ahhh"s and "isn't she beautiful"s. They had walked down the red carpet of the Church of the Seven Sisters as independent, isolated, singular people who completely believed in love and in one another; and walked out, hand in hand, her face and eyes glowing, his cheeks flushed red with stress and anxiety, but both smiling, content in the knowledge they had become one, united in a holy place, setting off on the biggest adventure of their lives together!

Trista wiped away a tear and took another sip from her pink bubbly wine.

"So sad, so terrible," she muttered, and started forward down the carpeted corridor, her pink shoes silent against the thick pile. She passed several broad oak doors, each one a portal into another realm of wealth and luxury. This really was a fabulous place. A palace, almost! No expense had been spared in making every detail exquisite.

Trista stopped, and stooping awkwardly in her gown, placed the fluted crystal on the carpet by the wall. Her painted lips had left smears, marking the crystal. She stood. She wiped away another tear. Moved again down the corridor, stopping finally at the very end door. The wedding suite. The most fabulous of all the fabulous rooms in this most opulent of buildings.

Trista reached out, long fingers touching the oak. *They are in there, newly wedded, their lives perfect. They are lucky beyond belief. They have a long bright sparkling future ahead of them. They have already consummated the marriage, maybe even now she carries his seed and will be with child. They'll have a plump bouncing baby boy, soon followed by a golden haired utterly perfect beautiful little sister. And the world will be so right for them. Their future will be an everlasting dream.*

Trista frowned, beautiful face scrunching up a little.

But…

But maybe their future won't be so perfect after all. Maybe he'll be out soldiering, on a raid or a mission, and get stabbed through the throat by a short sword, his blood bubbling along the blade as he watches his own reflected face twisted in horror in the sharpened steel. Or maybe she will be out in the market, basket on her arm filled with a selection of vegetables, and some nobleman's carriage comes thundering past, the horses spook at something, a screaming child maybe, the way horses often do, and change direction suddenly and she panics and before you know it, she's under the flailing hooves, then tangled around the axles of the carriage to become a bloody rag doll. She lies unconscious in bed for two days with broken legs and ribs and spine, mumbling incoherently, until finally her heart stops and she dies from her injuries, or from shock, or from long lost love. Or maybe their first child will have a terrible deformity that drives him to drink, and her slowly mad with the pressure, and slowly everything falls apart like an old dress at the seam. Falls apart. That's the key. Everything always falls apart.

She turned the door handle. Opened the heavy oak portal. Stepped through. Closed it behind her.

The room was dominated by a massive four-poster bed, each post ornately carved in ancient dark wood.

A single candle sat on a low table in the corner, burning with a steady flame. It threw long shadows around the room and gave just enough light to highlight the two entwined lovers, man and wife, holding one another beneath white silk sheets.

So sweet.

So loving.

So adorable.

I wish it could go on forever.

Well, maybe it can...

She pulled free a long, slender dagger. It gleamed black in the candlelight. Trista wiped away another tear from her beautiful cheek and advanced on the bed. Both newlyweds, man and wife, were breathing deep; no doubt after a wild couple of hours consummating their marriage in the obvious way. Her arm was across his chest: slender, pretty, pale white, like a long thin worm.

Trista moved around the bed, staring at them, dagger in one hand, the other trailing across the light, gauzy curtains that hung from the top of the bed. Silently, carefully, she reached out and lifted one of the gauze curtains, pulling it over her head so that she was *inside* that special domain; an intruder, within the new nest. A scorpion amongst the chicks.

"I'm sorry it has to be this way," she murmured, and lifted the dagger.

Candlelight gleamed from cold hard iron.

The groom's eyes flickered open and met hers, and for long seconds she could read the confusion there. He recognised her, but did not realise where he was, did not understand why he was awakening to see her face. His mouth opened forming a question, but the dagger swept down, cracking through his breast bone and skewering the heart beneath. Blood fountained, covering the bride, Trista's pink gown, the gauzy curtains and the wood of the ornate four-poster.

The groom thrashed, hands clawing silk, then died swiftly on the bed.

The bride came awake. She was worse the wear for wine, eyes bloodshot, face scrunched in confusion. She felt the warm blood on her and saw Trista first, drenched in blood, and opened her mouth in a silent scream. But nothing would come out. Then she glanced at her new husband and put both her hands to her mouth, blood-stained breasts bobbing.

"I'm sorry," said Trista.

"Why... oh why? Why do this?"

Trista leant forward, the blade lifting again. The bride read her intention and tried to back away, head shaking. Trista climbed onto the bed, eyes narrowed.

"Come here. I am saving you. I am purifying you. I am making sure your love remains pure; that it lasts *forever*..."

The bride began to scream.

The blade slashed left to right, a back-hand horizontal stroke that opened the woman's throat with medical precision. She toppled to her side, hands scrabbling at the gaping second mouth, blood flushing down her breasts and belly. Her legs thrashed for a while and Trista sat down, watching her die, watching the light fade from her eyes, studying the confusion and the shock and the questions.

Her leg kicked, and then the bride was still.

Wearily, Trista climbed off the now sodden, blood-soaked bed. It was a charnel pit. A butcher's block. She gave a great sigh and a weight greater than the world settled across her shoulders like ash from a volcanic eruption. She moved to the door.

The first man entered at a run, and Trista's blade punched into his belly, exploding him with an "oof" and sending him rolling into the bedchamber. She moved out into the corridor, where she could hear a commotion down the stairs. She padded forward, eyes fixed, face showing no emotion. Two men appeared at the top of the stairs, half-dressed and carrying swords. Trista stepped between them and her knife slashed left, then right, seeming to almost float past them. But its razor edge opened them like gutted fish and she was on the stairs, descending, a pool of blood following her from step to step to step.

A scream echoed behind her, high and shrill.

Followed by, "Call the City Watch! There's been murder, bloody murder!" But by then, Trista was out of the building, into the darkness, treading through fresh-fallen snow in her glossy pink shoes. She was out and gone, swallowed by the night, vanishing into the peaceful white snow flurries that conspired to mask her terrible crime.

Trista sat on the edge of the fountain, trailing her hand in the water where she'd cracked the ice. Her ballgown was a crumpled heap beside her, and she wore slim-fitting dark clothes and thigh-length black boots. The fountain tinkled, powered by some underground spring which forced pressurised water up a central spout and out over varying diameters of carved white stone. The surface of each platter had turned to ice, but water still moved beneath. The bottom pool, however, was pink after Trista washed the blood from her hands, and droplets of crimson peppered the front section, staining the ice.

Trista lifted her face to the falling snow, and tears rolled down her cheeks.

She did not act like she'd heard the figure approach; if she had, she did not acknowledge.

"Trista."

"Hello, Kiki."

Kiki moved forward and seated herself on the edge of the fountain. "We saw what you did. We were too late to stop you."

"I know."

"The City Watch are looking for you. They will hang you."

"I know this, also."

"And you'll let them?"

Trista gave a small, tinkling laugh, and avoided an answer. "What are you doing here, Keek? You're a long way from home and the honey-leaf."

Kiki gave a frown, and her eyes hardened into ice.

"Dalgoran is reforming the Iron Wolves. The mud-orcs are back. Along with terrible, twisted creatures made from horses and men. I know you probably have other things on your mind, right now, but I'd suggest staying here in Timanta isn't your safest option."

"They'll never find me. Never catch me."

She turned, and with sudden ferocity stared into Kiki's eyes. "Do you understand? Why I did it? Can you read my motives?"

Kiki bit her lip. Then gave a little shake of her head.

"They deserved the honesty death brings. They loved each other too much; and they deserved to love one another forever, not see it destroyed, not see it all fucked up. Narnok would understand. Ask him, later."

"Because of his wife?"

"Yes. And his face."

"You've met him? Since he received his... scars?"

"Several times our paths have crossed," said Trista, sadly, looking down at the ground. Then: "I loved him, you know. Loved him more than anything, more than life itself, more than the stars and the universe, more than the glow of a new-born's face, more than a single perfect snowflake."

She pushed the long, slim, black dagger into her boot. It had been cleaned since it carried out its murderous work.

"But they leave you. They always leave you in the end. The spark goes. The fire dies. People get fat and bald and old and ugly. Men run away with other women, women run away with other men; people move on, move out, move up. And love never survives, Kiki, can you not see that?" She looked up then. "Love only exists for the smallest fraction of time; the tiniest of connections. Like a splinter in the universe."

"Yes. I can see that," said Kiki, gently.

She reached out, slowly, as one approaching a passive tiger. She placed her hand on Trista's arm.

"And that's why you can capture it. Freeze it. Distil it. Yes, there is pain; there is always pain. But what is a little pain and blood against an unending backdrop of eternal love? In death, death after ultimate, mind-blowing, all-consuming love, you can capture that moment. Like diamonds in ice. You can see that, can't you, Kiki?"

"Come on. Dalgoran is here. The others are here. We need to move."

Trista glanced about, possibly concerned, or not, that somebody – a guard – might spot them. Dawn was breaking, the sky growing light beyond the light fall of snow. It wouldn't be long before they came looking for the killer in the pink gown. "Why should I come with you?" she said, suddenly, head snapping up.

"Because," said Kiki gently, "I love you. I have always loved you. I will always love you."

Trista stared into Kiki's eyes, and they remained like that for two, maybe three minutes. Trista smiled, then. A sudden movement. "If you'd been lying, I would have killed you."

"I know."

"I love you too, Kiki. And the others. But you're special."

"Thank you. Come on."

They stood. Trista prodded the ballgown with the toe of her boot. "I won't do it again. I promise. I won't do it again."

"Hush now. Come with me."

And holding Trista around the shoulders, Kiki gently walked her away from the fountain of blood and ice.

ZUNDER

The Iron Wolves rode under a bloated yellow moon, huddled in cloaks, heads bent against a savage, ice-filled wind which howled across the bleak, volcanic landscape surrounding the mighty dormant volcano, Zunder. They had said little to one another when Kiki returned with Zastarte and Trista; there were no warm greetings, no slaps on the back, no hearty guffaws and reminiscing of days gone past. Just a gathering of hardened middle-aged men and women, dressed in blacks and greys, wrapped in oiled leather cloaks, their eyes moving across one another with suspicion and guilt and a catalogue of old memories; bad memories.

"It's been a long time," said Dek, as Zastarte rolled his neck and stared disapprovingly at the cloak proffered by Kiki.

"Not long enough," smiled the dandy, and the good humour fell from Dek's face like a shadow under sunlight.

There had been a few mumbled greetings, and Dalgoran had fought well to disguise his massive disappointment at this, the ultimate, final reunion of his elite squad – the Iron Wolves – in all their decadence.

And now, they rode across a bleak and savage landscape, displaying the psychopathic wrath of Nature.

In silence.

It wasn't supposed to be like this, he thought, and shook his head.

So many years, so much pain; so many crimes not accounted for.

The bitterness was ripe in Dalgoran's mouth like he sucked a bad fruit.

The sadness hung heavy, in his soul.

I came looking for old heroes, he realised, pulling his cloak a little tighter. I came looking for *my* heroes. And instead, I found heroes crippled by their deeds, haunted by their past, twisted and broken by the noose of honour which once hung around their necks and had now constricted, choking their honesty; choking their honour.

He looked up at the yellow moon. It looked sick and pale.

What have I done? he asked himself.

What, in the name of the Furnace, have I done?

Within minutes they noticed signs of pursuit, and the Iron Wolves kicked their mounts into a gallop, riding hard away from Timanta with a group of City Guards on their heels, eight in number, wearing half-armour and pushing their mounts like men possessed. After a couple of miles of breakneck folly, as the rough trails through black igneous rock and dust grew narrower and they approached a steep valley of angular volcanic walls, Dalgoran gestured to Narnok, Dek and Zastarte, who nodded and drew up their mounts abruptly. The General continued with Kiki, Ragorek and Trista, seeking shelter, for huge storm clouds threatened the horizon beyond the towering, threatening bulk of Zunder.

Dek drew his sword and rolled his shoulders, as Narnok hefted his axe and Zastarte weighed his rapier. Zastarte was smiling, his long curls whipped by the wind, and he grinned at the two big men. "Hey! Just like old times!"

"Fuck old times," rumbled Narnok.

"But why such a sour face? Sorry. Sorry!"

"I don't appreciate your nasty humour," growled Narnok, throwing Zastarte a glance with his good eye. "I've cut off men's heads for less. Used their hollowed out skulls as plant pots."

"Narnok, my friend, we're on the same side!" he wailed with a theatrical toss of his hand, and as the guards approached at a gallop, their numbers forced into three abreast as the valley walls narrowed the trail, so the three Iron Wolves dug heels to flanks, and charged...

Dalgoran found a narrow channel which wormed between high walls of towering igneous rock. Zunder was there, an ever-present shadow blocking out the fading daylight, and the ground was bare, lifeless, angular and sharp, and devoid of any living thing. They followed the narrow trail to a dead end, and the rocky walls were possible to climb in an emergency, although each protrusion looked brittle and dangerous. Ragorek built a small fire as Kiki and Trista unrolled a tarpaulin and draped it over wooden poles wedged into the rocks to give a makeshift shelter.

Trista got a fire going and Kiki made a chicken soup from stock and vegetables. Trista was sullen and silent, lost in memories, lost in dark thoughts. Kiki felt no need to breach the mood, for she was suffering with her own problems. Suza had crawled back into her mind like a toad onto a dead black lily, taunting her, mocking, her tinkling laughter an ever-present soundtrack pushing Kiki to the borders of sanity. And on top of this, she had begun to suffer chest pains. Mild at first, and she'd put it down to withdrawal from the honey-leaf she still craved, combined with a renewed necessity for battle. In truth, the pain terrified Kiki. It was directly over the scar where the surgeons had cut into her chest, missing her heart by a finger's breadth. It did not bode well for her future, and her mood was dark.

Dek, Narnok and Zastarte returned as the sun was sinking behind the dormant volcano, Zunder. They brought with them extra mounts, weapons, armour and supplies from the guards' saddlebags, which they had looted with care. Some soldiers had been known to booby-trap their kit in the hope it would cause damage if in the wrong hands.

And now, as darkness fell, all sat around the fire, eating soup and watching one another. There was an uneasy atmosphere, as if seven starving lions had all been put in the same cage with one chunk of meat.

Dalgoran coughed, finally, and stood, putting hands on hips. He was illuminated by the flickering flames as a harsh wind howled around the outside of their little tunnel carved through the volcanic landscape. In the firelight, Dalgoran looked old, older than his seventy years, a worn out man: a shell. A man who had gone beyond his natural longevity and was simply waiting to die. He was pale, and heavily lined, with dark hollows under his eyes and a weariness to his face and stance. He glanced from one wolf to the next to the next, and with a sinking feeling inside, Kiki realised how disappointed he was in them all.

They had let him down.

They had killed his dream.

Fucking *murdered* it.

"You were my heroes, once," he said quietly, face softening into memories. "We stood together on the walls of Drakerath Fortress and we shook our fists; not just at the enemy, with its legions of mud-orcs; not just at Morkagoth, that evil bastard who wanted to take our souls; but at the *world!* We were proud and defiant, and believed we could never be beaten, no matter how large and fierce the enemy. We believed we could change things. We believed in truth and honour."

He stared at them all.

"When the seer gave me the prophecy, and I knew in my heart the mud-orcs were coming, I believed, I truly believed that reforming the Iron Wolves was what was necessary; in my arrogance, I thought I was the only man who had a solution. Maybe I was wrong. Jagged has petitioned King Yoon. Maybe we will arrive at Drakerath and this whole pointless reunion will have been for nothing. Maybe Yoon has reformed the army, and even now forty thousand Vagandrak warriors line the walls. If that doesn't repel the mud-orcs, I don't know what will." He smiled ruefully.

"If you believe that, then why continue with all this horse shit, old man?" rumbled Narnok.

Dalgoran gave a half shrug. "I can feel your disbelief. All of you. Those who want to be here are pandering to an old fool and his unfathomable, erratic conclusions based on – what? I have no evidence. Just half-connected clues which may well lead to a different outcome. I thought I had everything so clear in my mind. Now, it is filled with confusion. Some of you are here for money, or to run away from gods only know what horrific crimes. I look at you, now, here, like this; and I feel like I have created a monster. It is a very sad day for me."

He sat down.

Kiki stared around at the faces flickering in the fire. Each was unreadable; hard, and hard to be broken. She frowned then, and licked her lips, and was about to speak when Dek raised a hand and coughed and rolled his neck with a crackling of released tension.

"You are wrong, General," he said in a strong, proud voice, looking around at the other Iron Wolves.

"Aye? How's that?"

"Maybe you have no hard evidence concerning the mud-orcs' return. Maybe. But you have the heart of your country, and the heart and well-being of your people at the forefront of your mind. Most people are selfish by their very nature, General. By all the gods I've seen it, and done it. All of us here are normal men and women, and yes, we were great fighters in our day and we stood on the walls of Drakerath and defied the enemy. But that does not make us inherently good people; it never did. You, like everyone else, fell in love with the legend until you couldn't see the reality. We haven't changed, Dalgoran. But by the same breath, we *have changed*. We all here respect you more than any other, for you are our role model; you are our brother; and you are our father. I know I speak for everybody, in saying that we *will* follow you, and we will not let you down."

"Well, *I'm* here for the cash," said Zastarte.

"And to save your worthless stinking scrawny fucking neck," rumbled Narnok.

"Stop!" commanded Kiki, voice strong, eyes hard. "Dek is right. Nobody is forcing any of us to be here. We follow Dalgoran out of respect and honour and loyalty, no matter what our twisted mouths spit out." She turned on Zastarte. "You are one twisted fucker, Prince. I know this. I know that deep down inside that damaged heart, you are not a good person at all. Well then. You say you're here for the money? I'm telling you now, there is none. So, if you wish to walk away, now's the time to make that decision. Go on. Fuck off."

Everybody looked to Zastarte, who lounged back, an easy grin on his face, long dark curls glossy by the firelight. His eyes glittered with comedy. "Oh, Kiki, how terribly dramatic! You are a fabulous storyteller, spinning your wonderful yarns of good and bad, law and order, the darkness in men's souls. Ooh!" He gave a little shiver. "Even if there is no money here, now, there will be; when once again we build the legend of the Iron Wolves! All we need is to fight back another evil slathering horde and the kings and wealth and ladies will be lining up to be abused and robbed. You know this is the case." He turned on Dek. "So, you can talk about honour and nobility and building the ego of a pointless old man, but I for one am in this for the cash and the infamy, dear boy."

Dek growled and moved to get up. "Why, you pup, I'll beat the likes of that talk from you with my bare hands."

"Ah yes, our famous pit fighter shows his true colours. Anything that cannot be conquered via the intellect must be mashed under the battered fists. I abhor your painful pointless brutality, Dek; you are an insult to the name of education and civilisation."

"An insult, am I?" snarled Dek, face turning purple. "I'll fucking educate you, you fanciful, pompous fuckwit!"

"Ooh, I do declare my fear… no, wait, I believe I gave a tremble." Only Narnok caught the glint of the slender black dagger already in Zastarte's fist and half-concealed by a lace wrist ruff.

Dek surged up, but Narnok grabbed his arm in an iron grip, and pulled him back. "He has a blade," murmured the giant axeman.

Dek gave a nasty smile. "Yeah? Well, I can handle that."

"Stop it!" snapped Kiki. "This is ridiculous. Vagandrak is under threat from an age-old enemy. Come on. We were attacked by those deviant horse creatures, and we were attacked by a marauding group of mud-orcs. *That* doesn't happen randomly. *That* hasn't happened for twenty-five damn years, since we slaughtered that bastard Morkagoth! There's no smoke without fire. We know the score here, we're not battle virgins. Stop bloody squabbling and let's make an effort for the people of Vagandrak; let's do what we do best: fight, and kill, the enemy; but most of all, let's show Dalgoran his faith in us is not misplaced! Are you with me, Wolves?"

Dek stood. "I'm with you, Kiki. General." He nodded at Dalgoran. "To the death."

"Me also," rumbled Narnok, climbing ponderously to his feet. He stared hard at Dek. "I hate this bastard here more than life itself, but will put aside my feud until we are clear of this new threat." He hefted his axe, and Kiki swallowed. One day, their fight to the death was coming. And it would be an awesome, terrible battle.

"Trista?" Kiki's voice had dropped in volume, was now gentle, as if dealing with a delicate child.

Trista looked up. Her face was unreadable, but she gave a single nod. "I have a need in my soul; a need for repentance. I have done so many bad things, I recognise my soul is cracked. I am damaged in here," she clenched fist to breast, "and I'm struggling to put it right. But I will come with you. I will stand with General Dalgoran. After all, he is my father." She gave a cold and brittle smile.

Kiki gave a nod and looked finally to Prince Zastarte. Still, he lounged, like a lizard, a snake, but she could read the subsurface coiled tension in him: like a tightly wound spring, just vibrating and waiting to uncoil with a sudden burst of violence. Maybe he felt his back was against a wall, and the only way was to fight free? This little hollow in the rock was certainly claustrophobic to a large degree. And Zastarte was a creature of chaos, perhaps more than anybody here, Kiki realised.

"You tug at the heart strings, my sweetie." He smiled, but his eyes were hard. "Truly, you do. And you fight a good battle. But, like Trista, I feel my soul is darkened with shadows and death. Stained, I am. I am a bad man through and through. I believe I would do nothing but sully and poison your noble cause."

"You would strengthen it and cleanse your soul," said Kiki.

"I think my soul is beyond redemption," said Zastarte, smiling.

"Fight with us," said Kiki. "Come on! You complete us! Complete this unit!"

"Do you all feel like this?" asked Zastarte, eyes moving to meet the others in the group. They all nodded, and Dek squatted down before him.

"I confess. Yes, the velvet pantaloons disturb me. Yes, the lace ruffs disturb me. Your stinking perfume is capable of drawing in every fucking mud-orc for a three mile radius, and this disturbs me more than anything, you dandy bastard. But I still love you." He punched him in the chest, rocking the man. "We all do. We'd die for you. You're our brother, Zastarte, despite your... crimes. You're an Iron Wolf."

Zastarte nodded, smiling, eyes glittering. "Indeed, I do believe you have brought a tear to my eye. And that was something I thought impossible." He stood, and gripped Dek's arm, wrist to wrist, in the warrior's handshake.

Suddenly, something large, thrashing and violent landed in the middle of the fire, launched from above, sending coals and burning wood exploding outwards. Talons lashed out, striking sparks across Narnok's breastplate and sending the axeman staggering back against the volcanic rock wall. Its long tail, barbed with a sting, jabbed for Kiki's face and in reflex she swayed back, sword hissing free of scabbard, blade slamming up and through the thick mid-section of tail. The sting and writhing tail landed in the fire, still squirming.

"Back!" yelled Dalgoran, drawing his own sword, and the Iron Wolves circled the splice as far as the constrictive tunnel would allow.

It reared up in the flames, parts of its fur and flesh on fire, and glared at them, growling in a low rumble as its head lowered and it surveyed the Iron Wolves and their general; it was huge, bigger than the other deviant creatures they had dealt with, and muscles bulged under thick skin more like armour than flesh. It wasn't obvious what had created the splice, from which beast it had clawed its way out, kicking and screaming; there was part horse in there and part wolf. But also something else, for its arms and legs had armoured black plates with thick black hairs, and its eyes were a jet black, glassy, emotionless. But what sent shivers vibrating down Kiki's spine were the tiny pincers emerging from the lower jaw, constantly juddering and clicking, as if this horse and wolf had even, maybe, also absorbed an element of *insect*.

"By the Seven Sisters," murmured Ragorek, hefting his sword.

The splice cackled, head swinging around, covering all of them. It turned, claws crunching through glowing coals, and then launched at Narnok and Dek who kicked apart, weapons slamming out to clatter from armour. Even Narnok's axe was deflected, although it wasn't a clean strike and was delivered with an element of panic. Narnok had never been scared of another man in his entire life. But this… *thing* disturbed him to his very core.

It whirled, too fast for its size and bulk, and talons slashed for Kiki and Zastarte. Kiki took the blow against her shortsword, but the power forced her back against the wall with a grunt. Zastarte rolled with elegance and agility, rising with a knife in each fist. He threw them, and one glanced from a black-plated head sporting tufts of fur, whereas the second embedded in the centre of the splice's left eyeball. Its pincers clicked with incredible speed, but there was no cry, no sound of pain. The stump of its tail thrashed, like an angry scorpion deprived of its poisonous barb.

"You pointless, petty humans," it snarled and clicked between its pincers, as a great black tongue lolled in a maw filled with broken yellow teeth. "You think to stand against the Horse Lady? Look at me. Imagine a thousand like me. Imagine *ten thousand* like me! Your days are numbered, little people. You are nothing more than walking, talking, breathing corpses."

It lunged, but Narnok batted away the claw. Then Ragorek, longsword in both hands, screamed a battle cry and charged forward, sword slashing down, which, against a human, would have been a strike from clavicle to hip-bone. The sword raked against armour and the splice punched out, claws curled into a fist; the fist rammed Ragorek in the ribs, just below his lungs, smashing through chainmail vest and deep *into* the cavity beyond. Dek hammered his own blade into the splice's neck, where it hacked through flesh and blood arced out in a shower. Narnok's axe cleaved through the limb embedded in Ragorek's body as he gasped, and coughed out blood, and staggered back to hit the wall where he slid to the ground, face ashen in shock, both blood-splattered hands gripping the severed limb embedded within him as blood poured and frothed at his mouth.

"Ragorek!" screamed Dek, as the Iron Wolves attacked the beast.

DESEKRA

Desekra Fortress. Guardian of the south. Vast and mighty protector of the Pass of Splintered Bones. A thousand years old, and built by the direct ancestor of King Yoon, the mighty King Esekra the Great, who had grown old, and cynical, and weary of pitched battles against the then Zenta Tribesmen of the south.

A keep and four protective walls which spanned the Pass of Splintered Bones to the south; nearly four thousand men had died protecting the building site as the first wall was erected and constant waves of tribesmen attacked; then, a thousand trained archers had wreaked havoc on charging tribesmen, who retreated to watch and contemplate and cogitate and the wall got higher, black and grim, and foreboding, like a mammoth version of the Pit, Vagan's main prison deep under the city. Each wall was fifty feet high and twenty feet thick, huge blocks carved from the very mountains themselves. Huge steps of stone serviced each wall, and the battlements were wide, the crenellations high enough to give good cover for archers and to make life for prospective attackers just that little bit more difficult.

A wall was only as strong as its gates, and King Esekra had considered this problem well. Never anticipating a huge need to leave the fortress south in a hurry, the first wall had a single gate through which a mounted cavalryman, or a narrow cart, could pass. The outer door was made of stone blocks that fitted flush with the wall and ran on wheels of iron thicker than a man's waist. Behind this were four more foot-thick oak gates, and finally, for times of war, there was a small stone compound beside the tunnel, which was constantly stocked with mortar and large blocks of stone. In times of siege, the tunnel could be blocked solid in very little time.

Each wall was named after a hero from Vagandrak Legend. That first wall held the name of the greatest hero of all time, Sanderlek the Slayer, also known as Sanderlek the Black; supposedly carved from stone, he'd hunted the last of the shapeshifters which crept into children's bedrooms and stole them for food.

The second wall was Tranta-Kell, the hero an old warrior of the axe who made a name for himself during the Southern Zenta Wars. The third wall was named after Kubosa, a Battle King of fearsome reputation who had conquered the Plague Lands before they *became* the Plague Lands. And finally, wall four was named after Jandallakla, a warrior princess who had wed the King of Vagandrak and brought not just five strapping sons, but a love of sword, bow and spear from the northern ice wastes. She was a fearsome warrior in her own right, a formidable hunter, and became engraved in Vagandrak folk lore, her deeds exaggerated by the travelling bards of the time.

Finally, was the Keep. The Last Stand. Simply named *Zula*, an ancient word from the Equiem which meant "peace".

The melancholy of Zula was not lost on Torquatar, cavalry captain and now a bearer of two well-used iron shortswords as he turned his gaze back from the distant keep: massive, stocky, brooding, and dominated to either side by the sheer frightening scale of the violent mountain cliffs which rose up and up and up, forcing Torquatar to lean back, craning his head, gazing up towards the lofty rugged black peaks.

"Quite a sight, isn't it?" said Tekka, his appointed sword-brother. Each man had a sword-brother tasked with watching another's back in the event of a wall breach. Tekka was a short, squat man, quite sullen and rare to smile. It wasn't that Torquatar disliked the soldier, it was just he'd rather choose his own accomplice in battle.

"Vast," agreed Torquatar, returning his gaze to the plain below Sanderlek. From their vantage point, the plain seemed to roll away for eternity, dominated by a bloated red sun sinking slowly over the horizon.

"You think they'll come tonight?" ventured Tekka. His voice was steady and sure, but Torquatar could read the subtle fear in the man. It was in his eyes, in the occasional tremble of his hand. But Hell's Teeth, every man had a right to feel fear waiting for battle, right? Every man.

"According to King Yoon, they will not come at all."

Tekka hawked and spat, wiping his bearded mouth with the back of his hand. "That's what I think of the king's prediction. Let's see him talk his way out of this one! There's a rumour around the fortress that some of our cavalry intercepted a group of mud-orcs; a scouting party, no-less! They charged through, lost a few men, then came screaming back here to deliver the good news. What do you think of that?"

Torquatar pictured the drooling, snarling, savage mud-orcs. He remembered the impact as his lance speared one high in the chest, driving through chainmail vest and puncturing a lung before smashing out the other side in a shower of gore. Still the mud-orc tried to attack, and it had taken two blows from his sword to half-sever its head before his horse was free and pounding the thick grassland plains...

He smiled. "I'd pay less attention to gossip, if I was you, friend," said Torquatar, carefully. Sworn to silence by Vorokrim Kaightves in order to try and dispel any panic rising in the fortress whilst they waited for urgent news from King Yoon, Torquatar was unsurprised to find news of their encounter with the mud-orcs had leaked out. Bad news travelled fast, especially in a demoralised army waiting for an enemy they had only read about in their school books.

Tekka nodded. "Maybe. Maybe. We'll see, Torq." Then his face shifted, and his eyes stared off to the distant horizon. Something in Tekka's face changed; it was a subtle shift, but it stirred something deep in Torquatar's soul. He felt himself go cold, and he lifted his head, and turned, and looked to the horizon.

The first ranks of the advancing army marched in a massive crescent, at the centre of which sat a tall, pale woman on a massive, twisted, deviant horse-beast. It whinnied, and howled, and drooled, and pawed the grass with great buckled iron hooves the size of plates.

As Torquatar watched, the line of black figures expanded outwards to either side as more of this vast crescent became visible, slowly spreading as far as the eye could see, left to right, a giant stomping sweeping line of mud-orcs, many thousands across and bearing jagged swords and battered axes.

And then their marching boots and hooves came booming over the plains, a rhythmical thunder that went on, and on, and on, and grew and grew as the marching ranks expanded in size, and the plain behind was filled with yet more, thousands upon thousands upon thousands of mud-orcs snarling and growling, drooling saliva and bearing their evil, twisted weapons. Amidst the ranks came units of splice, padding like huge lions, sometimes limping, sometimes making twisted lurches as damaged limbs and spines and bodies advanced, gradually, upon Desekra.

Torquatar watched, mouth clamped shut and dry and bitter, as the enemy filled the horizon, filled his vision, filled the world beyond the tall black walls of Desekra Fortress. And still they came on, thousands upon thousands of mud-orcs and beasts, like some terrible nightmare made real; like some dark and twisted plague magick.

"An ugly bunch," growled Tekka, and spat between his boots, hoisting his spear, intent clear in his shining eyes.

"How..." Torquatar coughed, and glanced to Tekka. "Gods, man. How many *are* there?"

"A lot," said Tekka, face grim.

A runner arrived at a sprint, face screwed up in pain, breath hissing between clenched teeth. "General Kaightves requests your presence, Captain."

"Right away."

Tekka grinned at him. "Now, then, no running away, Torq. I'd hate to have to face these bastards on my own."

"Like I could ever be that lucky," muttered Torquatar, marching for the Keep.

Further along the wall, Jagan and Reegez watched with open mouths as the mud-orcs massed, and advanced, their howls and rumbles and boot thuds terrifying to hear, their vast ranks seeming to fill the horizon like a distant seething army of ants.

"By the Holy Mother and the chains of the Furnace," breathed Jagan gently, his eyes wide, face pallid, breath coming in short gasps. His knuckles were white where he clenched his spear, and his hand went to the hilt of his sword as his dry stalk tongue licked bark lips. "Have you ever seen such a sight?" he managed.

Reegez snarled something incomprehensible, as the massed ranks of mud-orcs grew larger, and larger, filling the horizon, filling the world. And then the drums started, a simple, single beat to which the mud-orcs marched and the splice limped, a deep thundering intonation as if the mountains themselves had opened up their throats and were grumbling at the gods for the abomination of this day to come…

"It's all for fucking show," growled Reegez. "Look at the width of their line? You watch, Jagan. You see how Esekra built this place? Set back from the mouth of the pass? It's a funnel. No matter how wide their lines, they'll have to funnel in to the width of the walls."

"But… there're so many! Ten thousand? Twenty?"

Reegez said nothing for a moment. All along Sanderlek the Vagandrak soldiers were staring with open mouths, haunted eyes and sweating palms. Fear swept along the wall like a forest fire at the height of summer. Tears rolled down cheeks. Men were making the sign of the Protective Cross and the Seven Sisters.

And then Sergeant Dunda leapt onto the battlements, and screamed, "Don't you worry, lads! We'll give these bastards a taste of Vagandrak fucking steel they'll never forget! You all stand here on Sanderlek, named after Sanderlek the Slayer – well, my granddad knew that grumpy old bastard! He told me the stories first-hand! And you know what Sanderlek would have done at a time like this?" And with a swift downward motion, Dunda dropped his pants and showed his big hairy backside to the enemy.

Laughter rippled up and down the wall, as other sergeants, lieutenants and captains moved amongst the men, offering words of encouragement and exhorting them to "stand steady". The archers were called forward and notched arrows to bows as the Vagandrak soldiers waited, watching the charging mud-orcs.

Faces could be made out now: bestial, feral, pale green skin streaked with crimson smears like tribal tattoos; hairless round heads sported large howling mouths ringed with rows of razor teeth, and with many showing short curved tusks. They were bigger than men, and moved with great agility across the uneven terrain.

And in their midst were the splice, deviations of horses and men and wolves, charging in discrete units to the booming thud of hundreds of drums.

At their centre, atop a massive splice formed from man and lion, sat Orlana: the Changer, the Horse Lady, pale white, high cheekbones, haughty and beautiful, with short white hair and black eyes. Her tapered fingers held huge tufts of tawny hair, a tattered mane, a cruel smile on her face at this, her advance, her attack, her impending slaughter.

Jagan stared down from the high walls, horror a fist in his heart.

"Who is that? A queen?" he said.

Reegez spat again, eyes sweeping across the charging ranks. "She looks like a bitch to me," he snarled.

"Will she want to stop... maybe talk?"

"I don't see no general going down there," said Reegez. "I think this is a straight attack, lad. I think they're coming over the walls!"

"ARCHERS!"

Jagan and Reegez moved back, allowing the archers to take up positions. All along Sanderlek, five hundred quivers touched cold cheeks and the archers regulated their breathing. They focused on targets, but this was not going to be difficult. The seething mass below filled their vision, filled the plain, and turned blood in the veins of the soldiers of Vagandrak to ice.

"I'm frightened, Reegez," said Jagan, staring hard at his friend. "I honestly didn't think it would come to this. I thought the men in power would sort things out. I thought King Yoon would stop this happening."

Reegez gripped Jagan's arm and squeezed hard. "Stick with me, lad. When them bastards come over, you watch my back, I'll watch yours. Can you do that?"

"I can do it," whispered Jagan, fear deep in his eyes.

"LOOSE!" screamed Captain Yoran, arm sweeping down.

Along the Sanderlek wall, the archers loosed arrows which arced high, then slammed into the advancing mass of mud-orcs and splice. Yew shafts punched through eyes and mouths, into chests and arms and legs and a whole line went down like wheat under a scythe. Mud-orcs and splice stumbled over their comrades, slowing the charge as a second volley of arrows cut through the air taking down another line. More arrows followed, and the charge was slowed by the onslaught of shafts and steel barbed heads. Mud-orcs went down screaming and clawing at eyes and throats, blood pumping out in huge crimson spurts. Splice were hardier, taking many arrows to slow and fall. But the sheer weight of the charging army pushed them on, and the drums slowed their beat as ranks fell and were trampled, then leapt, and the charge picked up pace again.

Jagan peered out, and saw the ladders and grappling irons bearing forward.

More shafts hissed through the air like black rain, steel hail, but there were simply too many mud-orcs to create an area of dead ground. On they came, and now with quivers spent, the archers stepped back and took up short swords. All along Sanderlek the defenders prepared for battle.

Jagan jumped as a grappling iron sailed over and bit into the stone of the battlement crenel, and he reached forward, but Reegez grabbed him. "No! It'll take off your fingers!"

The mud-orcs were howling battle-cries that drowned out the drums, and below the charge had faltered, slowing as the mud-orcs were channelled into the pass. Every soldier turned and grabbed large cobbles, which had been piled along the battlement walkways, and along the wall different sergeants screamed the command. Men started dropping cobbles off the battlements, to devastating effect against the climbing mud-orcs below. Many climbing were knocked from ropes and ladders, whilst those below had heads caved in, dropping instantly with crushed skulls and leaking brains.

Jagan and Reegez lobbed their pile of cobbles from the walkway, panting and sweating, hoisting the great lumps of stone onto the parapets then rolling them free. Below, hundreds of mud-orcs were crushed and injured. But then the cobbles were gone, and the defenders, seeing the seething mass of screaming, howling creatures, felt massively under-prepared. They were not ready for such a huge battle. They were not ready for war.

"STAND STEADY, LADS!" boomed Sergeant Dunda, shoulder against the parapet, shortsword in his gloved hands. He fixed his eyes on Reegez. "I see you there, Reegez, you dirty young pup! You owe me two silver pieces, so don't be fucking dying on me, you hear?"

"I hear you, Sarge!"

"They're coming!" breathed Jagan.

A slobbering head with black tusks appeared suddenly and Jagan stared into the black eyes, mouth open. Reegez's sword slammed past, a blur, slamming between the mud-orc's eyes and sending it sailing backwards.

"Kill them!" screamed Reegez.

"Thanks," said Jagan.

"Fucking kill them!"

And then the mud-orcs were appearing up and down Sanderlek, hundreds of them breaching the summit along the wall's entirety – and swords and clubs beat down, smashing them back, until a huge feral mud-orc breached the rise bearing a vicious heavy club with many iron spikes. The great weapon swept left and right, scattering defenders, crushing heads and snapping limbs. The mud-orc roared, moving forward and allowing a gap behind for more of its brethren to fill. The wall was breached.

"Jagan, to me!" screamed Reegez, seeing the danger, and ran at the huge mud-orc, fear ripe on his tongue, worms in his mind, and as its eyes turned on him and that club whistled an inch from removing his face, he felt himself fall into a calm well of serenity. He dropped himself, sliding under the swing of the club, and his sword hacked out once, twice, three times at the mud-orc's legs, cutting one free beneath the knee. It toppled across him, snarling and hissing and spitting and trying to bite his face off. Reegez screamed, but Jagan and Sergeant Dunda were there, swords plunging down as other soldiers cut and hacked, blood flying, limbs severed, until the breach was driven back and the mud-orc corpses cast from the battlements.

"Well done!" snapped Dunda, hauling Reegez to his feet. Then, "LOOK READY, LADS! THERE'S MORE OF THE BASTARDS COMING FAST! CUT AS MANY ROPES AS YOU CAN! AND PUT OUT THEIR EYES!"

Reegez and Jagan stood shoulder to shoulder, both men covered in blood and gore, both sets of eyes hardened, their lips grim compressed lines as below the mud-orcs howled and chanted, the drums beat hard, and with horror they realised it had only been an hour since the mud-orcs were sighted against the horizon.

Reegez looked up at the weak, wintry sun. He rubbed a hand through the blood on his face, and realised deep in his heart, deep in his soul, the very great mistake he had made in coming to Desekra Fortress.

For deep down, he knew the massive stone fortress would be his tomb.

THE DRAKKA

"Ragorek!" screamed Dek, as the Iron Wolves attacked the beast... weapons raised and hacking down with ferocity and need.

"Take it alive!" bellowed Kiki over the melee, and the Iron Wolves hacked at the splice, cutting at limbs as Dalgoran pulled a coil of rope from his pack and tossed it to Kiki. Amongst the scattered fire they battled and bludgeoned the splice, cutting free all four limbs in a frenzy of slamming sword and axe strikes... until it lay there, panting, single remaining dark insect eye fixed on them, glistening, intelligent, understanding...

Dek ran to Ragorek and crouched by the man, crouched by his brother. Ragorek was breathing fast and shallow, staring down at the limb like a thick spear inside him. He looked up at Dek and understanding passed between the two men. Ragorek was dying, and dying fast. There was no way Rag was walking away from a wound like that; to pull the limb free would be to unplug a river that would empty him like a bucket gushing free.

Dek held out his hand, and Ragorek took it in the warrior's grip. His grip was awesomely tight and he grimaced at Dek, blood frothing at his lips.

"I'm sorry, brother."

"I know, brother."

"I never meant it to end like this. Between us, I mean."

"I know that as well."

"I don't want to die with us full of hate."

Dek lowered his head and looked at the ground, and Ragorek realised the pugilist was crying. His head lifted slowly and through his tears, Dek growled, "I forgive you, Ragorek. Anything I said before, I said it in anger. All those hot words of fury, I cast them away. You're my brother and blood is thicker than water. We sent her away together, my friend, and at the end of the day, I reckon that's enough."

Ragorek nodded, and his head tipped forward a little. More blood frothed at his beard.

"I'm so thirsty," he croaked, and Kiki was there, passed Dek a canteen. Dek allowed water to dribble inside Rag's mouth, and he spluttered for a moment, then drank a few swallows.

He looked up suddenly, eyes bright and feverish. "It's gone dark, Dek. Why's it gone dark?"

"The clouds have covered the moon," said Dek, squeezing his brother's hand. "Don't worry, mate. I'm here. And soon the sun will be out."

"Good. I... like the... sunshine."

Dek nodded, holding his brother's hand as he had held his mother's, watching his brother die as he had watched his mother die, and a great and massive weight moved slowly down through him, like ink poured into water; like a devil gnawing through his soul.

"I'm here for you, Ragorek. Just like you were there for me. When we was kids. Remember that mine shaft? I fell down that, sat in the dark for a full day until you found me and rescued me. I'd be dead if it hadn't been for you."

"Yes. I remember." He smiled, a weak smile rimed with pink froth.

"Somebody's coming. Across the black desert."

Dek gritted his teeth, muscles squirming along his jaw. "Who is he?"

"He's wearing black armour, and a black helm, and rides a huge black stallion with no eyes."

"Bring him here, brother, I'll kill him for you."

"My sword, I need my sword!" screamed Ragorek, suddenly, hands scrabbling, and Dek grabbed the man's blade and pressed the pommel into Rag's quivering fingers. His hands curled around the weapon and he relaxed back with a deep sigh.

Then his eyes closed.

And his breathing stopped.

Dek sat, holding his hand for a long, long time, until Kiki put her hand on his shoulder. "Dek?"

"Hm?"

"Dek, we have the splice. Thought you might like a chat with the twisted bastard?"

"Oh. Yes."

Reluctantly, he released Ragorek's hand and stood, stretching his mighty chest. Then he turned and looked down the corridor of rock, to where they'd dragged the splice and bound what was left of the creature more tightly.

Dek strode towards the beast, Kiki close behind, and he pulled free a knife and knelt beside it.

"You killed my brother," he said, breathing harsh.

"It is the consequence of battle," said the splice, great jaws working hard to pronounce human sounds; the sight of this beast speaking seemed unreal. Surreal. Impossible even.

"Well, now you will give us some answers."

The splice stared at him from that one remaining insect-like eye. "As you wish," it rasped, then its jaws worked soundlessly, drooling. It squirmed a little bit, but Narnok had been excessive with the ropes and the knots.

"Who sent you?"

"You already know, little man. I told you." Its pincers clicked together several times, tongue lolling within its mouth.

"Remind me."

"The Horse Lady."

"Orlana," said Dalgoran, stepping forward and crouching beside Dek. "She is known as Orlana the Changer; also the Horse Lady, because she takes horses and uses the old magick. She turns them into beasts like *this*."

Dek nodded. "How many of you are there?"

The splice's eye met Dek's, then shifted to Dalgoran. "You are too late. We are coming."

"How many?" growled Dalgoran.

"Mud-orcs? Fifty thousand. A hundred, maybe. We are still growing, you petty, shitty little human." It cackled, thick tongue like a black sausage rolling around within the cage of its massive jaws. "And there are thousands of splice. We will riot over your walls. We will crush your army. We will ransack your world. There is nothing you can do, human."

"You will hit Desekra Fortress?"

The splice grinned at Dalgoran. "In days. If we are not already there. How does it feel to be a member of a soon extinct nation? An extinct species?"

Dek weighed the knife thoughtfully. "How do we kill Orlana?"

The splice's mouth lolled, and it did not answer. That eye was watching the knife.

"I can make your death last for days," said Dek.

"Do what you wish," said the splice.

Dalgoran put his hand on Dek's arm. "I know of Orlana. She is a creature of the Furnace. Like Morkagoth, killing her will not be easy."

"You talk of your own magick," rumbled the splice, and Dek stood and reached towards Narnok, who frowned, then nodded in understanding and handed the pit fighter his huge, double-headed axe.

"And how do you know of *our* magick?" said Dalgoran, voice stiff.

The splice grinned again, a most terrifying sight. "Orlana knows of you, Iron Wolves. And she knows of your… talent. She knows of your *threat*. She knows of your *curse*. We have been sent to kill you. To remove you from the equation."

Dek rolled his shoulders. "You said 'we'?"

"I am the first. More will follow. You will see. I was the test. I am one of the weakest."

Dek glanced sideways at Dalgoran, who gritted his teeth in a snarl. "Make it quick. We ride for Desekra Fortress at the Pass of Splintered Bones."

The axe smashed down, cleaving the splice's skull in two. The Iron Wolves did not bury Ragorek, but instead collected rocks which they piled about his body, after first removing the splice's claws and throwing the limb onto the fire. More rocks piled up until only Rag's face remained, and Dek lifted a large, rough-edged chunk of black volcanic rock, staring down into Rag's features, relaxed now in death.

"Goodbye, brother. Rest well in the Hall of Heroes."

Then he covered his brother's face, and the man was gone. The Iron Wolves rode hard, for long, long hours. Using the mounts from the pursuing guards killed by Dek and Narnok, they were able to swap between horses every couple of hours, resting one group of mounts whilst pushing themselves on without sleep.

Thankfully, the snow had stopped falling, but the world was a cold, bitter place, every tree and rock and wooded hollow and rolling grassland peppered with a thin scattering of snow or ice. The wind howled mournfully over moorland and shivering grass, a sorrowful sound of death and desolation.

Hooves cracked icy puddles and streams, and the following dawn saw them strung out in single file, tired, riding in silence, by instinct, each man and woman lost in their thoughts.

They were angling south and west now, towards what was known as the Drakka, Old Drak, a deserted and supposedly haunted city, and the shores of the Plague Ocean beyond. This would then cut them west, fast, taking a narrow path through the eastern arm of the Mountains of Skarandos, to emerge in the Pass of Splintered Bones where they could finally travel the rocky, bone-strewn valley floor, to join their comrades at Desekra Fortress.

Dalgoran was looking older than ever, hunched inside his cloak against the cold. Kiki rode in grim silence, the weight of Ragorek's death like a chain of guilt about her. If it hadn't been for their mission to reunite the Wolves, then Ragorek would never have died. That sort of shit always burned her worse than any brand.

Narnok rode next, axe across his lap, scarred face up and stern and focused, the milky eye in his face giving him an even more savage look. Ragorek's death had not touched him, for he had seen many men die – many in far worse ways. But Dek's pain touched him. After all, once *they* had been brothers. Now, brothers in hate, but still brothers. Then came Zastarte, his mood curiously dampened, his thoughts dark and old and lingering. Trista rode in silence, shivering against the cold despite her woollen clothes and fur-lined leather cloak. Her features were deathly pale, icy, and asleep she could easily be mistaken for a corpse. A beautiful one, but a corpse nonetheless.

Finally rode Dek, lost in distant dreams of childhood, his mind flooded with memories of an older brother he had looked up to for so long, despite the constant jibes, and jokes, and his apparent annoyance at every question Dek had ever asked, his enquiring mind simply eager for knowledge and, more importantly, acceptance.

They had not been the closest of brothers, and after their father had died Ragorek had taken Dek under his wing – or so Dek thought. But it soon became apparent that his eager questions, despite their innocence and good meaning, were an annoyance to his older brother, and so Dek had shifted inside himself, becoming more and more introverted. His moods had darkened, and at school he'd started getting into more and more fights, brought on by his bitterness at isolation, the death of his father, and the useless wreck his mother had become. He still loved her dearly, but his father's death had hit her hard, and she was barely a use to herself, never mind her fifteen year-old son. And so Dek had glided further and further from the right path, getting into more fights – most of which he won, until he started training hard, running, lifting rocks, putting himself about the village doing heavy lifting tasks, chopping wood, anything to earn a little money and simultaneously increase his strength and speed and fitness. Soon, he did not lose any fights. Soon, he'd made a name for himself and the big boys from other villages came looking for him. He broke them all, sometimes savagely, until one day a visit from the City Guard and a threat of tossing him into the dungeons and losing the key made him start to think of his future. Where was he going? He couldn't keep breaking noses and cheekbones, coming home with bloody knuckles and broken fingers. A kindly City Guard captain, Captain Horsell, had taken him to one side and given him a good hard talking to. He said a young man with Dek's... *enthusiasm* should channel that energy into something positive. He suggested the army, under King Tarek. Said he'd even write the young man a glowing reference, because he'd known Dek's father and Dek was a good person at heart. Horsell said it was a shame how some things turned out, and without a father, Dek needed guidance.

The next day, Dek had signed up. Been taken in as a grunt, a foot soldier, and quickly stood out not just as adept, but as a natural born warrior; a natural born killer. He'd been propelled forward until Dalgoran noticed him. And the rest was history.

Now, with the threat of Orlana and the mud-orcs and splice hanging over them like a heavy pendulous blade, it almost felt as if they were riding together on one last final desperate mission.

To help save Vagandrak. To help save their souls.

Darkness was falling fast as the Iron Wolves breached a massive hill, and looked down over the vast sprawl of Sayansora alv Drakka. Nearly twenty leagues wide in places, much more in some as it spread south towards the Plague Lands, this dense, vast forest ran from the southern edges of the Rokroth Marshes all the way through Vagandrak, until it effectively blocked any passage between the Plague Ocean and the Plague Lands. From north to south, the Drakka was probably a hundred leagues in total, and the core of the forest was rumoured to be at least a thousand years old, with massive ash, beech and oak forming many sections which were truly impassable, along with a proliferation of *stinga*, large, nasty thorn bushes which could cause serious allergic reactions in people. There were three main roads through the Drakka, although it wasn't the roads that were the problem.

Sayansora alv Drakka was silent. It was lifeless. Nothing stirred or moved in the vast places filled with ancient trees. No squirrels gathered nuts, no wolves prowled for prey, no birds sang and twittered.

Sayansora alv Drakka. The Drakka.

The Sea of Trees.

The Suicide Forest.

It was not a place for the delicate, the mentally unstable, or the spiritual. It was spoken in hushed whispers that the Drakka was a haunted place; haunted by the angry spirits of those trapped by their own suicide hands.

Kiki shivered.

"It looks dangerous," observed Trista, squirming a little in the saddle.

"It is dangerous," said Kiki, turning to look at her old friend and comrade-in-war. She smiled at the pale woman. "You'll be fine. With me."

"I was thinking more about the danger to the *bandits*," said Trista, offering a cold smile, colder than the grave.

"Bandits are not the problem," said Kiki slowly. "There are three roads through, but none are troubled by outlaws or brigands. Nothing lives down there. Nothing at all."

They sat, staring, for a long time.

"It's totally silent," said Trista, eventually.

"Yes."

"Why do no birds sing? Why no sighing of trees?"

"The birds and the wind choose to ignore this place. I don't know why."

"I don't bloody like it," muttered Narnok, moving his horse forward. The beast seemed a little skittish and stomped its hooves. "It's a bad place. A place of ghosts."

"You've been here before?" asked Trista.

Narnok nodded, milky eye seemingly fixed on the dreamy, silent world below. "We made it halfway through before two of our party… well, one man cut his own wrists, and a woman called Annabel – she disappeared. It took us three hours to find her. She'd hanged herself from a twisted old oak." Narnok drifted into silence.

"So, it is a haunted place, then?" said Zastarte. "I have heard rumours, of course, but one casts such things aside as waffle and dribble from those who've partaken of too much port and brandy." His smile was weak.

"Maybe. But still we must go through." Kiki bared her teeth in a skull grin. "We'll lose days if we have to head back north to circle the forest *and* the Rokroth Marshes. We have very little choice if we want to arrive at Desekra before the bastard mud-orcs invade."

"You still harbouring that dream, sweetie?" said Trista.

"As long as you consider the dream a nightmare, then yes."

"I've heard of this place," said Dek suddenly. "The Sea of Trees. It's spoken that when you sleep, the tree roots come to life and strangle you before retreating, leaving your death a mystery. And hundreds come here every year to take their own lives."

"Why would they do that?" asked Trista, dreamily. One hand had lifted, fingers entwining with her golden curls. Her eyes glittered like misty diamonds. "They must have been very unhappy with their lives to even contemplate such an act."

Dek shrugged. "I don't know. But why kill yourself, when there're plenty of other bastards willing to put a knife in your belly?"

"Still. It has a certain... romanticism to it, don't you think?"

"What?" snorted Dek. "Being found six months later, your body rotted away to bones and skin and dust, old shit still in your pants, your eyes eaten by the fucking birds? No. I'll die on a battlefield, thank you."

Suddenly, Dalgoran toppled from his saddle and hit the ground hard. The Iron Wolves kicked from their mounts and crouched around him. Narnok tossed aside his axe and stooping, lifted the general in his arms. "He's frozen. Let's find a hollow in the lee of this hill, build a fire, get some hot food into him."

They moved swiftly, working together. Dek galloped off to the edges of the forest with a spare mount, collecting wood which he piled onto the saddle before tying it tight with rope. Arriving back, he found the others had dug in two poles and made a lean-to with the tarpaulin. Dalgoran was lying on blankets and coughing harshly as Dek arrived, stripping the wood from the spare mount and tossing it to Narnok, who was building a fire in a ring of stones.

Kiki knelt beside Dalgoran, who was trembling, before he went into another coughing fit. When Kiki glanced around, her face was sombre.

"What is it?"

Kiki showed Dek a white cloth which was soiled with blood. She tipped water from her canteen onto the cloth, dabbing it at Dalgoran's mouth. His face was pale and drawn, and when his eyes opened they seemed very, very old.

"You understand, don't you?" he said, softly.

"Of course I do," murmured Kiki. "Lie back, get some rest."

"There is only one way to avoid criticism, Kiki; do nothing, say nothing, and be nothing. I cannot stand back and let evil flood the world in the guise of the mud-orcs; in the name of Orlana. I cannot be that man." He gripped her arm. "You do understand?"

"Yes. Shh. Lie back now. Get some rest."

Away from the old general, the Iron Wolves gathered in a small circle. Narnok looked off down the hill, towards Sayansora alv Drakka. Everything was still and completely silent. The forest seemed to give off an ancient, brooding atmosphere.

"Tomorrow," said Kiki, placing her hand on Narnok's arm.

"If he lives," said Narnok.

"If he lives," agreed Kiki.

General Dalgoran was made of harder stuff than that. With the dawn he opened his eyes and gazed at Kiki sat beside him, propped up, her own eyes closed. Immediately her eyes flared open and Dalgoran smiled at her.

"I thought I'd died and awoke to see an angel," he said.

She blushed. "You mock me."

"Not at all. I have never seen you more radiant. More beautiful."

"I... watched over you. I was frightened for you. You seemed so strong. I didn't see that one coming."

"You saw the blood?" said Dalgoran.

Kiki nodded. "We share a common enemy. The one that hides inside our bones and chooses our time for us."

"I think he will kill me first," smiled Dalgoran, and reached out, taking Kiki's hand. "I will not live to see

Desekra. You know this, and I know this. So let us no longer beat around the bush, Kiki. And anyway, in my dreams, I was visited by... an old friend."

He smiled, picturing General Jagged. The smile faded when he recalled Jagged's words in his dream; for their worst fears had been confirmed. King Yoon was not just insane, but in some way in league with Orlana, the Changer. Jagged was sure of it. He was totally unconcerned about an army of mud-orcs marching to his front door. To what bigger end, what deviated game such a collaboration would play out, they did not know. But Jagged had been murdered by Yoon – Dalgoran had seen the event clearly, as if it had been in bright sunlight and he stood but a few feet away. King Yoon's arm lifting with the shortsword, then slamming the blade down to cut a huge wound in Jagged's throat. The second blow severed Jagged's head, and Dalgoran shuddered at the powerful vision that had so troubled him in the night...

Jagged's final words echoed in Dalgoran's mind, spoken like oil-smoke from a mouth no longer connected to the body of his oldest, dearest friend...

"Seek out Orlana, and use the Wolves, Dalgoran... use their magick... then turn it on Yoon. He is a cancer at the heart of this country and he needs to be excised. Use the Wolves, Dalgoran... then lift their curse. They have earned that much."

"General?"

Dalgoran blinked and rubbed his stubbled chin. "What I wouldn't give for a hot bath, a shave and a fine beef dinner."

"You mentioned an old friend?"

"I was visited by Lord Jagged. In my dreams. He was murdered by King Yoon and the king plans no good for

Vagandrak; he will stand by with thirty thousand men and watch Desekra Fortress sundered. We need to get to Desekra."

"Yes, I know this," said Kiki gently.

"If you... use the Wolves, use their power to kill Orlana, to send back the mud-orcs, then we have agreed. We can lift the curse."

Kiki stared at him.

Eventually, she said, "You can do this?" Her mouth was bitter like ash.

"Yes. Jagged was the last one through which the magick of Morkagoth was bound. With him dead, now I am able to release you."

"And what if you die?" said Kiki.

"Then I will give you instructions on how to achieve it. But first, promise me you will fight Orlana. She is not of this world; she is from the Furnace, and at the very least she must be sent back."

"Tell me how to lift the curse?" said Kiki, iron eyes glinting.

"Promise."

"I promise."

"Deep below Desekra Fortress, beneath Zula, the keep, far far below there is a chamber. A hidden chamber. Inside it there is a chest. Everything you need to lift the curse is inside that chest." With shaking hands, Dalgoran lifted a key attached to a chain around his throat. "Help me unlock the clasp." Kiki did so. "This key unlocks both the chamber and the chest. You will understand, when you see it."

Kiki stared down at the ancient bronze key in her hand. It was still warm from contact with Dalgoran's fevered flesh.

He slumped back, seemingly exhausted. "I'm sorry, Kiki. Sorry it took so long. You were all heroes and yet you were punished by that very thing which saved you; you saved Vagandrak! You did not deserve to be chained for decades. But now you can all be free. It will be so, I swear."

Dalgoran coughed again, and this time there was bright blood.

"One more thing," he said.

Kiki looked down with tears in her eyes. "I never realised you were so weak," she said. "You fought the mud-orcs!"

He waved his hand. "Ha. When you have as much experience as I, you learn to conserve your strength. And it was only these last days I have felt my strength ebbing away. I am seventy years old, Kiki." He smiled weakly. "I think, at last, I have truly had enough. But I would ask you one last favour."

"Yes."

"Don't tell the others. About the key. About lifting the curse. If I am gone, I... do not trust them all. I fear one would take the key and seek to cure only themselves. You must rely on yourself, Kiki."

"And you trust me?"

Dalgoran chuckled. "You're my captain, Kiki. Always were, always will be. I'd trust you with... my life."

Kiki took Dalgoran's hand, wrist to wrist, in the warrior's grip. "We'll see this thing through together, you and I. You might be the general, but you don't have permission to step down just yet, old man. Vagandrak needs you. The Iron Wolves need you. And *I* need you. You are strong. I know you can see this thing through to the end. We will kill Orlana together and send Yoon packing with his tail between his legs. Are you with me, General?" There were tears on her cheeks. Dalgoran nodded. "Then get your shit together, soldier, and let's move out."

Tiny wisps of snow fell as they reached the edge of Sayansora alv Drakka. Kiki led the way, followed by General Dalgoran, Narnok, Trista, Zastarte and Dek bringing up the rear as requested. After the loss of his brother he wanted – needed – a little solitude. Well, thought Kiki as her horse padded the dead pine needles blanketing the wide trail into the Drakka, this is certainly the place for that.

Within a hundred metres the entire world descended into a softness, a silence, a terrible calm. The trees were quite densely packed, very old, towering above the group for hundreds of metres in places. Light filtered through from high above, but it had a surreal, unearthly glow, like something from an eldritch dream.

The Iron Wolves rode in silence, like intruders in an alien place. Through each ran different emotions.

Kiki slowly felt herself descending into a morose mood. Suza entered her mind, dark and brooding but saying nothing, like some evil ferret crouched on her chest as she slept, stealing her breath, sucking out her life and humanity and waiting for the opportunity to chew out her windpipe. The silence surrounded Kiki, invaded her like a mist, and she tumbled yet further into herself. She thought about the tumour close to her heart, feeding from her, a parasite the surgeons could not remove. She missed the tender, giving, nurturing love of the honey-leaf, its delicate and slightly bitter taste under her tongue, its pungent aroma in the drug pipe; after all, was it not the honey-leaf which had taken away her pain all those years as the tumour grew? Was it not the honey-leaf which masked her constant bitterness at the curse under which the Iron Wolves had been placed, in the name of honour and duty and doing the right fucking thing for their country? And Dalgoran had taken it away from her. On the one hand she cursed him for that, because he simply wanted her to fulfil his own ends. But then, he *was* her father; her adoptive father; the man who had showed her so much love and comfort after her own parents had… no. Don't go there. But you must go there, for now Dalgoran is dying, it could be weeks, or days, or even hours… your father is dying, Kiki, your father is dying…

Narnok pictured his face in the mirror and bitterness ran down his throat like acid. It burned him and scorched him inside out, because look what they did to him, just look what they'd fucking done: putting out his eye, he still remembered the fire, the sound of it popping, that bastard Xander leaning over him, stinking of sweat and lavender perfume in the hope it would mask his putrid stench, the grinning, leering face and the shiny bright tools of his trade… and all because of Dek, all because of Katuna the bitch, may she rot in the Furnace… but why hate, why hate at all? Hate accomplishes nothing in the end. Except maybe hate for oneself. Look at your face, your twisted carved up scarred face used as a totem to scare little children. Evil Narnok. Bad Narnok. Look at his face, he must possess true evil in his heart to end up with a face so cruel, a face so evil!

Trista, bright and beautiful Trista, but she'd never been bright and beautiful enough. Not for *him*. Not for *that bastard*. Oh he'd brought her flowers and chocolates and she'd been wooed by his pretty words, his silver tongue, when really it was the tongue of a serpent and she'd courted him, let him into her bed and life and love and heart, and they had married and it would have been perfect, for she was *with child*. How could it have gotten more perfect than that? But then the pains came, and the baby died inside, and how could she be a normal person after something like that? It made you want to… kill yourself. But not him. Oh no. He looked at her now with hate and disgust, as if she'd done something wrong, as if the death of their child was something she'd actually wanted! His days out, at work in the city, grew longer and longer and she knew he was seeing other women but did not care, for a while. But then, slowly, her energy came back and she followed him. He had three other women, one in every quarter of the city, and he would circulate through them, cycle through them as if they were fucking different sweetmeats to be sampled at his patronising leisure. He'd take them flowers and chocolates, just like he'd brought for her; and no doubt as he slipped his maggot into their sweet honey quims he'd whisper silver words into their ears as they groaned and slimed under his slick oily caress. The bastard. Well, she'd shown him all right, skewering him with a long blade as he fucked one of his mistresses, then crouching down in front of him and meeting his eyes and grinning as she watched him die, watched the life-light bleed from him like fluid from a punctured liver. And then – the others. The other women! Oh how they'd all died. Horribly died, begging and bleeding in front of her, offering her anything they could think of as she skinned them and cut off bits and put out their eyes. Oh they hadn't understood, but fuck them, why should they? Finally, she'd preyed on the newly married. She couldn't have the love of her life; so why should anybody else? They would only cheat on one another and watch their bright brilliant love turn to horse shit. So, she immortalised them after their greatest night of joy, because it never gets that good again, does it, and – horror, now she was here and yes, she'd said she would never do it again but – but – she felt herself drowning, in self-disgust, not for committing the murders but for *going back on her promise to herself, for telling Kiki she would never do it again* and her eyes glinted dark and evil under the surreal glow of that forest canopy, and she despised herself for being weak, hated herself so much she wanted to fucking *puke*...

Zastarte rode through the forest light. He lifted his head and allowed rays to fall upon his perfect skin. It felt warm after the cold wind of the savage hillsides, felt bright and orange and he felt... at one with the world. Faultless. Synchronised. Like a perfectly timed clock, tick tock tick tock ticking. He closed his eyes and orange bathed his eyelids, and the orange was warm, and glowing, and flickering, and it was the flames, the flames leaping up around him or more precisely, licking at the clothes and flesh of the men and women chained in his cellar. I love to see you burn. I love to look into your eyes reflecting the demon of beautiful understanding firelight; to see the demons dance, see them burn, smell the flesh as it cooks, hear the screams as it roasts, all like pig-meat, perfect perfect roasted pig-meat. Why do you cook them? Why do you burn them? Do they deserve the fire? Do they deserve to burn? Do they deserve to roast like a beef joint in the roasting oven, fat sizzling and running yellow and hot? Well of course they do. Who doesn't deserve to burn? Who hasn't had an impure thought or word or deed? The whole population of Vagandrak is corrupt, my dear. People step on people step on people. Nobody looks out for others any more. Nobody looks after their neighbours. Family are just selfish fucks interested in money and power and position and their own petty advancements; families used to be about close-knit communities, but not any longer; now a family is nothing but a family in name. There's no honour there, not like there used to be. I look at Dek and listen to him whining about his mother, and his brother, and it makes me laugh and writhe inside like I'm filled with rancid maggots; because he does not understand, nobody fucking understands, not like me, not like Prince Zastarte. And so, to make you people understand I take you, I move you from your comfort zones and I cut you, yes, and I hurt you, yes, and I introduce the concept of pain, yes, and I bring to you – after many hours and days and perhaps weeks of constant physical abuse – I bring to you a clarity, an understanding, a fucking purity of soul which has been driven out by the social conditions in which you live like pigs snuffling at a rancid trough. And yes, I may burn you; I may burn you until you die. But that's all about the purity. That's all about purification. Because there can be no greater crime than being impure. And you, Zastarte. Are you pure? Or do the toxins run through your veins and mind and soul? Are *you* part of the impure breed you so seek to burn? And he laughs. He laughs, because there is nothing else he can do. Because there is nothing he can possibly say. Because he is all part of the same corrupt and broken social system; all part of the same fucked up world with its twisted politics and deviant structure. Do you deserve to burn like all the rest, Zastarte? Of course I do. Of course I deserve to burn. And if there is ever any choice in the matter, if I ever get to choose my own passing, then that's the way it's going to be. I'm going to burn in the hot flames. Smoulder on the coals. Cook like soft braised beef. Because in fire, there is light, and heat, and cleansing. A cleansing of body and spirit and mind and soul. It's purification, my sweet fucking bastard. Purification of the highest possible order.

Dek rode at the back of the group, his resentment building with a fury he did not think possible. They were up ahead, he thought, laughing, joking, talking, and nobody was serious anymore, nobody had fucking *honour* or *respect* or *nobility* anymore. It was all about the flesh and the prize and the money and the sex and the power and the glory. Fucking insects. They might as well be fucking insects. He'd stamp on them and watch them crushed under his boots. His mother had told him as much, between her words of love and understanding and caring. She'd brought him up well, with a strong moral code, and even now he was breaking that code by thinking of the bad words, the evil words, the words that invaded a man's soul and made him far less than human. *You should never swear,* she would say. *It demeans you. Makes you less than whole. It's not necessary. If you cannot say it with the normal language offered by the Seven Sisters – well, don't say it at all.* And he believed her. He trusted her. As did his brother. As did his family. For she had been a good mother, standing strong and tall when his father died. She was all he had left. All any of them had left. And she fed them and cared for them, made sure they had shoes and clothes and went to school; instilled in them the good moral code. As it should be. As it always should be. So, how then, after all the years of effort and selflessness, after the fucking *decades* of giving, fucking giving with absolutely no questions asked, no need for repayment of any sort – how was it everybody turned against her?

How was it his brother, and sister, and nephews and nieces – how was it they all ignored her in her hour of need? Dek's rage was big. Bigger than him. Bigger than Vagandrak. Bigger than the fucking world. It was something that would slumber, and burn him like hot coals in his eyes and heart and soul. Rage, yes. And a lack of comprehension. How could people – how could family, fucking *family* – be so... callous, and uncaring, and pathetic, and weak, and ignoble, and traitorous, and shameful, towards the woman who had shown them nothing but love and caring and generosity? The rage expanded. Engulfed Dek.

Because... because they were selfish fucks caught up in their own petty woes and moans and plots and whines and difficulties, and they could not see the picture, could not see the bigger picture, could not see the wood for the trees, could not give their precious fucking time for an old woman on her death bed. Shame filled Dek like a smith's firepot, poured full of molten iron. And when it cooled, it would be hard, and maybe brittle, just like Dek's mind. Ragorek was dead. Poor, poor Ragorek. Well fuck him, thought Dek. Fuck that back-stabbing bastard. He deserved to die. He deserved the ignoble pile of shit that waited him at the end. Because he abused Trust. He abused Honour. And he abused Love. And now? Caustic laughter echoing between the ancient, twisted trees older than him; older than Vagandrak; older than Time. Now, there is only one answer for my lack of understanding, my lack of care, my lack of justice, my lack of love. Now, all I can do is roll over and die like I should have done twenty years ago under Morkagoth's blade and the twisted magick of the Equiem.

Horse hooves were muffled in the gloom of Sayansora alv Drakka.

Dying light spilled across slack, exhausted faces.

Night was coming; they needed a place to camp.

Kiki found it, in her half-aware dreamstate. It was a small clearing in the woodland, within a circle of small standing stones. Each stone was half the height of a man, and worn for centuries by the elements to smooth arches.

They slowly dismounted, as if limbs were filled with lead, heads overflowing with old dreams and older ambitions and dark bitter memories. They hobbled the creatures, which moved slowly, as if awaking from a great sleep, and then laid out blankets under the trees. It was warm. Warm enough after the snow and harsh winds of the wildlands. They laid out their blankets and ate oatmeal cakes in silence, drank water in silence and lay down in silence. The melancholy was like some deep and embittered music. Nostalgia flowed like wine. Confusion was a rug, a welcome drug, and each individual member of the Iron Wolves were not just lulled by the forest, they were tugged into it, became a part of it, became a part of intertwining memories; became a part of… history.

They lay down on comfortable blankets.

The forest was silent as the grave. Deserted as a tomb.

And closing their eyes, each member of the Iron Wolves gradually fell to slumber: to sleep, to sleep.

Last to go was General Dalgoran. In him there was no bitterness. In him there was no hate. In him, there was no need for power or money or glory or battlelust or retribution of any kind. All was gone and done and dead on a distant battlefield a million years previous.

Everything fell away like dust brushed from the lapels of an old army jacket.

Dalgoran remembered the first time he saw Farsala. With her long dark curls, her full lips, her large gold jewellery, she had the look of the wild travelling women in their ornate caravans of red and green and gold. She'd been cocky, strong-willed, wild, and Dalgoran remembered every single moment of that first conversation, each word a honey drop on his tongue; he remembered every nuance of gesture, every tilt of her head, every flutter of eyelashes, every smile or half-smile or twitch of her lips. She was a demon in his soul, invading his soul. Worse than any demon, for she took him in an instant and crushed his future into her own without the slightest bit of effort. And he did not object. On the contrary, he welcomed it as something he'd never before dreamt as possible. Within minutes they were in love, within days they were pledged to one another eternal. It had been a swift wedding ceremony. They weren't interested in pleasing pointless family; only in expressing their everlasting love for one another. They'd lived a long and interesting life. Borne fine strong children. They'd worked hard together, played hard together. Making love had been gentle and fulfilling, or wild and exciting. Tending the gardens had been an act of harmonious joy. Raising their children had been a long and beautiful procedure, filled with a million tiny intricate joys, a subtle smile, first time walks, first words, giggling slurps, thrown chocolate cake, amusing mispronunciations, then watching them grow tall and strong, bright and intelligent as the years flowed by and Dalgoran rose in rank and trained the armies of King Tarek. There had always been a low-level constant threat that was part of being a soldier; the constant possibility of death lurking, either thrown from a horse during a cavalry charge, a misplaced arrow, a savage sword blow in the heat of a skirmish with Zakora. But it was as if Dalgoran was blessed. He'd taken cuts, but nothing ever serious; nothing mortal. And he'd killed men, but it was always about keeping the peace, always about protecting the good people of Vagandrak. Everything had been so good, so right, the pieces of a puzzle locking into place.

The years rolled by...

And then Farsala died.

Tears rolled down Dalgoran's cheeks. Above him, the trees shifted in a kind of ethereal witch-light. Around him, the Iron Wolves slept in complete silence. No movement, no snoring, no rustling.

They slept like the dead.

Slowly, Dalgoran reached down under the blankets and pulled a short dagger from a sheath in his boot. More tears rolled down his cheeks and a single bright pinprick of light focused his entire mind, his being, his soul. He relaxed back in his blankets, and exhaled, and the world felt right, the time felt right, and the trees moved above him like a soothing lover, and he hardly felt the bite of razor steel as it crossed his wrist. A flood of warmth eased over his arm, then over his chest where he held his clenched fist to his breast. He could hear the beat of his heart, a rhythmic thumping, and there was no pain, there was no hate, his mind was bright and white and clean, and Farsala would be waiting for him on the Other Side.

They would spend eternity together.

He listened to the beat of his heart. Gradually, it started to slow.

Dalgoran closed his eyes.

He smiled.

He remembered Farsala's first smile.

Their first kiss.

Their first child.

And his heart stopped, and General Dalgoran died.

A DARK AND DANGEROUS PATH

Kiki had moved Dalgoran's chilled lifeless body to the centre of the stone circle, and the Iron Wolves sat in a semi-circle around the old man. His tunic was stained with blood; a lot of blood. His face was grey, hair white, face relaxed and completely at peace. Winter sunlight glimmered from above, from between the high branches of the eerily silent trees, and for a few moments dancing patterns of light played across Dalgoran, as if some ancient God was blessing him for the last time from on high. Then the light shifted, and the baubles of glowing gold spun away and were gone, and winter returned, and the bleak cold of the forest rushed in and filled the Iron Wolves with its desolation.

"Why?" said Kiki, softly. She leant forward on her knees and took Dalgoran's hand in her own, and squeezed his freezing dead fingers. Her eyes strayed to the other hand and the wrist with the neat razor slash. She turned and stared at the faces of Dek, then Narnok, then Trista, and finally Zastarte.

"This place got to him," rumbled Narnok. He shuddered. "I had very, very bad dreams."

"Me also," said Dek.

"Did you want to kill yourself?" Narnok turned his harsh scarred face on Dek, who flinched, seeming to shiver, then looked down at the dead pine needles on the ground.

"I'm... not sure. I was filled with hate and melancholy." He glanced up suddenly, head swaying left and right, eyes sweeping the trees. "It's this fucking place! It's... evil. There's something here that wants us to die; to join it. Them."

"Angry spirits?" said Trista, softly.

"Maybe," said Dek.

"We can't leave him here. His body, I mean." Kiki glanced around.

The others stared at her. Finally, Narnok said, "That's ridiculous. We'll bury him here and be done with it. We're not dragging a corpse across half the damn country."

"It's not a corpse, it's Dalgoran," said Kiki through clenched teeth.

"No, my dear, it's simply dead meat. Dalgoran has gone."

Kiki stared at Narnok. "Don't cross me on this, Narnok."

"We are not taking his body across Vagandrak."

"You try and fucking stop me, and I'll cut out your other eye."

Narnok scowled. "You think you can threaten me and I'll stand here and take it?" He hefted his axe. "You really think you've got what it takes, bitch?"

Kiki stood and unsheathed her sword. She stared at them, slowly, one after the other. "I'm taking Dalgoran out of this place. Anybody stands in my way, I'll kill them. I can't say it clearer than that."

Dek rose and placed a restraining arm on Narnok. "Leave her be, Big Man."

"Or what will you do? Find another way to stab me in the back?"

"Guys, guys, guys," said Zastarte, standing, tossing back his dark curls, holding both hands out, palms flat in some form of supplication. "This is ridiculous. Sayansora *does this* to people, can't you see? This place wants your souls. It wants your blood. Instead of standing around squabbling like a bunch of village idiots, we need to mount up and *get out*. And I kind of agree with Kiki; there is no honour leaving Dalgoran in a place such as this. It could well be a condemnation for his eternal soul."

"Who are you calling a fucking village idiot?" snarled Narnok, rounding on Zastarte.

"Er. You?"

"I'll carve you a new quim, mate."

"Thus I rest my case."

They stared at each other, and Zastarte's hand inched towards his rapier.

"Touch it and I'll remove your hand," growled Narnok.

"The very same words spoken by the last man I tortured, disembowelled and set on fire whilst he was still breathing. He stank like a burning pig as he screamed and begged. I had his skull mounted in a glass case in my home. Go easy with your threats, Narnok One Eye, or maybe you too can experience the pleasure of my dungeon."

"Wait!" snapped Kiki. "Truly. There is no need for this. I will take Dalgoran's body and bury it myself when we leave the Drakka on our way to the Pass of Splintered Bones."

There was an uneasy silence, and Kiki looked at the Iron Wolves once more. Then she frowned. "What is it?"

"You say it," muttered Dek, nudging Narnok.

"Well," rumbled the large axeman, "the thing is, this mission to Desekra, it was all based on Dalgoran and his prophecy and shit. The thing is, he offered us gold, lots of gold, and now he's dead."

"So?" Kiki's words were acid.

"*So*, we was wondering if now Dalgoran is dead, would we still get the gold? I mean, who's to say what he promised us or not? We might get there and do all this fighting and save the fucking realm again, and still be penniless afterwards. That King Yoon, he's supposed to be crazy, so they say. Why would he back us up? Why would he honour any debt? Why would anybody honour the debt of a dying old general?"

Kiki stared hard at Narnok, then at Dek, and Trista, and Zastarte.

"So, you're all here for the gold?"

"Not all of us," said Dek.

"But it would come in handy," said Trista. "It always does. And let's be honest, we are mercenaries. Each and every one of us."

"Dalgoran is... *was* my father."

"So?" said Narnok. And gave a semi-toothless grin.

"Are you refusing to come with me?"

"No, of course not," said Dek smoothly. "I'm with you, for one. For old times' sake. For the years we spent as the Wolves; for the past, the present and the future. I'll stand beside you, Kiki. I love you like no other."

"You loved my wife more," mumbled Narnok.

"Shut your mouth, fat man, lest I hack out your tongue."

"Guys, guys, really, I implore, we need to leave this place. Before it kills us."

They nodded and started to move to their mounts, but Kiki gave a cough and held up a hand. "Wait. There is one last thing. Before he died, before he *committed suicide*, Dalgoran told me one thing of great importance."

"Spit it out," rumbled Narnok.

"He told me how to lift the curse."

There was a stunned silence.

Eventually, Dek spoke. "But he said it was impossible! After we made the binding, after we spoke the lore, after they used their magick; it was a one way process. Dalgoran and Jagged, Meyton and Dalgerberg; they said it could never be taken back. We were cursed. For eternity. Or at least, till the day we died."

"Apparently, they lied."

"Give me his body," growled Narnok, hefting his axe, "I'll cut up the old fucker right now!"

"Back!" snapped Dek, his own blade singing free. "Can't you hear what she's saying? Don't you fucking *understand*, you big oaf? She can free us." His eyes were gleaming as he looked around at the Iron Wolves. "She can free us all!"

"Are you sure, Kiki?" asked Zastarte. His face was impassive, but his eyes were shining. "He told? Told you how to do it?"

"Yes. I swear it. By the Seven Sisters."

"How?" growled Narnok.

"Yes, how?" said Dek.

Kiki gave a narrow smile. "I'll tell you when we reach Desekra."

"Reach..." Narnok gave a broad, nasty smile. "So, you're holding us to ransom to get where you want?"

"You said to Dalgoran, each of you said you would come to Desekra and help turn back the mud-orcs and the Changer. What else has altered? Only now I offer you a greater prize. I offer you your..."

"Freedom," said Dek, eyes narrowed.

"You must tell us, sweetie," said Trista, moving close. But Kiki stepped back and lowered the point of her sword to Trista's belly.

"Drop the fucking blade."

Trista sighed, and the concealed iron dagger hit the frosted ground.

"And the other."

A second knife followed.

"If you kill me, you'll never find out. If you help me, we can all win this game."

"Sweetie, I was simply going to mention that *if you die*, on the journey, for example, if we are attacked by mud-orcs or splice, then the secret will die with you. We will always be cursed."

"And a few moments ago, that was the way you thought it was always going to be. So, nothing will have changed, will it? *Sweetie*." Kiki swept an angry gaze across the group. "I thought better of you people; I thought we were locked in kinship by bonds of honour stronger than any iron chains. But I see I was sorely mistaken. You were the Iron Wolves, but you have fallen a long way since then, fallen faster than any dark angel plummeting to earth and the Furnace deep below. I see I will have to watch my back. But listen, and listen good. The only way I'll help lift the curse we all suffer is if you help me get to where I want to be. We have a common goal. Do we understand one another?"

"I'll stand by you," said Dek, voice hard.

"And I," said Narnok. "You can rest easy, Little One. I'll see nobody harms you. I want this dark magick out of my blood. Out of my soul. I would cross oceans and kill armies to achieve it. If that's what it takes."

Kiki nodded. "So, not for honour and old times' sake, then. But for personal gain. But I can live with that. At least I understand the mercenary part of your soul." She turned on Trista and Zastarte. "And what about you two? Do I have to worry about a knife in the back, or can we agree that for your help, I can help purify your blood? And your souls." She gave a narrow smile. "You know only I can do it. You know only I hold the key."

"You have me," said Zastarte with his easy flamboyant smile. "No catch. I'll do what it takes. You want us to fight? Be the Big Heroes? Drive out the mud-orcs? Slay Orlana? We can do all that. Or die trying."

Kiki nodded.

"And you, bitch?"

"No need to get personal," smiled Trista, running a hand through her golden curls. "I, like the others, would like my… freedom returning. You all know, as do I, how this affects our everyday lives. I would enjoy living my final years as a… *normal person*. That would give my life a certain… equilibrium."

Silence followed.

Kiki nodded. "Mount up. Let's get through this damned forest as quick as we can."

They rode as fast as the forest trails would allow. Still the silence was oppressive and complete, and Kiki felt the eroding consequences of the place; her mind turned more and more to her mental torture by Suza, to her need for honey-leaf stimulation, to the cancer that was wearing her down and, finally and ultimately, to the death of her beloved friend and father-figure. Dalgoran. Gone. She could not believe it was possible! It was heart-wrenching, terrifying, horrifying and deeply, deeply heartbreaking. So sad she wanted to crawl into a hole and… (*hush*) die.

They stopped mid-afternoon for a much needed rest, and Dek helped Kiki ease the body of Dalgoran from the back of the general's mount where he had been tied. Narnok went about making a pan of stew, as Kiki took a long drink of water from her canteen and gazed about her.

Motes of light danced through the forest.

It was a beautiful place, but terribly sombre; utterly melancholic.

She shivered.

Truly, it was a place to die.

They sat and ate from wooden platters, and then scratching his stubble, Dek mumbled about going for a piss. He wandered a short way from the makeshift camp and urinated into a bed of ferns, sighing to himself as he laced up his trews and cursed Narnok for not adding more salt to the stew. It's what every good stew needs, he thought, a good bit of generous salt. Adds flavour and replenishes lost reserves. Nothing like a good bit of salt to really make a meal stand out.

He turned, and screamed…

The others came running, weapons drawn, poised and ready for combat with mud-orc or splice, and stopped dead. Dek was staring at them, face ashen, a fake smile on his taut face. "Sorry about that," he said, deepening his voice. "Gave me a bit of a shock, it did. Not what you're expecting when you're stowing your cock back in your trousers."

The Iron Wolves stared at him, then slowly turned to see what had startled the pit-fighter. It was a body, strung up by the neck. A woman, by the clothing, although it was now impossible to tell from the features. The withered skull, still with a covering of paper-thin dead skin, was a pale brown in colour, with sunken sockets containing no eyes. A grey rope fixed the corpse in position against an ancient, twisted tree trunk, and the belly and legs seemed curiously bloated, expanded, whilst the arms had withered away to little more than bones. The hands, also, seemed bigger than they should; probably an effect of the skeletal limbs. One hand was missing, and the arm seemed to end in a tuft of grassy tendons. The clothing, a flowery dress, was muddied and torn. The feet wore expensive boots, crusted in mud and pine needles.

"By the Seven Sisters," murmured Kiki. "That is truly horrific."

"It gets worse," rumbled Narnok, who'd taken several steps ahead, up a short embankment and between two massive ancient oaks, which seemed to act as pillars bordering some great portal into…

They scrambled up the soil and leaves, and stood, mouths open, eyes wide, staring out at a massive glade of hanging corpses. There were perhaps seventy or eighty bodies, each hung by their own hand on short tattered ropes, wearing a disarray of clothing, dresses and shirts and trews, some in boots, some barefoot, all crusted with mud and dirt, as if they'd been hanging for years. Poppies grew all around the glade, adding bright red clusters to a very sombre place.

Nothing moved in this mass place of suicide.

Nothing moved at all.

"I think I'm going to be sick," said Trista, quietly.

"What would make so many kill themselves?" whispered Kiki.

"We need to leave," said Zastarte, no smiles, no flippancy, only a core-deep urgency which spoke to the rest of the Iron Wolves. "Right. Fucking. Now."

They moved back to their makeshift camp, packing swiftly and lifting Dalgoran to the back of his mount.

"How long till we leave the forest?" asked Zastarte, suddenly, his eyes haunted and glittering as if he suffered some kind of fever.

"Two days," said Kiki. "Maybe a day and a half, if we kill the horses." She gave a weak and bittersweet smile.

"Then we need to kill the horses," said Zastarte, brutally. "Come on."

They rode fast and hard, pushing their mounts with little mercy, then swapping to the spare horses and pushing them with the same relentless need. But still the day wore on and gradually the sun dropped lower in the sky above the tall trees, the green diffused light getting weaker and weaker and weaker, until the Iron Wolves could do nothing but acknowledge the fact they were going to have to spend another night in Sayansora alv Drakka – the Forest of Suicide. The Forest of Angry Spirits. The Sea of Trees…

They rode late into the night, until exhaustion threatened to cripple one or all with a serious fall. They dismounted, warily, in the unending total blanketing silence. Narnok mumbled something about gathering firewood, and Kiki gestured to Dek to accompany him.

"None of us goes anywhere alone," she said.

"So, if I need a shit, you'll come with me?" grinned Zastarte.

"Prince, I'll even wipe your backside if it stops you drawing a razor across your windpipe." His smile fell, then, and his handsome features creased into a frown.

Narnok and Dek built a raging fire and dragged various fallen logs to form a semi-protective barrier. Narnok made another of his dubiously famous stews, this time using wild onions Dek had discovered in the forest. This time, when Narnok was not looking, Dek added more salt.

They sat around the fire, eating, and then thinking. The horses, tethered to one side, seemed docile, drugged even. Kiki crossed to her mount, a grey mare, and stroked her muzzle. The creature nuzzled against her, but soon lowered her head and stared at the ground.

"It's even affecting the horses," noted Trista.

"Yes." Kiki retook her seat, and warmed her hands against the blaze as Dek added more chunks of wood he had, along with much moaning and carping from Narnok, hewn using Narnok's fabulous double-headed battleaxe.

"It's not for chopping wood," moaned the large axeman.

"Shut up, or we'll freeze."

Now, with the blaze lifting their dampened spirits, Trista started to sing, a lilting sorrowful tune, melodic, haunting, spiritual, in the long dead language of the Equiem. Eventually her notes faded into silence, and the forest crept back to fill their souls with the emptiness of the void.

"It's just unnatural," grunted Narnok, finally.

"What, Trista's singing?"

"No no! That was beautiful. I'm talking about this place. This bloody silence. It gives me the damn and bloody creeps."

"More than a glade of eighty corpses, you mean?" said Kiki, one eyebrow raised.

"Point taken," muttered Narnok.

"Listen," said Zastarte. "Here is the plan."

"What plan?" said Narnok.

"The plan I'm going to tell you if you listen, axeman."

"Oh. Well, why didn't you say?"

Zastarte stared at him. "I remember. I remember this," he said.

"Oh? And what does that fucking mean?"

"I'd forgotten. Heh. But now I remember."

"You'll remember my boot up your fucking arse, lad."

"Ahh, and now straight to the terrible anal insults. Narnok, you need to relax, my friend, and let people speak, and then, and only then, engage your brain before you open your mouth. I see the last twenty years has done nothing to expand your horizons, nor increase your intellect."

"Eh?"

"Look. This place is haunted… or infused with… demons, or whatever the hell this phenomena would claim to be. I suggest two of us keeping watch at any one time throughout the night. It'll be safer that way."

"But we'll only get half the sleep," moaned Narnok.

Zastarte gave a tight smile. "We'll do it your way then, shall we? And one of us will submit, lay down and commit suicide. Then you'll get all the sleep you need – for an eternity. How does that sound?"

"Point taken. No need to go on about it."

"It's a good idea," said Kiki, wearily. "We'll sleep in shifts, keep one another awake, watch the others for signs of... anything untoward. Who's going first?"

"I will," mumbled Narnok, casting an evil look towards Zastarte. "As long as I don't have some dandy popinjay to keep me company, boring me with tall tales of his exaggerated sexual exploits. Or then I *will* fucking hang myself."

"I'll sit with you," said Trista, and beamed him a smile.

Narnok stared back, his heavily scarred face impassive. "As you wish," he said.

Within minutes the others were asleep from sheer exhaustion, and Narnok and Trista sat across the fire from one another, watching like two tomcats across a cooked chicken leg. It was Narnok who broke the silence first.

"Why did you volunteer?"

"Why not?"

"You're a slippery eel, Trista. You always were."

"You had an eye for me, back in the day," she said, smiling seductively.

"Just the one eye for you now," said Narnok, pulling his axe close and hugging it like he would a lover.

"Why don't you come over here and sit next to me, Big Man?" she said, beaming another smile and patting the log beside her.

"No."

"Why not?"

"I seem to remember that falling in love with you was like a death penalty. How many men died because of you? In the *good old days?*"

"It is not my fault young handsome chivalrous heroes chose to do battle and duel over my exquisite beauty."

"Ha! You played them for idiots. Gullible fools falling over themselves for a simple kiss or a glance from them fluttering eyelids. You used to make me sick."

"Only because you never got a slice of my cake," she smiled.

"I was good looking enough, back then, right enough," said Narnok, staring at her.

"I have one question, then."

"Go on."

"Why did you never try for me? I think you would have found me extremely accommodating."

"I got pissed once in Vagan," said Narnok, staring into the fire. "Ended up sharing a bottle of Vagandrak Red with a professor from the university. An expert on insects, he was. Ha! What fucking use is that, I ask you? What point? Anyways, he tells me this story about this little black spider, can't remember its name, horrible black legs, red markings on its back, deadly as they come. Send you screaming and begging for mercy with one little bastard bite. Deadly to humans. According to this professor type, can't remember his name, forked beard, cross-eyed, probably from the chemicals. Anyways, he reckons this spider would fuck its mate, get impregnated, then kill him." Narnok glanced up then, more to see if Trista had fallen asleep than to see if she was really listening to his tale. She hadn't, and she was.

"Go on," she said, voice soft.

"Or, more precisely, this little bugger would have sex, then *eat* the male partner. Sex, then dinner, so to speak.

Except the father was the main course. Sexual cannibalism, this professor type called it. Horrible!"

Narnok shuddered, then looked long and hard at Trista. "So?"

"That's you, that is," said Narnok.

"What, a 'sexual cannibal'?"

"Yeah. Sex and death, hand in hand." He grinned at her. "That's why I never went near you. I like a good fuck as much as the next man; but unlike this little black spider fellow, I ain't willing to give my liver and lungs for the privilege. *No* woman is *that* good."

"Ha! Maybe you should try it. Maybe I'd surprise you."

"Or maybe you wouldn't. Tits are tits and quim is quim. It all gets a bit the same, after a while."

"What happened to your eye, Narnok?"

"Some bastard put it out. I made him eat his own eyes before I chewed out his throat."

"A shame. And the scars to your face? Cut you up bad, did he?"

"He did."

"This because of your wife? The one who fucked Dek?"

"I think this is getting too personal," said Narnok. "Now, what I'd suggest for a happy watch is shutting *your* mouth before I *cut off your head*."

"And you think you could?"

"I'd make a pretty good stab at it. So to speak."

Trista smiled sweetly. "I'm sure you would, honeycake."

They descended into an uneasy silence, watching one other across the fire. Neither spoke for a long time, and eventually Narnok fished out his whetstone and started honing the blades of his axe with short, easy strokes.

"You love that axe, don't you?" said Trista, eventually.

"More than any woman."

"Really? Why's that?"

"This true love has never let me down."

"I wish I knew that feeling," sighed Trista, and closed her eyes, rubbing her eyelids.

Narnok honed his axe blades. It relaxed him. It reminded him of years ago, in the army, waiting for battle. Always waiting for battle. Ninety-nine days out of a hundred, always waiting for a bloody battle.

The whetstone hissed across steel.

Narnok felt his eyelids heavy. And it felt nice. It felt good. It felt… right.

And… gradually… he slept.

Kiki awoke with a start. She'd been dreaming about her brother, who slipped a noose around his neck and stepped off a bench. The rope made a snapping sound as it cracked tight. At the top of the stairs she screamed, lurching forward to save him…

And she blinked.

Was it real? Did it happen?

Smoke curled from the embers of the fire. Kiki stared at the sleeping figures of Narnok and Trista. And then… Prince Zastarte, who stood, rapier drawn, his eyes gazing down into… the fire.

"No," murmured Kiki, and leapt from her blankets, lurching across the short space and grabbing Zastarte as he stepped forward – into the flames. He blinked, and looked first at his rapier, then down into the glowing embers, then up at Kiki. Confusion flooded him and he rubbed his jaw, then his eyes, and coughed and stepped away from the fire.

"What was I doing?" he said. And he was like a child again. Lost, and lonely, and alone.

"You were going to burn," said Kiki, gently.

"That makes sense."

The others came awake. The night forest was, if anything, more ethereal and deeply frightening than during the wintry daylight, such as it was. The only light came from the slumbering fire. Orange ignited the features of the Iron Wolves. They stared at one another, like newborns, like amateurs, like the idiot naïve.

"What happens next?" whispered Trista.

"We get the fuck out of here," said Kiki, voice level.

And the trees... groaned. For the first time in nearly three days the trees *spoke* to them. Branches shifted and creaked, leaves hissed, and the forest seemed to come – alive. Like snakes through grass, tree roots curled along the ground and Kiki danced back from several questing tendrils. Branches bowed as if blown by the wind, leaning down towards the group and Dek snarled, "This bastard place wants us, wants to keep us!"

And a high-pitched gibbering sound sailed between them, like an army of ghosts, like a battalion of the murdered. *Stay with us be with us play with us; we want you we need you, you are ours to see and touch and hold and taste and be with for evermore. Stay with us and play with us, you need us like nothing you ever needed before, you can feel our love and our understanding and our purity. Come and be a part of something bigger, something great, something eternal, an essence you could never understand, a calm place, a loving place, join with us, you can feel what it's like on the other plains of reality... we praise the Equiem, and worship those who existed Before.*

"No," said Kiki, forcing growled words between stubborn lips.

And the sighs and joy and laughter turned to serpent hisses and groans and the cries of the tortured.

You WILL stay with us, fuckers, you will become a part of this place; for you have invaded our realm and the only way to survive our realm is to become a part of it, to exist here, to worship here and understand and become part of our Ancient Lore…

They came, from the darkness, the hung, the gouged, the cut, the bled, the poisoned, the dismembered, the sad, the necrotic, the dead, the dead, the dead, the dead. Moving slowly, many trailing the ropes of the noose, they advanced slowly from between the trees, coming from the darkness, hands outstretched, eyes white and blank and lifeless…

"No!" screamed Kiki, as all around her the Iron Wolves stood, motionless, unable to react, unable to do *anything*. And the slaughtered, the murdered, the suicide cases from the last hundred years emerged and tugged and nagged and muttered and persuaded…

Narnok stepped forward, axe slamming around, and a head was cut from stooped shoulders. There was no blood. The body collapsed, deflated, to the woodland floor. The spell was broken, and the Iron Wolves drew weapons and, back to back, faced this new enemy, this spirit of the woodland, these victims of a dark, invasive possession.

"We need to get to the horses," growled Kiki.

The Drakka dead shuffled forward, gathering the coils of their nooses as weapons, and with a scream Kiki launched herself at the moaning, shuffling throng, sword slamming left and right cutting limbs and heads from bodies without blood, without screams, without emotion; like a fishmonger pares pale white fish flesh. It was quite the most sickening slaughter Kiki had ever delivered, and she felt like she wanted to puke. There was no joy in battle. No sense of bettering a foe. It was just sick. And sorrowful. And pathetic.

The others followed, weapons cutting left and right through the walking dead, a tunnel through the resurrected flesh of the forest until they reached their mounts and Zastarte, Dek and Trista formed an iron wall whilst Kiki and Narnok tied Dalgoran to his mount.

Then they leapt into saddles and were galloping through the gloom, panicked horses knocking aside the pale rotting bodies as their own panic started to rise. There were hundreds of forest corpses, and as they flashed past, stumbling from the depths of the dark woodland, Kiki started to see weapons in brown mottled hands: suicide blades, daggers which had been used to cut own throats or wrists or groin arteries. Her heart was in her throat. She wasn't breathing. She knew to gallop down this dark trail was suicide in itself, and it would only take one fallen tree to bring them all collapsing down...

A figure loomed ahead, and Kiki leant forward in her saddle, over the neck of her mount, and slashed down a vicious strike with her own blade. The young, dead woman, with pale fish flesh and panther black hair, eyes purple rings, her throat gaping wide like a yellow second mouth, was bludgeoned aside and fell back into the forest to which she already belonged...

And then they were free, and no more came, and Kiki slowed her lathered mount and glanced back. The other Iron Wolves stared ahead, mouths grim, and they walked for a while.

As dawn was breaking over the Drakka, so they emerged from Sayansora alv Drakka and breathed deeply, like struggling swimmers coming up for air. Their mounts plodded up a hillside and they stopped at the summit, turning to look back on the sprawl of ancient forest behind.

Narnok dropped from his saddle, breathing deeply, and looked up at Kiki. "One day," he said quietly, "I'm coming back here. I'll bring a cart filled with barrels of lantern oil. I'm going to burn those poor, lost souls."

Kiki nodded, but did not reply.

Exhaustion was her mistress, and Suza floated into her subconscious like a bobbing corpse on a river.

You were lucky, bitch.

"Oh yes?"

That place is… strange. It knows you. It wants you. It will hunt you down and see you become a part of its legend. It has tasted you, Kiki; you and the other Wolves. It will never rest until you are a part of it.

Kiki snorted a laugh. "Well, it'll have to join the queue. I've got an army of mud-orcs and splice to wade through first. If I make it through that, then I'll worry about some haunted fucking forest coming and knocking on my back door."

As you wish, you dying cancer whore. But don't say I didn't warn you…

Kiki glanced around at the others, then she pointed west towards the distant Mountains of Skarandos, visible even from this distance: massive, black, foreboding, peaks and upper flanks encased in ice and snow.

She imagined, for a moment, that she could hear the sounds of battle.

She imagined, for a moment, she could hear the noise of the screaming, the dying, the ring of steel on steel, iron on iron, the snarls of a feral enemy, the high pitched laughter of Orlana, the Changer, the Horse Lady…

In a cold, bleak voice, she said, "Wolves, mount up! Let's ride."

CONFLICT

Reegez blocked a slash of claws, and the mud-orc's face thrust towards his, fangs and tusks dripping saliva, the fetid breath blasting him like an evil wind from Hell. He staggered back under the sheer force of the blow, and the mud-orc's axe lifted and battered down at him, his sword slamming up to block the blow which nearly forced him to his knees and sent pain searing through his spine. Again, the mud-orc lifted its axe, but Reegez back-handed his sword across its throat. Blood bubbled out of cut open flesh and it took a step back, eyes raging with hate. It dropped to one knee and Reegez kicked it in the face, then twitched left as a long, black spear thrust at him, the point inches from his right eye. An axe hit the wielder between the shoulder blades and the mud-orc went down, but on the blood-slippery ramparts it twisted, grabbing the Vagandrak warrior's legs and dragging him down to the stone with it, where it pulled him into a bear-hug and bit off his screaming face. Reegez leapt forward, his own sword plunging into the creature's eye, and heard a cry to his right. His head snapped round and he watched two mud-orcs with wicked curved swords hacking at Jagan, the former farmer desperately defending against the blows as he backed away towards the steps that led down to the killing ground between Sanderlek and Tranta-Kell. Reegez ran forward, slipping on blood, and wielding his sword double-handed, hacked it into the skull of the attacking mud-orc. It cried out, a high-pitched keening sound, but did not go down until Reegez hacked again. Jagan cut the throat of the beast before him, then stood there panting, blood dripping from his sword, his armour bathed in crimson, his face grey with exhaustion.

For a moment, they'd cleared the ramparts.

Reegez stared off down the length of Sanderlek and the tangle of bodies, both Vagandrak soldiers and attacking mud-orcs. He breathed deeply and watched several young men come forward with buckets and cups. He took one, thankfully, drinking most of it down then tipping the rest over his lank hair and rubbing his wet face. His hand came away smeared with blood.

"You look like a demon," said Jagan, and gave a half-hearted grin.

"I feel dead inside."

"I don't know how much longer I can go on."

"They're breaking us, wearing us down," said Reegez, bitterly.

"WELL DONE!" boomed Sergeant Dunda, striding along the battlements. "WE CAN HOLD, I PROMISE YOU. NOW READY YOURSELVES, THE BASTARDS ARE COMING BACK!"

"Great," muttered Jagan staring up at the winter sun. It was past its zenith, but there was plenty more daylight left. Plenty more killing to be done. Plenty more dying to be done.

The archers ran forward with refreshed quivers and, as the mud-orc army roared and advanced, so shafts slashed through the air and punched hundreds from their feet. But still they came, like a great tide of insects, and the

drums beat and beat and beat and Jagan clutched at his
head, thinking he must surely go mad.

Reegez grabbed his shoulder. "Hold it together, brother."

"I want to see my little girl again," said Jagan, with tears
in his eyes.

Reegez gave a simple nod. There was nothing he could
say. No words to ease the pain.

The mud-orcs accelerated, and more ladders thumped
against the wall, with hundreds of vicious iron spikes
curving over the battlements, pulling tight against the
parapets with squeals and sparks and injuring a few of the
defenders in the process.

Jagan felt something take hold of his brain, and he
felt a kind of madness descend upon him like a fallout of
ash. It was like nothing he had ever felt before, nothing
he'd experienced; he could suddenly feel the thump and
echo of his own heartbeat in his chest and mind and taste
salt on his lips and hear the drums pounding as if they
would eventually pound in his skull. The mud-orcs were
screaming and roaring and the Vagandrak soldiers were
waiting in grim silence as final shafts were loosed, and the
mud-orcs let out a terrifying bellow and came scrambling
and leaping up the ladders like great agile cats, their claws
raking stonework to be met at the summit by daggers and
swords in eyes and brains, great warhammers and axes
thudding down to knock them flailing and screaming all
the way to the pile of corpses at the foot of Sanderlek.

"HOLD STEADY!" boomed Sergeant Dunda, and the
words swirled around Jagan's mind like a whirlpool of
reverberating noises and a mud-orc appeared and he
leapt forward, sword thrusting through its eyeball, and he
saw the spittle on its lips heard the shrill cry of its curses
and hate but it came on, claws grabbing the sword and

trapping the blade inside its own head as Jagan was forced back by the sheer weight and ferocity of the creature, his boot slipping on blood-slippery stone and he went down, still gripping his sword pommel, the mud-orc forced atop him, its feet claws scrabbling at his lower legs tearing skin as it wrenched the sword from its own eye leaving a great gaping wound that dribbled blood and eye jelly down onto Jagan's upturned face, and he was screaming, he realised, as the beast drooled over him, its claws slashing for his face. From the corner of his eye he saw Reegez battling two mud-orcs and he, too, went down under a flurry of claw slashes and Jagan's head tilted left as claws raked his cheek, opening it like a zip, to clatter off the stone. Jagan's hands came up, grabbing the mud-orc's wrists and they locked for a few moments, struggling, with the beast's fangs snapping and clashing in front of him and it forced towards him, muzzle straining to bite a hole through the middle of his face.

Red mist descended on him and the sounds of battle drifted and merged into a background hum, with no individual sounds. His entire world focused on this creature before him, atop him, its strength greater than his, its ferocity greater than his; and it was snapping and grinding and pushing and straining, he head-butted it suddenly, savagely, snapping a fang against his forehead, then butted it again as he twisted and squirmed, trying to throw it off, but those fangs came back so he dropped his head a little and pushed his head forward, teeth meeting its neck and he bit; he bit as hard and as deep as he could and the thrashing of the creature above him changed suddenly, from forcing itself forward to pulling itself away as Jagan tore out a mouthful of rancid bitter flesh like rubber and spat it aside, and the mud-orc screeched and he went in again, chewing into its throat as claws scrabbled against his breast-plate and leg-greaves, tearing one free to be cast back, clattering across the battlements between the legs of battling defenders. He bit down again, and as he held the creature by the throat he reached down, drawing a dagger from his boot and slamming it up and sideways into the mud-orc's head. It froze, muscles spasming, locked tight above him. And then, as if it had turned to stone, the creature toppled sideways and lay still. Jagan rolled to his hands and knees, scrambled for his sword, stood and with a scream attacked, sword slamming left and right, hacking heads from bodies with neat precise powerful movements. He cut his way to Reegez, who had dispatched one mud-orc but was losing a savage swordfight to the second, and with a neat stroke Jagan split its head vertically in two, like chopping open a melon. The mud-orc froze, then dropped to both knees, curved sword falling from its fingers.

Reegez sighed a thank you, but Jagan was gone, cutting a path towards the battlements, a trail of heads and limbs behind him, the mud-orcs parting as his dazzling show of skill made them stumble back. A spear jabbed at him, but he batted it aside, blade cutting the throat of the mud-orc. Then he reached the battlements, and hacked off a clawed arm that was just reaching over. He leapt up onto the stone platform, gazing out over the swarm of creatures beneath him, and all he could picture at the heart of his red-mist madness was little Janna, sweet little Janna, at home with her mother, unaware her father battled for basic survival. To hold those fat little fingers again, to stroke her baby-soft skin, to kiss the crown of her head.

"COME ON!" he screamed at the army of mud-orcs. "COME ON AND FUCKING DIE!"

As if in response to his invitation, the enemy army surged forward.

Kiki and the Iron Wolves rode like the possessed, passing the shores of the Plague Ocean but avoiding the glittering, metallic waters lapping the distant shore. To drink the water was to die a horrible, painful death within a single minute, puking up lungs, stomach sack and bowel. It was not a good way to die. To sail on such an ocean was, by definition, an act of insanity, which resulted in the lapping waves taking an average of two to three hours to eat through the timbers of any hull... whereupon the ship sank and the entire crew died with their lungs ejecting in lumps from behind their melting teeth.

Again they rode, swapping mounts every hour, and had only made one stop to give General Dalgoran a hasty burial. It was a shallow grave in a grove of sycamores, and Kiki made a promise she would return with flowers and a headstone; if she survived.

Now, night had fallen, but the roads had improved and they halted at a tavern for a meal. It was quiet, the landlord a jovial, rotund fellow, but sporting a foul mood. He eyed the Iron Wolves with distaste and an unfriendly air as they removed heavy overcoats and seated themselves around a large, rectangular table of rough pine.

After ordering food and ales, the landlord returned with their drinks, once again eyeing the group suspiciously.

"You ride in from the west?" he asked.

"Aye. We came through Sayansora."

The landlord made the sign of the Protective Cross. "You did well to walk from that place alive."

"It was not a pleasant experience," agreed Kiki. "Tell me, is there news from the Desekra Fortress?"

The landlord nodded, wiping his hands on a dirty rag. "The mud-orcs are there, killing the good men of Vagandrak. People from these parts have been fleeing north. Never has our war capital of Vagan had such an influx of refugees. Unfortunately, there are many terrors out on the night road." His face was grim, eyes hooded.

"Mud-orcs?"

"And beasts, so I have heard tell. Creatures from nightmare. They have been roaming the countryside, killing men, women, children, dogs, pigs, whatever they can get their stinking claws into." He looked shiftily to one side, then said, "Not King's Guard, are you?"

"Mercenaries," said Dek swiftly. "Beholden to no man, nor king."

"It is said King Yoon and an army of thirty thousand have camped just north of the Bones. Yet he will not take his men to aid the defenders. Only a rumour, you understand," he added swiftly, "but if you are seeking paid work, I am sure they will greet you like long lost brothers on those cursed walls!"

"Thank you," said Kiki, tipping him, and taking a hefty drink.

"We can get there by the morning, if we ride all night," said Narnok.

"Will we be welcome, is what's praying on my mind."

"Who's in charge there?"

"Vorokrim," said Kiki. "Or he was when Dalgoran rode out to reunite us."

"And he's loyal to Dalgoran?" said Dek.

"Yes. So I believe."

"We'll soon find out," said Narnok, thanking the landlord as a large bowl of stew was placed before him.

"I'm sorry," said the landlord. "Meat is in short supply, but the stew is good. My wife's family recipe."

They ate in silence, each lost in their own thoughts, and after tipping the landlord generously, headed back out to the stables where the ostler had rubbed down their mounts, giving them oats and placing blankets across their backs.

"You are leaving already?" said the man, small and ferret-featured, his eyebrows forming a frown.

"We are heading for Desekra Fortress," said Kiki, placing her hand on the muzzle of her mount.

"These beasts are exhausted," said the man.

"That may be so. But we are needed there... urgently." She smiled.

"So be it. But I'm warning you, ride easy, or you'll kill them." He patted the beast's flank. "These beasts are too noble to ride to death like that."

They mounted up and left the small village behind, exiting on the western road towards the Mountains of Skarandos and the Bone Channel that would take them through a long, winding valley to the Pass of Splintered Bones.

Snow began to fall again.

Kiki huddled deep inside her cloak, thankful for the filling meal and the ale warming her belly.

The road was wide and well made, and the night stretched off into infinity. As they rode, Kiki thought about her life, her youth training with sword, bow and spear thanks to her father's military aspirations; she thought about her mad sister, sane back then, normal then; she thought about Desekra Fortress, the Pass of Splintered Bones, and the sorcerer Morkagoth.

Morkagoth. That bastard.

He'd raised an army of mud-orcs through sacrifice and murder. Fed innocent people to the Old Gods, the Equiem, in exchange for an army summoned from the mud. Old magick. Evil magick. And in order to beat him, in order to send him screaming and begging back to the Furnace, a group of the best military minds, scholars and those who had studied not just the Equiem, but the old magick, came together and hatched a plan. A plan of magick... Or rather, what turned out to be a curse.

Nobody could get close enough to Morkagoth to deliver the killing blow. Not that a killing blow would actually sever him from life, but more likely, would open a portal or pathway of recognition – allowing the guardians of the Furnace to find him, to chain him, to drag him back to an eternal oblivion of torture and pain that was the Furnace.

And so the Iron Wolves had... been cursed.

They had welcomed it. Welcomed the power.

But then, what a curse it turned out to be...

Kiki smiled at that and drifted to thoughts of Suza – the bitch – then beyond, tranquil now, nostalgic, floating and gently happy as if taken by the heady fumes of drugsmoke found in the underground dens of Rokroth and Drakerath. And the honey-leaf. *Ahhh, joy*, the honey-leaf. Her eyes misted over and her mouth became dry. Gods, she missed it. Missed it like a child taken from her. Missed it like a lung ripped out. To take that precious leaf, and put it under her tongue, and allow it to slowly dissolve, thick juices carried by thicker saliva running down her throat. To feel that tingling in her fingertips and toes, gently spreading through hands and feet, accelerating into a rush of pure joy, pure orgasm, slamming through her veins and taking her spine in its fist and smashing her down into a well of total beauty total joy perfect harmony; an equilibrium with the stars and the people and the gods and the shit; a total understanding of the universe, of humanity, of life and death and love and death.

They rode on, through the night.

The vaults of Heaven were endless, and vast, the stars blotted out by heavy cloud.

The mountains loomed close.

Snow fell.

Kiki dreamed, and laughed, and reminisced. And realised, in a strange way, that this could be it. This *must* be it. What it felt like to realise, *finally*, one's own mortality. At first she had been an incredible warrior. Then she'd been cursed in order to defeat Morkagoth; many, she knew, would have seen the ancient magick as a blessing; but she and the other Iron Wolves now knew what it was. No blessing, but a curse. A fucking *curse*. Increased strength, agility, speed, all wonderful, yes. They had become incredible warriors. Unbeatable. But then there had been

(*hush, my dear, it's time to sleep*)

the rest.

"Kiki," said Dek, riding in close, and she snapped upright. "You were dozing. Falling asleep. Last thing we need is you toppling on your fat head and breaking your stupid neck." He grinned like a young boy to take the sting from his words.

"Indeed," she said, almost primly.

"How do you feel?"

"Like the weight of the world lies across my shoulders. Like the whole of Vagandrak is waiting with baited breath.

Like it's not my fucking problem." She glanced at him, and smiled.

"Do you really think it'll be like the last time?"

"With Morkagoth?" She considered this, then shrugged. "I don't know. Dalgoran believed so, and he was one of the bastards who summoned our… curse. Our oblivion. He'd read the books. Studied the lore. Done the math. Ha! The old dead bastard."

"I think you need a drink," said Dek, and uncorked a small, steel hip-flask. He took a long draught, then handed it over, reaching across the pommel of his saddle, which creaked.

Kiki took it and knocked back a large drink. Then she choked as fire exploded in her mouth, throat and belly. She handed the flask back, eyes watering, and coughed again. "What, in the name of the Seven Sisters, *is that*?"

"They call it Zunder Fire. 'Made with the lava from the Great Volcano!'" he quoted, and chuckled. "Hits the spot, right? I bought it back at the tavern. Thought it might warm our bellies against the snow."

"Warm our bellies? I think it's burned out my insides."

"It has that effect as well, yes. How do you feel about the coming battle?"

"The mud-orcs?"

"Yes."

"Tired. Lost. Alone. Dalgoran's dead and, to be honest, Dek, the whole world no longer feels real. This whole thing? It feels like… a dream. Like I've smoked a bowl, chewed the honey-leaf, and I'm still fucking dreaming two weeks later. But you know what the worst thing is?"

"Go on."

"I don't want to wake up. I want the dream to go on and on and on, and unto death."

Dek considered this. "What you need is a man."

"Oh, you think so, do you?"

"I don't mean rutting beneath the blankets, girl. I mean a lover. A friend. A husband." He stared at her.

The humour fell from her face. "I'm dying from a tumour inside my chest, alongside my heart," she snapped. "Last thing I need is some back-stabbing bastard breaking the other half."

The mountains grew ever close, and through the freezing wind and whipping snow, Narnok guided them to the Bone Channel. They entered the narrow aperture cautiously, fearing it may be guarded – either by Vagandrak infantry and archers, or something more terrifying. But there was nothing but a cold, mournful wind crying in mock sorrow down the long, freezing corridors of rock.

As dawn broke, the Iron Wolves walked their horses, gazing up at the sheer massive walls of granite rearing around them. Impossibly high, vast, unforgiving, this cleft cut through the mountains seemed incredible, artificial, as if man had used some giant saw blade to hack a rough path through the mountains themselves. But they all knew this was impossible. No such tools could exist.

"Maybe it was magick?" whispered Narnok at one point when they stopped to drink ice-chilled water from canteens that were cold to the touch. "Maybe some great magician cast a spell, blasted the rock away and made this narrow road through the mountains?"

"I don't believe any man could be that powerful," said Dek, rubbing at his stubble.

"I think, dear love, you'll one day realise that's exactly what the ladies think of me," piped up Zastarte, as if awakening from a melancholic slumber. He'd been pretty much silent since the death of Dalgoran, and the attack by the suicide victims of the Drakka; now, it seemed, his humanity was slipping back into place. He had surprised himself by how much Dalgoran had meant to him. But then, Dalgoran had saved him on occasions the others knew nothing about. If it hadn't been for Dalgoran, Zastarte would have been dead and buried many times over...

"What, lacking in power?" chuckled Narnok.

"No, packing so much love they believe they will explode in ecstasy the minute I walk in the room."

"You're full of shit," said Narnok, scowling.

"No, I am full of love."

Trista looked at him. "Really?"

"There's not a woman who would not bow to my supremacy."

"And you *really* believe that?" she said.

"Of course," smiled Zastarte, with easy charm. "It is one of my core principles."

"Try me," said Trista.

"Ahh, but then you are not a woman."

Narnok snorted on his water.

"What the fuck am I, then?" snapped Trista, rattled.

"Indeed, do not trouble yourself to be upset. I would merely suggest you are *more* than a woman. After all, you have the exalted rank of Iron Wolf; I would wager that only one in a hundred thousand ever earned such a position. Thus, you are not simply 'woman', you are indeed a kind of 'super woman'."

Trista stared at him. "Are you taking the piss?"

"Oh no! I would never dream of such a travesty."

"Well. That's all right then." She stared at him some more. "Sometimes, you have a golden tongue," she said.

Narnok nudged her. "Heh. He'd better be careful. There's people I know who'd want to cut that out."

"Precisely," said Trista, looking down her nose at the old, scarred, one-eyed axeman.

They crept through the chasm. Not because they had to, but because Narnok reminded them of a particular mission where a mountain decided to try and collapse on them, mainly due to Dek and Mola's rowdy drinking songs. They'd nearly died under the savage rockfall. There was nothing like learning a lesson the hard way.

The passage towards the Pass of Splintered Bones was long, and narrow, and straight except for a couple of angular jerks through the rock, cut-out switchbacks which caused the horses a few problems due to the sheer confines and severe angles. But they managed it, with a lot of cursing and gentle talking to the beasts.

It took several hours to negotiate the narrow channel through the mountains and Narnok especially was a moaning old goat. He claimed he was too old, too wide, too tired and too grumpy to be undertaking such adventures. He said he wanted a clean, nasty battle with the enemy stood before him, somebody he could really hit with his axe.

With little humour, Kiki pointed out that that was exactly what he was going to get.

Narnok thought this hilariously funny.

Eventually the pathway became so narrow they had to dismount and lead their horses in single file, snorting with ears laid back. Occasionally, trickles of rock fell from high above, rattling down the near vertical walls.

Gloom and darkness closed in. Occasional snowflakes fluttered down into the impossibly deep valley.

Dek, in particular, was in sour mood at this confined traverse. "It feels like I'm in a coffin and they're closing the lid," he mumbled, words echoing to the others from the sheets of black granite to either side. "It feels like the mountains are waiting to chuck a billion tons of rock on our heads."

"Maybe they are," said Kiki, softly.

"Well, I'd rather die on a battlefield with a sword in my hand. A good clean death! Not this, buried by rock as a random act of Nature. This place is wrong, I reckon. It shouldn't exist. It wasn't made by natural means, that I can tell you."

After another hour, they saw a long straight tunnel with daylight at the far end. They unconsciously increased their pace, until Narnok's boots stepped cautiously out into wintry sunlight, crunching bones underfoot, head snapping left and right to check for possible threats, axe head glittering menacingly.

"We're clear," he said, leading out his horse, and one by one the others emerged to stand at the centre of the Pass of Splintered Bones, breathing deeply as if they'd just emerged from under a black ocean and were gasping for breath.

Dek tilted his head, listening. "What's that sound?"

"Drums," said Kiki.

And the sounds of distant battle drifted to them down the pass, intermingled with the booming of mud-orc drums and a mournful howl of the wind. There were clashes and smashes of iron and steel. Screams and wails and growls. All interwoven like a song by the croon of the wind down the pass.

Mountains reared above the Iron Wolves, dizzying and vast.

Kiki looked at her companions. With a grunt, she mounted her horse.

"Iron Wolves. Let's ride!"

Approaching Desekra Fortress from the Vagandrak side of the pass was unnerving for all members of the Iron Wolves. Only Narnok had been back during the past two decades, and even Narnok's journey had been nearly fifteen years previous. The huge black walls of the keep, Zula, loomed gradually into view alongside an increase in the song of battle. Huge gates stood centrally in the keep, and archers guarded the wall high up, winter sun glinting from helms.

Narnok reined in his mount out of range, and lifted his hand, bellowing, "We seek General Vorokrim! We have been sent by General Dalgoran, greatest hero of the War of Zakora!"

"Approach the gate!" came the shouted reply.

Kiki led the wedge now, and they walked their mounts, iron hooves crunching bones, eyes taking in the vast, sheer walls of the keep. She was painfully aware of at least a hundred arrows trained on her, and sweat trickled down the middle of her back. *What if King Yoon was here? What if, as everybody claimed, he had gone insane? What if he was cooperating with Orlana, the Horse Lady? Maybe he had ordered their deaths...*

The great gate opened enough to allow entry, and once inside the sounds of battle increased exponentially. They were relieved of swords and knives, their mounts led away to stables, and a heavily armed group of soldiers surrounded them.

"State your business," snapped an irate captain. He looked exhausted, eyes red-rimmed, a shade of stubble on his face, a fresh cut on his neck.

"We have been sent by General Dalgoran. We are here to see General Vorokrim Kaightves. He will see us immediately, when he hears our names." Kiki gave a narrow smile.

"That is of little concern," said the captain, flicking his hand to a man by his side. "Escort these *people* to the dungeons, the general is a very busy man. We are fighting a war! He will see you at his convenience."

Kiki stepped in fast, a blur, grabbing the captain's throat and dragging him close so he was suddenly off-balance, arms waving. "You don't understand; I am Captain Kiki Mandasayard, leader of the Iron Wolves, the soldiers who saved your parents' lives when we fought the mud-orcs and killed Morkagoth twenty years ago. You will take us to General Vorokrim right now or I'll break your neck, we'll put down your men, and walk there ourselves. Understand?"

She released him, and he staggered, and coughed, and looked around, face pale. The armed soldiers had backed away a little, a ring of steel surrounding the unarmed Wolves.

Narnok leaned to the closest man. "If you keep pointing that sword at me, laddie, I'm going to shove it up your quim, hilt first." He gave a broad wink, although there was no humour in his scarred face.

"Back away, back away, er, lady, if you and your companions would… would like… to follow me."

Narnok growled, "And tell those idiots to bring our weapons. We'll be needing them on the walls soon enough."

They climbed steep steps and thankfully were met by a sergeant who recognised Narnok. He shook the giant axeman's hand, a look of awe on his broad brutal features, and took over from the shaken captain, leading them deep into the fortress keep; deep into the belly of Zula.

Within minutes they were ushered into a high room which looked out over the four massive walls of Desekra Fortress, and the battle which raged on Sanderlek. For long moments Kiki, Dek, Narnok, Zastarte and Trista stared out at the carnage. Siege engines were being pulled towards Sanderlek, creeping forward by inches, and archers had braziers and arrows with oil soaked tips. As they watched, men with slingshots sent clay balls of oil hurtling across the massed mud-orcs, to smash against the huge siege towers, closely followed by hundreds of fire-tipped arrows, a glittering hail which arced above the battle, above the struggling defenders on the wall. With a roar and blast of billowing fire five of the six towers went up, raging as their timbers burned and fell, igniting or crushing the mud-orcs standing beneath hauling on massive ropes. The whole scene was suddenly one of mayhem, as if the fires of Hell had suddenly visited the world.

On the walls, the defenders slaughtered the remaining mud-orcs and hurled bodies from the battlements. A ragged cheer went up as the mud-orcs retreated out of archer range, defeated for the moment.

"They're still testing us," said Vorokrim, rubbing at his eyes and standing, smiling weakly. "Captain Kiki. You look in fine health! Dek, always a pleasure. I've won a lot of silver pennies when I've wagered on your fights. Narnok – is that you, Narnok? I heard about your... *injuries*..."

"Don't worry. You should see the other fucker."

"I can believe it! Trista, beautiful as ever, and hopefully as deadly as ever! Your lightning blade will not go amiss in this damn fortress. And Zastarte! I see you still haven't got a bloody haircut, but as long as you can wield a blade I'll overlook the insubordination. Unless you'd like me to send for the barber? By all the gods, it's good to see you. We are in dire need of help. Any help!"

"Have many lives been lost?" asked Kiki.

"Two thousand souls, sent screaming to the void by these green-skinned bastards. We are undermanned, and Sanderlek is too long. It's a rancid whore to defend without full fortress battalions, and my captains are urging me to pull back to Tranta-Kell where the walls narrow. But this will hammer morale, I know it. Still, these siege engines appeared this morning; if they manage to get them up to the walls we'll have to withdraw. We will have little option."

Kiki nodded. "Have you seen Orlana, this witch who leads the mud-orcs? Has she attempted to make any demands?"

"No. None. The mud-orcs arrived, and they attacked almost immediately. We sent out messengers to try and seek some sort of parley, but they were returned tied to their horses and minus their heads. We've sent treaties to King Yoon begging him for more support, but he has gone silent – indeed, as he has been for the previous five weeks. My scouts tell me he's moved up to camp his thirty thousand men by the mouth of the Pass of Splintered Bones; I assumed they were coming to our aid, but now I am not so sure. I do not know what strange game is being played here, but I feel it is some kind of test." He stared hard at Kiki. "Sometimes, I think I'm going out of my mind."

"Is there anything we can do to help?" rumbled Narnok.

"Is Dalgoran with you? I could do with his sage counsel."

The Iron Wolves exchanged glances. "He didn't make it," said Kiki, and watched the expression drop from Vorokrim's face.

"Oh. That's… very bad news," he muttered.

"We could go and pay Yoon a visit," said Kiki, gently.

"I sent Captain Veragesh at dawn this morning. When I heard you on the stairs, that's who I thought was returning."

There came a clatter of boots, and Captain Yoran appeared. He saluted General Vorokrim. "Sir. The enemy have changed their lines. They've abandoned the siege engines, and the mud-orcs have shifted back. Those huge bastard creatures have moved to the front. And the drums have started again."

"Are they a mix of horse, man and wolf?" said Kiki.

"Yes," nodded Captain Yoran. "This is the moment we've been waiting for. The hour we've been dreading. I think they mean to take the wall today… I'll order extra men from the reserves, but we're starting to run low on arrows."

"I have wagons coming in shortly from Vagan," muttered Vorokrim. He rubbed at his temples. "This is a nightmare!"

"Come on," said Kiki. "Let's escort Captain Yoran back to Sanderlek. I feel the need to stretch my muscles."

The others nodded and, as they reached the doorway, Vorokrim said, "If I hear from the King, I'll send for you."

"You do that," said Kiki, and closed the heavy, iron studded door.

Walking across the killing grounds brought back floods of memories. Training with sword, spear and bow. Running the length of the walls carrying logs and sacks of coal and other assorted awkward objects guaranteed to "make you bloody fit!" and "strengthen those bloody legs!"

"Remember Sergeant Scorptail?" grinned Dek.

"Bloody remember him? Course I bloody remember him!"

"What a bastard," chirped in Narnok.

"Only because he was stronger than you!"

"Not for long," rumbled Narnok.

"I think he fancied Trista," smiled Dek, and Trista pulled a scrunched-up face.

"She broke his jaw in the mess hall," said Narnok. "Best left hook I ever saw! For a woman, anyways."

"I can always show you another, sweetie," smiled Trista, eyes glittering.

The air was chilled and smelled of fire, mud-orc and latrines. Dark clouds towered over a sky bigger than the world. With the sun sinking towards the west, the long shadows of the mountains fell over Desekra Fortress, giving it a gloomy, melancholy air. The drums started, and the Iron Wolves each grabbed a small round shield from a pile lying on a weapons cart behind the second wall, Tranta-Kell.

"Long time since I've had use for one of these," said Dek, grabbing both handles tight and flexing his shoulders.

"Need a helmet?" said Narnok. "There's helmets over there."

"No. They obscure my hearing and my peripheral vision. Better without."

The drums boomed louder, and with the rhythm came a cacophony of bestial snarls and squeals and growls like nothing they had ever heard. They ran up the steps to the battlements, heart rates increasing, adrenaline pumping, and the full extent of the plain opened before them like some terrible vision, with thousands upon thousands of mud-orcs ranged in unit squares, but at the front, like snarling leashed giant rabid dogs, were the splice; not in their tens, or hundreds, but now in their thousands, many pawing the ground with twisted iron hooves, many lifting great broken jaws to the heavens and howling long and high and mournful.

"They're too big to come over the walls," said Narnok, slowly.

"You think?" said Kiki, weighing her sword.

All along the wall soldiers were nudging one another, and muttering, and flashing them smiles. Several men pointed.

"Word gets around fast," said Dek. "You'd better make a speech."

"What, me?" said Kiki, frowning.

"We're the heroes from the War of Zakora! There's not many fought the mud-orcs, Kiki. Our soldiers will be expecting something!"

"We're here to test the enemy, observe the attack, not make new fucking friends," she snapped.

"He's right," said Narnok, nudging her in the ribs. "You need to speak."

"I am *not* speaking to these men!" snapped Kiki, shaking her head. "You bloody do it!"

"Ha! Be my pleasure," grinned Narnok. With Dek's help, he hauled his bulk up onto the battlements and stared down at the sea of faces. He scratched his heavily scarred face, then shouted, "Ha! I see you there, Dunda you young pup! Who the fuck made you a sergeant? They need their heads seeing to!"

"You did, Narnok!" he roared, and laughter rippled along the line.

"Now then, soldiers of Vagandrak, I am Narnok; some of you may have heard of me, some of you might not; and it's true I ain't a pretty sight, lads," he boomed, voice projecting well, as if he were a born orator. "But I'm prettier than the sisters of these here motherfuckers attacking the fortress today." He gestured with his thumb behind him. "I ain't one for speeches. I usually let the other prettier ones do the talking, but you've been doing a grand job here without us; don't think we're anything special, we're just here to help out some old friends and protect our country. Just like what you're doing. Now, it looks like they're sending in these splice creatures, and we've fought a few now on the road here, and we killed them dead. They die just like any other bastard. They might need a bit more stabbing because they're bigger and fatter…"

"Like you, old man!" shouted someone from the back.

"Heh, come over here, you little weasel, I'll show you who's old and fat! I've been killing men and beasts since before you were suckling on your mother's tits, but that's probably only a few years back anyways, judging by the lack of real hair on your chin. The point is, don't be frightened by these bastards. We stood here twenty years ago, the Iron Wolves, and built ourselves a legend. Left with so much gold our horses had buckled legs by the time we reached Vagan, and the never-ending parties beyond. Just think of the wine, the women, the riches, the honour and how once we were normal soldiers just like you. We fought for our brothers and sisters and friends and our country; and we left as heroes!"

Just then a roar went up from the mud-orcs and splice combined, a terrifying primal scream that slammed across the killing ground like a wave of terror.

"YEAH!" roared back Narnok, "THAT'S THE SOUND YOUR SISTER MAKES WHEN I GIVE IT HER GOOD!"

He leapt down to laughter, and then the line spread out, soldiers readying themselves for the onslaught.

"You didn't mention the King," said Dek.

"Eh?"

"You know, for King and Country, that sort of thing?"

"Ha. Fuck him. He's a dick."

"They're coming," said Kiki, and watched as the splice formed into two columns and the mud-orcs arranged themselves about the splice, once again carrying ladders and grappling hooks.

"What are they doing?" muttered Narnok.

"The splice are going to attack the gate tunnel," said Kiki, realisation dawning. "Sergeant! Has the gate tunnel been sealed?"

"King Yoon has forbidden it."

"So, we're relying on the gates?"

Sergeant Dunda nodded, and Kiki cursed.

"Here we go," said Zastarte, tying back his hair and tightening a borrowed breastplate. He suddenly grinned at the other Iron Wolves. "Just like old times, hey?"

"Just like old times," agreed Kiki, lips compressed, eyes narrowed, and the mud-orcs and splice charged with a howling cacophony she would have believed impossible. Archers sent hails of arrows arcing over the battlements and down to punch hundreds of enemy from their feet...

And the attack began afresh.

KING'S GAME

King Yoon walked his war charger down the Pass of Splintered Bones, head held high, eyes burning, hand on the hilt of his silver-steel sword. Behind, in rigid disciplined columns, rode a hundred of his elite guard in full black armour, helms pulled over eyes, black plumes flowing from angular helmets. They appeared like insects. Almost. The King's shaggy black hair was swept back, oiled and heavily perfumed, his face painted white, his lips red, and he wore a shaggy black pelt from some jungle cat, and expensive soft leather riding trews and boots. Around his throat was wrapped a lavender scarf. On each finger, a glittering jewel of some different family of gems. In contrast to his dandy image, his elite soldiers oozed malevolence and dread and violence. They were battle hardened, each man tested in real combat, in army training and real-world gladiator battles, in skirmishes with Vagandrak enemies and in secret military manoeuvres King Yoon would have discussed with no man.

They approached Desekra as befitted the King of the Northern Realm, and Yoon ignored the challenge when it came from the ramparts. "If a man doesn't recognise his own monarch," he muttered, "then that man deserves to hang!"

Yoon was met at the gate by a gaggle of nervous commissioned officers, who quickly escorted Yoon and his ten personally chosen warriors up the stairs of the Zula

Keep and into the audience chamber of General Vorokrim Kaightves, who was standing, surveying the valiant efforts of the defenders below.

Mud-orcs were swarming over the battlements.

Splice were snarling, screeching and digging through the gates. Those more agile clambered up ropes, or simply cut grooves into the stonework with razor claws, scrambled vertically up the wall and attacked... to be met by sword and spear and mace. They took a lot of killing. A *lot* of killing...

Vorokrim turned, and his heart caught in his mouth. He approached his monarch, knelt and kissed the proffered Ring of Kings. Yoon bade the general stand and Vorokrim did so, as Yoon swaggered across the large chamber, finger trailing across maps on the massive oak desk, until he stood, swaying slightly, and surveyed the battle below.

"So, this is Zula. This is Desekra. And these are the mud-orcs I keep hearing so much about."

"Yes, Majesty," said Vorokrim carefully. "As you can see, your men fight valiantly to protect the realm. They give their lives for you, and for their families and the good people of Vagandrak."

"Indeed they do," observed Yoon, nose turned slightly up. "You know I have thirty thousand men camped but a league from here?"

"I do, Majesty, and my burning question is *why* you do not bring them *here*. Not a year ago you reduced the full complement of this fortress. Not a problem in peacetime. But now, Majesty, you ask the impossible from your remaining men. You ask the impossible from *me*."

"You seek to question my judgement?"

Carefully, as if walking a high wire, Vorokrim said, "Not your judgement, Highness; I just see an obvious answer to all our problems, camped but a few miles from here, and idly wonder what could possibly stay your hand?"

"I do not have to tell you, you know." Yoon's voice was petulant.

"Of course, Highness." Vorokrim was sweating, and decided that for now the best policy was silence.

"What I want to know, my dear Vorokrim Kaightves, is exactly *who* this Orlana the Changer really is. I want to know *why* she wishes entry into Vagandrak. I want to know *exactly what* she wants. And I want to know it *today*. Why have you not found out?"

"F... found out?" stuttered Vorokrim.

"Why have you not been out there and spoken to this woman?"

"I, well, I don't think she's exactly approachable, Majesty. After all, she's brought damn near a hundred thousand mud-orcs knocking on our front door with their swords and axes. I think that's a pretty clear statement of intent."

"And I reiterate, *General*, this is your command; you control Desekra; why have you not spoken to this, this *upstart*?"

"What do you want me to do?" snapped Vorokrim, a frown on his face. "You want me to open the gates, stroll out there amidst her thousands of feral twisted creatures intent on our imminent destruction and have a simple chat?"

Yoon turned, and smiled at Vorokrim; a friendly smile, like a gesture of love between two very old friends. "Why, yes, General, I think that sounds like a fabulous idea. Go and see what she wants. Report back to me in an hour."

Yoon turned his back on Vorokrim, gazing out over the defenders. Men went down under a unit of splice that had made it over the walls, fists and hooves swiping heads from shoulders, claws disembowelling screaming men, twisted fangs biting and twisting off arms and legs and skulls.

"King Yoon," said Vorokrim, his throat dry, his voice cracked. "You cannot really be ordering me to open the gates to our attackers, stepping out into their midst, and seeking to communicate with somebody who threatens bloody extinction to your country? Really?"

"Are you disobeying a direct order from your King?" said Yoon. He turned his dark eyes on Vorokrim, and the general saw the demon madness lurking in their glittering, sparkling depths.

"Yes," said General Vorokrim, softly.

"You dare to question my judgement?" said Yoon.

"I dare," said General Vorokrim, forcing his back ramrod straight. "You have enough men camped close by to hold these damn walls for a year – and yet you chose to sit them down and play games whilst their brothers-in-arms are slaughtered on these bloody walls. You come here and ask me to open the gates – an act of treason against national security. And then you order me to effectively commit suicide. Only somebody who had lost his mind would order such a thing."

"Open the gates," said Yoon, moving closer, baring his teeth in a smile that was not a smile. Yoon glanced to his ten elite soldiers, who subtly shifted hands to the hilts of their swords.

"No," said Vorokrim, staring hard into Yoon's eyes.

"Open them."

"Open them yourself."

"That, I will do, ahhhh, yes, that I will do," said Yoon, half-turning from Vorokrim who felt himself slipping, felt his body and mind and will slipping into a great void of insanity. How could men stay sane in such cauldrons of pressure and madness? How could a straight military man make the correct decisions when faced with such ludicrous demands?

Yoon turned, fast, faster than most warriors, and the dagger stabbed sideways into General Vorokrim's throat. It was a long, thin, black-bladed dagger. It slid easily through flesh, through tendons, through Vorokrim's oesophagus.

Yoon turned away and gazed out of the window as Vorokrim dropped to his knees, one hand coming up to almost idly explore the steel through his neck, and through his windpipe. He opened his mouth to speak, but no words would come out. His voice no longer worked. Slowly, blood dribbled down the corner of his chin as he explored the alien metal inside his flesh.

"I am so disappointed in you, Vorokrim," said Yoon, inspecting his painted fingernails. "So very, very disappointed. I thought you were made of sterner stuff. I thought you had intelligence and an understanding of the finer details of military strategy." He tutted. Then turned. He smiled and moved close to Vorokrim, reaching down to touch the hilt of the blade.

"Oh dear," he said. "It looks like you have a little problem." Yoon smiled reassuringly. "I think we can both agree, at this moment in time, my old friend, you are ably removed of your command."

Vorokrim toppled sideways and lay still on the carpet.

Yoon's head snapped up. "Captain Dokta!"

"Yes, Majesty!" He snapped to attention. Good. Good. Yoon appreciated the man's lack of tardiness.

"You have come far in these last few months. I have grown fond of your strength, your ambition and indeed your ruthlessness. Please, go downstairs, take the rest of our elite guard, and open the gates."

"Open the gates to the mud-orcs?" said Captain Dokta.

"Exactly so."

Captain Dokta hesitated, but only for a moment. He saluted. "Yes, Majesty. As you command." He disappeared down the steep stone steps.

Yoon turned back to the panoramic view of the battle. "But my, this is a fine vision," he muttered. "I must have something similar added to the top floor of the Tower of the Moon. It offers a most pleasing light! Most rousing and heroic! Quite a magickal spectacle to be sure!"

Kiki flowed with the battle. She was at one with her sword and shield. She danced amongst the defenders, light, fast, agile, her sword a spear of lightning flickering between the attacking mud-orcs like some demon blade, a simple cut here, a slash there, a stab, parry, thrust, cut, slice, block, stab. She moved with elegance and perfect balance. A dancer. A dancer on the stage of death, shifting between the enemy and hardly seeming to inflict a wound, yet leaving a trail of destruction in her wake, leaving mud-orcs kneeling on the battlements trying to hold their throats together, or slipping and rolling around in their own spilled entrails.

In contrast, Narnok used his prodigious size, weight, power and ferocity to cut a two-handed bloody path through the enemy. Whilst the mud-orcs were on their ladders and ropes, his terrible axe made short work of any head or claws that appeared in an attempt to gain a handhold. On other areas of the battlements, when a breach was made Narnok, often with Sergeant Dunda by his side, strode into the breach great axe smashing left and right, cutting heads from shoulders, gouging huge horrific flapping wounds down chests and bellies.

Dek used a combination of his sword and the pit-fighting skills he knew so well, punching, kicking, eye-gouging and head-butting to stun and blind, before using his blade to finish off whatever unfortunate lay squirming at his feet. Unlike Kiki's cool calculated attack, and Narnok's bellowing hate-filled bludgeoning, Dek walked a path somewhere in between, his responses more like the soldiers around him, more like the men dying around him. At one point, a soldier's sword broke, and he was borne to the ground by a mammoth mud-orc all slashing claws and frothing jaws. It strained for the soldier's face as he desperately tried to hold it away, its teeth snapping and clashing inches from his. Dek hacked halfway through the mud-orc's neck and it squealed high and long. He front-kicked it from the soldier and plunged his blade through the creature's eye, skewering its brain. He hauled the man to his feet.

"Thank you," spluttered the warrior. "I am Reegez!"

"Dek," growled Dek. "Your turn to watch my back now, lad!" and he grinned and slapped the man between the shoulder blades.

Trista and Zastarte fought as a team, side by side whilst assaulting the attacking mud-orcs, and back to back when a breach in the wall occurred. It was as if they were psychically linked in battle, finishing one another's sword strokes, defending one another from attacking blows of sword and spear and claws. Watching them, they were like entwined ballet dancers re-enacting some amazing scene of battle on the stage; only this stage was not filled with props and fake blood, this stage was in the theatre of war, and only dying men and slippery entrails and beheaded mud-orcs formed the set against a backdrop of stone and sky and screaming aggression.

The mud-orcs were attacking with renewed ferocity now, and below they had great shields of leather and iron, stretched out over a large group of splice tearing at the great wooden gate and hacking around the stone with huge picks and chisels. More and more mud-orcs were breaching the battlements, and at one point nearly ten pockets of savage fighting broke out as the mud-orcs poured onto the battlements and the defenders fought to save the wall and the mud-orcs battled to link each individual pocket into a fighting line. The Iron Wolves waded into these pockets, dispatching enemies with skill and speed and ease, seemingly untouchable and they danced and shifted and moved like ghosts amidst the action, amidst the savagery, amidst the dying.

After twenty minutes of insane battle, Narnok threw the last mud-orc from the battlements and leapt up onto the stone, adrenaline pumping strong in him as he waved his huge axe and screamed something incomprehensible, something primeval and inhuman at the withdrawing beasts.

He dropped down to the stone, bathed in blood, his face like that of a demon. Kiki approached. "Why the withdrawal?"

"The bastards know when they're beaten!"

"No, they don't. Look out there! One hundred thousand of the fuckers! That's not an enemy that's defeated, that's an enemy that is regrouping to try a different tactic. I'm wondering what it is."

"We'll find out soon enough," said Dek, wiping blood and orc-gore from his face with an old towel that looked better placed in a charnel house than on a fortress wall. Although, in all reality, that was what the place had become.

Stretcher bearers carried the wounded and dying from Sanderlek, all the way to the large hospital blocks attached to the Keep where surgeons worked tirelessly in grim and terrible conditions. Soldiers were removing the dead, tossing them down to carts below the wall and scattering buckets of sand across the walkways. Wounded mud-orcs were dispatched with cuts to the throat or dagger blows to the brain, then tossed over the wall to further hamper their comrades below.

Young lads with buckets of water were doing the rounds, and the Iron Wolves gratefully received cups of water, drinking and then washing blood from their faces. Then they sat, backs to the parapets, and Kiki placed her hands flat on the stone battlements.

"Can you feel it?"

The others looked at her.

"Eh?" said Narnok.

"The magick," she said. "The curse, it is here, within the stone. It emanates from this very structure."

"What *did* Dalgoran tell you?" rumbled Narnok.

"I will explain. When the job is done; when we achieve what we came here to achieve."

Dek stood, climbed onto the parapet and stared out, shading his eyes. The enemy stretched for as far as the eye could see, and he shivered when he saw the units of splice, many lying down and tearing at chunks of meat which looked suspiciously human.

"Do you see her?"

"No. They have war tents set up, right far back. It looks like yet another fucking leader who leads from the rear."

"We need to get to her."

"I have a plan about that," said Narnok, and grinned.

"You're obviously thinking of the mines. But do they go

far enough? No point popping up in the middle of a party of splice and having our heads ripped clean off before we even get near the bitch."

"They'll get us close enough," said Narnok. "They did last time." He stood and shaded his eyes next to Dek. "You see the rocks, off to the right. There's one of the exits."

"We'd still need to sneak through ten thousand mud-orcs."

Narnok nodded. "I thought about that as well. We skin some of the mud-orcs, wear them like a suit."

Kiki stared at him. "That will convince nobody, Narnok. Have you been on the honey-leaf?"

"In my experience," the axeman said, somewhat haughtily, "the mud-orcs have poor eyesight and track more by sound and smell. Well. *Stench*," he corrected himself.

"I'm not sure that would work. But maybe… if we soaked ourselves in mud-orc blood, that would disguise us. To some extent."

"Sounds good to me," rumbled Narnok.

Kiki pulled back her hair into a tight pony-tail and tied it up. "We'd also need the gate keys."

"Dalgoran had the keys!" said Zastarte.

"Yeah, but that's twenty years past," muttered Narnok.

"We'll find them," said Kiki.

Just then a runner arrived, panting. "You're the Iron Wolves?" Kiki nodded. "General Vorokrim requests your immediate audience back at Zula. He says there has been an amazing breakthrough! King Yoon has finally become involved and sent soldiers!"

"Come on," said Dek, reaching out and hauling Kiki up. "There's no rest for the wicked."

"Yeah. We've had that all our lives," muttered Kiki, and as they descended the steps she noticed a large group of armoured warriors heading for the gates. They wore black armour, which was nothing incredible in itself, except it looked more ceremonial and had not recently seen battle. Too smooth. Too polished. Unusual, for soldiers in a fortress under siege.

They walked through the cold chill across the killing ground between Sanderlek and Tranta-Kell, passing through the narrow tunnel with its massive oak portals and piles of stone waiting on the other side to seal the tunnel closed when the time came. Up a steep incline towards Kubosa, (after all, no need making it easy for an attacking enemy, is there?), through that tunnel and towards Jandallakla, then on towards the Keep. Here, the runner halted, hopping from foot to foot.

"He said for you to go up."

Kiki nodded, and led the Wolves up the first set of stone steps. Here, there was a short platform and a stern faced man waiting for them, backed by five other stern faced men. They all wore neat, black, armour which had seen little or no battle. Kiki gave a quick narrow smile. So then, a set-up, she thought idly.

You deserve nothing less, bitch, said Suza in her mind, and gave her a long, low, mocking laugh. *They're going to cut you up and spit you out, bury you all in unmarked graves for not complying with the King. He's gonna gut you like fish. Cut out your insides, including that funny little tumour friend you've got poking at you in there, and leave you hung and helpless from the battlements to appease Orlana and beg her forgiveness. Then he's going to open the gates and just watch those lovely splice come pouring through...*

How do you know this?

Just call it female intuition.

"I am General Rorgell, of the King's Elite Guard. King Yoon is here. In the name of His Majesty, the King of Vagandrak, give up your weapons and follow me."

Kiki handed over her sword and daggers to the waiting soldiers, and slowly the other Iron Wolves complied without comment. Briefly, each of the Wolves met Kiki's gaze and each of them had the same understanding. This was a trap.

They followed Rorgell up the steps and into Vorokrim's chamber. It looked much the same as several hours earlier, except with one major difference. Now, Vorokrim sat in his chair, eyes open and glassy, a thin black dagger through his throat, from side to side, as if he were a skewered kebab.

Kiki wanted to gasp, but held an iron stance. She strode forward and folded her arms as the other Iron Wolves fanned out behind her. There were another five armoured men in the room bearing naked blades, and the five from the steps filed in behind. The Iron Wolves were effectively disarmed and surrounded.

And there, against the window, was King Yoon.

He turned, and gave them a sickly smile.

"You had General Vorokrim killed?" said Kiki, gently, her eyes meeting those dark glittering orbs of her king.

"He disobeyed a direct order," said Yoon, voice rich and vibrant.

"Of course he did," said Kiki smoothly. "No man, no matter what rank, should ever question his king."

Yoon smiled at that. "Yes, yes. Quite right, my dear. And you are, of course, Kikellya Mandasayard, Captain of the Iron Wolves, and these," Yoon spread out his fingers as if introducing them to his court, "are Narnok of the Axe; Dek of the Fighting Pits – boy, I've won many a gold crown on your exploits; Trista, such a shame you no longer frequent my court functions, but at least now the mortality rate of my guests has improved considerably; and finally, the elusive Prince Zastarte."

"Your Majesty," said Zastarte, and gave an elaborate bow.

"What intrigues me, my friends and loyal subjects, and I do hope I can call you my loyal subjects, is in the wondering of what you wish to achieve by coming here. As we all know, you are the heroes of the War of Zakora some twenty years past, and you fought the mud-orcs back then. You also slew the sorcerer Morkagoth." He clapped his hands several times, but his face held no mockery. "Well done. You saved your country! And your country was thankful! However, here, and now, we have this situation under control."

"You call that under control?" growled Narnok, pointing to the mayhem on Sanderlek. "Carts full of dead men who will no longer kiss their wives, no longer hold their children; mourning parents having to bury their first born sons; widows weeping over their only children?"

Kiki placed a hand on Narnok's arm.

"You're starting to sound like Vorokrim," smiled King Yoon, making them all feel very, very uneasy.

"What is it you want from us, King Yoon?"

"I wish you to leave. Your presence was neither requested, nor is it needed. I fear it may upset... negotiations with Queen Orlana."

"*Queen* Orlana?" spluttered Dek. "So, you have met?"

"We have had, shall we say, some communication. The next step is to open the gates and welcome her into our country. This attack was unnecessary. She makes very grave and important promises about the safety of our people."

"You will not open the gates," said Kiki, eyes hard and focused on King Yoon. She heard the gentle movements behind her as the black armoured soldiers prepared to attack.

Yoon frowned. "You dare to question your King?" and he gave the signal.

The Iron Wolves leapt into action, spinning and attacking in fluid fast movements even as the soldiers launched themselves forward, swords hacking down. Kiki twisted, as the blade whistled past her and she grabbed the man by the throat, lifted him from his feet and punched him three times in the groin. She lowered him, taking his blade and slamming it through his neck. He went down hard, gurgling, as the man behind lunged a jab for Kiki's eye. Her blade slashed up, deflecting the blow with a clash of iron and she stuck the point of her own blade in his throat. He, too, gurgled as he fell. Narnok slapped away a sword with his forearm, the razor edge cutting a long line across his flesh, and he punched the soldier in the throat with such power he killed the man, leaving him choking and purple curled on expensive rugs. Dek front-kicked a soldier with his blade in the air, pulled a hidden knife from his boot and descended, landing atop the soldier's breast-plate and plunging his dagger through the helm, into the eye and brain beyond. He took the short sword, blocked a savage cut from another soldier, reversed the blade and cut through the attacker's leg, severing it just below the knee. The man toppled, screaming, scrabbling at the stump, blood flowing out over the stone and rugs. Zastarte and Trista worked together, feinting, jabbing, as Trista pulled a long pin from her hair and pushed it through a soldier's eye. Within seconds the Iron Wolves had swords and cut their way through the rest of the soldiers in just a few more seconds. The only people left standing were King Yoon, who had backed away with hands raised at the sudden violent onslaught, and General Rorgell, who held his longsword in stunned disbelief at the savagery and ferocity of the Iron Wolves taking out ten of his elite men.

Narnok grinned at him, scarred face glistening with sweat and blood. "It's what we do, brother," he spat.

Face pale, Rorgell screamed and attacked.

And lay dead at Narnok's feet, a third of his head cut free in a diagonal slice.

Dek ran and bolted the door, with three heavy sliders of iron. Then they turned on King Yoon and advanced slowly across the chamber, the five of them spreading out.

"Tell me what happened to Vorokrim," said Kiki.

"I told you! He disobeyed a direct order from his king!"

"Was the order to open the gate?"

King Yoon remained silent.

"WAS IT TO OPEN THE FUCKING GATE?" screamed Kiki.

"Yes, yes, yes. Please, don't kill me! I implore thee!"

"Narnok?"

"Yes, Kiki?" He was grinning broadly.

"Put a bag over this fucker's head, take him down, and lock him in a faraway dungeon."

"My pleasure," he said, and reached forward, grabbing Yoon. Yoon struggled, and Narnok head-butted him, breaking his nose. Blood flowed down his chest and Yoon howled. Yoon pulled a hidden dagger from his sleeve and Narnok took it from him like sweetcakes from a child. He waggled the dagger before Yoon's eye. "You try any more tricks, sunshine, and I'll pluck out your eyeball. Then you'll look like me." He grinned through his scars. "Only a damn sight less pretty."

"Dek. You and Zastarte gather together a few captains, get down to the gates. I've got a feeling Yoon's elite guards are in the process of opening the tunnel. Stop them. Kill them, if you have to, but I'd prefer a surrender. It's bad for morale, men killing fellow countrymen when there's tens of thousands of mud-orcs needing a blade in the skull."

Dek saluted her. "Yes, Lady. And, Lady? I really am glad to have you back."

"Good to be back," smiled Kiki. "Meet back here as soon as possible. We need to take out Orlana. And we need to do it tonight."

"Er," said Narnok, suddenly. "We have a problem."

"What?"

"Look!" he snapped, pointing...

As below, the mud-orc horde advanced... led by the splice.

Led by *all* the splice.

"They've opened the gate," hissed Dek.

"Get down there!" yelled Kiki.

"You're too late, honey-leaf whore," said Yoon through his mask of blood, grinning, as Narnok found a hood and slammed it over his head. He punched Yoon three times through the cloth, and the King of Vagandrak went silent. Silent and limp.

"Change of plan," said Kiki. "Get him to the fucking dungeons; the rest of you come with me."

THE IRON GATES

The splice poured through the open tunnel, and the King's elite guard stood to one side as hooves and paws and claws gouged the earth and stone and the beasts invaded Desekra Fortress. Ten, twenty, thirty, forty... the Iron Wolves, backed by a thousand Vagandrak men arrived, fifty bearing heavy crossbows, and shafts hissed and snarled through the air, punching splice from their feet, bending them over double and slamming them back into their comrades. With battle cries, King Yoon's elite guards drew swords and charged the Iron Wolves, but more heavy crossbows smashed them in half, three hundred thick yew shafts cutting through the enemy and breaking them against the stone. Splice snarled and screamed and crawled over their comrades, as more bows were loaded and archers peppered them with arrows. Kiki led the charge alongside Narnok and Dek, and they hit the front splice in a blur of aggression and hacking violence, swords and axes cleaving skulls and brains and limbs, skewering eyes and sending blood flowing into the soil.

"We need to seal the tunnel!" screamed Kiki.

"I can do that," bellowed Narnok. "Just get me deep inside."

They fought their way through splice, the brave soldiers of Vagandrak covering their backs, and hacked and hewed their way through walls of splice flesh until they stood within the narrow confines. Narnok put his axe through the skull of a wolf splice, then another, and the bodies blocked the narrow portal. He turned to Kiki.

"Get back!"

"What are you going to do?"

"GET BACK!"

Kiki retreated, and Narnok looked up. "Come on, you tender little whore, open your legs for me," he said, and spat into the palms of his hands, one by one. He hammered his axe upwards, chipping stone. Then again, and again, and again, and again. A splice made from horse, man and wolf, snarling and drooling, crawled over its felled comrades and as it was about to leap, received an axe head between the eyes. Brain, skull and blood splashed up the stone.

"Come on," said Narnok. Ten more times he hammered the axe at the roof of the tunnel, and dust trickled down, then tiny stones. Outside Sanderlek the splice were massed, the defenders stood on the parapets, archers firing down into their milling ranks. But they took the arrows. They took hundreds of arrows, and their ferocity and dark magick carried them on.

Again and again Narnok hammered his trusty axe upwards and he knew it, could *feel* it, could feel Iron Wolf magick coursing through his veins, vibrating through his boots, surging through the very soul of the fortress. Desekra was built for the men and women and children of Vagandrak. And Narnok was a portal for that magick. His legacy. His curse. His pride. His sacrifice…

He screamed, and the axe rammed upwards, the blades buckling, folding down into a hammer.

"COME DOWN ON US YOU FUCKING WHORE!" he screamed, blow after blow after blow echoing through

Desekra, iron smashing stone, metal beckoning the fortress itself to collapse, to help them, to aid the defenders in their desperate hour of need...

And Desekra responded, and groaned, and stone blocks shifted, and more splice forced their way through the tunnel opened by King Yoon and crawled over dead and dying comrades as Narnok, like a man possessed, muscles bunched and curling like writhing snakes, his lips moving in silent incantation, bludgeoned the weapon he could no longer call an axe into the roof of the tunnel... and splice snarling with bared fangs and razor claws scrambled like cats over their fallen comrades and leapt at Narnok to tear off his face...

As the fortress rumbled.

The Pass of Splintered Bones *groaned*.

And the roof caved in.

Narnok turned to flee, sprinting with all his might. Stones fell down, huge blocks of granite booming and tumbling, and he managed a few more strides then felt himself go under. The whole of the Desekra Fortress rumbled and groaned, as if some great earthquake was taking it in gauntleted fist and shaking it. As a warning. To the future.

Outside, Kiki watched the wall shudder, trembling and groaning, the whole tunnel collapsing with great bellows of grinding screaming stone. Dust pumped out as if from some natural explosion, and Kiki was hit in the face by a hundred chips of stone.

Slowly, the wall groaned, and sagged just a little; like a man's mouth after a stroke.

Dek stepped forward and went to move again. Kiki blocked him with the flat of her sword.

"He's gone," she said.

"But… he's Narnok! He can't fucking die!"

"He's gone," she repeated, and the sorrow in her voice was that of a thousand mourners chanting the loss of a hero.

She turned, and grabbed Dek's jerkin. "Focus! I need you! We have to travel the tunnels. We need to reach Orlana!"

"You really think we can kill her?"

"I am beginning to understand," said Kiki.

"The curse?"

"The fortress. Desekra. The curse of the Iron Wolves does not lie within us; it lies within Desekra. We are not trying to free ourselves, we are trying to separate ourselves from the legacy of the king who built this tomb. Esekra. Esekra, the Lost."

She did not know why she said it. But it sounded right. It sounded… *true*.

"What next?" panted Trista.

"We head for the mines," said Kiki, voice grim.

Each carried a brand which sputtered through different colours as they descended into the lower dungeons. They had confided only in Sergeant Dunda, who had grabbed two of his most trusted men to help, Reegez and Jagan, both hardened by the last few days fighting on the first Desekra wall, with blades drawn and faces grim, as if the whole sanctity of the nation depended on their actions. Which, maybe, it did. They approached Dalgoran's old living chambers in Zula Keep warily, and inside found everything preserved as the old general had left it. Kiki headed for the chest at the back of the room, under the polished oak desk. Inside the chest, she found the thick bunch of keys for the gates in the mines. Without them, they would never negotiate the vast portals known as the Gates of Iron.

Now, as they descended into the dungeons, into the mine labyrinth, flames burned yellow, then on another level blue, another green, another red. As if each subterranean level beneath the Desekra Fortress was composed of different air, different chemicals, different atoms, different *magick*. The levels went down and down and down and down. Eventually the steps stopped, and became corridors, and halls, and caverns, and sometimes arched walkways over vast bottomless chasms. Darkness flooded in, so that even the brands seemed to illuminate little, providing only small circles of light in a vast unending darkness that surrounded the Iron Wolves. Flames sputtered and spat. The cold increased, not the cold of a savage winter containing snow and ice, but the cold of the deep; the cold of the grave; the cold of a bottomless tombworld.

"I hate it down here," said Trista. "Where is the sunlight? Where is the world? Where is life?"

"We'll be out soon enough," said Kiki.

"These mines are unnatural. The internal magick of the mountain drawing on the weak, of mind and spirit and flesh. They were not a place designed for human presence. There is a great evil down here." Trista shivered.

Kiki nodded, and they pushed on, finding the first huge portal. It was a gate of iron, intricately carved, maybe ten feet high and over a foot thick. It must have weighed a hundred tons. Within the ornate ironwork was the intricately formed shape of a howling wolf, head lifted to a full moon. The key turned easily, with a heavy clunk. As Kiki touched the metal, tiny sparks ran along the aged black iron and discharged against her skin. She felt this power pulsing inside her. She felt like it was exploring her. She felt magick tingling in her veins.

Desekra Fortress knew she was there, she, Kiki, Captain of the Iron Wolves. Finally, the Great Fortress seemed to come awake and it *knew*; knew all the Iron Wolves were alive and wriggling in Her belly, in Her womb; like tiny embryos. Her unborn. And She, Desekra, started to feed them; an intravenous delivery of energy, strength, power, *magick*. She fed the Curse inside them all.

They moved into the corridor beyond the massive iron portal, and the tunnel narrowed here so it could be defended, if discovered. Following protocol, Kiki turned and locked the gate behind them. They all exchanged a solemn glance. There would be no quick retreat when this thing was done; or not done. And if the splice were hot on their heels following a failure, they would be trapped, quite literally, between a rock and a hard place.

They followed the narrow winding tunnel, which sometimes sloped steeply down, sometimes climbed until their leg muscles were burning. All sense of direction and depth were soon lost and gone, drifted away like smoke. The Iron Wolves forced themselves to trust the winding tunnel, and when they came to hubs where tunnels spun away like complex spider webs, they then relied on Kiki's memory.

They came to another gate, then another, and another. Each portal ten feet high, over a foot thick and carved with a different representation of a wolf every time; on one, a pack hunting; on another, two wolves fighting for supremacy; on yet another, a wolf standing above a man, fangs tearing into his throat. The black iron gleamed and the workmanship was intricate and incredibly detailed and showed no rust, despite the cold and damp atmosphere in which they existed.

Finally, after passing through twelve gates, the ground rose up steeply, and Zastarte muttered through his sweat and lank hair, until they reached the final gate; the thirteenth.

Through this they passed, Kiki solemnly locking the portal, and then they climbed again, feeling a cool breeze drifting down to meet them. They stepped into a cave with a soft sand floor, itself burrowed deep within a giant standing stone. Carefully, they edged around a series of vertical pillars that hid the tunnel from the cave mouth and that, Kiki knew, gave an optical illusion of a solid wall when viewed from the entrance.

Warily the group stepped free and drew weapons. Night had fallen during their journey, and they could hear a rumble of drums, smell fire and woodsmoke and roasting meat. They moved to the entrance to the cave, and stared out at the other huge standing stones – as they had twenty years earlier.

The mud-orcs were camped in a vast arc stretching away into the night. In the distance, they could see Desekra Fortress, fires burning on the walls, the slick granite glowing under the pale light of a full moon.

"This is where we see if it was a good idea," muttered Kiki, and pulled a large flash from her pack. The others did the same and, grimacing, especially Zastarte who started making retching noises, they began to smear mud-orc blood on their faces, hands, arms, clothing, armour, and rubbing the foul-stinking liquor into their hair, massaging it down to the roots.

"This is the worst thing I have ever done for King and Country," murmured Zastarte.

"Even worse than the secret mission where you had to make love to a syphilitic whore down by the docks?" queried Trista.

"At least there was a little pleasure to be gained from such an activity; this, my love, hardly climaxes with joyous ejaculation."

"There'll be a joyous ejaculation of your head from your shoulders if you carry on talking," hissed Kiki.

"Now keep your mouths shut. We all know what we have to do."

They stepped within the lee of the huge standing stones, and a cold wind snapped at them like a dog. They watched for long, dragging minutes. The mud-orc camp was a bustle of activity. They were indeed, as intelligence gathered by Vagandrak scouts suggested, getting ready for a night attack – the first of its kind, and the first time Orlana had tried such a tactic.

The Iron Wolves waited, until with a roar the lines of mud-orcs flowed out across the plains and hundreds of arrows arced into the sky from the Sanderlek battlements, a dark hail against the moonlit heavens, thudding home and taking down a huge swathe of the enemy. Growling and howling the mud-orcs flowed on, a green sea of bile and hate, and grappling irons sailed over the battlements and ladders thudded against parapets as the enemy swarmed up Sanderlek and the brave defenders of Vagandrak met them with sword and axe and spear.

The remainder of the army was reorganising into units, huge leader mud-orcs snarling and spitting in their grotesque language. Kiki set her eyes on the white tents of Orlana and, taking a deep breath, led the Iron Wolves from the protection of the standing stones.

They skirted the rear of the camp, moving slowly, the energy of Desekra Fortress flowing in their veins, the might of the magick, of the curse, filling all four up to the brim with a bubbling power that threatened to spill out, to overflow at any moment...

There was a central tent, larger than the others and fashioned from white Zakoran silk. There were guards outside the front but they seemed excessively relaxed; after all, *they* were the ones attacking the enemy.

Kiki signalled in military sign. *That one*.

Advance, came Dek's reply. Zastarte and Trista brought up the rear.

Reaching the rear of the tent and hunkering down, Kiki produced a dagger, and glancing left and right, cut into the silk a short distance from the ground. Silently, she opened the silk with a razor edge.

Inside the tent was dark, with just a single brazier burning, allowing soft golden shadows to flicker inside the silk walls. The sounds of battle were close here, screams, cries, the clash of iron on iron, all echoing back from the battle on and below Sanderlek, and rushing across the Zakora plains like an ocean of misery.

Kiki unfolded, delicately, like a rose opening its petals.

There, lounging naked under silk sheets, was a tall woman with short white hair, and a powerful man with a forked black beard and thick, bushy black hair, whom she recognised with a start; it was King Zorkai of Zakora. There was considerable trade between Vagandrak and Zakora – or there had been, before the attack of the mud-orc army. Kiki had travelled to the capital city of Zak-Tan on several occasions during the last decade, and on her previous visit had seen him address his people of the desert.

Kiki's fist clenched around her sword pommel, and with Dek to her left, and Trista and Zastarte to her right, the Iron Wolves moved carefully, silently, across thick rugs and between piles of gold-embroidered cushions towards Orlana, the Changer, the creature known as the Horse Lady…

WOLVES UNITE

Narnok coughed and choked on dust, and wondered for a split second how much being crushed to death was going to hurt. He hadn't wanted to die so young, although he acknowledged he was far from being a spring chicken. Indeed, most days he felt truly invincible, despite his age, despite the scars, despite having only one eye! But here, and now, acting like a damn fool hero in a role he should have left to the young and the strong, to those more readily willing to carve themselves a pedestal in the Hall of Heroes, he'd gone and got himself fucking killed. You stupid old fool, he chastised himself.

The fortress around him rumbled and groaned, shaking, filled with dust and falling stone, and for a moment it felt like the whole of Sanderlek had come down on him. The world was rocking as if in the throes of a huge earthquake, and Narnok tried to turn and run but was swiftly battered down, hit in the head by a huge block which knocked him sideways and instantly unconscious.

Narnok's dreams were sweet. He dreamt of Katuna, holding her close after making love, his seed in her womb, praying that it would find its way to her egg, so they could produce children, so he could become a father! He smelled the oil in her dark curls, and she slept with his great arms around her, protecting her from the evils of the night; the evils of the world. Even in the dark he could see her olive skin, soft and smooth and gorgeous, and he ran his fingers down her arm, marvelling that a woman so ravishingly beautiful could have not just taken him to bed, but chosen him to spend the rest of her life alongside; partners in crime, for the rest of eternity. "We will die together, my sweet," he whispered to her sleeping form, "and we will be buried together at the old cemetery on Heroes Walk." Then Xander's face flashed into his mind, mouth wide and screaming, teeth sharp like daggers and plunging down to tear off his face…

He woke up coughing, in a panic, trying to turn but realising he was trapped, pinned down by Xander who had his razors sharp and ready and the acid in its bottle dripping to burn out his eye.

He breathed in deep, confused, choking on dust, and panic was his master for several minutes and he screamed and heaved and pushed and struggled and tried to escape. Gradually he tired enough to pause, and engage his brain, and think, and retrace his steps.

Mud-orcs. Splice. Invasion.

Sanderlek. Tunnel breach!

He'd brought down the roof. Ahh. *Ahhh!* Horse shit.

Narnok lay there for a long while, and he could not feel his legs. That wasn't good, that wasn't. He flexed both hands, and could move them, and most of his arms. The darkness was complete around him, so utter and total and black he could be lying in (shhhh) *his tomb.*

Fear gnawed at him. Like a rat feeding on his intestines.

Yes, there had been the possibility of being crushed alive when he embarked on his foolhardy bloody stupid attempt to bring down the roof and seal the tunnel from the splice. He'd kind of romantically imagined he would flee along the tunnel, rocks tumbling down behind him, before making a last desperate dash and flinging himself out onto the winter grass beyond. The soldiers would laugh and pat him on the back and call him a hero. He'd beam at them like a village idiot, and say something inane and uproarious. "When I party, I always bring the roof down!" Har har har. Indeed.

What he hadn't anticipated was being buried. Truly. *Buried* alive.

"HEY!" he shouted, but the sound reverberated back, stinging his own ears with its amplified volume and he winced. He quietened down and listened, to see if he could hear any sounds of digging. Surely they'd rescue him, wouldn't they? But then, they *were* in the middle of a battle. Would they even have time, between fending off mud-orc attacks and simply trying to stay alive?

Of course they wouldn't. They'd assume him dead. And they all had their own problems.

"Damn. Damn and bloody bollocks," he muttered, and touched the stone above him. It was a huge flat slab. Subtly, he felt it shift. His hands explored the parameters; it was a damn sight bigger than him. If it came down, it'd crush him like a bug under a boot.

So, what now? Dig my own way out?

He lay for a while, wondering what to do, before he realised there was nothing he *could* do. He was good and trapped. Good and buried. Good and fucking dead.

He touched the block above him with both hands, tracing the smoothness of the stone. When they had been *made* Iron Wolves, Dalgoran and the others, the magick makers had explained that the magick came from the bones of the thousands slain in the Pass of Splintered Bones. It was part of the death-magick that ran through the very bedrock of the mountains. And Desekra Fortress was *part* of the mountains; part of that bedrock, built and created from the very stone infused with the power of life and death and law and chaos.

"Help me," he said, staring into the darkness. "Desekra! I am one of your Iron Wolves. My friends are heading into the heart of darkness and I need to be there with them! I invoke you! I invoke the power of the Iron Wolves!"

And it came to him, he felt it, the magick in the stone, the energy stored deep within every atom of this massive fortress. And Desekra did not speak to him; there were no words or thoughts or ideas, simply a *feeling*. And that feeling was: *prepare yourself*. And Narnok prepared himself, and felt that surge of raw power like which he had not experienced for so many years; he felt the magick of the *shapeshifter*, and it started deep inside his bones, at their core, and he felt them turn to iron. They began to grow, and Narnok readied himself for the *pain*, and readied himself for the *change*, and readied himself for the absolute total *agony* to come.

Queen Orlana had stood outside her war tent, breathing the cold winter air of this human world. She watched, a little in dismay, as the tunnel was brought crashing down and she realised: King Yoon's favour was gone. Either by understanding, or death, or betrayal. It did not matter. The fool with whom she had communicated was no longer in control. The idiot with whom she had *bargained* was no longer in a position to bargain. And she smiled. At least it had been an *interesting* situation. To watch one in such a position of power crumble like cheese.

Still. It mattered little.

She gazed across her ranks of mud-orcs. Ninety thousand strong and still growing as her scouts scoured the lands of Zakora for more flesh to feed the mud-pits, feeding the magick, growing the mud-orcs, creating the soldiers she needed to achieve...

Ahhh.

No need to know that, just yet.

Yoon had amused her greatly. "What do you want with my land? My home country? My Vagandrak?"

"I do not want your pathetic world," she'd said.

"Then why invade?"

"I want what is beyond."

"Explain?"

"Use your mind, man! It was what you were born with!"

And still he did not understand. And now, probably, he was dead. She shrugged. She examined her fingernails. It did not matter. Tomorrow, she would throw everything at Desekra. She had three thousand splice in the Skarandos Mountains, and surely thousands had died. But many would have survived, and would mass behind Desekra, where it was at its most vulnerable, where they least expected attack. She would hit them from both sides. Take the damned place. Overrun it, and head...

Beyond.

Into Vagandrak.

And *beyond*.

But now, she stood and enjoyed the evening air of this alien place. This alien world. She had summoned two of her generals, and chuckled to herself as she realised one was not necessarily a *general*, but considered himself a *king*. But then, all idiots realise the truth too late, she thought. All are consumed by arrogance and ignorance and vastly exaggerated self-importance. It was simply the way of the world. From politicians to academics to the ones supposedly *in power*.

For Orlana, it was one of humanity's greatest triumphs.

A natural order, an in-built pre-programmed aptitude for self-destruction.

The need to better the next man, to the exclusion of all fellow men.

It made her life *so much easier.*

Zorkai had been taken to bed, and Orlana fucked him like she'd never fucked him before. He felt them fuse together, as one, as he pumped himself inside her and felt himself turned inside out, and he saw black stars in a black endless universe and suddenly understanding came to him: she was using him for something elemental, something to do with earth and blood and soul magick. And after the long hours, when she finally allowed him to withdraw like a withered, shrivelled shell, he felt utterly dirty and used and usurped. He was no longer the King of Zakora. He was no longer king.

He turned over on the sheets, head on his arm, and listened to the distant sounds of battle. Where once it had been music to him, now it was pain. Where once it had been a prelude to immortality, now it was a prologue to oblivion.

Zorkai rolled from the sheets, where Orlana slept like a pale white statue, and slowly he reached for his short sword. His brow furrowed. Yes. It was decided. He would run the bitch through, and go home... and the Vagandrak soldiers? Well, they were all big boys. They weren't his problem. He'd had enough. Enough of the slaughter of his people. Of the stench of the mud-orcs. Of the squealing and drooling of the splice. But most of all, most sickeningly of all, of being the bastard pointless puppet of another human being. Well. Another *creature*, he told himself. And shuddered.

He lifted the blade. It felt good and solid and real in his hands. He would decapitate the bitch. Remove her fucking head. See if that didn't send her flowing back to whatever shit-hole she'd squirmed from like a poisonous cold-skinned reptile...

That's it. That's what she reminded him of.

A snake. A big, white, albino snake – in the shell of a woman.

And the best way to kill a snake was to remove its head.

He eased forward in total silence, the sword lifting a little as he readied himself for the killing stroke.

"Better leave this one to us, Zorkai," came a low, husky voice from the gloom at the back of the tent, just behind him.

Zorkai blinked, as his eyes adjusted, and he saw... four soldiers, and yet they were *not* soldiers. Even as he watched they were changing, their skin darkening, hairs like iron bristles starting to ease across their skin.

Orlana suddenly rolled from her sheets, completely naked, crouched on all fours, and her mouth folded back open until her whole head was nothing more than one huge fang-rimmed hole. She screamed at Zorkai, and the blast picked him up, stripped fat streamers of skin from his flesh, and blasted him backwards through the wall of the tent.

She turned on the Iron Wolves, face rolling back to a rough approximation of a woman like melted wax down the soft flanks of a candle; and she grinned at them. Slowly, she unfolded from the crouch and looked down her nose.

"Welcome. I've been expecting you."

"Didn't look that way to me," growled Dek. "Looked like you were asleep, snoring and having dreams of happy slaughter." His voice was thick, rolling slowly around his gradually emerging fangs. His face, also, was changing, as progressively a muzzle pushed its way from the lower portion of his face. And when he spoke, his teeth were no longer white, but the silver grey of polished iron. "Easy meat for the swords of the Iron Wolves."

"I have been expecting you, because my splice failed to neutralise your threat. And after that dead fool Dalgoran revealed your existence to me through the lines, and illustrated exactly what you did to Morkagoth... Well. I have been awaiting this time. This meeting. With some relish, in fact." She smiled, showing perfect teeth.

"I like it when a murdering bitch acknowledges her impending time for death," said Zastarte. His curls were no longer curls, but a great dark mane. His eyes were larger, had shifted more around the sides of his skull, and were the gleaming colour of iron. His arms were longer, and thicker, and his fingers had turned into claws.

"You carry the old magick in your bones," said Orlana, words almost a whisper. "Which is impressive. *Eain doam shalsoar*. The Art of the Shapeshifter. And yet you are not as dangerous as you think... You are merely kittens, mewling helplessly for their mother. You are newborns, without true control of your power. Indeed, without any understanding of the power you possess. You think the *shapeshifter* is simply about becoming another creature?" She laughed, a short cruel bark as the Iron Wolves tensed for battle. "But then, this is no time for debate. Or education." Her eyes gleamed and her voice accelerated in volume. "TUBODA!"

The huge splice was there in an instant, appearing through the silk tent flaps to loom over Orlana protectively, like a mighty lion over its cub. Compared to the others, he was truly huge, his muzzle bent, fangs and claws twisted and broken, rippling with huge muscles and a jaw and bite bigger than any puny lion.

"This is Tuboda, my Prime," said Orlana sweetly. "He will explain things to you. He will... educate you."

Tuboda roared, head lowering and moving from left to right and back, a massive scream of air flowing back through the thick fur of the Iron Wolves. Now they dropped their weapons as slowly their bodies completed the transformation, as they shapeshifted from human to... not wolves, exactly, but some nightmare artist's impression of a cross between wolf and demon. The curse was complete.

"Dek," said Kiki through a muzzle thick with fangs.

Dek and Tuboda leapt at the same time, hammering together above Orlana's bed sheets with a mighty *smack* of impacting flesh and muscle and bone. Amidst savage snarling fangs they snapped and slashed at one another, great limbs wrapping around like two big cats wrestling. Tuboda's claws slashed, cutting a long line down Dek's flank and he howled, ducking a swipe of twisted paw as his own claws raked Tuboda's mighty chest. Claws flashed and slashed, and Dek stepped back, lowered a shoulder and charged Tuboda, but the splice saw the move, side-stepped and grabbed Dek by the scruff as he charged past. With toss of his head, he threw Dek from the tent and charged suddenly at Kiki, Zastarte and Trista, his fangs snapping, claws slashing, and for a moment everything became a chaos of razor fangs and flailing limbs, lethal claws and powerful thudding blows. Tuboda was fearsome indeed, smashing Trista aside, then Zastarte, and aiming himself straight for Kiki's throat, huge expanded lion's muzzle chewing and straining... Kiki leapt at him, her own head smashing Tuboda's aside as Dek appeared back in the tent, grabbed the brazier between both claws, lifted it and hurled it at Tuboda. A raft of glowing coals hit the splice, igniting its fur, which went up in a sudden blaze, setting fire to the tent, which itself went up within a heartbeat. Flames screamed through the tent and the Iron Wolves rolled from the blaze, out into the cold night, and waited... Tuboda came charging out, fur on fire, roaring an attack straight for Kiki's throat. They slammed together, going down in a snarling hammering smashing ball of violence. And then Orlana strode from the flames, naked, unmarked, head held high, a smile on her lips. Dek launched at her, claws slashing for her throat, but she shifted with a subtle movement, and punched him in the heart sending him accelerating across the rough ground to roll over twenty or thirty times before coming to a halt in the dust.

As Kiki fought for her life against Tuboda, their claws raking at one another, heads smashing together, fangs seeking to get a hold on the other's throat to deliver that killing blow, so Zastarte and Trista, working as a team, attacked Orlana. Hardly seeming to move, she punched them from the air, one then the other, massive blows of energy that sent them flailing across the dry earth in ploughed furrows of mud.

With a roar Dek charged Tuboda's side, knocking him from his dominant position above Kiki, and Dek's muzzle drove deep into Tuboda's flesh, snapping ribs and chewing through meat in search of the beating heart within. Tuboda screamed, great mouth lifting to roar at the velvet heavens, and Dek pulled out, snarling chewing muzzle dragging free muscle and tendons and splinters of bone. Tuboda spun around, but Kiki leapt on his back, jaws fastening over his head and biting down with all the might of her iron fangs. A huge chunk of Tuboda's head came away with a crunch, and Kiki spat out a rock-sized lump of fur and skull and brain. Tuboda hit the ground with a thud, and lay there, panting, great tawny eyes watching them. Dek's claws slashed Tuboda's throat, ripping it free trailing skin and muscle. Blood pumped out, staining the soil. In a great shuddering spasm, Tuboda died.

The Iron Wolves padded to stand together, facing Orlana. She was smiling at them. "You cannot stand against me," she said, simply.

"We will try," growled Kiki.

"The prophecy said 'Wolves unite'. You are not united. There is one missing. One buried beneath the fortress."

"This is true." Kiki's iron eyes fixed on Orlana. "What do you want here, Orlana? Why attack our people? Why invade our land?"

Orlana laughed, a rich peal. "I don't want your pathetic country. I want to take my army through the Pass of Splintered Bones and... beyond. I have my own agenda. One that does not concern you."

"But on the route, you will slaughter thousands?"

"The Mud-Pits need to be fed if I want more mud-orcs. And I will always need more mud-orcs. They serve my purpose, Kiki. You are powerful indeed, Iron Wolves. If you joined with me, if you helped me with my cause, you would be very well rewarded."

"I do not think so," said Kiki, head lowering.

"Dalgoran cursed you well, with the magick of the Equiem."

"It is a curse we will lift. When we have killed you."

Orlana laughed again, that beautiful, tinkling sound that cut through the grind of savage battle like a diamond blade cutting glass. "I am a denizen of the Furnace," she said, the smile falling from her face and her dark eyes fixing on Kiki. "I cannot be killed."

"Let's find out," said Kiki.

Kiki, Dek, Zastarte and Trista spread out, growling. Each was bigger than any wolf, their fur like iron bristles, their teeth silver iron, their claws razor daggers, their huge shaggy heads towering above heavily muscled bodies. Moonlight glinted from their metallic fur, and their saliva drooled like mercury spools.

They charged, as one, but Orlana lifted both hands and her eyes closed for a moment. There was no sound, no bright fire, no explosions or sparks or screams. Just a silent *pulse* of energy, of Equiem magick funnelled up from the bedrock of the mountains and channelled *at* the Iron Wolves. They were picked up and sent spinning away, end over end, to hit the ground hard, rolling over in the dust and the mud, stunned and bruised. They leapt up, snarling, and widened their circle, charging in at Orlana from different directions. Orlana spun like a ballerina, both hands outstretched, and again the Iron Wolves were blasted away to lie in heaps, battered and stunned. If they had been human, they would have been broken and crushed into an easy death.

Across the battlefield, where the mud-orcs marched and the units of splice waited for their chance to rend and tear and murder, something was happening under the light of the full moon. There was a disturbance, as *something* slammed through their lines with an unstoppable force. The mud-orcs seemed to notice little, as they were advancing on an enemy fortress and not expecting the enemy to be coming the other way; and, as events became clear, it was obvious the creature appeared – superficially at least – like that of a advancing splice.

Narnok, now changed to an *Iron Wolf*, charged between the ranks of advancing mud-orcs, his muzzle low to the ground, his powerful legs pumping, his iron-dark eyes seeing everything with a ghostly aura. He spied the mud-orcs, the splice, the war tents with the central one still roaring with flames – and there was Orlana and *there* were the other Wolves and a connection rioted through him, and he accelerated yet more, claws pounded across frozen grass and soil, for he had the *message* and he had to get the *message* to Kiki…

Splice seemed suddenly aware of him, and charged at Narnok. Snarling, with eyes full of rage, he shouldered them out of the way, sending them squealing and wailing into fires and one another. Closer he came, closer and closer. He watched Orlana spinning, sending out pulses of raw energy and he felt them and absorbed them for he carried the power of the Equiem. He carried the magick of Desekra.

"KIKI!" he bellowed, as the Iron Wolves gathered for another charge.

"Join with us!"

"No, that is not the way! I was trapped under the tunnel and Desekra joined with me; filled me with her Knowledge! You are our captain because you are *shamathe*, you are in tune with Nature and the elements and the Old Magick! You must use the power of your youth, of your childhood… think back, travel back, *regress*… you are not like us, because for you this is not some magick imposed curse. You were *born* like this. You are shamathe, one of the Old Shaman, and you command the power of the World Tree!"

Orlana screamed, the pitch so high it could not be heard by human ears and then dropping fast so it instantly rendered anything within a league's radius temporarily deaf. Kiki's mouth had dropped open, and for a moment everything seemed to click into place. It was like finding the final piece of a puzzle.

Desekra, Dalgoran and the Equiem had not *cursed* her.

No.

She had been born this way. It was part of her bloodline. Part of her descendancy.

She was a shamathe.

One of the Old Protectors.

With the power of Nature in the palms of her hands... She did not have cancer, she did not have a tumour expanding alongside her heart. No. That growth was her *second* heart. The heart of the magicker. The heart of the Old Shaman.

Orlana's scream was blasting out, and the Iron Wolves were cowering; in fact, the battle had halted with the suddenness of a lightning strike. Mud-orcs had covered their ears, which were bleeding, slammed dead in their tracks; the splice were writhing in the dirt with blood pouring from every orifice; and every living organism on the vast plain before Desekra Fortress was disabled and down and slammed to earth...

Except for Kiki.

She walked forward, slowly, cowed a little by the power that flowed through every atom of her body, and the vast and profound understanding which surged through her, like blood in veins, sap in trees, spirits in the wind... like magick through the heart of the leylines that criss-crossed the world.

The whole of creation and its energy opened up to her.

And she finally understood the true nature of Desekra Fortress.

It lived. It breathed. *She* lived. *She* breathed. She needed to be saved, before this savage horde born of evil and sacrifice and murder and death took her and spilt so much blood it would stain her stones for an eternity; she would never be clean again. Not because of death on her walls, but because of the nature of the enemy. Because of the way they had been summoned, created through genocide, born through an act of pure evil.

"I stand before you," said Kiki, looking up defiantly at Orlana, the Horse Lady.

"Kill her!" screamed Orlana, pointing, but the splice and mud-orcs stayed down, and she was alone on the plain of battle. She was alone in the world, as she had been alone in the Furnace and the Halls of Chaos.

"You cannot kill me," said Kiki, softly, and slowly the magick of the shapeshift began to regress; the fur shrunk, her limbs returned to human proportions, her muzzle retracted, the claws and fangs of iron disappeared. Kiki was a woman again. Kike was a girl again, with the strong, rhythmic beat of two hearts in her chest. The beat of the human, and the beat of the mystic.

"Then we have a stalemate," said Orlana.

Kiki tilted her head. "You think so?"

"No weapons of iron or steel or wood or fire can harm me. You have neither the power nor the understanding of the magick that flows through your veins to be able to do anything worthwhile; and we stand here facing one another. *Join me, Kiki!* Join me, and together we shall rule not just this world, but we shall conquer the Furnace. We shall rule the tombworld together as well. Together, we will be unstoppable. Like no force this universe has ever seen. Liken nothing since the creation of the stars!" Orlana's face was wide and open and totally beautiful; perfectly fired porcelain. Perfectly created flesh.

Kiki stared at her. "No, Orlana. For you are born of pain and hatred and bitterness and despair. I have felt those emotions, yes, but ultimately I was born of pleasure and love and honour and kindness. I could never be like you. I could never rule alongside you."

"Wretched child!" hissed Orlana, stooping a little, eyes flashing with lightning, hands with their long perfect white fingers curling into claws. "I will cast you into oblivion! We shall see how your magick serves you there!" and her arms came back and she seemed to grow, to stretch upwards towards the heavens, her whole body elongating, her arms and legs stretching out as her eyes flashed silver with stored lightning and her fingers became long jagged silver swords.

Kiki stood her ground, staring up, as Orlana mouthed the most powerful incantation ever seen on the face of the world. The skies grew dark, huge towering black clouds scudding across the sky as lightning flickered and the mountains groaned and rumbled and clashed like titans at war.

Orlana screamed, and fire erupted from her mouth, smoke from nostrils and eyes and ears and quim. She screamed, and both arms came together with a thunderous smash, both fists joining into one meld of flesh and bone and sinew as dark power and dark magick poured from her, channelled from the roots of the world; from the Beginning. From the Equiem.

Kiki turned, looking down at her frozen, pain-riddled friends: the Iron Wolves.

Then she glanced back at Orlana as the magick hit her, and she opened her mouth and swallowed the pulse. Her teeth clacked shut.

Orlana blinked.

Kiki smiled.

"Now it's my turn," she said. And she lifted her head and stared at the sky, where red streaks smashed through the black of night. Then she stared at the towering vast range, the Mountains of Skarandos. And then her eyes came to rest on Desekra Fortress, the creation of a Great Mage: Esekra. She reached out a hand towards the fortress and felt the magick stored there, as if in a great battery. This was a Well of the Elder Shamathe. A Well of the Equiem.

Words would not do it.

Nor screams, nor tears, nor blood, nor sacrifice,

Slowly, Kiki lifted her hand. And she smiled. *No.* Kiki did not lift her hand. Kikellya Mandasayard Dalgorana du Tebija lifted her hand, and she summoned the mountains and the roots of the world, she summoned the lightning and the power of the storm, she summoned the forests of Vagandrak and the spirits of the dead. The world gave a sigh. The mountains groaned and trembled. Desekra Fortress shook.

Orlana stared at her in disbelief. "No," she said, holding out a hand. "No, it cannot be! You cannot do this!"

"But I can," said Kiki, and her clenched fists came together, and then came apart again, and it was like the dying of worlds. The earth began to violently shake and she felt both hearts beating as one, and power surged through her, she became a channel, she became a portal, and yet she controlled the portal and the ground and mountains shook and a roaring grew from out of nowhere, vast and titanic and overwhelming. The whole world and the mountains groaned and moved. An earthquake took the Pass of Splintered Bones, and the Desekra Fortress, and the Mountains of Skarandos, and the Plains of Zakora, and began to hammer them in a clenched fist, hard and fast, and it built and built and built until the world was buzzing, humming, a mammoth charge of non-discharged power. And Kiki stared at Orlana, and she screamed, and her mouth became a vast white hole, blinding and searing like white fire which radiated out as the earthquake increased and built and roared and the whole world was shaking, wailing, dying. And the plain before the Desekra Fortress started to collapse with mammoth roars and a grinding of rock and a smashing of mountains collapsing, and suddenly a huge pit opened up and swallowed a thousand mud-orcs screaming down into the fire and churning rocks and wrath. More pits opened up, and jagged lines ran from the Sanderlek wall of Desekra right up to the war tents of Orlana the Changer, and Kiki stood with arms above her head, foaming at the mouth, her eyes rolled back in her head showing nothing but fresh new-forged silver iron. The earthquake smashed across the plain, eating the army of mud-orcs with a feral mouth of collapsing rock and dirt and fire. The splice were taken dragging screaming and clawing into the bowels of the opened world. Fire billowed up in high columns as tall as the mountains. The sky went blacker than black. The stars were put out.

And then Kiki stared at Orlana, the Changer, the Horse Lady, and she pointed, and her arm became black fire, her arm became retribution and lightning and rock and the earthquake all screamed and roared as the land beneath her feet suddenly crumbled, and her eyes flashed silver as she spoke words of power long lost, and the ground distorted, and Orlana was sucked away down in a sudden fast river of collapsing rock and soil and fire and lightning. Down down down she was dragged, deep beneath the world; and in the blink of a splice's eye, she was gone.

Slowly, Kiki came around.

She stood on an island of rock. A pillar, amidst a sea of collapsed earth and rock and world. At her feet lay Dek and Narnok and Trista and Zastarte, all staring up at her in awe; true awe, shining in their eyes alongside fear, and horror, and raw terror.

Then Kiki fell to her knees, and her forehead touched the warm rock, and around her the earthquakes gradually rumbled to a halt. Gradually subsided. More rocks and columns and walls fell away, crumbling into the huge pits which now formed the majority of the plain before Desekra. And yet the fortress itself remained unharmed. The pits and chasms ran in jagged lines all the way up to the foot of Sanderlek, where they had swallowed many thousands of mud-orc corpses.

Kiki looked up, and Dek took her hand.

It began to snow, and amidst the snow was black ash.

"What did I do?"

Dek grinned at her. "You tore apart the world."

Kiki stared at the insanity before her, the chasms and voids and random zig-zagging walkways of what remained of the plain. She turned her head, from left to right, astounded, truly astounded, by the act of destruction.

"I did this?"

"Yeah. I wouldn't like to be on the wrong side of *you* on a bad bloody morning," said Dek.

"Nonsense," grinned Narnok, slapping Kiki on the back and nearly pitching her to her face. "She's the Captain of the Iron Wolves! She's our friend! Our comrade! Our ally! We have nothing to fear! Not like those sorry bastards down there!" He peered over the edge, and stones trickled treacherously.

Kiki smiled, then pitched to her side, shaking uncontrollably. She frothed at the mouth and her eyes went blank.

"Let's get her to the surgeons," said Trista, quietly.

"Agreed," said Dek. "Who will help me carry her?"

And together, they bore Kiki's unconscious body across the narrow, jagged walkways of rock, above mammoth fiery chasms filled with bottomless drops and raging fires and crumbling stone. She was limp, and spent, and done, and empty.

And happy. Kiki was happy.

Orlana was defeated. Vagandrak was saved.

EPILOGUE
SOUR TIMES

Dawn broke, cold and full of ice. Snow fell heavily across a silent, broken, collapsed plain before the fortress of Desekra. Dek, Narnok, Trista and Zastarte stood on the battlements of Sanderlek, staring out at a fractured, malformed world beyond.

"We won," said Dek, half in disbelief.

"Kiki beat them," said Trista, grinning. "She fucking beat them."

"What did she do?" asked Dek, voice filled with awe.

"She used the power of the elements, the power of Nature, the magick of the Equiem, the magick of Desekra," rumbled Narnok, slowly. "She is a *shamathe*. A bloodline descendant of the shaman who used to rule this world. Remember Zunder? That bloody volcano? We should have known then."

Dek shook his head. "She said she did not remember her childhood. Her early childhood."

"Did not remember, or chose to repress?" said Narnok.

They were quiet for a while, staring out across the fractured plain. The world had changed. The Iron Wolves had changed.

"She sure killed the shit out of Orlana," said Zastarte, softly.

Narnok looked at him. "I'm not sure she did," he said.

"Meaning?"

"Meaning just that. Powers like Orlana don't just simply die. She'll be back. Mark my words. That bitch will be back. With her army. We've not seen the last of those mud-orc bastards. Gone, but not forgotten, eh?"

"Well," said Dek, rolling his shoulders, "I don't know about you, but I think we've earned a fucking drink."

"Damn well said!" snorted Narnok. "But it has to be said, Dek my pretty little pit fighter, you're buying!"

"And how do you work that one out?" snapped Dek.

"Because of what you did to my wife."

"Ahh. Fair enough. But... you'll never let that one lie, will you?"

Narnok stared hard, with his one good eye. "Never, ever, you back-stabbing bastard."

Dek slept the sleep of a man after eighteen flagons of ale. When they came for him, he was ill-prepared. The helves beat down breaking his nose, eye-socket and jaw; breaking his arm and shin, and fracturing three ribs. They dragged him groaning to the dungeons of Desekra, where he was chained up tight against the wall and, still stunned beyond belief, wondered what the fuck had hit him.

Days passed. Days, melting into weeks.

Gradually, Dek learned that the others were in adjoining cells. Trista. Zastarte. Narnok. Kiki. All had been taken in their sleep, beaten to within an inch of their lives, then chained up in the dark and the damp, waiting for... what?

It came, after a month.

King Yoon, in all his finery, his silk, his lace and his velvet. He strode in with Captain Dokta and several others of his elite force. Yoon stared for a long time at Dek, who eventually spat vaguely in Yoon's direction.

"What do you want, you fucker?"

"You dare…!"

"Oh yeah, fucking save it for the people. You were going to sell us out to the witch, and Kiki saved your backside and your kingdom. We all fought for you. Fought to save your lands, your palaces, your riches. And what thanks do we get? Broken bones and chained in your dungeon."

"Well," whispered Yoon, moving in close, "you're going to like the rest of it, then, Mr Iron Wolf."

"I think I might not," said Dek, meeting Yoon's gaze in utmost hate.

"You saved us, yes. But nobody here knows that. The soldiers out on the walls think they were saved by a simple earthquake; a random act of nature! Of course, you and I both know different, but I can't have a random psychopathic bitch like Kiki running around with that sort of… *power*." He stared hard at Dek. "Or indeed, any of *you* with that kind of power. So, you have been tried. You have been found guilty. And you have been sentenced."

"Sentenced?" snarled Dek.

"Sentenced to death. By hanging. On the morrow."

The sky was the colour of iron. The clouds were bruises inflicted against the sky. A cold bitter winter wind blew down the Pass of Splintered Bones, howling, mournful and desolate; and low as a tomb. Carpenters had erected a makeshift gallows on Sanderlek, protruding out so that the victims would be hung out over No Man's Land. Without honour. In complete disgrace.

The convicted Wolves stood on the battlements where, only a few weeks earlier, they had fought, giving their lifeblood to defend their nation and its people.

A thousand soldiers of Vagandrak lined the walls. Sergeant Dunda stood to one side, face solemn, impassive, his great hands clenched behind his back, his armour and boots polished to an unholy shine.

Standing, chained, with black silk hoods over their heads, were the Iron Wolves.

Kiki. Dek. Narnok. Zastarte. Trista.

"The Iron Wolves have been found guilty on twelve counts of treason against His Majesty, King Yoon of Vagandrak," read a small, pompous fat man from a vellum scroll. "These counts amount to theft, extortion, the murder of General Dalgoran, the kidnapping and imprisonment of various members of the royal family…"

"I'll fucking show him imprisonment," murmured Narnok, bristling.

"If you hadn't had your pants round your ankles, we wouldn't be in this mess," snapped Dek.

"Thus proclaims Mr Two Kegs," growled Narnok. "Maybe if *you* could hold your ale a little better, you might have heard the stampede to your door?"

"Silence amongst the prisoners!" squawked the bureaucrat.

"Or what?" bellowed Narnok. "You'll fucking hang us?" His laughter roared across the walls of Desekra Fortress.

The list of misdemeanours continued, and Yoon watched from a specially erected stand built from oak and nails.

Eventually, the five members of the Iron Wolves were led to makeshift gallows. Rope nooses were placed about their necks.

Yoon watched on, impassively.

"I hereby pronounce a sentence of death," whined the bureaucrat. "You five, members of the Iron Wolves, Kiki, Dek, Narnok, Zastarte and Trista, will hang by the neck until dead. Have you any final requests?"

"A longer rope?" boomed Narnok, laughter echoing.

Nobody answered his jest.

"I have one thing to say," came the demure, measured voice of Kiki. Yoon made a throat-cutting gesture, but it was too late. Kiki continued, "Orlana the Changer, the Horse Lady, is far from dead. She will be back, Yoon. Back real soon. And who will protect you from her Equiem magick then?"

"Now," said King Yoon, dark eyes flashing dangerously at the hangman. "Do it now. DO IT NOW!"

The hangman reached out, and with trembling, gloved fingers, took hold of a brass lever that operated the simple pulleys, which in turn dropped the trapdoors beneath the hooded victims.

Silence and shame rolled out across Desekra Fortress. Across the sundered plains of Zakora. Across the waiting, breathless World.

ACKNOWLEDGMENTS

As ever, there are a host of people to praise (and a host to curse, but we won't go there today). I want to thank my wife Sonia for her strength and love. I want to thank my children, Joe and Olly, for always making me laugh and showing me the constant joy of being a father. I want to thank Ian Graham, as ever, for his constant support and camaraderie – the grizzled, stinking old goat. Thanks to Kevin and Lyndsay, for all the good times in the last year (and by God, I needed some of those). Angry Robots: Thanks to Marco, for commissioning this book and being one of the Good Guys; to Lee, for looking so very, very sexy ("Bring out the gimp" / "Gimp's sleeping" / "Well, I guess you're gonna have to wake him up, now, won't you"); and Darren T, fellow NMA fanatic, gardening and real ale fan, for being such a good Anarchy contact. I'd like to thank "Mem", whom inspired me with Aokigahara, and also for agreeing to be locked in shackles in the boot of my Jag (a very long story). And finally, I'd like to thank all the actors in my first feature film, the fun of making it helped bring me back from some very dark places.

ABOUT THE AUTHOR

Andy Remic is a British writer with a love of ancient warfare, mountain climbing and sword fighting. Once a member of the Army of Iron, he has since retired from a savage world of blood-oil magick and gnashing vachines, and works as an underworld smuggler of rare dog-gems in the seedy districts of Falanor. In his spare time, he writes out his fantastical adventures.

andyremic.com

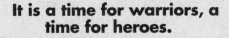

**It is a time for warriors, a
time for heroes.**

THE
**CLOCKWORK
VAMPIRE**
CHRONICLES

ANDY REMIC

KELL'S LEGEND · SOUL STEALERS · VAMPIRE WARLORDS

Chuck Wendig has raised the bar of the urban fantasy genre.
New York Journal of Books

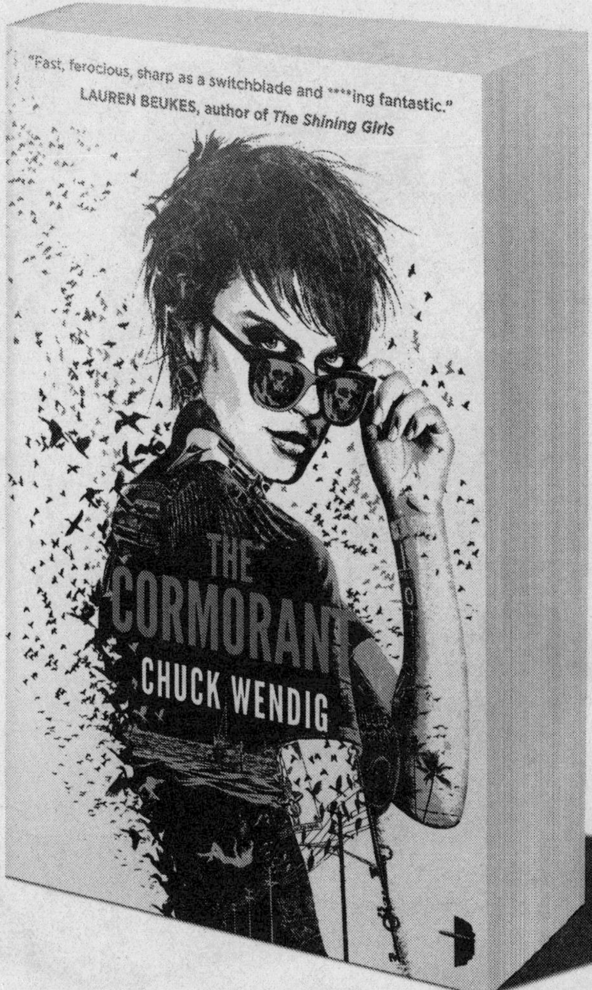

The quest for the Arbor has begun…

HEARTWOOD

FREYA ROBERTSON

The quest for the Arbor has begun…